CRUMBLE CITY JUNIOR COLLEGE

Debra:
I am pleased
that you are reading
my magnum opus.
Enjoy!
Harold Kaplan

385-KAPL

CRUMBLE CITY JUNIOR COLLEGE

Harold M. Kaplan

and

Joyce Lundeen

Library of Congress Number:		99-90480
ISBN Numbers	Hardcover:	0-7388-0404-5
	Softcover:	0-7388-0405-3

This book was printed in the United States of America.

To order additional copies of this book, contact:

Xlibris Corporation
PO Box 2199
Princeton, NJ 08543-2199
USA

1-888-7-XLIBRIS
1-609-278-0075
www.Xlibris.com
Orders@Xlibris.com

We express our appreciation to Kathleen Jones, a colleague, who contributed from beginning to end not only to the technical production, but to the quality of the book, with her high standard of excellence and vigor that inspired our efforts.

PREFACE

Crumble City Junior College was a mythical organized disorganization nestled in euphoric complacency at the far end of some wagon ruts in darkest America. It was established as an act of revenge on the natives after they voted to turn all their State officials out of office.

The College was founded as a fully discredited institution. Its charter stated that this condition be perpetuated so that no student would need to develop a sore brain from studying.

Fendrick Poltroon, long-time College Archivist, sold many of the notes for this opus to the present writers who in turn embellished the tale with additional blubberings during psychiatric questioning under light pentothal anesthesia. The writers admitted collecting everything written herein from an untrustworthy source and the tale is thus only as much of a mis-history as their mischievous informant could conjure up. When the writers recovered from the truth serum at their final therapy session, they stated that Fendrick was the biggest liar south of the north pole.

As for the daily antics on the scene, the writers' accounts may evoke a visual imagery which on stretch could be classified as humor if the readers are crocked on the same wavelength.

Crumble City Junior College is a work of fiction. Names, characters, places and incidents are imaginary. Any resemblance to real events, locales, or persons living or dead is entirely coincidental.

FACULTY NEWSLETTER

Assistant Instructor Emeritus Primeval Confusion has invented an eight-sided lollipop, with a cement covering that could occupy a child for days. He says that this will be received with at least as much enthusiasm from mothers as that attending Thomas Crapper's invention of the flush toilet. One must admit that Crumble is an outstanding place for the nurturing of geniuses.

Professor Radford Hanky has protested to the Administration that a sophomore in the Printing Service has invaded his research privacy. Hanky is an authority on the five-toed Jerboa from Eastern Siberia. The sophomore has already outpublished Hanky on the four-toed Jerboa. Hanky has expressed fears about the safety of his position and well he should. The matter may have to be adjudicated by the Board of Trustees.

Wendy Hindfin, a graduate in Theatre, has a promising career. Her role as an anchovy in the Crumble Players production, "Don't Sleep in the Deep," has won rave reviews. She displayed outstanding dignity and courage as she waved goodbye to the audience while being swallowed by a killer whale.

A patrol carrying firearms has been temporarily assigned to the colloquia in the English Department. It started when a janitor studying remedial English insisted that gorse and furze are the only true English synonyms. The janitor was lucky; he had only three of his fingers mangled by an opposing visiting lecturer from Mexico. The earlier reports that he had his head bashed in are simply not true.

Still more. Opponents of Garbled Syntax, voted "Best Teacher" by his students, had to be subdued when Garble refused to change "The pipe was unloosened from the clamp."

The CCJC Chemical Foundation, which manufactures new chemicals for sale, guarantees that if your laboratory is on an island, their chemicals will reach your island dry. No other chemical manufacturer has ever yet issued such a sweeping statement.

The Flikachickens, our recent man and wife team in the Department of Anthropology, came to a tragic end yesterday in the Museum. They were playfully jousting with some of their excavated material. According to eyewitnesses, it all wound up by each one killing the other with His and Her spears which they had lovingly given to each other just a few weeks previously.

Refried Beans, expert in exotic cookery, has been banished from Home Economics. His last concoction burned a hole right through the wedding pot just before he turned the light on under it. His major crime, however, was that he backed up a safe distance while he watched the floor dissolve.

Dean Catcabbage of the School of Agriculture has found it necessary to discipline Wallago Carpetbeetle , an international authority on tomatoes. The Dean dreamed that Wallago threw a rotten tomato at him while the Dean was emceeing a banquet. Wallago was called in the next day to explain his actions, but he stated that it was the Dean's dream, not his. The Dean informed Wallago that according to the second law of metaphysics the substance of a dream involved all persons appearing therein. Also, according to the universal academic principle of lèse majesté which Wallago should have known exists between a dean and his staff, Wallago's insufferable behavior could not be tolerated. Wallago will apologize at the next faculty meeting.

The interdepartmental dinner meeting held last night is a model for future meetings. Leaking Faucet of the Philosophy Department stated that the theory of counterpoint could not adequately describe the beauty of a fugue. Pyromaniac Suburbia, representing the College Fire Department, took exception and observed that Leaking's theory of cosmogony has been reclassified as bullshit, category unknown. McRooster, Professor of Dead Birds, noted that the conversation had reached a level at which he could participate. Instructor Putressin, a protagonist of Pyromaniac, remarked that McRooster had already been silenced by his critics and should remain anonymous for several years for the good of the College. What was announced as McRooster's Law of Dead Birds was neither a law nor a discovery by McRooster and furthermore it was difficult not to discover a dead bird.

Other business was routine and the meeting adjourned after the fried raccoon was consumed.

We believe it to be our duty to pretest the extent of the crass sense of humor of people who read this stuff. Much more sophisticated evaluations than the following will be presented as we develop our testing skill.

Weegie Senseless, an astute upper level major in Logic, but a low achiever otherwise, laughs until she cries when catsup shoots out of its bottle and in perfect symmetry of arrangement sprays the entire front aspect of her husband's new jackets. This happens frequently with any bottle not nailed to the table.

Don't send us your opinions. Nobody asked you to read this.

Upchuck Daily has been appointed Superchairman, Department to be founded when he sees an opening to remove a competitor. It is said that if he were an earthworm, he would be a veritable Einstein among them.

Burnt Rubber, Instructor in Automotive Engineering, is also an author in his spare moments. He made one major mistake in his article, "Why Are Secretaries Better Looking Than Wives?," citing evidence in his Preface that he writes from experience. He is currently hobbling on one crutch since his wife bent the other one over his head. Burnt says that his next tome will be on "How To Pot Pansies." His wife is writing a scientific paper on "Crisis Intervention." She hopes that it will get her a job in marriage counseling.

Dean Catcabbage presided at the faculty retreat at Hogan's Frog Farm. The Dean was optimistic. He opened the conference by sagely observing that the future is ahead of us and we must all go forward to get there. He wanted the faculty to be the first to learn that Crumble had this very week been rated by the Accreditation Body to be the leading backward college in the country.

Bam Bam LaTossie may be the new Chair of the Theatre Department. She so outbehinded the present incumbent, Priscilla Prim, during chorus rehearsal that the male students are demanding Priscilla's immediate ouster. Priscilla counters that Bam Bam is no prize hen's chicken and she should be returned to the nearest whorehouse, preferably by overnight mail.

The Physiology Chairman announces a semester appointment to his staff, Visiting Lecturer No Tinkle, a urologist. Tinkle created an international stir this year with his paper "Urination is a Personal Matter," published by the Journal of the Pipefitters Union, current issue. This contribution has already influenced the design of latrines in the fire station in South Cornfield Tinkle is working feverishly on a process which could be an item of universal importance. From the only information that we are allowed to print, he has developed a formula in which a solution of fermented turkey wings in volcano sauce is a super-solvent for clogged drainpipes.

From the meticulously kept archives of the History Department, circa 1200 A.D.

Our staff is in disagreement about the punishment meted out to the fellow (below) whose head was affixed for one week to a lighted pole on London Bridge.

Queen to the castle plumber: Go fetch your honey dipper, the one with the extra-long handle, and clean out the royal dungpit.
Illiterate plumber: At your cervix, m'Lady.

President Timkens at Convocation:
"Crumble is at the cutting edge of excellence. "
Campus cops:
"Let's go get him and find out what he's smoking."

Direct plane service has been established between the local campus and the new Marco Polo branch in the Arctic Circle. This will allow mail and other items to be sent in the College's diplomatic pouch that is immune to customs' inspection. The newly installed vice-president at Marco Polo is presently sending his laundry in the pouch.

A fight broke out at the weekly colloquium of the Music Department. Trumpeteer Giovanni Tremulo insisted that in the next concert the start of "La Donna e Mobile" was to be sung forte instead of pianissimo. In the ensuing fracas, two violins, a harpsichord and a cello were completely demolished. Fragments of human hair and a whole scalp were found on the harp strings.

President Timkens has asked the faculty not to become alarmed over the recent number of items stolen from the College. He observes that our crime rate is still well below that occurring in the State House.

Picololi Frenzo of the Music Department is considering an apology to a student who has spent four years as a Music major.

He told her in class that her voice sounded like a mixture of sand and shit being ground up at low speed in a cement mixture.

Attila Ferocio, Instructor in Mannerly Behavior, is about to be reduced to a lamb chop. He was summoned to President Timkens' office on a charge of hitting School of Education teachers on the head with an oversized dictionary when in talking with him they made any mistake in English. The thumpings were frequent.

Timkens has put Attila on Pay Withheld Status until Attila sends him 10 jokes written by Julius Caesar. This could be a long assignment.

Ferd Airball, Consultant in Animal Behavior, forgot about the territorial rights of his dog and went to sleep in the doghouse. His dog surveyed the situation from all angles, dragged Ferd through the house and locked the door on him.

Ferd believes that he might get back for a clean shirt if he can get the dog caught for jaywalking or shoplifting a bone from the nearby supermarket. He told his class that the dog has the wrong choice of priorities but the class thinks that the dog and Ferd have poor communication.

The English Department has introduced its newest member, Benjie Witless. Benjie is infamous for his books written with flair under various pseudonyms. Thus, The Flowing Stream by I. P. Standing; The Grasshopper's Lady by Erasmus B. Green; The Wildcat's Revenge by Claude Boobs; and other goodies too numerous to mention.

A quickie: Instructor Fizzle has had it. The only two neurons left in his brain are in danger of separating. The College maintenance team has been given the task of gluing them together.

WEEKLY REPORT FROM THE HIGH POTENTATES IN ADMINISTRATION

President Timkens will attend a legislative hearing to be held in enemy territory at Downstate University. Because of the danger involved, the Registrar and the College Attorney will ride shotgun on top of Timkens' Rolls Royce.

The elected faculty representative, Frisbee Bodkins, Professor of Paleontology, was called into President Timkens' office yesterday. The transcript of their conversation follows:

Timkens: "Are you ready for the conversation?"

Bodkins: "Yes sir."

Timkens: "Brush off your pants, you're dirtying the furniture. Now, Bodkins, are you fully aware that Paleontology is a luxury here at Crumble?"

Bodkins: "Yes sir."

Timkens: "Let's not waste precious time. The Legislature has only given us $67,432,540.37 which is 30 dollars short of our last budget. We intend to retrieve this deficit and stop this raiding of our resources. As far as we in this office are concerned, all administrative personnel will cry all day in the Senate gallery next week. The entire faculty will assemble in the basement corridor of our beloved State House our first day there and we will fast for the next two days. We are flying in two swamis from another country to train the faculty to fast professionally. You, Bodkins, will walk the faculty the 230 miles from here to the State House They will look more ragged than now, if possible. We need to create a good impression. If this fails, you will have to turn in your starfish to the Zoology Department.

Bodkins: Count on me, Sire. For God, Country and Crumble.

President Timkens had to sharply rebuke Faculty Assistant Boory Thump who was recently caught playing footsie with the President's secretary. Timkens reminded Thump that he had violated the second law of thermodynamics, which states quite simply "Don't defecate where you eat." Thump has been put on probationary curfew.

The Great Crumble Hedgehopper Airways has temporarily had its franchise suspended by the College. The pilot delivered President Timkens' caviar one day late from the Caspian sea. Timkens complained that the combination of pheasant with domestic caviar made him ill.

At the last faculty meeting, Timkens had to chide the entire group once again. He observed that the faculty march out of the assembly hall following the recessional at the Commencement exercises closely resembled the Bongoland army in full retreat.

Lower Dean Fartsey has just had a transplant of an unburied dinosaur brain and he is recovering with even more than usual mania. He is showering the entire country with applications to become a university president.

Vice President Downhill has discovered the customary survival technic for administrators whose positions and accomplishments are coming up for a five-year review. First, you do your homework internally, making sure that your judges are all people whom you have nominated to be on the Board of Trustees and whose special exotic brand of liquor you know with certainty. Secondly, you collar all the college and downtown reporters, handing them treatises on how you intend to make your college one of unique excellence, dismissing the fact that for the past eight years you could only be found in London or Paris. And thirdly, you never omit your intention to get the faculty an 18 percent raise, which you couldn't do even if you fired all the janitors.

The Administration is taking appropriate action concerning the disappearance of the last four Psychology chairmen. Experts in the Department of Astrophysics are sure that the chairmen have fallen into a black hole. If the hole can be located, all the chairmen will be found in there, mumbling incoherently to each other. Only other psychologists will be able to tell what they are saying.

A blue-ribbon search team is being formed. One million dollars have been allotted to the project, one half being for the presearch dinner meetings of the team. This is the customary sum needed for the generation of an idea.

The Trustees have also taken up the matter of Bosley Straightlace, Director of the Curriculum in Public Administration, who wrote the famous text "The Moral Degeneration of the College Student." Sadly, he has been found guilty of evasion of his income taxes. When questioned by the Board as to his course of action, he stated that he intended at this time to cry profusely. He also indicated that he would appeal to the students to see what system they used for their demonstrated success in evading everything.

Since the Director is temporarily not with us, because of difficulties with bail, a minority student has been hired from the High School to take over his work.

Dean Catcabbage of the College of Agriculture was driving his state-owned automobile down Main Street this morning when it burst into flames. Our quick-thinking Dean, whose capacity to meet an acute emergency has brought him to his present exalted position, immediately swung the car into a nearby garage. It is regrettable that the mechanics and other personnel ran for their lives, and the garage along with the rest of the block burned to the ground. The loss is estimated at $250,000.

The Dean's forthright action can only be commended. He will be given a citation at the annual Dean's banquet following his release from jail.

President Timkens has as usual efficiently solved the problem of how to temporarily banish all administrators in adjacent offices when he becomes displeased with them. Several times this month, Dean Dingleberry, his desk, rug, secretary along with her desk and rug, have been fork-lifted to the backyard close to the briar patch. The fork-lift operator may have to be put on the permanent payroll.

President Timkens, with the help of the Crumble Corps of Engineers, but particularly his secretary, Vera Scrum, has set up an experimental system to discourage the professorial nuisances who object to change of any description in or about the College and who immediately enlist a whole cluck of campus clones to espouse their common cause.

The scenario develops as follows: The righteous professor is first made to sit for computer-controlled 2.500 hours on a backless hallway bench. If he leans back, he falls out of a loose window. Timkens is an expert on gravitational forces. Each 20 minutes a computer voice tells the still forthright professor that his turn is only a few minutes away. Should he leave, he forfeits three months to the next possible appointment. Since it is the purpose to enlist Timkens' support to leave the city dump untouched so that the rats will be allowed to survive as an endangered species, the professor waits patiently, rehearsing his speech.

In stage 2, the victim is led into a long, violet-illuminated room facing, at the far end, Vera, who is perched behind a huge King Henry the VIIIth desk flanked by Great Crumble and other flags on either side and a dragon spitting fire on top of her chair. This abruptly slows the professor to milli-steps while diverting his attention to how to murder everyone involved. His primary mission has already been attenuated.

In stage 3, the professor is asked to state his name and show his I.D. card. This lowers his self-esteem by an indeterminate increment, his rage increasing when Vera asks several times if he is sure that the vowels in his name are not misplaced.

If Vera hasn't completely mastered the situation, she asks him to step back and walk through a metal detector which is rigged to sound like a fire alarm, people from other offices running in with extinguishers and stretchers. Vera then asks the victim if he has stolen some books from the library and if he will agree to be searched by the janitor.

When Vera is sure that the victim's pulse rate is not over 150, she informs him that the only other clearance test necessary, since he has done so well, is an obstacle course set up by the Corps of Engineers. This involves a dam, a raging waterfall, and a chain of rocks obstructed by a number of smashed canoes and some partly eaten dead dogs at the far end. The whole thing is a feat of genius.

We can only report that even the most intrepid have never completed the course. During these sessions, Timkens can usually be found in what appears to be a benign coma. Even his cat is in full hypertonic extension. Both are confident that Vera (recently elevated to Trusted Administrative Assistant) has the situation well in hand.

The Unslum the Neighborhood Committee held its meetings in Poverty Square, but in a four month period only three pages of minutes were available. This was because of member Unrestrained Effusion who objected every two sentences to colons, semicolons, commas, verbs and whatever else constitutes a speech. A solution to the problem was at hand. On leaving the building, the permanently unemployed loiterers outside were informed that Unrestrained was loaded with fresh cash and it could be added that he was disruptive.

After the next meeting, at which Unrestrained was prominent by his absence, the tribal chief outside discreetly told the group that the service was meticulously performed. The client showed an appropriate attitude adjustment prior to his clinical discharge. More clients would be appreciated.

Professor Eucrites Bronzite, Assistant Chairman
Department of Geology
Dear Professor Bronzite:

It has come to my attention that Geology Janitor Dirty Lavatory successfully refuted your theory that chrondruls are metamorphosed garnets. It is all the more serious that he completely convinced a large group of onlookers that your opinions are bizarre and outmoded. I have additionally before me excerpts from your lecture of last Tuesday where you confused pigeonite with hexahedrite and you also omitted the "e" in plagioclase.

I am elevating janitor Lavatory to Acting Chairman on a two weeks trial basis. You will serve as his assistant for that period of time and your capacity to learn will determine your future here.

Above all else, the truth must prevail in Geology.

Cordially yours,
Dean Dingleberry

MEMO TO: All department heads in the Hall of Science

Please post the following notice on your bulletin boards:

The Department of Microbiology is searching for three dieners to care for its rat colony. They will be fed the same nutritious food that the rats receive, water-soluble pellets. It will be necessary for the dieners to wear masks to avoid contaminating the animals. The caretakers and rats will all be tattooed for identification with two letters, one in each ear. There are excellent supplementary benefits, including free post mortem examinations. At all times simplicity will be emphasized to correspond with what we have to put up with.

The National Association of Embittered Faculty Members has

just voted Foon Repoochy, Crumble correspondence course alumnus, its highest community award "Solid Citizen of the Year." This is a most deserving honor, since Solid Citizen Repoochy pulled himself up by his own bootstraps and he didn't have any bootstraps.

Let us review Foon's sordid life. At birth he was named after an ethnic curse. This is nothing to be laughed at. To say that he was born in the slums is an understatement from out of town. His early life was passed in a cave on the bank of a river in a section called the Five Corners. At this intersection shit from five cities came flying in at high speed. Foon learned never to duck but to lean toward the most fashionable sewer. Obviously this didn't always work.

Following his first bank robbery, during which his cerebrum was appropriately dented by an unsportsmanly bank teller, a downright unfriendly judge remanded him to the pokey. Foon soon won his freedom on the logical plea that the barbed wire was unduly hindering his exercise, which consisted of digging a tunnel to the outside.

But Foon again became a victim of legal foul play. Due to unexpected delays in plans to rob another bank, he had to feed his starving family, and he was apprehended while taking home a stolen seal from the city aquarium. Foon admitted that he never should have taken the subway.

> *[Ed. note: We are forced by the cost of paper that could be put to more useful ends to cut short this woeful tale. It need only be stated that Foon took correspondence courses from Crumble, became an expert locksmith, and as you would suspect he hasn't had much financial trouble since. The current tidal wave to elect him county sheriff led to his citation by the NAOEFM].*

Grimsby McFinch
Department of Sociology

385-KAPL

Dear Author McFinch:
Our refereed comments of your manuscript are as follows: "We don't need your book to lose money. There are better ways."

Since our astute Board of Reviewers have been expertly trained to separate making money from saving souls, we recommend that you buy a small printing press and peddle your thing from the back of a truck. It's been done with fish.

Yours with finality,
Forby Doo Doo
Editor, The Great Crumble Press

Chi Square Dingdong
Statistician and Punchcard Straightener
Computer Service
Dear Chi Square:

Your manuscript is most interesting, especially since it proves that faculty members exposed to speeches by Dean Dingleberry suffer measurable brain damage.

My secretary, who has nothing to do but cannot be fired, will be given the task of editing your work to improve her English and yours, too.

Your friendly editor,
Forby Doo Doo

Mr. White Soda
Temperance Lecturer
Dear Mr. Soda:

I am writing to you only in respect to your position as Housemaster of Freshman Dormitory No. 154. Our field agents have reported an item of deviant behavior that necessitates immediate correction.

It has been observed that you eat noisily. Apparently uninhibited, you make humming or mumbling noises, something like "um-yum-yum."

Let me draw your attention to the fact that only uneducated persons and members of primitive tribes eat noisily.

Would you kindly make only unobtrusive chewing movements as your contribution to good training for our students. We will follow your progress with interest.

Bon appetit,
Noodles Fettachini
Nutrition and Toilet Training,
Department of Lower Education

TO: All faculty
FROM: Vera Scrum, Trusted Administrative Assistant

You are invited to the birthday party for Dean Dingleberry to be held at the President's house next Wednesday. Come at 4:30 p.m. so as not to interfere with the Dean's bedtime.

We would appreciate a small token of love for our Dean. In view of the condition of his gums, we suggest that you bring Girl Scout cookies.

Fetid Pigeon
Laboratory Assistant in Ornithology
Dear Laboratory Assistant Fetid:

We note your appeal to the State Board of Education to close the College since you have been denied continuance on our faculty. If you decide to persist in your case, let me remind you that our Department of Investigation of Faculty Delinquency has uncovered the following facts.

1. You were logged urinating in the Crumble reservoir on three separate fishing trips. Signs have been posted there today closing the reservoir until it is found free of pollution. The only

exception is its use as a tribal waterhole by some homeless, deranged college students.

2. A copy of the 75 A.D. writings of Pliny the Elder was photographed on your coffee table. You are clearly to be suspected of communist leanings.

3. You have been seen in the College dining hall eating with other males. The connection with homosexuality is obviously strong.

4. Last Thursday, you misplaced a decimal point in deriving the square root of 3. This is serious misinformation for ornithology students. One such student has complained that the amount of extra work this has caused him in trying to get at the correct answer has given him severe stomach pains, tentatively diagnosed at the Health Service as an ulcer. Do you have malpractice insurance?

5. Two weeks ago, when your student worker in the Serpentarium was bitten by an ular kapak bodoh, you slapped a wet chicken on the wound. Although we do not question the treatment, we deplore the fact that you were practicing medicine without a license.

6. Additional evidence given to me is admittedly weak, but it is being pursued. Meanwhile, a one-way ticket to the next state has been purchased for you, and I am confident that you will pick it up promptly.
   With best wishes for your success—somewhere else.
   Smiley Timkens

Laryngeal Fidget
Speech Correctionist
Dear Dr. Fidget:

Your students and colleagues are complaining that your voice emphasizes woe and desolation with every note. An experienced housewife who is a student in your class says that your voice sounds like falling crockery.

I am asking you politely to go to the Audiovisual area every afternoon and listen for one hour to a tape of my voice which is reposeful, serene and purring, veritably a symphonic orchestration.

Compassionately,
Smiley Timkens

The graduating seniors presented Dean Dingleberry with a sled at the Commencement exercise. There is a strange silence in the Taj Mahal section of the Administration Building.

ADMINISTRATIVE ACTIONS OF THE WEEK

A task force has been set up to resolve a foregone conclusion. The following are the circumstances that led to the tragedy.

Dean Ollie Underbright arrived at his office at the usual time, 11:20 a.m. To his surprise, a sign "Women's Toilet" was hanging on his door. Ollie retreated behind a curtain to check the traffic pattern. After seeing no entrant females the whole day, he rashly walked into his former office and was at once seized by security guards and hustled to the city pokey on a charge of immorality.

By merciful decree Ollie was restored to Dean's status and allowed to return to his office. Three months later, when he arrived promptly at 11:20 a.m., he was blocked by about three tons of hay on the floor. The janitor had received orders to get ready for a horse show and to convert the office into a stable. There was also some talk about the room becoming a grain elevator. The Dean told the task force that this was the last straw, no pun intended.

Several administrators intervened for Ollie, but two months later a Chinese delicatessen was moved into the Dean's office. The President told the task force that a course in International Grocery Management had been established and it was urgently necessary to find space. Also, the Dean had been given a hook in the steam tunnel to hang his hat and umbrella. The Dean cleverly countered that his secretary's desk was three blocks away. The President nullified this argument, however, by noting that a letter had been sent to the staff to take compulsory exercise and that walking would be credited as partly satisfying the Dean's work load. The task force then struck the Dean's objection from the record.

The Dean told the washroom attendant that he began to harbor the feeling that he wasn't wanted. The President replied that nothing justified this attitude and that the Dean was obviously coming into a spell of paranoia. This was dangerous to the community and could result in the Dean being quarantined in a steam tunnel for an unspecified time. The President rested his case.

The task force is working on the briefs and will submit the expected report of a presidential committee.

MEMO FROM TIMKENS TO HIGH LEVEL ADMINISTRATORS, BUT NOT INCLUDING STAFF LOITERING IN THE OFFICE

Due to the national energy shortage, all persons above are forbidden to drive the Isotta Fraschini and the Mayback Pullman Cabriolet. No action is yet taken on the Rolls-Royce. The Chancellor may have access to the motorized wheelbarrow if approved by the President's secretary. Deans may drive the 1928 Hudson, and an Edsel is available from the Museum if the wheels can be straightened out.

State Capitol the IXth, whose ancestors owned the State, is finding it more difficult to steal everything. There are just too many competitors. The IXth has scheduled a meeting with the Political Science Department to modernize his procedures. (Editor's note: Whoops! Prepare for a tax increase on skimmed milk, day-old-bread, hot water, scrubbing boards and once-free, unburied cheese.)

The Administration once again warns that dogs are not allowed on the grass around campus buildings. All violators will be prosecuted.

Freshman Desiccated Haddock is leaving Crumble. He says that he is a technopeasant and has only enough money to buy a pencil. All his classmates have computers and associated hardware so that when they add 2 plus 3, colored lights flash all over the place; bells ring, doors open and close, and they get their jollies even without their customary hallucinogens.

English instructor Murky Cliché is being sued by a former student who claims that Murky analyzed every line in every book to the extent that the student can no longer read anything. In a new book, the student cannot figure out by himself what deep meaning the author had on each page so the student dreams that he is flunking English exams. He contacted one prolific writer who replied that he writes only when he is stone drunk; he has to ask his wife what he wrote and he couldn't care less.

This will serve to introduce you to Intern Gleep. He is now at our Health Service, following his banishment from the Great Crumble Hospital. His odyssey should be of interest to any of you who like to travel downhill. At the time of this writing, all his diagnostic memos can be found in a pile of rubbish labeled "Danger to Health—Don't Read This." If you stand near the incinerator this weekend, you can watch his stuff get sucked in.

Dear President Timkens:

Some of your students may wish to transfer here for proper and mannerly education. We have three unused scholarships, each for $137.12.

The only condition is that the recipient must be an illegitimate descendant of a Confederate soldier who fought in the Battle of Antioch.

Please post this in a conspicuous place, with a light under it.

Old True Friend,
(General) Lee Beauregard Ciderjug, President
Burpo Jenkins Teachers College
Southern Branch, New Thebes
Assistant Instructor Borden Toiletseat
Dear Borden:

Parking your car in the space marked "For President Only" might have been due to your weak eyes the first time, but is obviously due to your weak brain the twelfth time.

I have instructed the Campus Police to ignite a sophisticated bomb under your car when it next appears in the lot, and to kick your ass before you get up too much speed making your escape from the burning wreckage.

Smiley Timkens

Creamed Codfish, by his own admission the highest authority in professordom on the theory and practice of education, has notified Dean Dingleberry that he could, albeit begrudgingly, spare 10 minutes to solve all the academic problems of Crumble. Codfish's secretary will brief Dingleberry on how to cringe before and after the session. Also, how to exit upon the run when hearing sounds from Codfish such as "harrumph." Codfish's fee will be commensurate with his pomp and circumstance.

> *Editorial Comment: Hot air rises. Don't be surprised if you see a self-appointed genius floating slowly toward the ceiling.*

The legislature sent an investigative team to Crumble following faculty complaints about administrative excesses. The following is an excerpt from a tape recording.

Legislator: You are a Vice-President?

VP: Yes, Your Holiness

Legislator: How much time do you spend at Crumble?

VP: About three weeks per year. It is essential that we go to meetings so that subject matter can be obtained to proliferate more meetings.

Legislator: Where do you go?

VP: New York, San Francisco, New Orleans, San Diego in the winter.

Legislator. Where do the faculty go?

VP: Dogwalk, Oklahoma; Litchfield, Illinois; Fitchburg, Massachusetts.

Legislator: Excellent choices all around. My only suggestion is that you turn down the thermostat in the administrative washroom at 6 p.m. All told, you are following an approvable schedule.

Colonel Craven Surrender
Department of Military Tactics and Strategy
Dear Friend Craven:

A bill is enclosed for the damage you caused falling down a flight of stairs in the Armory. Worse, all your troops obediently repeated the act, ruining the freshly laid cement in the first floor patio.

Your excuse that you have amblyopia ex anopsia will do you no good. In fact, I have asked that you be demoted to a private as of this letter since all our administrators must now measure up to sufficiently tough physical standards to intimidate their faculty as a logical step in riot control.

Since your logic as well as your physique seems to be weakening. you have been given appointments tomorrow, first at the finance office where Henry Nickelbiter, our genial Bursar, will bring you into balance with your financial debts by demanding cash payment for floor repairs. Then at the Health Service you will receive a performance booster. This injection is painless and it has worked in rats.

Smiley Timkens

Heard at the Faculty Club:
Local Anonymous Professor:

I heard you buried your wife last week.

Visiting Professor from Oxford:

Had to. Dead, you know.

One of the student members of the band called The Undesirables blew out an inguinal hernia during a pelvic gyration while blowing his horn. He is the first student to look like a Crumble professor.

The Administration has received copies of the following letters from Chief Ketchum of the Great Crumble Police. They are presented below for no valid reason.

To: Fafnir
Skid Row, Crumble
From: Chief Ketchum, Great Crumble Police

According to Norse mythology, you were supposed to have been killed by Sigurd. Please explain why you are currently walking around Crumble as a vagrant. Putting you in the slammer costs us money which could be better used in our weekly coon pie supper.

To: Chief Ketchum
From: Fafnir

I got tired being typecast as a dragon guarding the goddamn Nibelung treasure. They told me I would be safe here because who in hell ever heard of Crumble. My advice to you is to keep away from Norse mythology and start reading the books here on Pornograph Square. They will improve the circulation in your feet which can help you catch real criminals. Keep in touch.

To: Chief Ketchum
From: Irate mother, also a taxpayer

What do you mean, kicking my son and his girlfriend out of the park just because they were fornicating. And worse, you embarrassed them by telling them that they were too young. Haven't you ever heard of Daphnis and Chloe who made love even before they had nuptial-size sex organs? Oh, for shame!

TO: The Faculty
FROM: The Great Crumble Press

You and your dear ones are invited to tea to honor our eminent author, Helmut Schnaglefoogle (or is it Schnooglefagle).

Whatever his name is, he is acclaimed for his text, "Screw 'em All but Four." His coming sequel, The Hell with Everybody"' is even better.

Administrator Pinwheel held a yard sale of all rocks and minerals in the Geology Museum while the Museum instructors were on spring vacation. We have heard that Pinwheel has been whisked out of the country since it is rumored that the Museum Director is looking for him with a telescopic rifle.

Assistant Instructor Numberless says that he was the only friend of Lesser Dean Hobbledehoy at a time when the Dean was a student and shunned as the class idiot who could be contagious. Now that the Dean is suffering a common delusion that he is in authority, the truth being that he is only allowed to sort out red and white Indian nuts for the cafeteria, Numberless is classified as persona non grata and can see the Dean only by prior arrangement with the room janitor.

Student Shanahan McMurphy, a name that a shame never was connected with, lived the life of Riley with considerable exuberance and his family drummed him out, which is the reason that he matriculated at Crumble under the Simon-pure name of Smith.

Whoever tells the truth is chased out of nine villages

—Proverb

The Ides of March
Thaddeus Chickensoup
Department of Foreign Languages

Dear Chickensoup:

Your recent letter to me that you are doing away with Latin and suggesting that you can assist me in getting temporary work in the cranberry bogs has been disposed of with the rest of the excrement following its proper usage on my derriere.

You are a son-of-a-bitch

Sincerely yours,
Scrambled Prose
Reader in Ancient Languages

The Calends of April
Scrambled Prose
Reader in Ancient Languages
Dear Reader Prose:

I am in receipt of your crapulous eructation dated the Ides of March. This is to inform you that I am taking back my offer to locate you in the cranberry bogs.

In the interest of the academic community, I recommend that the best way you can relate to the Department is to commit suicide.

As always I stand willing to help you solve your dilemma.

Happy Holidays,
Thaddeus Chickensoup
Chairman

Memo to: Thaddeus Chickensoup and Scrambled Prose
From: Hot Urine, College Ombudsman

Copies of your letters have come to my attention. May I commend both of you for maintaining a dialogue in the face of crises.

Copies of my commendation will be sent to President Timkens. These will become part of your permanent record which will accompany you as you both seek new positions.

Memo to: Professor Injured Fox
Wildlife Training Institute
From: Dean Ollie Underbright
School of Education

According to the President's Office, you will be expected to retire in 14 years from the present date. Let me remind you that it is not too early to think about your replacement.

If you wish to comment, please leave your reply in the third stall in the faculty men's room.

From President Timkens' apothegms, this time quoting from Konrad Adenauer: The good Lord set definite limits on man's wisdom, but not on his stupidity.

WEEKLY REPORT OF THE HEALTH SERVICE

Dr. Wobbly Lubdub, our astute cardiologist, has presented the College with a picture of the right coronary artery taken at autopsy from CCJC President Felton Tingle who reigned from 1940 to 1945. No other photo of Tingle is available to hang in the Administration Building. The Trustees will consider the offer.

The Health Service is fortunate in obtaining the service of Dr. APEOTFZ as visiting ophthalmologist. He has already sent his bag of lenses to the clinic.

The Health Service recommends the drinking of clear chicken broth from the College Cafeteria after mud wrestling. This can be poured over your head between spoonfuls, exerting a cleansing effect without calories. Such soups as mulligatawny or clam chowder are discouraged.

The Health Service refuses to sponsor the preparation called alpha sesquialiate, whose essential ingredient is tree drippings. The formula was developed by the Chairman of the Health Education Department who likes to think he's a doctor.

The College psychiatrist has declared the entire Department of Psychology to be insane. President Timkens has brought in a new chairman, Pointed Head, a clickswitcher who lived three years inside a Skinner box so that he could feel authentic about the research of his staff.

A coed, whose name is being withheld, puzzled all the doctors at the Health Service by complaining that for the past month she was urinating in four streams. Intern Gleep solved-the mystery. Upon vaginal examination he pulled out a fly button. The coed has been advised to buy her boy friend an updated pair of pants.

Following the advice of our neurologists that Dean Dingleberry is dyscoordinating, the Campus Police have painted on all the windows, doors, hood and roof of his auto "Watch out for sudden stops." A similar sign is being made for the Dean's hat. Our beloved Dean has been under close surveillance since he drove his car through the Business Office, totaling all the machines in a single maneuver.

The Health Service would like at this time to apologize to the Dean who was somewhat put out by last night's news release on his accident. The report read "X-rays of the Dean's head show nothing."

Ungraceful Heaveho, the College riding instructor, was admitted to the infirmary today. While demonstrating to his class the proper way to ride, he had a small mishap. His horse fell on him after it tripped over a cow.

Business major Troglodyte is experiencing what might be called an internship in his field. He was caught at 2 a.m. by the police inside the Great Crumble Department Store stuffing merchandise in a huge laundry cart. He explained that he had read that there was going to be a 100% markdown sale and he wanted to be there early. Confusion reigns in the Department of Mathematics as to whether to defend him.

The Health Service was this week called into consultation in the case of a coed who claimed that a horse chased her on the fourth floor of her dormitory. She insisted that she escaped through a skylight in the roof.

The adroitness of Health Service officials has served to clear up difficulties that have been going on for months between Health Educator Razzell Thyratron and his students. The class frequently complained that Thyratron was dropping corn and cliches all over the place. When questioned at the Clinic, Thyratron stated that he had solved "The Case of the Clandestine Cation." The examiner asked him what he had solved it with. "With mustard, of course," replied Thyratron. Prof. Thyratron is presently receiving shock treatment and a frontal lobotomy is under consideration.

Memo to: Hilary Groinstrain
Family Practice, Health Service
From: College Ombudsman
Subject: Warning of possible dismissal

The following has come to my attention. Yesterday, you extracted a corn and the patient hollered "uncle." Obviously, you failed to observe the humane code of Hammurabi which we all hold sacred at Crumble.

Worse, after you fitted glasses to our Clinical Professor of Ophthalmology, he couldn't find his way out of the Health Service and was found on the roof dangling by his toes, head down.

Gideon Twit
Executive Janitor at the Health Service

Your manuscript "Don't Eat Filched Fish If It Resembles Your Girlfriend" has been endorsed by our reviewer in The Great Crumble Madhouse on Screwview Avenue and we now accept it. You need to expand the passages reading "Locks and keys, keys and locks, the white immortal note." It is unclear why a bear attacked you at a reception desk and how a wasp counterattacked the bear and saved your life.

Fendrick Poltroon, ex-ghost writer, will edit the manuscript.

We can only pray that the whole thing will not become indescribable.

Deliriously yours,
Forby Doo Doo,
Press Editor

The weekly clinicopathological conference at the Health Service was attended by Physiology classes to emphasize how scientific medicine must be pursued. The first case was a boy with a skin rash. One physician said that it was squawmint. Another claimed that it just had to be pheasant's eye. An expert called in said it was yerba-de-pasmo. The boy's mother noted that he always got a rash after eating cucumbers and what was all the excitement. The physicians all left by the back door.

Ferna Grub, internationally famous authority on standardization, gave the Health Service seminar this week on the specificity of cockroach blood. When asked what species of roach she used, she answered "I don't know, they live in my kitchen." The Health Service Director told the Bursar not to pay her for the lecture.

Alex Drainstuffer, College Plumber, is being considered for Family Counselor at the Health Service. He has accumulated evidence that fornication is the chief cause of fatigue in 98-year old people. His findings make Counseling an objective science, like Wave Mechanics.

The Health Service is introducing a psychoclinical advice column. Address your query to "Myron, Sage of the Health Service." The following excerpts illustrate the value of the letters received.

Dear Myron.

I am an instructor here with sub-starvation salary and I am asking for sympathy. Advise quickly. Haggard

Dear Haggard: I once saw the word "sympathy" and I asked my secretary to look it up. She said that the dictionary had such a word, close to shit and suicide. You now have two choices.

Dear Myron:

I am going with an ugly student, although real dreamy and he has a cool convertible. His wife is coming here Saturday, but we have a date for Saturday. What right does he have to stand me up? Angry Coed

Dear Angry: Find a fellow today, more of your own type. You will recognize him by his pointed head.

Dear Myron:

I have been caught shoplifting because of inability to make up my mind what to steal. Please suggest correct behavior. Happy Face

Dear Happy: Itemize your intended loot in advance. Such advanced logic confuses the police.

Dear Myron:

I am Happy Face again. I forgot to tell you that I stole a cement mixer and a snowplow. They have been parked behind my dormitory but nobody has asked any questions. How do I uncomplicate this situation?

Dear Happy: The best thing for you to do is to get them around to the front lawn and leave them there. They will blend in harmoniously with everything else on the lawn and nobody will ever find them.

Dear Myron:

My proctologist told me that he would have to pass a colonoscope when I next come in. What is a colonoscope? Frizzled Janitress

Dear Frizzled: The colonoscope is a tube that visualizes your rectum and lower bowel. If you are lucky, there will not be an asshole at both ends.

Dear Myron:

I hate my Department Chairman. Shall I floor the son of a bitch or run the risk of developing high blood pressure? Anonymous Diener in Paleontology

Dear Anonymous: We are working up an All-College Hate Day which will meet behind the gym next month. The meeting is being convened by a recently discharged member of the Philosophy Department who hates more people than anyone else on campus does. He says that this is a disease of intellectuals and he wants you to be his guest.

Dear Myron:

I have been so sweet to all the faculty members and now they have voted to expel me from all faculty meetings. They don't answer my letters. How can I avoid a clinical depression? Melodious Tinkle

Dear Melodious: You failed to heed the proverb "Make yourself all honey and the flies will devour you." Bring a hatchet to the next meeting. Go after the Committee Chairman first. This will quickly empty the room of grieving faculty members and you will emerge as one who can solve all problems. Nobody will grieve for several months which will put you in line for promotion.

The Health Service reports that Dean Dingleberry's house has again been red-tagged by the Board of Health. This time the cockroaches failed to eat the maggots out of fear of counterattack. This has upset the long standing balance of nature, particularly in the Dean's pantry, and this situation might conceivably have spread and unbalanced the whole neighborhood.

Chief Intern Blue Acne at the Health Service has been suspended for 24 hours. He could not find a vitamin B-12 pill to give a patient so he gave him two B-6s. The Department of Mathematics is protesting the suspension.

The pathologist at the Great Crumble Hospital is spending the week with the District Attorney. He did an autopsy on a fellow who was taking a nap.

The pamphlet by Myron on "How to Protect Yourself Against the Doctor After He Arrives" will be distributed Thursday in the rear of each dormitory next to the dumpster. Please rush for your copy before the garbage collector arrives.

Dean Dingleberry was mercilessly mowed down by a tricycle yesterday. It was hit and run. What appeared to be a five year old driver hastily departed from the scene of the disaster. The Dean is being massaged with arnica every two hours.

Delayed Yawp, Exercise Physiologist, has been admitted to the Health Service because of a severe head cold. It is expected that his autopsy will be held next week.

NOTICE: All students who were injured in the shit storm that unexpectedly hit Crumble last night will come in to the Health Service only by way of the laundry.

The Head Nurse at the Health Service quotes from a bad experience "Never enter a pissing contest with a skunk."

Helpful Thoughts for this Week Only:

1. A boil on the stove is worth two on your behind.
2. Eat shit, 100 billion flies can't be wrong.
3. Avoid tranquilizers. You may find yourself being nice to people you don't even like.

SOME INCIDENTALS—JUST DUG UP

Aged Cheese
College Literary Consultant
Dear Cheese:

I am too busy to be receiving complaints about smart alecks who tell our students to return to the third grade for a course in writing. Also, you are practicing medicine without a license. You told a student who couldn't smell an overripe tomato that he had a failure in the addimenta cerebri mammillaria.

Your terminology is obsolete. The proper 15th century usage is failure in the carunculae similes capitibus mammillarum or something like that.

You are hereby transferred to the Foreign Language Department as a temporary student. If you pass a test in Latin and Greek roots, you will be considered for return to your misinformation desk.

Veritas
Smiley Timkens

Dean Catcabbage claims that the quality of horse manure in Crumble is deteriorating seriously and the School of Agriculture may have to close. He has asked Non Sequitur, Assistant to the Assistant Instructor in Genetics, for emergency assistance. Nonnie is also an authority on taste so he should be an excellent choice.

Nonnie has had some interesting experiences. At one time some of his not so loving colleagues invited him to a "Hey Nonnie Nonnie and a Hah, Hah Hah" forgiveness party, at which one of them tried to kill him but fell over a barrel and shot himself in the leg. Nonnie retreated at full speed to a more hospitable environment .

MORE LETTERS TO MYRON

Dear Myron:

My Histology instructor asked me if I had read about Ruffini's end organ and I instituted charges of sexual harassment. I later looked in the book, which is a new experience for me, and I found that it was a skin heat receptor. What do I do now? Precious

Dear Precious: You have had it. Buy a portable prayer stool and hope for the best.

Dear Myron:

Our dormitory had better be watched closer than I am now able to do. The girl across the hall keeps practicing mouth-to-mouth resuscitation on a cat, our resident counselor is having an affair with the janitor, and my room-mate thinks she is Joan of Arc. Please advise me what to do next? SIGNED: Junior Coed

ANSWER: You're doing O.K. so far, but who does your homework?

Dear Myron:

My fraternity brothers and I have become embroiled in an argument. They claim that we should all learn to protect ourselves from the wind of a cannon ball. How can this be done? SIGNED: Fletcher

ANSWER: During the siege you must dip fast or you will follow your turban into the trench.

Dear Myron:

I want to transfer to Shebanse Polytech next term, but their catalog states that "Advanced students must be deeply studied in physics." What physic shall I take? —Peripatetic Sophomore

ANSWER: I am sending you a loaded pistol. Please shoot yourself in the head. Your brain molecules are out of line.

Dear Myron:

Is the Health Service reasonable in its charges? I am a partially starved sophomore with a chronic vitamin deficiency and would like to visit your clinic.

Dear Partially Starved Sophomore: By all means come to see us. We do our best to bring illness within the reach of everyone.

Dear Myron:

I have incurable hiccups which interfere with both my studies and my sex life. I am appealing to you in final desperation. SIGNED: Despondent graduate student

Dear Despondent Graduate Student: I have referred your note to a professor of history and found that in the 1800s a Lady Waterford of England chained her father-in-law to a wild bear to cure his hiccups (the father-in-law's hiccups, not the bear's). Please give me one week to get a bear and I will make an appointment for you at your pleasure.

Dear Myron:

I am a cured alcoholic, but my roommate insists every night that I drink Scotch with him so that he can cure his insomnia. Please advise. SIGNED: Troubled Sophomore.

Dear Troubled Sophomore: When he next urges that you drink, say yes, accept the drink, unbutton his coat and pour it in his breast pocket. Watch your teeth as you back away smartly.

Dear Myron:

You have been preaching proper health habits to survive to a ripe old age. However, even at 10 years old, I was considered to be a mutation and a certified lunatic. At 30 I was a compulsive embezzler who blew the family bankroll on an ill-chosen horse. To what do you ascribe the fact that in 1965 I am 100 years old? SIGNED: Professor Rancid Kipper—Dept. of Philosophy

Dear Rancid Kipper: I ascribe it to the fact that you were born in 1865.

Dear Myron:

Upon playfully palming my girl friend's derriere, she shouts "oof." Please explain. SIGNED: Perplexed Sophomore

Dear Perplexed Sophomore: This is called the "goosing syndrome" and is a sex-linked genetic trait expressed in females characteristically from puberty to menopause. If hyperactive, your girl friend has "gans." There is no known cure, but remission is spontaneous with age.

Dear Myron:

How do you manage to write with such sophistication about sex? SIGNED: Admiring Coed

Dear Admiring Coed: It's all very simple. I just start with a clean piece of paper and a dirty mind.

Dear Myron:

I was smart in high school, but something keeps happening. I seem to be afflicted with attacks of sudden stupidity. How can I tell when I am cured? SIGNED: Stupefied Freshman

Dear Stupefied Freshman: Sudden stupidity is a manifestation of the wrath of God. Sacrifice a horse and make a urine stew. If you drink it you are not cured.

Dear Myron:

My husband is a student and I am left home to do housework that is driving me mad. What can I do to relieve the monotony. SIGNED: Frustrated Sarah

Dear Frustrated Sarah: We will have to start therapy slowly. As your first approach, vacuum all rugs from east to west on Mondays and Wednesdays. Then change your approach from north to south on Tuesdays and Thursdays. Prior to your husband's return on Saturday afternoon, break all dishes remaining from the previous Saturday's therapy. Call me for the next stage in your cure, but quickly if your husband approaches you with a cue stick.

Dear Myron:

About two hours after my husband goes to bed, he looks as white as a ghost. I can't get him to go for treatment. Advice needed. Puzzled Housewife

Dear Housewife: Stay calm. Our night staff prowled your premises. They noted that your husband pulls a sheet over himself exactly two hours after he zonks out. Tuck him in with safety pins tomorrow night and with a fireman's lift drag him to our psychiatric ward. We will spray him with ice water until the deconditioning produces a cure. It won't take long.

Dear Myron:

I love every player on our football team. How can I narrow the field down to the guy I am going to nail? SIGNED: Hopie Hopeless

Dear Ms. Hopeless: Wait until the crime wave ends. If one of them is still not in jail, rush into your act. But don't let him join the basketball team.

Dear Myron:

My boyfriend left me, but he forgot to take his jockstrap. What shall I do with it since I am very honest. SIGNED: Perplexed Coed

Dear Perplexed: Advertise for another boyfriend who can fit into it. Something like that happened to Cinderella.

Dear Myron:

My fiancee died during sexual intercourse. How can I grieve appropriately? SIGNED: Parboiled

Dear Parboiled: Wear a black condom for one month during your next encounter.

Dear Myron:

We wish to express our deep sympathy about your being gored by a bull and trust that you will recover speedily from your accident. SIGNED: Health Service Staff

Dear Staff: It was no accident. The godamn bastard did it on purpose.

CAMPUS POLICE NOTES

The Department of Physical Education states that the following items have disappeared from its inventory:

1 Dolly Madison four-poster bed; 1 color television set; 1-750 pound safe; 1 walk-in cold room, 20 x 40 feet including all contents and one human research subject riding a stationary bicycle; 1 chemical bench, 10 x 100 ft. including drains and about 75 pipes and fittings; 1 forty foot cabin cruiser, in dry-dock behind the laboratory; and 1 thirty-five cent pinchclamp.

The faculty is using the bicycle paths as emergency devices to save their lives from the cyclists who ride full speed on the sidewalks reserved for pedestrians. The casualties are not reportable since the faculty members are classified as expendable commodities. Furthermore, the administrators cannot be burdened by trivia other than what they generate themselves.

The campus police have given up their dog which was purchased to reduce sidewalk crime on the campus. It seems that a stray cat backed the dog up a tree. In spite of the urging of the cops to have the dog come down, while telling it that history was on its side, the dog refused the advice.

Loaded Diaper, Chief of Campus Detectives, has failed as usual to solve a recent train robbery in which three bushels of tamales and refried beans were taken from a derailed freight train at the Crumble campus. Apparently, the robber in a fit of conscience gave himself up at the police station, confessing his guilt in broken Spanish. Diaper warned the robber that he was too busy trying to solve the train robbery and that if he didn't get the hell out, he would be booked for disturbing the peace. The robber left, thanking Diaper for his quick trial and exoneration, consistent with all he had heard about the great American system of justice.

The bust of Dean Dingleberry in the Library Memorial Room seems to attract vandals who are skilled anatomists. The bust was first desecrated by a split in half, the two halves being labeled "frontal section." A replacement bust was cut to two parts labeled "perfect lateral views." A third was "oblique longitudinal." The most recent work was labeled "disarticulated and as seen upside down." The Trustees are considering the construction of a headless cement post marked "Dean Dingleberry was here."

Ishmael Hawkbeak
Junior Clerk in College Business Office

I have read your letter to the District Attorney, stating that I have cleaned out the surplus million dollars in the cash register and that you are breathlessly awaiting my indictment.

It is written that into each life a little rain must fall. I am about to treat you to a thunderstorm. Upon receipt of this friendly note, start running for the front gate. You might just outrace the first tidal wave.

At your post-mortem would you like your skull cleaned medium-well or lightly breaded before it is shellacked?

I suggest that you get the ark ready,
Timkens

STUDENT HAPPENINGS

Fawchee Subnormal is reopening for the sixth time. Low student enrollment is the problem. Although confessed morons are surfacing at more frequent times, most of them are now being accepted at better colleges.

To celebrate the grand reopening, two deans will be given away. If you come late, you could avoid the prize.

Unworkable Hopper, Admissions Obstructionist
Upper Flushbox Institute of Plumbing
Dear Unworkable:

I recommend Malcolm Lardo with enthusiasm as a transfer student to your institution. His scroungability and physical stamina are extraordinary as witnessed by the fact that he once got a question answered here at the Bursar's office.

Vocal Misuse—Speech Pathologist

The Economics Department reports that its accuracy in predicting by polls is awesome. In its latest poll, 86% of the faculty answered that yesterday was Friday; 100% of the students were sure that it was Friday.

Two-Piss Mortadella, toughest student at Crumble, was K.O.'d in one punch by a clinically anemic female lecturer whose hat he threw out the window when he had enough of the lecture. To make sure that the class understood the importance of reinforcement in conditioning, she floored him again with one hand behind her back. Class attendance has abruptly decreased.

POTPOURRI

Offbeat Steamwhistle, conductor of the Great Crumble Symphony Orchestra, is applying for Picololi Frenzo's position at the College. We remain neutral but we suggest that you watch our notices for the conclusion of this epic struggle.

In accordance with the wishes of one-time President of Crumble, Dr. Foutsch Dingle, the epitaph on his tombstone in the Great Crumble Cemetery now reads "I told you I didn't feel good."

President Timkens is acquiring an impressive reputation as an oracle. If you oppose him at his weekly press conference, he at once tells your fortune.

By administrative directive, the two newly matriculated cannibals will need further indoctrination. They ate a professor last week, and one of them said "Well, anyway, its better than the food at the Student Union."

The Administration announces that Dented Cannonball, a retired general, will come to the campus as Professor of Military Tactics. He once started a war, but nobody showed up.

The Campus Police are in heavily armed search for the Mad Snork. He has been dropping fortune cookies containing obscene statements down the Dean of Women's fireplace. One view holds that he is a spin-off from the Malevolent Society. The only clue is a manuscript entitled "Footprints of a Duck," presumably dropped by accident down the chimney along with a ham sandwich. The campus will be alerted with daily bulletins.

President Timkens' superb respect for keeping to a strict time schedule was evidenced again at the last Administrators breakfast. When Dean Underbright, seated next to Timkens, persisted in a conversation while Timkens was presiding, Timkens plastered Underbright's face with a prune Danish. With his belief in reinforcement, he then massaged Underbright's head with some apricot yogurt, while continuing his call for a question on the floor. Underbright was admonished not to speak nor to leave the meeting since respect for time and the need for a quorum were essential to an orderly meeting.

Alumnus Contrived Hokum, who just received his law degree from Downstate University, has recently had his first case. The College is suing him for non-payment of back tuition.

Herman Fenderbender, our in-house automotive expert, is showing some clinical problems. Last week he was tightening a bolt on President Timkens' new super-luxury auto and he crashed through the windshield, slid over the hood, and landed in good swimming position in an open tank of motor oil. Yesterday he drove the auto, top down, during a violent but expected shit storm. Timkens has surveyed the disaster from a respectful distance and he is thinking about turning in the auto or Fenderbender, but not necessarily in that order.

From the unexpurgated edition of the Holy Book, compliments of the Camel and Goatcheese crowd, "The college president is the shepherd of his flock and the dean is a crook on his staff."

Malcolm Goose-Egg has been appointed Dean of the Curriculum of Losers Program. This is democracy at its finest, providing an education for all. At the start, only multi-flunkers from the prestigious colleges will be admitted. Thereafter it will be all downhill. The Dean has conclusive statistics that such students are most apt to become presidents and chancellors.

The Council of Deans has complimented the Dean of Freshmen for the freebie sign over his office door. It reads:

Office of the Dean
Mocha Cola

Coed Melba Toast has thrown in her hat, and bra too, as a candidate in the coming race for Mayor of Crumble. The Malevolent Society endorses her and this is a plus. The Society notes proudly that Melba has been stewed, tattooed, not to mention other activities against the mores, and its members want to know how Mayor Slusher Weakling has the gall to compete with such first class talent.

Slusher counters that Melba is being treated for Herpes, she can't sing the second stanza of God Bless Crumble, she doesn't know how to bake coon pie, and this is just for openers.

Brother Dominic, the write-in candidate, has wisely withdrawn from the race.

Frozen Cogwheel
Transportation Service
Dear Frozen (or is it Broken) Cogwheel:

The recent incident in which you grounded our paddlewheeler, the Fairy Queen, gives some evidence that you cannot be trusted with a boat. This is the third steamboat that you have racked up. The Coast Guard says it has to use another river to get downstream.

Please turn in your captain's hat.

Farewell to the sea,

Smiley Timkens, Emergency Commodore

The Malevolent Society proudly submits its innovative brochure "How to Decommission a Ferocious Teacher." Following Step 1, which necessitates kidnapping, four people are to sit on him while a fifth, preferably disbarred from Zoology 101 for illegal frog surgery, performs a chromosome change on the electee (currently called a "guest"). Having reduced the amputee from a lion to a lambchop, he is, in keeping with the preservation of his dignity, to be renamed Buffalo Bill. A numerical system may have to be set up to differentiate a succession of Buffalos. The new name of the reconstituted winner will be noted on a forged birth certificate which can be placed neatly in the administrative files by a shoeless secretary trained to walk on tiptoes.

If a peon-type faculty member receives a deanly boot, is he the subject or object of this maneuver? The English faculty will meet even in midnight session to resolve this important question.

The off-section of the music faculty has taken over the Great Crumble Symphony Orchestra. Everyone is-invited to their next concert. We have a special treat. World-famous Picololi Frenzo will be the conductor. All people in the first two rows will be given free haircuts. At intermission, take the square headbowl that you find under your seat and present it with this notice or a reasonable facsimile to Professor Frenzo.

The attack on Ollie Underbright in the alley behind the opera house has been explained. Professor Frenzo heard Ollie sing in church this past Sunday and that did it. The professor sneaked up from behind and hit Ollie square in the mush with his rubber frying pan. Frenzo told the police that he had such perfect pitch that he couldn't stand hearing Ollie deviate from the required frequency. Ollie was not only giving him an aversion to music, but was making him an atheist. There is no question about Frenzo's religious faith as well as his logic and we can only applaud his release from custody.

Chief Ketchum of the Great Crumble Constabulary has nominated Sam Slosher for the best driver of the New Year's weekend. Sam, who is a charter member of the Checkered Shirt/Multiple Beer/Loud Guffaw Club, drove on the right side of the road and didn't have a single head-on collision in the entire weekend.

From Intern Gleep's log:

The patient was never ill before but he is now. He woke up dead.

Demosthenes Blabberbarrel
Department of Speech
Dear Demosthenes:

Students complain that you mumble in your lectures. Please send a letter to me detailing your marital history along with a Health Service report of your blood and urine chemistry.

For the next two months you will practice the following:

Round the rugged rock the ragged rascal ran.

Methodist Episcopal

Peter Piper picked a peck of pickled peppers.

A lumbar puncture and ventriculogram will be arranged for you. You will then report to Vera Scrum who will referee a dialogue between you and one of our intelligent students.

Sternly,
Dean Dingleberry

Dubious Validity
Department of Mathematics
Dear Dubious:

Although you are keeper of the Sacred Scrolls of Crumble, you have refused to acknowledge that the structure of pineapples obeys the Fibonacci number sequence. This is unbounded intransigence.

Obviously, you are not an adequately acceptable, Crumble-type staff member.

We are assigning you to the appleknocker section until you learn more about fruit. Report at Barrel 1 tomorrow.

Not too enthusiastic,
Dean Dingleberry

Flaky Whitefish
Department of English
Dear Teaching Assistant Whitefish:

We are again returning Chapter 1 of your manuscript entitled "Detoured by Diarrhea." There is no further point in your arguing in favor of your own English and, despite your threats to castrate me, we are now stating plainly that the following corrections must stand firm:

On page 3, line 9, "to whom he should of" should be changed to "of which he should of."

On page 9, line 4, "who he worked with" should be changed to "for whom he worked for."

On page 9, line 11, "regardless where he came from" should be changed to "irregardless from whence he came."

Your book has some good points but our staff cannot agree on their location. Because of the reputation of this Press, we cannot tolerate whimsies in language.

The Janitor
During absence of all the staff
The Great Crumble Press

To: Marlinspike Foof
From: President Timkens

You have been cloistered in your office reading "Ba Ba the Elephant" for days, apparently drowning the sorrow of your own stupidity. When your house was finally paid for, you should have been sober during the victory party when you burned the mortgage and unfortunately the whole house with it, and all this three hours before you renewed your fire insurance policy.

Our records indicate that you are hell-bent for trouble. Your latest book *Saints and Other Psychotics* has just lost our Outreach Center its accreditation in the Horseshit Ridge Public Schools.

Please start hoarding pennies in anticipation of your retirement. In the meantime, report tomorrow to the Defectory at the back of the Health Service where our neurosurgeon will check the alignment of your brain.

TO: Lichtenstein
FROM: Office of the President

This is to inform you that you have been appointed to the newly created position, Director of Corridors.

We found recently that we had money left over just sufficient to hire one more administrator. After an unbroken session of over ten hours of deliberation by our top level staff concerning where best to spend our budget, we concluded that the problem of corridors has never been explored elsewhere. Administrators are generally concerned with staff and classrooms. This post will be an innovation and will be the first in this country. Again we lead.

You will be housed in the Administration Building next to the President's office so that he may keep in hourly touch with your plans.

A committee meeting will be called immediately concerning the urgent problem, shall we label the hall pots cuspidors or spittoons.

Please give this your serious attention and come to the meeting prepared to talk sense.

Your friendly secretary,
Vera Scrum

From: Dean Dingleberry
To: The Faculty

I am sending each of you copies of a recent letter from our Governor to President Timkens. After reading this we all know that you will willingly make the small sacrifice so gently requested.

From: The Governor
To: President Timkens

An acute shortage of several million dollars has been discovered in our operating funds. We are asking every state institution not only to limit expenditures, but to help in a personal way to restore our financial stability.

From: President Timkens
To: The Governor

Unfortunately, your letter has just reached me while I am on a much needed vacation on board the Flagship Queen Mary the Seventh. Obviously we are prepared to tighten our belts and return the state to solvency. Crumble never fails when the Governor calls. I have cabled our kind-hearted Dean Dingleberry to sound the alarm and cut 10% from the salaries of all faculty members who do not shovel coal elsewhere after hours. Our faculty would give more, but I am taking the initiative to prevent them from their own over-generosity.

Even I shall participate in a most extreme way. After reaching Tibet, I have decided to sharply reduce the number of sherpas who will climb Mt. Everest with me. Also, on the way back, I have cut my swimming lessons on the Riviera to just three weeks.

To: President Timkens
From: Psychology Staff

When you recommended Rufus Scratchbottom to us, you

stated that he was poised on the edge of tomorrow. Apparently he fell into yesterday. We have partly solved the problem by putting him in a barrel at any faculty meeting. The lid is inserted as soon as he starts to talk.

To: The Great Crumble Quality Control Laboratory
From: Social Secretary, President Timkens' House

Our milk is now tasting peculiar. Would you analyze it?

To: Social Secretary
From: Quality Control Laboratory

We analyzed the milk. Someone is pissing in it.

To: QCL:
From: Social Secretary

The President wants to know whose piss it is. And how many. We are submitting another sample with the name of suspects. Hopefully, we will not have to piss-type the entire faculty.

SCOOP RELEASE

International Wire and Horseracing Service is proud to announce the following scoop release.

Shebanse Polytech, the brightest star in the spreading state educational system, will shortly announce its new president, Dauntless Dan Shmirts.

Dauntless Dan was for several years the head of Wrong State University to the east. He attained his greatest fame by stabbing the governor. Something about a ten dollar bill. The everforgiving governor has freed him to develop Shebanse into an institution which will strike terror into Downstate University.

We have advance information that Dauntless Dan's first act of defiance will be to build a dormitory 2 miles long and 3 feet high. It will be entirely underground. This will allow ample parking for legitimate and illegitimate purposes in the woods above and please the ecologists by allowing freedom of expression for beer can throwers throughout the preserve.

Also, it will allow moles to attend classes. We know of no other college which moles can attend. Try to beat that for area service.

As soon as we get additional information about Shebanse Polytech, and also who won the third at Hialeah, we will have another startling release.

STUDENT NOTES

Mr. Dill Pickle, an unclassified senior, was called in to the Dean of Men about being perpetually drunk. Mr. Pickle explained that he was a polytheist and it was essential to pour a libation to the Goddess of Victory, to Kris Kringle and to various other divinities who needed to be placated any particular evening. The Dean agreed that he ought not to interfere with such a noble purpose. The Dean, however, campused Pickle for setting fire routinely to paper napkins at every table in the dining hall. Pickle agreed that he would try his best to limit this bad habit only to holidays.

Mr. Blix Cottonrat, who has just come to Crumble as an exchange student from Bongoland, has told reporters that he has American blood in his veins. His father ate a missionary.

Mayor Slusher Weakling, in his semi-weekly Sanitation Address, stated that if the students don't stop beer-bottling the town, he will personally break a new bottle over each student's head. To expedite this, he requests that all students leave the campus Tuesday only by the main gate. Suspicious-appearing ones will be given the therapeutic treatment. Slusher offers his usual quotation that "Thems which is innocent I will apologize to; thems which is guilty deserve what they get."

To: Admissions Office
Re: Lycanthrope Catwink's character

Mr. Catwink has a character. I recommend him for going to

colledge, mostly as a freshmin, even less. Thru Personal contack as my kitchen scrime boy he was as honest as can be expextid. He is upwright and a churchgoer, His teacher says he has a good record in study hall.

I would recomment him to anyone. His ambishin is to be a teacher in Crumble High School.

Slusher Weakling
Mayor of Crumble

The mayor also noted in another communication that intermarriages between townsfolk and Crumble City Junior College students would henceforth be permitted without penalty. The mayor observed that this was the new right of any Crumble City taxpayer—if he could find a college student fit to marry (which the mayor doubted).

The Biology Building janitor wants a student investigated. He says that this student spends most of his time beating up glassware. He does it in his laboratory on the second floor. Every day you can hear him in there, dropping pipets, smashing beakers, and kicking around centrifuge tubes. The janitor thinks this student has a grudge.

The Department of Physics has broken Teaching Assistant Felix Malarchy so that he is now an undergraduate. In his lectures to students, Felix simply was unable to equate mits with stilbs. Worse still, Felix finally admitted that he never heard of either one of them. Felix will have to write 10,000 times that 1 mit is 10^{-4} stilbs and he has agreed to accept all other similarly appropriate punishment.

A Writing Sample from a Test in the English Department:

"Woman meticulously dressed, hair done obviously by Pierre Andre of Fifth Avenue, carrying a copy of Aesop's Fables in one hand and a sandwich board reading Down With President Timkens in the other hand."

Directions to students: Write a one-page essay about this passage. It is admirably matched with your convoluted adolescent minds.

People are bringing folding seats to watch the goings on at the Great Crumble Mattress Factory downtown. Wall-to-wall bedbugs have seized the premises. Expert exterminators from the Entomology class at the College have been called in and they have surrounded the building with spray cannons. The leader issued his final ultimatum with a bullhorn "Come out, you bastards" but the only response was thousands of bedbugs peering out the windows to see what Crumble students look like. The whole matter is touch and go.

All students are advised to read the new sign posted in Obstetrical Lane in the Crumble Cemetery. It reads. "Please keep your clothes on when a funeral is passing by."

The fraternity that complained it didn't have a pot to pee in or a window to throw it out of was given wide-mouthed bottles by a local philanthropist. A drive for a window should solve the problem.

To freshmen living in Economy Dormitory in Alligator Swamp: Make friends with a plumber. Ingratiate yourself.

Daisy Doolittle, who prefers not to live alone and her definition includes females, has invited 10 males to share her apartment. She is also looking for a cashier.

The Student Council has requested surplus cheese for the students in Economy Dorm. There will have to be an investigation of Housemother Cruella and her daughter, Crumbette.

Boorsby Chimneysoot, a wheelchair student, who always surfaces exactly 10 minutes before any of his classes ends, ran his chair full speed downhill to get to the last three minutes of a lecture which was on the importance of punctuality. This time he smashed into his instructor who as usual had forgotten that he had a lecture. Both are no longer concerned about getting to class since they have been assigned to washing frogs for the remainder of the semester.

We just retrieved a misplaced letter to Myron:

Dear Myron:

I am going into oratory full speed and to hell with your advice except to find out what the greatest clinical dangers are in my new field. Unfettered Sadie

Dear Unfettered: The outstanding clinical danger for you is hoof-in-mouth disease. Get a job in a morgue where you can be away from the live ones.

The Committee to Restore Student Rights has been disestablished. The Administration declares it to be a misrepresentation. The students never had any rights to begin with.

Students will be glad to know that Crumble's newest restaurant "FLOG A DEAD HORSE" will open shortly. When Dean Dingleberry heard the news, he went into a swivit. Research ophthalmologists are watching his eyeballs oscillate.

The Health Service advises students that when they become frustrated, it is therapeutic to throw a college vice-president out of the window. Such administrators must expect to be thrown out of the window from time to time and this should be taken with good grace.

Crumble's leading research student is leaving the College. He spent seven years on a genetic study with fruit flies and he claimed his study was of Nobel Prize quality. Just before he obtained the final results, the Janitorial service sprayed the building, acutely terminating the monumental work.

From: Football Coaching Staff
To: Committee on Admissions

We very much regret your attitude toward the boy whom we convinced should come to CCJC from Horseshit Ridge High School. He ranked first in a class of seven students and there is no disgrace in admitting valedictorians. This statement is especially true for fullbacks. It is certainly not our fault that he now ranks next to last among 11,000 students. Given a fair chance he will probably flunk high. We believe that he deserves every opportunity to flunk on his own accord and in his own time, and a fair time allotted for this should be the next four years.

The course in Advanced Writing for Prospective Authors, English 502, is just chock full of useful gems. Even at the first meeting, the lecturer warns the students never to write on both sides of the manuscript paper, especially if it is toilet paper. This caveat, alone, is worth the tuition. Keep in mind that the course is open to the student who cannot afford a brain evaluation when the magnetic imaging van rolls slowly through the neighborhood.

More effective action is being requested by the local pawnbroker against Bog Whortleberry, an unfrocked Honor Student. According to the pawnbroker, the dialogue went something like this at 2 a.m. last night.
Bog: "Whassa time?"
Pawnbroker; "Why do you call me at this hour?"
Bog: "You have my watch."

Bog has some redeeming trait. When asked by a motorist "Have you lived here all your life," Bog replied quick as a flash "Not yet."

This month's national collegiate prize for non-interpretable quotations went to Crumble, as expected. A student majoring in Logic said "Live it up while you can; you will be dead the rest of your life." His brother, also a half-wit, said "Of the five smartest students in Remedial English, I'm in the top 10."

Fishkettle Socrates, Diener in Remedial English and Something in Philosophy, asked Physical Education student Pogo Twister to write an essay defending both "Look before you leap" and the contradictory "He who hesitates is lost."

Pogo lost some sleep pondering the problem, but with good judgment came to class the next morning, sized up Fishkettle carefully, leaped, and then decked him forthright.

The Disciplinary Committee agreed that Pogo had satisfied all conditions and that his putting it in writing would have wasted his valuable time.

Crumble's intercontinental football star, Nawrocki, is now markedly diminished in his phenomenal reputation. He started as the superstar in the line-up for Crumble versus Fawchee Subnormal. This contest rivals that of subway workers versus airplane baggage handlers, Robin Hood versus The Sheriff of Nottingham, or even Abdul-el-Bull-Bull Amir versus Ivan Petrofsky Skivar.

By the third play of the epic contest, Nawrocki had brought the ball down to the one-yard line on fourth down and a decision was made to attempt a field goal. With his most mighty effort Nawrocki missed the ball, but he kicked the internationally famous referee Teetertotter who just missed sailing over the goal post.

Nawrocki, sad to relate, was a victim of the immutable rule

covering that kind of unsportsmanlike conduct. He was undressed, even including his jockstrap, and an electrologist was hastily summoned to erase his penile tattoo reading "Varsity Superstar." He was then unceremoniously removed from the stadium in a go-cart pulled by a mule at funeral-type speed.

From an old Pro: If you have the need to accrete useful knowledge, don't keep working in your office. Get out into the corridor or head for the front steps. That's where the action is.

ALUMNI NOTES

Outstanding alumnus, Shakershooker Snickersnacker, is as American as apple pie, motherhood and Hoolihan. He married his cousin because her name was July Fourth. According to the neighbors, the police appear regularly to quell the vocal firecrackers. Parental guidance determines whether the neighbors' children are permitted to be part of the listening audience.

July is pregnant and wants to name a possible son "John." The Spondee Society, which encourages balanced syllables in names, says that it will excommunicate Shakershooker for irreligious conduct if he allows this to happen.

Dr. Fishball Windbreaker, '46, has been made Visiting Professor. Fishball is the world's greatest authority on wormy mackerel. He has published 150 papers on this matter, although 147 of them are apparently identical. Fishball says he may turn his attention to some other earth-shaking research when he reaches Crumble; for example, he is currently showing a small interest in the parasites of the aardvark and is submitting 20 manuscripts to indicate that this is only a pilot study. This is obviously now his territory and all other investigators are hereby forewarned to keep clear.

114 Overhead Door, class of 1950, has left the country and opened a restaurant in Formosa. 114 is finally a success since all the Chinese truckdrivers stop there.

Squirrel Cage Public Schools
Office of the Superintendent
Dear President Timkens:

This is in anser to yore litter about jobs for Crumble alumny. We have jobs here for two of yore recunt grsdjits in English. They have to see me to tell them about our supurb indoctrinatshun course. They need thes before we give them a certificit in English. Don't send us A studints; they are troublemakers.

I was very luky here. Because I had an English majur at Crumble, I was first made Charemin of English in the High School. My speshalty is Beowulf and Anglo-Saxon Filologi. The Schule Commity liked me so much they made me Soopintendent instead of Principil.

Hard work pays,
Horace Greeley
Class of 1950

Knickerbocker Greenteeth '25 received the following note: Please do not come back to any more reunions. Your urine has retarded the setting of the cement on the new sidewalk back of the library. Of course, there is the possibility that we could use you to unclog drains. This would allow us to discharge the plumber in the Philosophy building who must be a communist to work with that gang.

Sludge Lagoon '52 has completed his master's thesis at another university but he won't tell where. He says that he has enough thesis material left over for two of his friends who he will meet at the coming reunion.

SOME INCIDENTAL CATCHUPS

Assistant Diener Truncated Cerebrum sent President Timkens a bottle of wine with a screw cap for Timkens' birthday. It is our considered opinion that Truncated may stay in rank for the rest of his unfortunate life. Timkens can get very stern about the status of social maturity in postpuberal staff members.

The story is told about our bravest military alumnus, Colonel Gideon Floy, during an incident in his wartime service.

Colonel Floy: Men, as soon as you meet the enemy, fight to the bitter end and give no quarter. Even when entirely surrounded, remember that you are the main hope of your fellow men. If, however, the situation is obviously totally hopeless, you might turn around and run. I'm a little lame so I'll start now.

Architect Subliminal, who designed the Crumble city hall that disappeared into a mine shaft, has got into it again. This time he put Doric instead of Corinthian pillars on the portico of the new horse barn at the School of Agriculture. When questioned about this, Subliminal said "Who the hell cares?" Greek professor Thanatos threatens to firebomb Subliminal's motorcycle.

The Faculty Club in an admirable change of pace served a choice between brindled gnu and dik-dik last night. The cook is congratulated on his research boldness and should be promoted to Lecturer in Zoology.

TOWN AND GOWN

Dr. A. Kooky Strategy, Assistant Instructor in Political Science, ran for dogcatcher in a precinct full of cats and won, paws down.

The Crumble Office Furniture Co. has been found playing the Shawnee Switch. The point of the game was to sell a roomful of desks to CCJC, steal them back during the night, then sell them back at a higher price due to the prevailing scarcity. The furniture outfit deserved to get caught because it disobeyed the cardinal rule of the game, which is that the goods must not be stolen back more than twice.

Appeal from the Mayor's Office:

Help make our junkyards more esthetic. Throw something beautiful away today.

The Great River Crumble has dried up following installation of the new dam under the direction of the School of Engineering. It is now estimated that it will take two years for a fish to learn to swim.

Dean Dingleberry is being honored again. The Crumble Popcorn Vendors Association has inscribed his name in its golden book of all-time greats. Such names as Obadiah, Socrates, Lorenzo de Medici, Napoleon, Fingers McGurk and Paul Revere are in the same book.

The Crumble security patrolman who directed the polite safeblower how to reach the bank at 2 a.m. Thursday will have three years leave without pay.

Condemned Bait, retired fisheries expert, was seen today in a police car, completely bound in chains. He couldn't make his monthly payment for his 1906 watch to soft-hearted Sam, owner of Crumble's leading loan company. Sam's wife, Piranha, says they will press the case until justice is done. Please call the Bastille for visiting hours.

Mayor Slusher Weakling proudly announces that Middle Swiddlepuddle Academy will relocate in Crumble. This may take some time since the Academy's deportation notice has not yet been signed by the Governor and Board of Health.

The mayor was busy in the suburbs this morning. He cut the ribbon on the new dirt road connecting Yokelsburg to Bad Eggsville. There might have been somebody watching, but no one knew how to get there.

Instructor Beerkeg has again advanced Veterinary Medicine. He has given irrefutable evidence that a tightly wrapped medical journal is the best ammunition to throw at a disagreeable cat.

Director Fearless of the Great Crumble Antivivisection Society has a Great Dane called Howl and the dog has an obedience score of 0.3 on a scale of 1 to 10. To date, the director has had his collarbone displaced into his ankle and three unexplained bones jutting through his skull, and this only on walking the dog. The director hopes that the dog will never encounter a squirrel. We can only hope that this doesn't happen downhill.

Immoderate Diseasepot, whose academic specialty is the destruction of proverbs and maxims, has now done in "Two heads are better than one." He found that his two stupid physicians multiplied his disease by two and, much worse, it cost him twice as much.

President Timkens is to be commended for his verbal dexterity. At the commencement exercises he exhorted the graduates to use their skills and profound knowledge attributable to the unsurpassed faculty to go forth and meet the enormous opportunities awaiting them in the outside world. He had just told the same faculty, who had to attend the graduation exercises as an obligation, that if they don't pay on time for their rented caps and gowns, they may face the dismal probability of being thrown out into a hostile world in which jobs are hardly existent.

The note above should also serve as a warning to the faculty that attendance at commencement is a must. An absent person will have to submit letters from his physician, attorney, and also from a clergyman who can attest to the defendant's godliness. The whole thing must be signed by a judge. We cite the devious attempt of a staff member who surreptitiously stepped out of the processional formation and was immediately jabbed by a spear wielded by an alert dean who was charged with surveillance from a position under a seat.

FACULTY REPORTS: WE JUST HAVE TO PRINT THEM

Our legal staff has mixed opinions on the following case. We have no commentary from the Health Service. The convicted criminal who murdered 10 people wasn't put in the electric chair on the appointed day because he didn't feel well. We don't need any more comments. Read it and shut up.

Since we provide non-requested commentary on academic trivia, we pause to note that our Physics Department agrees with the comedians who hold that an egg can be unscrambled by feeding it back to a hen which in turn organizes a new egg. Organization implies a lessening of entropy (energy loss) to the universe. This defies the Second Law of Thermodynamics which holds that the energy of the universe is going downhill. The loss, however, fails to be compensated by the hen's heroic action because there are energy-rich wastes produced in the processes involved in evolving a new egg. The net loss is thus in keeping with the tenets of the Second Law.

In this imaginary fray, an elegant compromise has been offered which claims that although a hen may not be able to restore a single unscrambled egg to its pristine condition, a several egg omelet that includes shells might work, thus confirming the validity of the Second Law.

We applaud the fact that this dreamed-up scenario (SCIENCE, v.249, p.228, 1990) reveals a healthy sense of humor among scientists even though there are no Nobel prizes awarded.

The Great Crumble Players, who have been seized and removed to the city jail frequently for their somewhat overzealous moonlight cast and crew parties, are finding it difficult to rehearse for a play about Rome circa 50 B.C. This is because everyone knows that Romans when sober were very serious and they always spoke in somber, whole sentences. Thus, in the play:

Magistrate: Time prevents frivolity. By the way, whom shall we execute today?

Patrician: Horatius Minimus; he ran a red light.

A General (who just happened to be passing by): It is a dull day. Let us start a war.

Magistrate: State the charges. I will present the facts to the great and noble Caesar when he completes his three-day nap.

General: A plebeian in Carthage has failed to pay his taxes. He claims to have spent his money buying a goat.

Magistrate: Get the fleet ready. And as a bonus, General, over the Alps you go. Start now. The troops will follow next month when the shoemaker finishes heels and soles on their boots.

(Editor's note: Enough of the Romans for today. We could return to this but we probably won't.)

Electronic Fog, the latest Crumble addition and an expert in Biomedical Engineering, has had mixed inventive success or failure depending on your personal opinion. His thermometer, which requires two rooms of wiring, measures oral temperature and then only if the subject stands on his head. Another invention gives the pulse rate and requires that wires are wrapped around the entire outside of the building. Fog's colleagues on the second floor fear that he may get interested in electric motors and some have taken out earthquake insurance.

MEMO TO: Members of the Faculty Roundtable
FROM: Rigged Hornblower, Self-Appointed Chairman
The next meeting of the Roundtable will be devoted to emphasiz-

ing the need for greater democracy in electing the members of, and selecting the agendas for, the various College committees.

As a trusted member of the Roundtable, I am ordering you to come to a collusory meeting at my home Tuesday evening. The purpose is to ensure that the proper individuals will be nominated to all committees that decide anything.

Parkinson, a keen observer of academic life, established immutable laws of departmental behavior. We cannot refrain from confirming one of his laws herein. When the Political Science Department cannot ascertain the solution to a complex national problem, they call upon Sinbad, a staff member who is an expert on military disasters. Sinbad displays the Parkinsonian syndrome known as "reverse infallibility." He can always be depended upon to provide an answer. Immediately, the staff knows that just exactly the opposite is the correct answer.

Last night the Malevolent Society members celebrated their fifth anniversary with their expected creative genius. They captured Dean Dingleberry, put him in a cage, and lowered him into the Chancellor's office to test the air. Dingleberry had to admit that at desk level he found it difficult to breathe. The Health Service and Board of Health have put the chamber on red alert, but they state that the Chancellor and his office appear to be fully adapted to each other.

The recent meeting of the College Honor Society was not its most successful. Guest speaker Whitaker Woofer was asked by the chronic heckler group "Did Aholibamah go to bed with Bashemath?" Woofer responded that he knew nothing about sex, whereupon he launched into an endless monologue on the point. After 30 minutes, President Timkens smashed a plate over Woofer's head. This abruptly improved the quality of the meeting. It was the consensus, however, that Woofer could articulate nonsense comprehensibly.

The Trustees will address the question, "Should Dean Dingleberry be separated?" The question has arisen as to whether he is still capable of bringing in his truffles. Even the President is considering letting Dingleberry retire. An example is the following letter.

Dear Dean:

We would like to bring to your attention the fact that on July 10 we received a return-addressed envelope from you without anything in it. Would you shed some light on this?

Lighthouse Keepers of America

Eliot Parrotfish, Crumble genealogist, can trace faculty names back to the fourth century. Since Eliot murdered his assistant, his own name will be changed to Number 14,786 at the State prison and he might be difficult to trace.

The new baker at the Student Center is very polite. For example, he says to his supervisor "I don't really give a shit, Mam"; or "screw you." But he never swears on Sunday.

Gluteal Lurch, a perennial candidate who is never accepted for a job, complains that he was turned down for a post which was given to Magnolia LaDouche. Lurch says that in preparing for her interview she put on her killer dress, drew herself up to her full height, and with unerring confidence followed her breasts right into the room.

Intern Gleep's 20-year old cardiac patient has gone into a rock-a-bye baby status following Gleep's prescription for a new craze, the cholesterol on the rocks diet. Gleep's victim ate polar bear liver twice a day, washed down with a gallon of port wine. The bookmakers in the Zoology Department are taking odds on the date of Gleep's retreat at high speed.

The Governor
Your Excellency:

I wish to remind you of the recent legislation that all missing funds up to one million dollars are exempt from investigation. Our annual audit shows no more than $999,998.98 missing in this category. Thus, as always, Crumble adheres strictly to State law.

Exuberantly truthful,
Henry Nickelbiter, Bursar

Dr. Split Crotch
Professor of Obstetrics in the Health Service
Dear Orator and Wit:

Your supremely forceful tirade against Crumble in the last convocation just lost us another 350 students. In recognition of the bereavement of those surplus faculty members who must now leave us, and also in honor of your passing, I am asking that all campus flags be lowered to half mast while you are being escorted slowly out of town by the campus police to escape the charge of criminal trespass on college property. You are fired as of this letter. Please deposit your I.D. card in the trash barrel as you leave the front gate.

Fondest farewell,
Smiley Timkens

There is always a glitch in the plans of steam plant foreman Boilercrud. Today, with the mercury below zero, heating the College had to be scrubbed. A huckster sold Boilercrud a control box with nice dials on the outside. On the inside they found a note reading "If you're smart you'll throw the whole thing away."

A truly prospective Nobel Prize winner, Aseptic Fishworm, announced recently that he had discovered the universal solvent. There was some temporary confusion when a freshman in Physical Education asked him what he kept it in.

The Chancellor, who has been gone, God knows where (and probably couldn't care less), for two years, is back and is demanding a 25% raise in pay. He justifies this by the fact that the entire program of the college improved at once when he left. He argues that the improvement must be attributed solely and directly to him. The Philosophy Department is wrestling with the logic of the situation and will shortly present its position paper to the Board of Trustees.

MAINLY PRESIDENT TIMKENS

President Smiley Timkens
Dear Smiley:

Greetings from the State Capitol. We are always overjoyed to hear from you.

The request of your Board of Trustees for $225 million dollars to operate the college next year has been reviewed in the light of current austerity measures.

If we were the U.S. Government and you were in Kenya, we would have to grant your request by the sheer force of logic. We are fully aware that your faculty and students are poverty stricken, your region of the State is distressed, and your administrators enjoy unrestrained luxury. Moreover, the size of your request indicates your ability to get rid of the money.

Since you are in direct competition with other institutions and also with the limitless supply of unwed mothers who need most of our funds, we suggest that you revise your budget to 10 million dollars and resubmit it. We will then try to get you 5 million.

Your best friend,
Pendleton Finque, Lieutenant Governor

Proptosis Fleabane, cryptographer, has cracked Timkens' supersecret communication code. It was discovered that Fleabane read Trusted Administrative Secretary Vera Scrum's lips, because she mumbles while she types. Timkens is getting a mask fitted to Vera's face, but she will first be laundered by Crumble Intelligence to ascertain the depth of her transgressions.

Dr. Dominic Regurgito
Lecturer on Stomach Diseases
Health Service
Dear Dr. Regurgito:

The Antivivisection Society has amassed incontrovertible evidence that you have been shining an intense beam of light into your fish tank, causing unknown damage to the guppies but, worse still, to their progeny. The college cannot be exposed to unfavorable publicity through the wanton acts of any of its faculty members. I am therefore turning over your fish tank to the Deacon of the College Chapel. To insure your proper rehabilitation, I am placing you, for a probationary period, as animal warden for the Antivivisection Society. You will patrol the campus from midnight to 6 a.m. feeding stray cats.

As soon as infallible tests developed at Crumble show a decisive change in your behavior, you will be removed from leave without pay status and returned to the classroom.

Everyone loves guppies,
Smiley Timkens

From: President's Office Quickie
To: Dean Dingleberry

I am deeply appreciative of your desire to fire Assistant Dean Unscrambled Eggs immediately. You state that he lost the key to the master keyrack, which effectively shut down the entire Liberal Arts College for three days while the keyhunt was in progress.

Since this is the first time that Professor Eggs has crossed my radar screen I will as usual temper mercy with justice and merely warn him by fining him three months of his salary.

Because other administrators have complained that you failed to join the key hunt, I am fining you two months of your salary.
Trainee Indwelling Catheter

Health Service
Dear Mr. Catheter:

Your enemies are expressing great concern for your mental health. Enemies are the best source of singling out defects. They think, for example, that you have a book in your collection entitled "Intersexes in the Gypsy Moth."

Also, you have not published in the past 13 years. Your explanation is that it takes time to re-tool following each publication. This we can understand. Your theory about the cause of dowager's hump has been refuted, however, and this has detracted from the reputation of the Health Service.

At a recent cocktail party you engaged in a furious argument with the chaired Professor of Theology and at one point you were heard to shout "What the hell do you know about the Holy Ghost?"

The unforgivable transgression is that you were seen bending your identification card, which is treasured at Crumble. It will no longer be possible to process your salary check through our special and secret machine and this makes your position here untenable.

Fond farewell,
Smiley Timkens

Complete Triviality
Instructor in Bowling
Dear Mr. Triviality:

I am in grateful receipt of your new and widely acclaimed book *The Demise of the College President.*

Be fully assured that it will serve a most useful purpose. My housekeeper has been instructed to wrap fish in it, using only one page per fish. We will thus be fortunate to have your text in our home for at least a year.

Keep in touch with me if you put out a second edition.

Cordially,
Smiley Timkens

President Timkens
Dear Prexy:

I am hereby protesting your notification that I am in danger of being dismissed as Department Chairman because the monthly Health Service check of my urine showed the presence of mauve factor. There is no clear cut evidence that patients who have mauve factor differ from anyone else around here.

I regard the whole system as unfair. To cite one instance, Prof. Tummytamper has not been given his notice despite the fact that he passes two watery stools per day. There is also talk that he has griping abdominal pains every time he sees a student.

Miss Kitty Litter of the Home Economics Department is known to have dry mouth and scanty urination. She is also known to be particularly fond of lukewarm dog chow.

There is also the case of Mrs. Marigold van Loon. She climbs poles but she is not working for the telephone company. As a child she used to wet the ceiling.

And mind you, Prexy, the above cases are only within the circle of my closest friends. I request that you reconsider your hasty decision. Truth will prevail,

Fungi Ben Mushroom
Chairman of Botany

NIGHTLETTER FROM THE REGISTRAR

Lichtenstein:

The Committee on Exotic Minorities is being called into immediate night session. Come as you are.

A cryptic note, below, has just been received by carrier pigeon from the missionary CCJC enrollment center. Apparently there is the possibility of obtaining six applicants from Lower Kettledrum Province in Bongoland, and no expense should be spared to bring this about.

The applicants state: "Have heard of humanitarian work of great white father, Smiley Timkens, President of College and undoubtedly of United States. Our problem is, lazy relatives have bowel movements in bed, push it out with feet. More education needed. Urgent. Save us. Matriculation fee guaranteed."

At present, our plans are to have the Dean of Freshmen take charge of you as a group and form a safari. The party will hack its way through the 180 miles of twisted jungle. A helicopter will drop leaflets "We are coming."

STUDENT HUMDRUM

Ms. Jot Tittle
President, The American's American Society
From: Dean Dingleberry

We investigated your complaint that a student told you that another student told him in the washroom that two instructors are teaching communist doctrines to their classes.

One of the instructors has been in Sri Lanka for the past five years teaching an Agriculture class how to plant tomatoes. Students registered here in a class assigned to him by error said that he once surfaced on campus and asked where his raincoat was.

The second instructor is thought to be in Nepal teaching the sherpas how to better develop a second wind while climbing. We have been tracing how he manages to get his monthly salary check. He once told his class here that he wanted to be a sheep herder. Our students were diverting him from his grand purpose.

The arrest of Filch Hammertoe, a sophomore, sullies Crumble's impeccable reputation. The charge is that he hid stolen jugs of rum inside the carillon at the College chapel. The clanging that accompanied a solo by the carilloneur led to Filch's current sojourn in the city bastille.

Former student Yok Tommygun, a several time pardonee from the state prison, is now on security patrol in the College payroll office. The Bursar explains that it will be easier to identify the criminal when the crime wave begins.

The Secretary of the Student Council reports that two students shot each other fatally from opposites sides of a corridor in the Student Union. Out of respect for the dead, no names were taken.

Overheard in Freshman Commons:

Student 1: Why aren't you taking your dog for a walk this morning?

S-2: He isn't up to it.

S-l: How come?

S-2: He's dead.

Farly Sourstomach, a brilliant student, is in trouble. He lost his tuition money in a poker game. Presently, he lives inside an elevated Cola sign on Main Street.

Farly made his major mistake by taking in a roomer. The very smart roomer nailed a mailbox to the sign pole. One day the roomer complained that a special delivery letter was not received and he visited his congressman to demand dismissal of the postmaster.

Farly and his friend are reconsidering their position in the city pokey.

Some action will have to be taken about the cross-eyed cricket. He flies in to a classroom, takes notes for the first half of the class, then eats them. Worse, he eats the notes of students he hates. Yesterday he ate the lecturer's notes and since the lecturer obviously was not expected to remember anything, he had to dismiss the class.

Dear Unremitting Sin:

All-Purpose Standby Professor

Since you are now 97 years old and must prepare for judgment day, a long overdue behavior modification toward students is a must. You need to be aware that St. Peter, who guards the gates of Heaven, will peruse your vita line by line with a magnifying glass. In my opinion, your chances of getting into the big rock-candy mountain are slim. Just in case of trouble, I urge that you read Dante's INFERNO, especially his one-liner stating that the damned who abide in the seventh circle of Hell must stand neck-deep in boiling lava.

For your cosmic happiness,
Angelina Christmascake, Head
Division of Theology

The students are in agreement that the greatest advance in academia is the invention of the eraser. We are not asking your opinion.

Miss Susie Floogel
Campus
Dear Miss Floogel:

Our entire Sorority joins in the regret that we cannot ask you to become a member at this time.

In short, you have flunked the candid crumpets-and-tea test. An invisible protractor which hung over your head indicated that when you raised your teacup, the critical value of sine theta was exceeded for the allowable elevation of your little finger.

Also, among other things, you have given us the impression that your family once owned an alley-cat.

Cordially,
Harriett Strump
Recording Secretary

THE FACULTY—MERCIFULLY SHORT

Miss Serenade Appelstrudel
Department of Music
Dear Miss Appelstrudel:

You have been on our music faculty twenty seven years and I am willing to pander to your fantasies about your operatic abilities. In the last concert, however, I detected a wobble in your voice when you attained the whistle register.

As you are aware, our public image is important and it demands superb poise and confidence. An excessive tremulo signals impending senescence. I suggest that you immediately consult our hypnotist at the Health Service. He will realign your vocal machinery and restore your ego.

You will report to my office in exactly three weeks and be tested by our trusted administrative secretary for your ability to go from buffo to lyric.

Your wish is my command,
Smiley Timkens

A Day in the Life of an English Professor:

Professor: Wake up student Stenchitol. It is difficult to learn in the Trendelenburg position.

Stenchitol: Heard you twice the first time.

Professor: Who wrote the Charge of the Light Brigade?

Stenchitol: The Suburban Gas and Electric Company.

Professor: I'm asking you politely, please major in physical education.

Hamburger Whoosh
Meat Packing Area, Student Union
Dear Hamburger:

Your manuscript "English Has Been Had Man And All You Other Cats" has the distinction of being all alone in its class. Our most humane reviewer had to be given tranquilizers. I reviewed the opus and I have classified the language as "Contemporary Makeshift."

If you come here with an interpreter, we may be able to decode the sentences. We can then better advise you about the type of incinerator to throw the manuscript (?) into.

No charge for the advice,
Forby Doo Doo

Just retired, famous Professor Numinous, for years deferentially bowed to by everyone at Crumble, and unwaveringly arrogant as consistent with his exalted status, has just suffered the syndrome called "Instant Oblivion." He moved to another city where he sits totally unrecognized on a park bench while the fellow mowing the grass around him is having a ball conversing in fourth grade English with everyone present or passing by. *Sic transit gloria mundi.*

The chaplain of the College Chapel was robbed this morning by two unidentified students. One said he was not an atheist and used a bottle of Christian Brothers brandy to hit the chaplain over the head.

REPORT OF THE ADMINISTRATORS WINGDING

The High Administration held its banquet last night in the Platinum Room of President Timkens' home.

It was agreed that substituting Tasmanian wombat for the usual coon pie and dumplings was an excellent innovation. The honored guest, Grand Rubbish, Mayor of South Cornfield, stated that the horseradish could have been better.

The Director of Building and Grounds claimed that a general misconception seems to exist that the College is for faculty and students. Unless something is done, their presence will someday require painting of the buildings. Third Vice President Dingdong Featherbrain observed that he has seen this alarming situation elsewhere.

Uppermost Dean Dingleberry moved that Deans who attained their quota of discharging two full professors per year over a five year period should be invited to succeeding wingdings.

Statistical Director Fivetoes Plusorminustwo showed charts about the activities of the full professors. The members in that rank want their teaching loads lightened because it is a waste of superior brains to expose inferior students to superior intellects.

It was noted that all full professors loads had been cut in half one year ago. Analysis of this action upon the scholarly performance was as follows:

37 percent of the full professors have been home more often washing dishes; 40 percent are actively engaged in leaving town every Thursday for meetings which all agreed cut down their light and food bill at home; 2 percent are attendants at laundromats or car washes most of the week. The remaining staff have successfully eluded trace.

The College Attorney wanted to show how justicc prevailed in the Great Crumble Courthouse. Permission was granted.

Judge to plaintiff: Do you have witnesses that your husband floored you with a right hook?

Plaintiff: Definitely. There were two cats and a talking parrot present.

Judge: The parrot's testimony is admissible. The Court will adjourn and you will bring the bird here tomorrow to be sworn in.

Dean Dingleberry said that the subject of professors was beginning to nauseate him. Could he have some more wombat?

President Timkens spoke of the need for enforcing the nepotism clause which forbids anyone in Crumble from being hired. The point arose, Timkens said, after Dingleberry recommended his niece, Densie Ann, who then joined Timkens' secretarial staff. It seems that Timkens wanted to get rid of Dillsworth Chuckwagon who Timkens inherited from an uncle along with a bankrupt hotel. Timkens noted that Dillsworth's only virtue was that he sustained a visible body temperature. Timkens proposed that the Faculty cast a vote between Dillsworth or Chilbain Fench (Emeritus Trusted Presidential Assistant) for the position as Fourth Vice President. Densie Ann, the vote counter, couldn't spell Chilbain, so she eliminated him from the ticket and Dillsworth won the election. Densie Ann, unfirable, will be transferred to the Marco Polo branch in the Arctic Circle.

The Director of Buildings and Grounds said that a sewerpipe had to be fixed right away since a proctor had reported a flood about four hours ago in a coed dormitory. He would try to wake up a plumber. One of the Vice Presidents woke up and moved for adjournment. This was done following the singing of God Bless America.

MORE FACULTY NOTES—
SORRY ABOUT THAT

The State Department of Conservation closed the College pond today after exhaustive analysis resulting in a diagnosis of submarginal fish. Jonathan Rockbottom, Professor of English, whose family has lived on submarginal fish-heads for four years has circulated a petition to nullify this action which could change his entire life style.

Assistant Professor Bodkins discovered a leak yesterday in his basement chemistry laboratory. Students reported today that Bodkins was up to his neck in water. He had used the wrong form to summon assistance from the Department of Buildings and Grounds. Bodkins has been advised to seek assistance from the Coast Guard.

The English Department announces that Distinguished Professor Misplaced Diphthong, who wrote the text "The Ineluctable Oblivion that Awaits the Uncreative Mind" has completely disappeared. Police can find no trace.

The Legislature recommended that an increase in salary be paid to all those instructors who have had no increases for seventeen years.

The President and Board of Trustees dissented on the grounds that this action would separate this group off as a special entity within an academic society that should be homogeneous. Moreover, their report states, the current salaries of this group are still in excess of those paid to local egg candlers and this has already created enough ill-will in the community.

Dysgenesis T. Smith, Professor of Drama, believes in fate and he finally got his. He was having his routine 10 a.m. nap in his office on the third floor when two tons of coal fell on him. The Mobile Unit from the Health Service broke an axle while bringing him to the hospital, and the victim lost two more teeth.

Investigation has revealed that the College Architect insulated the roofs of several buildings with coal. Something about it being cheaper than conventional methods. In fact, Architect Benson had just published his findings in the national journal and stayed close to his telephone just in case he was nominated to the Hall of Fame.

The Professor is convalescing nicely. He refuses to return to his office until the Geology Department finishes its report on the depth of the residual coal deposits in the Department roof. Other faculty members have been supplied with crash helmets and snorkels.

The seminar by the Economics Department on Business Advertising was of particularly high quality. When your rival firm is claiming to have 26% free material in one of its products, your firm must meet this competition with vigor and the clear thinking worthy of a Crumble graduate. Just grind up some unwashed socks and incorporate them into the developing mash. When the weight is appropriately increased, proudly advertise your product as having a 30% freebie increment, not to mention an indescribable flavor. Always put a scientific analysis on the container label, designating the additive as tetra-hexa-methyl-umpha-umpha, of which only a pint exists in the world.

Shpritzen Wasser, who once failed a course in Public Speaking because of slobbering saliva while talking, is heading a national committee that is preparing a film on lecturing technics. Shpritzen has announced that in view of his extensive experience his committee although large will be entirely unnecessary.

Droopy Drone, Lecturer in bagpipes in the Music Department, has announced his latest song "Where There's a Hill, There's a Valley." This has received a citation for being the most logical opus of the year. Although there is talk of transferring Droopy to the Philosophy Department, the Botany Department has first claim following his thrilling work "If the Rats don't get it, the Bread Mold will."

Dr. Twerp Heady of the Department of Anthropology has revealed that he has the largest collection of shrunken dean's skulls in the Western Hemisphere. He intends to analyze the material for significant osteologic differences between greater and lesser deans.

The Faculty Playgroup has been forbidden permission to put on their production "Fury in the Greenhouse." This was based upon a factual account of a gunfight between the staff of the Botany Department and the employees of Buildings and Grounds. It started over who owns the rhododendrons. The Administration prefers that the incident be forgotten.

Randolph Sixtoes, Expert in Genetics, has just completed an exhaustive study of the faculty, relating the frequency of their use of swear words with their chromosomes. In normal conversation, when the word "dean" was presented to one group, it was found that the mean number of swear words used was 65 per 100 words. This was considered a control group. Evidence was presented to prove conclusively that control persons have an N gene (noncuss) limiting their cussing capacity. In the second, or experimental group, the mean number of swear words in discussing the dean was 93.7 for every 100 words used. These individuals were found to have a C (cussing) gene. The C gene appears to be dominant, as evidenced by an analysis of the children of N x C matings. No sex difference was observed. The Administration urges all afflicted persons to seek genetic counseling in the Health Service.

The Department of Economics proudly announces the appointment of Beef Stroganoff as Supervisor of Gourmet Cooking. Beef is the most innovative cook in America and comes on fortissimo in most places where he hasn't been kicked out of. It was he who first stuffed potatoes with potatoes. It was he who invented a Hunter's stew which contains anything that comes down the alley. Need we say more. Truly a goliath if the kitchen is not too well lighted. Beef succeeds Pork Cutlet who was traded to the Poisoned Arrow School of Taxidermy. The Deans, who are brave at heart, will be the first to try out their recipes.

Professor McRooster has developed a highly successfully technic for improving his staff. He singles out one staff member and prays for him the whole week. When the prayee is lecturing to his class, McRooster prays especially hard. Subsequent student evaluations show significant increase in the instructor's performance.

McRooster once prayed that God would kill the worst lecturer in the Department. The next day the instructor escaped unharmed from an auto accident, but began using nouns and verbs in his lectures. McRooster says that even though God missed, the divine message never fails.

The faculty is invited to the Social Pathology lecture tomorrow on occupational success. A typical case history will be presented. The career of Mr. X reads: grouse flusher, second hand auto dealer, mayor, full-fledged criminal.

Observations from the Computer Service: The fellow who has the bull by the tail gets 100 times more information than does the bystander.

Misplaced Decimalpoint, Assistant Instructor in Mathematics, has unveiled a theory called "The Principle of Unbelievable Endurance." The essence is that Crumble exists. Misplaced may be demoted for insisting that the second law of thermodynamics applies to Crumble, i.e., "Everything in Crumble is going downhill."

Sick Story—Anonymous
Eve: Do you love me?
Adam: Who else?

The Political Science Department quotes Simon Cameron that an honest politician is one who, when he is bought, stays bought.

The College Telecasting Department states that a 600 foot TV tower was stolen last night while the program was going on. If the tower is returned to the Scrambled Image TV Station, no questions will be asked.

To celebrate its tenth anniversary, the Health Service will award its lucky 100,000th patient a free cystoscopy, plus bilateral drainage.

Dr. Finkie-the-Frankie, internationally noted geneticist in the Department of Microbiology, was called in to determine why hoofs were dropping off the horses at the Agriculture farm. Unfortunately, it was discovered that Finkie-the-Frankie didn't know a horse's pastern from its fetlock. In fact he didn't know his own derriere from his elbow. A sophomore observed that the disease was diagnosed in 1295 A.D. as due to selenium poisoning. Finkie-the-Frankie explained to the Dean that it was no longer possible to expect anyone to keep up with the literature.

Your Roving Reporter notes that faculty members have been taking off for the long Labor Day weekend. President Timkens is visiting his 520 acre estate, Cheatwood. The Chairman of the

Botany Department is beating his way through the forest to reach his one room cabin at Bagworm-on-Spruce.

Okie Dokie has joined President Timkens Yesman Staff following a cosmic search. Okie's previous dismissals elsewhere are indeterminate since all his letters of recommendation are glorious in hallelujahs; this is standard technic to palm off a moron on unsuspecting victims.

Okie's fate at Crumble is already sealed. If he doesn't say yes with sufficient alacrity, he goes out the gate in a wheelbarrow. If he says yes too often, he goes out in the same wheelbarrow when the inevitable disaster, which will be laid on him, occurs.

The Crumble City aldermen, working with the CCJC Architectural Service, have decided to put welcoming signs at each of the approaches to the city. There is some trouble at the northern sign which reads "The City With Irresistible Charm." It appears that citizen Jeb Hackletwister refuses to move his outhouse off the property.

CCJC's new lake sprung a leak the first time it was opened. The level precipitously dropped while 1500 faculty and students were swimming and they quickly found themselves up to their belly in deep mud. The Governor, who had cut the ribbon at the far end and was delivering a stirring oration, was caught up by the current and washed over the spillway. The lake was built over an abandoned mine and simply fell into it. One spectator remarked that it was just like taking the stopper out of a bathtub. When the farmer who sold the lake was asked why he did not inform anyone about the situation, he answered "Nobody asked me."

Ogo Wormington, staff criminologist, was completing his research problem in State's Prison. He had been active four years and required ten more days to complete the crucial experiment needed to write his book. Unfortunately, the 15 prisoners he was working on were all paroled and took off in a cloud of dust. The writer talks of suicide and welcomes comments on a method.

McRooster, described by Dean Dingleberry as the most versatile staff member on the campus, placed his painting called "A Drowned Duck" in competition for a national prize. The painting was called an indescribable mess by the Academy of Art and even by the Society for Dead Birds. The Crumble Art and Literary Magazine "Disjointed" disagreed with these views. President Timkens, noted for his ability to straddle both sides of a controversy, stated "McRooster's ignorance is invincible."

President Timkens has discharged his wine steward after he shamefully belittled the omnipotence of Dionysus and Bacchus, the Greek and Roman Gods of Wine, who did so much for human pleasure. The steward can no longer be trusted.

President Timkens says that the faculty must be reduced in number, starting with the charity cases (translation: worthless teachers). He wants them to be paid in the same line as the unwed mothers, thus leaving more space in the Bursar's office for the higher grade loafers.

The Governor objects, claiming that the unwed mothers are now causing undue congestion at his garage entrance and his Rolls-Royce does not idle well at very low speed. There appears to be a standoff and the whole thing may never be solved.

The Microbiology Journal Club will not meet at Hokum's saloon this week. Extensive repairs to the slot machines inflicted by police necessitate temporary closure.

A dissident in the Speech Department says that a bore is a committee chairman who spends hours saying nothing. He also adds the comment of Jules Renard that a bore includes the committee chairman who can make you waste the entire day in five minutes. Unfortunately the faculty is given no choice.

We are compelled to insert this note which was sent to Myron at the Health Service.

Dear Myron:

My mother is unhappy with my live-in boyfriend, Poison Oak. I am taking him home this vacation to introduce him. I just know that she will love him as she does me. What do you think? Marmalade Hogfish

Dear Marmalade: If your mother says that she loves you, check it out.—Myron

Pansie Pinhead, the Registrar's chief secretary, will be questioned about her possible connection with forged student I.D. cards. Her fatal mistake was made traveling with Open Yap Hot Bun, a 13-year old foreign student. His I.D. card stated that he was prime minister of his country and to show him every courtesy of the United States, especially courtesy concerning entrance to taverns.

Joe Chaos, Senior Investigator in Geology at Crumble, goes to every scientific meeting in the world, but of late he can only be found in the corridors bewailing his grant-reductional fate. He may have to go back to Crumble and find out if they will give him some work to do for his pay. Chaos lays the blame on Geology Editor Primordial Slime. This fearless foe states that the last 300 manuscripts by Chaos are either totally wrong or are inconsequential to any known human endeavor. Slime has generously offered to tell Chaos where a high mountain is that he (Chaos, not Slime) can jump off, feet first. The instructional staff back at Crumble doesn't seem to feel any pain about Chaos not coming up trumps.

Crumble has another non-disputed first. We never cease being amazed by these kudos. Cornelius Dirtpan has developed the largest list of blasphemous words ever recorded in the English language since he was demoted from Chaired Professor of Theology to Janitor Emeritus.

The State Safety Officers meeting this week was truly informative. The famous lecturer, Curbside Slob, emphasized that radioactively contaminated bananas and oranges could be made safe by peeling them before eating them. The audience was spellbound.

CAVEAT: The easiest way to infuriate the office staff is to always get in earlier than they do. This may be the first unforgivable transgression against the acceptable mores. Our advice is that if you refuse to correct the error of your ways, then climb into the building through a chimney and hide in the President's office (he never comes in early) until the chimes of the morning strike.

Another example of bad manners is to arrive at a party after your Dean arrives and to leave just before he does. Who the boss is becomes blurred.

Another faux pas is to fail to show up at the office Halloween party or to arrive dressed as a normal person who is acceptable on the subway.

In a recent talk, Jayalkashmi Wentkatchalem, head of our newly formed seminar series, Nutrition for Americans, declared that the ratio of cases of dermatomalacia to Bitot spots was much greater in Hyderabad than in Coonoor. (Editor's note: We thought we would pass this along.)

To: Search Committee for New Vice President

From: Herman Sozzled, Secretary of the Board of Trustees

Certain procedures are to be emphasized in your search for the VP. The candidate must have an initial for his first name. His middle name should indicate baronial excellence, culture, wealth, and an authentic odor of aged cheese. A hyphenated surname might just put the candidate in like a porch climber.

As examples, I would cite: A. Wellington Hexapod or perhaps better, F. Manchester Dew-on-the Mountain.

Names such as Setscrew or Luckless will be laundered before such persons will be permitted to surface on the campus.

Subluxated Gyrus, clinical psychologist, who is occasionally discharged from the local madhouse, just won acclaim for his book *Screws in the C Valve*. This tome could rank with the dead sea scrolls. Subluxated's last book, *Gremlins in the Microswitch*, has been enthusiastically endorsed by a frenzied group of panting students in psychology.

Bugstew Hokum, Sophomore of the Year, complained that Dean Catcabbage treated him coolly at the reception last week. When Catcabbage introduced his wife, Fanny, Bugstew remarked that he could remember when Fanny was a girl's name. (We see no reason for the Dean's coolness and we can only suggest that he was constipated.)

Sociologist Compote Swindleton was born to do major research. His most recent scholarly endeavor was to test the view that "Strong fences make good neighbors." Like all solid research, this demanded a double blind approach. Thus, half the researchers walked on their own side. The other half threw rotten tomatoes and occasionally a dead cat or two over the fence into Brother John's yard. Brother John was not told which half included the offenders. The experimental protocol was obviously excellent. However, the experiment broke down. After kicking the shit out of all he could catch, Brother John said that he agrees with Slusher Weakling's position that "Them's which is innocent I apologizes to; them's which is guilty deserves their beating." The research team has abruptly decreased in numbers.

The Sidewalk Committee has resigned. Students hate sidewalks. Once one is built, they immediately create a parallel pathway through the rose bushes.

Miss Eileen Panfuss, of the Home Economics Department, has won the "National Dish of the Month" award. Its name is "Chilly Mess of Chaos " and is designed especially for the euphoric and untidy housewife.

The Campus Police were called in to quell a near riot last night at the Psychology Colloquium. A clinical psychologist who contended that psychic energizers were invented by Freud was attacked by experimental psychologists, obviously communists, who held stoutly to the view that the energizers were invented by General Electric. President Timkens has ruled that Psychology Hall is currently off-limits to the Department and will be used by the local Brownie troop, for basket weaving.

Mrs. Droney Pustule, whose husband works in the hospital sterilizing bedpans, is an upcoming teacher in the Zero Disadvantaged Program. She radiates brilliance, especially in the faculty meetings. Just as the most bored instructor is shouting for adjournment, she raises her hand and with sickening sweetness asks another question. Everyone expects her to say something like "We fry ours in lard" but she always narrowly misses this and comes out with some equally inane nonsense about a misplaced vowel in section 3, line 14 of the College constitution which nobody ever read. The chairman sternly silences the full professors, which ensures another one-hour dialogue. This is necessary since his wife cannot pick him up or probably doesn't want to.

The Chairman of the Design Department has much to answer for. Their latest design, a toaster, has consistently failed to eject jelly jump-ups. The Chairman has fallen from his days of glory. At one time he directed his students to make go-carts. One day a student accidentally made a go-cart. But, alas, this inventive direction now seems to be lost.

Great excitement appears to have arisen in the Administration Building. Oil has been discovered on the campus, in greatest concentration under the 14-1/2 million dollar library. Timkens has issued orders to start drilling right through the middle of the building.

Twisted Cable, Instructor in Safety, had bad luck in attempting to show a neophyte how to pilot one of the college's fleet of airplanes.

Twisted with good luck somehow managed to get the plane to the end of the runway before he took his inevitable double flip. Rescue squads crowbarred him and his student out of the wreckage in about 2 hours.

Twisted has been admonished not even to talk to students for the next two months, on the theory that some violent accident resulting from his advice will turn them into a crib-case.

The rumor that a dean was in the library needs clarification. The dean in question tripped on the sidewalk and was then carried into the library until the ambulance came.

The Student Union will open another bistro. After a pitched fist fight among members of the Building Committee, it was voted to name the restaurant THE RED STOOL. This is in honor of a deceased proctologist, Rancid Cookie, who died of unremitting diarrhea after faithful service as a food consultant in the main cafeteria.

Schnickle and Glintz, the consulting architects for the College, have expanded to Schnickle, Glintz, Yarf and Doubleschmeiss. This dilution occurred when Schnickle attempted to monogram the University Seal on Glintz's derriere after an altercation about the exact location of the second floor toilet in the Animal House. The situation is pretty much in hand now that Schnickle has been restricted to back yard privileges at the College Defectory. We are receiving reports from a tranquilizer salesman.

Dr. Perley Pessel has been invited to present the annual lecture to the Biology Colloquium. He will talk on the "Presence of Unidentified Objects in the Urine of Discharged University Presidents."

Dr. Lower Drainpipe, specialist in diseases of the anus and rectum, was introduced at the television show last night by the Chairman of the Department of Health Education. The Chairman logically noted that you can always tell a man's profession by looking at him.

Crumble's richest alumnus has promised a large bequest to the college with the proviso that his matriculating son be tucked into bed every night by a dean.

McRooster became involved in a heated argument with a student two days ago and his cerebral circulation is just slowing to normal. It seems that while McRooster was in the stockroom, a student asked for test tubes without color. McRooster asked without what color. The student wanted them without brown. McRooster insisted that he would have to take them without blue since he did not have any without brown. The attendants from the Defectory have not yet been able to ascertain what followed.

The Board of Trustees have finally decided that Assistant Instructor Sharkbait of Fisheries cannot be chided by his Chairman for his insistence that wrong ideas are just as important as right ones. Even though Sharkbait has been wrong for 30 years, and unquestionably longer, the Trustees have confirmed his right to be wrong by giving him the highest salary of the entire faculty. The decision rested on the fact that he generated more ideas, and who cares what, than anyone else in the College. The Board warned the Chairman that Sharkbait was not to be introduced at Department seminars as a "Festering Mass of Unsupported Assertions."

President Timkens, following an expected tantrum from the deans who are protesting elevation of standards, has announced that the rules allowing admission of the lowest tenth of high school classes shall be changed to read the lowest fifth. Heading the protests is Dean Dingleberry. He claims that his particular unit cannot afford to lose any more applicants because he may become unnecessary. Also, he is opposed to change for any reason. This appears to be a reasonable argument.

It is currently the nutritionists who quite effectively screw up the literature such that every red-blooded American who seeks longevity that includes biceps enhancement is slowly starving on bean sprouts or clogging up his intestines with oat bran. It may be necessary to turkey farm the guiding wizards into escape-proof cages in the subterranean areas of Home Economics buildings.

Even the hard scientists are at it, probably with some cause. It is now wrong to believe maps that show the north pole of every planet on the top side of the solar system. Henceforth, all students majoring in cartography or astronomy need to carry a card, if he/she cannot remember anything, the card noting that if you make a fist with your right hand and you align your fingers with the rotation of a planet (consult the nearest encyclopedia), your thumb will lie at the north pole. If the world gets topsy turvy, and who knows if it won't, immediately call the Astronomy office at Crumble. They will tell you how to realign your card even while you are upside down.

Dean Dingleberry
Uppermost Dean

You are a son-of-a-bitch. Please note the brevity of this letter. You once told me that I had to enroll in English As A Second Language. My writing skill has improved so much since I received my certificate in remedial writing that I have been offered another position, in Broken Latin.

Amor scribendi,
Melvin Two-teeth
Immediate Past Staff Member

McRooster, Professor of Dead Birds, has summoned the editor of the Faculty Newsletter for an interview. McRooster said that at one time he had intended to run for deanship when Dingleberry retired. This meant that he had to cultivate as many faculty members as possible. He found, however, that every time he memorized one faculty member's name, he forgot the name of one dead bird. McRooster theorizes that he is the only person at Crumble who knows exactly how much room he has in his brain. In view of this, he would prefer to bypass the deanship and run for higher office.

Wally, who comes from South Cornfield to make repairs on the electronic instruments, and who affixes a tag on each repaired instrument reading "A Wally Temporary," is facing loss of his job. Wally has protested, stating that his contract reads that the repair must last only until he has reached the city limits.

Director, Animal Quarters
Dear Ex-Director:

As of this letter, you are demoted to Animal Caretaker, scrime-boy section. You should have known better than to have talked back to a secretary both on civil service and the union.

In terms that you can understand, your tunnel-vision behavior confirms the historic observation that "the world of a flea is one square yard of a dog."

Accept your corrective appointment in the positive light that we try to fit everyone into a position appropriate to his talents.

Cheerio,
Dingleberry

We throw in here a caviat from Myron at the Health Service: If you are cast adrift in the Great River Crumble and nobody even bothers to look, be of good cheer. There is enough crap floating around you to keep you in nutritional balance forever. As a native of Crumble, you may even recommend the change of fare. (Editor's Note: Just for the information of those who like to enrich their store of useless knowledge, if you have to be cast adrift, the Baltic Sea is your best choice since you will neither bloat nor shrink. Also, you are not likely to be attacked by crocodiles. Remeber that we may never acknowledge that we could be liars.)

The headstone of our late Dean Emeritus, Rencher Turkey, was unveiled today in the hallowed College graveyard. We quote the epitaph thereon:

To venerable Dean Turkey, who during his life discharged 183 faculty members whom the Lord delivered into his hands. He was looking forward to his quota of 200 before the year ended when his luck ran out and he fell mortally ill.

The Board of Trustees announces that the College has bought a deactivated submarine base in the Firth of Clyde. The international aspects of the College are becoming increasingly evident.

President Timkens is becoming irked by letters sent to him from local citizens. An example of this deplorable tendency is given.

Dear President:

Your College serves no useful purpose except to embarrass me when my friends visit me in Crumble. My reason for writing is to ask you politely to discontinue operation. I would appreciate your cooperation.

Felix Cudoweicz
Drawbridge Tender

At the Summer Commencement, two forty year service pins were awarded. The citations are as follows:

To Instructor Abiah Yazook, a pious and prudent man. He was good but not that good.

To Assistant Instructor Schooley Fish. He was here 40 years.

Gaia, the Greek Goddess of Earth, who has been trying vainly to keep the environment optimal, has been advised to stay clear of Crumble. The students are proficient at spewing lethal extremes of filth hither and yon about the crampus, as much yon as hither. It is now necessary to keep the fog and strobe lights on continuously, particularly the laundry rooms.

Horseradish Peroxidase, an eco-ecologist in the day and securely locked in his airtight chemistry laboratory at night, is working might and main to solve the problem. He nearly got hanged when his first pronunciamento was to throw everyone out and start fresh. He has now changed his evil ways and declared that lots of rain could help.

The lecture on Developmental Stages of Poverty by the unsinkable Princeton Scraggs was well received. He described how delighted his parents were when they could afford a second set of loin cloths. Their upward mobility was even more obvious when they bought a tent. Scraggs explained that his recent reversion to a diet of fish heads was caused by the repossession of his pole and raft.

The harrowing experience of the traveling missionary from the Theology group must be told. He was caught by man-eating cannibals in the jungle. As he was being stuffed into the wedding pot along with a ladle to stir the impending stew, the tribal chief screamed some weird sounds. The soup-to-be victim asked his interpreter what the chief was hollering about. The polite interpreter replied "The chief wants to know whatever happened to Herbert Hoover?"

Ferdinand Maximilian of Austria, jobless at age 29, read in a newspaper that there was an opening for a king, or something like that, in Mexico. You may not believe it but he became Emperor of Mexico in 1864.

From: Quirkus Clinker, Defender of Causes
To: Director of Animal Care

Your Animal Welfare Committee should be dissolved at once, preferably in acid. It permitted a snake to climb into the bouillabaisse at the monthly dean's banquet. Put an impartial animal on the Committee, let's say a rat.

Bubbles Nakedemis, who once was the centerfold in a swine contest, has been appointed Instructor-Without-Portfolio. No Department has been assigned since nobody will let her in. The Maintenance Department says that she has some shingles missing from her roof.

The Campus Police are investigating a letter which does not compliment President Timkens. The letter has been traced to the Malevolent Society. We reprint it below.

Timkens
The Taj Mahal

I am tired of you referring to me as "Superstupid." The prefix is especially annoying. Following careful reflection, I have decided to kick the crap out of you at your earliest convenience and, being a fair man, I will do this with one hand behind my back. My credentials from the National Sluggers Association are enclosed.

The Faculty Club seems to be a place as good as any to stage your demise. Please respond.

Ollie Underbright, Dean

Heard in the School of Agriculture Chicken Farm:
First Hen: How much do you get a dozen for your eggs?
Second Hen: Eighty-five cents. What do you get?
First Hen: Eighty-seven cents.
Second Hen: I wouldn't strain myself for two cents.

Open Zipper
Reproductive Physiologist
Dear Open:

Because of my compulsive promptness, I am replying to your letter of 8 a.m. in which you state that you have had enough of "this benevolent dictator bullshit" and that either you go or I do.

First, I am pleased that you gave me a choice. It speaks well for possibilities in your character. Responding to the choice, obviously you go.

Preliminary perusal of your files indicates at once that you are not of high Crumble character. For example, there is no evidence that you have ever read Ageldorf's *Möglichkeit und Ehrfahrung* or that you have ever been to the Delaware Water Gap. We are not sure that you know the capital of Arkansas. Our janitors report that your name is never mentioned in the daily graffiti appearing on the west wall of the women's toilet. Obviously, your prestige index kept in our files has sunk below the red line. A serious charge against you is that you touched the No Touch machine set up in Dean Dingleberry's waiting room to assess faculty integrity.

The College will provide a van with curtains drawn together for 2 a.m. tomorrow so that in full justice and mercy you can leave town surreptitiously. The Dean will think up an appropriate excuse to explain your desertion.

Your friendly counselor,
Smiley Timkens

Director, Animal Jungle
Campus
Dear Director: .

Dean Catcabbage informed me that he had to reprimand you for a sacrilegious outburst in the presence of your innocent animal caretakers.

At Crumble we make no remarks against race, religion or people with money. You have broken a cardinal rule.

You will report to the College chapel for one week and write 50,000 times "Every morning, noon and night, thank God sang Theocrite."

Alfred Thunderbird
Assistant Chaplain

Untreated Boil, Plastic Surgeon
Health Service
Dear Friend:

Intern Gleep, a veritable fountainhead of discernment, states that you are disputatious. We have similar statements from a second year pre-podiatry student. The Linguistics staff could not believe that you have disagreed with Aristotle. Gleep also complains that you have never read Morgagni's "De Sedibus et Causis Morborum" even though this was published in 1761.

After thorough review of the facts, I recommend silence and very little of that, too, for one lunar month.

Silence is golden and other proverbs,

Igorot Scato, In the absence of the Chancellor

Ms. Fermented Anchovy
Assistant Diener in Psychology
Dear Ms. Anchovy:

It has come to my attention that you characteristically make extraordinary grimaces and undertake aberrant bodily contortions in those faculty meetings over which I preside.

As you should be aware, persons who so suppress their feelings of hostility and are unable to verbalize their emotions during stress are apt to suffer from an engorged, angry, red, fragile large bowel. This is in comparison with controls who express their feelings properly and in accordance with Robert's rules of parliamentary order.

Because you may not be able to measure up to the prescribed medical standards for remaining on our consulting faculty, I am hereby discharging you in the best interests of your health. The Bursar will grant you two weeks' severance pay without detailed questioning.

As usual with empathy—Smiley Timkens

The recent Director of the College Cafeteria, who got the job because the administration liked the sign on his lunchbox that read "Mommy makes good sandwiches" has picked up another job as scrime boy at Peter's Piss Stop in South Cornfield. For those of you who would like to visit him, take the road to the edge of Pothole Spur and Sandtrap Chasm Drive. Avoid the bettors sitting on the roadside bench who take odds on how many times your auto will completely revolve before landing upside down.

College Architect Benson made his first mistake and it was a lollapalooza. He built a house on the side of a steep cliff and he diverted a stream to flow directly through the center of it. One day in the midst of a torrential rain, the stream took a left turn through the kitchen. Within minutes all furniture was downstream. It was lucky that Benson could do the breaststroke, his only swimming maneuver. This allowed him to keep up with his kitchen stove. He has taken early retirement to nurse his bruises, but he is not yet able to write his memoirs.

With the student enrollment decreasing, Dean Dingleberry proposes a solution to reduce the excess faculty. He suggests eliminating Assistant Instructor as a rank. This will at once remove 37% of the staff. Each individual subsequently without such rank will be designated a non-person. As such, he will have no identity, thus causing no concern to anyone. The Dean terms this action "Cooperative Adaptation."

As one member of the Trustees put it "Isn't that nifty?" Another said. "Think of the toilet paper it will save."

The Department of Anthropology announces two unavoidable talks this month. Bobalik Isenglas, country unknown, will discuss "There is Nothing like an Old-Fashioned American Name." An Eskimo will talk on "Sexual Behavior in a 10-Occupant Igloo."

The Governor
State House
Dear Governor:

Your attempt to enforce an economy measure, which affects Crumble City Junior College, and particularly myself, is a horrendous travesty on our local tradition.

As you should have long known, no law should intervene between me and the riches the Lord saw fit to put in my lap. This statement has the support of all the local clergymen as well as the Democrats.

I am fully confident that we will be able to support you for a second term.

Couldn't be more humble,
Smiley Timkens

Smiley Timkens, President
Crumble City Junior College
Dear President Timkens:

Although you have been somewhat more than enthusiastic in your political activities as a Democrat, I did win the current election for Governor on the Republican ticket.

Because we must present a united front to the good people of our state, I would like to retain your able services. After careful thought I am offering you a position as Superintendent of the Dog Pound in Capital City. This is more in line with your capabilities and interests than your current humdrum position as College President.

Let me hear from you.
Cordially,
Roman Crockery
Governor

Governor Roman Crockery
State House
Dear Crocked:

I was pleased to hear of your election to office. If it had to be a Republican, I couldn't think of a better man and dearer friend.

Although you undoubtedly want me in Capital City, I must guide our College through the trying times ahead. Our people here feel strongly that destiny has placed me in a position to help them in their hour of need.

A count of our State legislators indicates that we Democrats have a high majority in both the house and senate. Fortunately for the welfare of our great State, they are all personal friends of mine. This includes the Comptroller of the Currency.

Not one to take it lying down,
Smiley

Dear Smiley

There has never been any question about your great leadership. Some of my best friends have children at Crumble City Junior College and they all testify to your infinite wisdom. We would never dream of turning over your office to anyone less capable than you.

Your best friend,
Roman

Visiting Lecturer Hinky Dinky Parlezvous
French Department
Dear Hinky:

Our auditors tell me that you have been here lecturing in some kind of broken English for three years.

Enough already. Go home. Your office will be turned over to our pigeon feeders as of 3 p.m. tomorrow.

Caretaker of State funds,
Smiley Timkens

Little Bo Peep
Kindergarten Expert
Dear Bo:

We have considerable evidence that you have consorted with other staff members, meeting downtown but especially in the subterranean grotto of the cafeteria, and maligning deans. Our evidence is indisputable since it has been reported to us by three service station attendants and a typist in the Crumble Sewer Department.

As you know, between the hours of 9 a.m. to 5 p.m. all conversation pertaining to the College belongs to the Management. In accordance with our policy to grant mercy and justice to first offenders, let this letter serve as a warning.

Your sympathetic counselor,
Smiley Timkens

The Trustees have agreed that future candidates for Dean must not only be tall but wide. The increased surface area will make them more menacing to faculty. It is recognized that brain size may not be in conformity.

Instructor Flounder,
Department Unverifiable
Dear Flounder

We are informed that you have just had a vasectomy. This is a bad example for the rest of our faculty since you are 95 years old.

Our College Attorney informs me that you could by our high internal moral standards be considered guilty of mayhem. This is because you have voluntarily submitted to a mutilating procedure that renders you unfit to fight for God, Country and Crumble, in that order, in the event of an emergency.

Since you did not obtain our written consent, I am relieving you of your post. Because justice must be tempered with mercy, you will simply be transferred to the basement of the Museum, where you will clean bones for the remainder of your wretched existence here.

Old Friend and Counselor
Smiley Timkens

Professor Oedipus Rex, Chairman
Department of Philosophy
Dear Professor Rex:

The Board of Trustees has wrestled painfully with the problem of where to locate the new fire station. It is altogether possible that the Philosophy building will be converted to this purpose.

As Chairman it will be your duty to appeal to the emotions of your staff in finding themselves other quarters, regardless of how irrational their pleas may be. It may be timely to remind them that Socrates taught from the stump of a tree.

I have unlimited confidence in your ability to have the building vacated in 24 hours.

For peace and quiet,
Smiley Timkens

Assistant Instructor Comma Sprinkler
Department of English
Dear Old Friend Comma:

I am deeply grieved that you have publicly announced that I am a dictator. We both graduated in the same college class and I have done everything in the past 30 years to insure your advancement to a position commensurate with your intelligence and training.

It is clear that you are unfamiliar with the words of St. Paul that "If the trumpet give an uncertain sound, who shall prepare himself for battle?" Obviously I have a clear mandate for action from the very fountainhead of the church. Your own failure to recognize this brands you as an atheist. Because of this deviant behavior, I find it impossible to justify your continuance at this institution. You will find your severance check awaiting you at the back door of the Bursar's office.

With deepest regard for your welfare,
Smiley Timkens

The School of Education is following the research of Visiting Lecturer Crazy Cantelope with great interest. He reads his notes to his class with every other word in reverse. The students take down his lectures diligently and they flunk the exams in the same way.

Memo to: Dean Dingleberry
From: Language Mangler, Chairman of English Department

I would like to recommend Unleashed Asparagus for the Instructorship in Remedial Reading. Among his positive assets there is ample evidence that he has read books that have hard covers. He has also lost his sense of smell and will like Crumble.

We have thoroughly investigated his past history and the only unfortunate incident in his career was when as a sophomore here he was caught sunbathing on the Great Crumble Flag. This led to no conviction, however, since only a few minutes prior to the desecration he had been hit by a ferryboat and was with fair presumption acutely addled.

If you wish further testimonial to his character, you may feel free to call his fiancee, Miss Chicken Gumbo, in our Department of Nutrition.

Captain Rodney (nee Irving-the-Wise), Lecturer on Military Tactics and Strategy, fully lived up to his squadron's expectations last night. Chased around the dining room table by his wife with upraised meat cleaver, Rodney dived through the nearest window. The only somewhat debatable flaw in his remarkably perceptive logic, which he says he will correct next time, is that he forgot he was two stories up .

Some of the faculty have protested against the view that faculty committees do nothing. It is contended that if they can screw things up, they do it proficiently.

Oedipus Rex, Chairman
Department of Philosophy
Dear Professor Rex:

We have read a report of the State Legislature that you have forty-three faculty members and only three students who are majors.

To solve this dilemma for the people of this State, we would be willing to take over the Philosophy Building and turn it into a foundry. Our primary product is drill jig bushings. The younger faculty could thus be productively employed probably for the first time. To ensure their scholarly development, we will offer two twenty minute breaks around the cracker barrel where they can discuss Aristotle, Sophocles, or kick the barrel to release their hostility.

For the senescing staff, who are not too adept at anything, we are contemplating a salt water-pretzel subsidiary in the east wing and they could be gainfully employed where a power failure wouldn't be too disastrous.

Our corporate management awaits your thinking with baited breath.

Sincerely yours,
Corroded Clutch, First Vice President
Universal Steel and Twisted Pretzel Corporation

Loose Photon, an exiled biophysicist, has received a medal called the Hefty Chesty, which is Crumble's salute to genius. This is for his book *Low Sperm Count—A Boon to Unwed Mothers*. Herman

Fenderbender, book reviewer at the Crumble Automotive Service, says that this text ranks with such works as Othello or Hamlet.

THE BEST OF STUDENT NEWS

Falling Watermellon, I.Q. 60, likes freebies. He responded at once to a sign on the bulletin board at the Student Union which read "Come and get yours." He got his without delay. He lasted three punches as a sparring partner against the champ before they wheeled him out in a laundry basket.

The Architectural Office has decided to lower the sidewalk curbs to accommodate coeds whose behinds hit the curb when-they leave the sidewalk. According to Catbird Clop, an authority on fruit flies, low chassis are an inherited trait due to intermarriage especially with Crumble instructors.

The Campus Police are cracking down on reckless wheelchair students. Lafe Troobnick is a frequent offender. Last night they found him dangling head down over Campus Cliff, only one wheel of his chair being caught in a rock and preventing the final disaster. A week ago he was being towed by a rope to the State of Maine Express. Troobnick's chair has been chained to the central flagpole until the Dean comes up with a treatment. Troobnick says that he will fight any decision all the way to the Supreme Court.

Miss Gouda Cheese of the Home Economics Department is sponsoring a long-forgotten concoction called "Defeaties, A Cereal for Losers." Miss Cheese claims that this is trendy since losers form an increasingly large segment of the Crumble population.

Superstar actress Vacuum Frontroom of the Great Crumble Players has been cast in the leading role of the play "Togetherness." In the first rehearsal she had to be separated by hot water from her lover. There is no question that Frontroom will live the part furiously.

Twing Soot had a run-in with Instructor Nasty of the Health Education Department. Nasty gave an unannounced quiz the main question being "In one minute discuss the hygiene of the alimentary canal." Soot, showing an unexpected touch of genius wrote "Brush your teeth and wipe your behind."

Tangerine LaBomba
Campus Ladies of the Night
Dear Madam (or do I have the wrong person?)

Your collected memoirs entitled "Phallus in Wonderland" is revolting. There will be a delay due to sanitizing it before it can be accepted in the mails. My secretary will not touch it with a 10-foot pole for fear of getting herpes or more. I have ordered tongs so that she can wrap it at a safe distance.

Forget that you ever heard of us
Forby Doo Doo, Editor of Press

Good Mimie who won a prize as Crumble's Queen of Love and Beauty got loaded with redwood rum last night and sawed down the campus water tower. Dean Dingleberry was taking a shower and he should be avoided for a few days. The Student Union will sell water if you bring a jug.

Crumble lost 365 to 0 in the television show called University Smarts where colleges compete in tests of knowledge. Crumble's opponent was the Bachigallupo School of Riveting. Our students say they were cheated out of three points and they are sending a protest to the station.

Wallaby Vroom, a major in Economics, has opened a general

store called "FROM DIAPER TO SHROUD." His expressive ability suggests a touch of genius.

At the recent convocation, the worst teacher of the year was announced. The dishonor went to Jocasta, Lecturer in Remedial Reading. Mercifully, she only received a plaque with the inscription "There are students who insist that she speaks English." Also, the students selected the worst dressed teacher with the comment "He always looks like he was dragged into class on a rope." The unmeritorious winners will be demoted for the semester and sent to Horseshit Ridge High School where they will be unnoticed.

The monthly report of the Director of the Animal Quarters is not good:

The antivivisectionists are getting bolder. Their most violent member, right here in our Zoology Department, has given his cat a private telephone. The number is unlisted.

As if that isn't enough. We heard the report that a dog shot its master. The dog had gone into a depression when it was losing speed in a fox and hounds race. The master is looking around for a dog psychiatrist. Obviously, our veterinary schools are not keeping up with the times.

The Botany Chairman told his class yesterday that they were so noisy that he couldn't hear his own lecture. He was at once informed by a coed in the second row not to worry since he wasn't missing anything. Then Truck Bumper, the varsity fullback, asked the lecturer what class this was. His coach told him that if he attended any lecture, he would be eligible Saturday.

The student body is urged to pay serious attention to the sign at the main campus entrance, just posted by the Department of Buildings and Grounds. Just so that all our readers will be informed, the sign states: "$25.00 to $50.00 fine for littering the main campus drive, depending upon how much you throw out."

The Speech Department is pleased to announce the opening of a new section in Speech 101 for freshmen. The instructor is Mr. Kslh. His first lecture is open to the public and is entitled "Better to Have No Need Than to Need to Have." Mr. Kslh is on probationary appointment.

The Dean of Students at Downstate University would like to remind all undergraduates that the Liars Bench on the west side of the Administration Building is reserved solely for postdoctoral fellows. They must have a common meeting place for profound discussion of their daily discoveries. Undergraduates are expected to intercommunicate at the back of various bowling alleys downtown.

The Zeta Gnu house has been taken over by the Department of Buildings and Grounds. It will be a warehouse for storing bibles. This follows the annual Bottled-in-Bond party in which Dean Underbright was thrown into a pizza oven where he spent the night. The Dean had been invited as the speaker and honored guest.

Plink and Plop, our new sound engineers on retainer, have been ordered to move off their street. They are too noisy as they hit each other over the head prior to an exhaustive decision.

Fenwick Grunch, a senior who was once caught robbing the student Canterbury House and later the Newman Center was arrested upon breaking into the Hillel House. He informed the Dean of Men that he hated bigotry and wanted to let the student body know that he was non-sectarian.

Nawrocki, Crumble's greatest football hero, did it again. He carried the ball right out of the stadium, followed by his team, the other team, the referees, and several dogs, then through the field house, over the opposing team's grandstand, back to the field and touchdown!

Dean Angelina Christmascake of the School of Theology says that in her role as Head Angelologist she is removing student Toodles Flambé from archangel status in the sophmore class. Toodles was identified in a centerfold, thus defiling the entire Theology building which must be aired out.

The field trip in Public Health proposed for next Thursday has been called off. In the last trip the rats chased the professor and his students out of the city dump. For a while it was touch and go .

Something will have to be done about the basement cafeteria in the Union. According to student Bulko, who ought to know because he eats lunch there everyday from 11 to 3, the food is so bad that the flies come in to commit suicide.

Ferkin Gherkin, a chronic hoaxter, entered a paper for oral presentation at the regional Zoology meetings. His paper title was incomprehensible and the results impossible. As expected, the paper was accepted by the Board of Geniuses. When the paper was called for reading, Ferkin's accomplice, Wendell, rushed to the platform and announced that Ferkin had just died in the hallway. The moderator assented to Wendell's tearful request that a 10 minute eulogy be substituted for the departed member and his proposed speech. At the close of the eulogy, all persons having risen for a minute of silence, Ferkin walked in, noisily chomping peanuts, whereupon he demanded the dismissal of the moderator for deviant conduct of a scientific meeting.

The campus bereaves the passing of freshman crusader, Smut Wowser, who took the semester off to do good aboard ship. Wowser called the crew together to talk about Save the Whales Day. During his impassioned address, he fell off the bow of the ship and was eaten by a shark.

Short Fuse, outstanding student in Motorcycle Repair, has been appointed Resident Fellow in Economy Dorm. He and his genial wife, Pixie, invite all students to an open house in their apartment, The Growlery, this Saturday.

Fungus Twillum, a third time freshman, puzzled the diagnosticians at the Health Service for two years, during which time he continually complained of a sore wrist. The case was only recently solved. Twillum was found to have spent every day at the racetrack tearing up losing tickets.

Alumnus Boobs has appealed to the student body for help. His surname has been truncated in the University scrolls to Boob. The Printing Service refuses to correct this. The Service claims that the deletion saves the College $4.80 per annum and that over a 100 year period the total savings will be significant.

Students and staff with truncated names in the files are asked to attend a meeting so that they may grieve communally. No visitors will be admitted.

For every group an anti-group forms. Surer than hell, a Goodie Society has been formed at Crumble. At its first meeting strong action was proposed against vulgarisms. The initial target was the battlecry to arms of the Malevolent Society, to wit, "Shit, Piss and Corruption." The meeting ended in a stalemate with a proposed antithetical slogan, "No Shit, Piss and Corruption." This was just too overwhelming for the supergoodie section of the Goodies. The matter will have to be adjudicated by a highly experienced anti-flesh and bone man and even he may have to make his statement in Sanskrit with the hope that nobody in the group can translate his opinion.

Ruptured Hamstring, second to Nawrocki as an all-round star, is having considerable trouble financing his way back to his native country because he easily failed all his courses. He wrote to his mother back home about his numerous successes at Crumble, ending each letter with the triumphant note that he had another feather in his hat. When the impending disaster materialized, he wrote to his mother for fare home. She answered promptly, telling him to shove all his feathers up his behind and fly home.

The students are petitioning to prevent the Dean of Students, a former tobacco auctioneer, from giving out degrees at commencement. He expedited the whole thing by selling the diplomas to the highest bidder.

Students are asked to consider this report very seriously. Saché Biceps, a major in Physical Education, used profane language in the chapel. Divine wrath came fast. He flunked fishing and pogo stick, both on the same day. He was hit on the head with a brick that the Dean of the School of Theology said was hurled from outer space. He lost his wallet in Alligator Swamp. A committee from Theology announced that he was the object of cosmic revenge. If repentant, they would unhex him. Biceps has accepted their advice and will limit his activity to silence accompanying a case of beer per day.

Quarterback Miscue—Victory Stadium

We have kept you eligible for 14 years as a sophomore, wearing various disguises, but it may be time to trade you to the tiddlywinks team.

We have recently discovered that The Brat, quarterback for the Disjointed Vocational Grammar School, has been totally wised up and he has changed his name 12 times to stay eligible. In the last game with us, he completed 87 passes to his wide receiver, Razzmattazz, to beat us 117 to 0.

Our closest score was when they defeated us by only 67 to 3, when you sank in 9 feet of marsh water behind our goal line as you tossed the pass which eventuated in a field goal.

Turn in your uniform today, including your last paycheck.

Tricky Kneecap, Coach

Students are warned to be cautious when eating at the Red Stool restaurant. A chemist says that their "hokey cheese spread" is preserved with 8-hydroxyquinoline. This is also used in contraceptives and rectal suppositories.

Because of the drop in enrollment, all students are advised not to plead guilty in the local courts. The enrollment has caused the Administration to change the next calendar so that classes will begin after other colleges have thrown out their flunkees. The Registrar's office will stay open all night during that period.

Following the admission of a white rat to the Psychology Department, a frog has applied for an Assistantship in the Department of Physiology. The frog claims that it knows more about frogs than any member of the Department does.

A vendetta is in progress on the campus. The Malevolent Society stole a showcase that was in the lobby of a fraternity house and submerged it in Alligator Swamp, with a sign reading "Underwater Shop." The fraternity then seized a stationwagon belonging to the Malevolent Society and sawed it in half. Last night the aggrieved Malevolent group climbed the roof of the fraternity house and reamed the chimney right off the building. Their carpenter declared that it was as easy and delightful as coring an apple. The Administration is negotiating a truce.

According to a wit named Charles Lever, who deserves immortality, there is nothing so useless as doing efficiently that which should not be done at all.

Hittle Midway, the enterprising student who recently opened a campus exterminator service, is being chased out of town. Hittle phoned Yarward, a first floor butler at President Timkens' home, and said "I hear you have rats."

Investigation of an outbreak of vomiting following a dinner for outstanding deans revealed that a self-proclaimed cook from the student Malevolent Society had spiked the soup with automobile brake fluid. The cook proudly accepted compliments for the exotic flavor. We agree that ingenuity was demonstrated.

Witty William, student comedian-in-training, is not yet entirely successful. We ask for your comments:

To his quiz instructor in Psychology: "What kind of an exam is this; all it contains is a bunch of questions."

To the Diener in Embryology: "My wife is delivering tomorrow. Can she play doubles in tennis this afternoon?"

To the warden at the city jail: "How about suspending my jail sentence until tomorrow? The Saloonatics are giving an excellent band concert tonight."

To his section man in Oceanography: "I heard that clams are happiest at high tide. Need your opinion, Doc." Witty was at loss for a rebuttal when informed that the ability of clams to stay clammed up contributed to their longevity.

In answer to the Dean of Men's questioning Witty about why he left town every other day, Witty said "It is essential for me to get a bowel of my mother's vitals."

We wanted the opinions of two experts , one a visiting professor from Scotland who replied "We don't want Witty in Glaucomora. The other said "Keep him out of Peoria."

We regret the incident that happened to an unfortunate coed last night. Upon being pinned by her fraternity boyfriend, her inflated bra shot out air at great velocity. In accordance with

Newton's third law of motion, F = MA, she was sent with equal momentum in the opposite direction and found herself in a tree.

Student Gruff, class advocate, wrote in the College newspaper that a mythical person would call Dean Dingleberry a horse's ass, grade zero. The College attorneys were directed to expel Gruff but they lost the case. The Department of Mathematics, always rising to the defense of quantitative logic, stated that a mythical person has the rank of zero since he does not exist. Ergo, all propositions involving combinations of zero must equal zero. The attorneys have been directed to send Gruff letters of apology and also to attend math lectures if they wish to keep their jobs.

We are delighted with the logic and mercy of the starving student who said to his girlfriend teller while he was robbing the Bursar's office "I usually shoot people for money; I like you so I'll shoot you for nothing."

We wanted to write about Jack Hyperemesis, Pretender in Medical Statistics, but we drew a blank. We will accept any suggestions.

Did you ever stop to realize that a schoolroom appears to be the only place where the consumer (known as a "student") wants as little as possible for his money. The situation needs research in depth, but don't ask the faculties. They could be part of the cause.

The luncheon meeting of the Student Blood Sausage, Head Cheese and Yellow Mustard Club was not up to its usual sparkling quality. The bus driver bringing the members to the wingding was avoiding a roadblock because of his hit and run tactics after demolishing several stray hogs the week previously. It took an extra two hours between sizzle and serve. Worse, the speaker never showed up. His wife just divorced him and he couldn't bear to leave the rubber duck that he now slept with.

Rent-A-Whore By The Week, a new downtown business run by the Malevolent Society, is stirring up controversy in the usual bastions of righteousness. Mayor Weakling, always for progress, says that the business is revitalizing the economic slump downtown. He also notes that the outfit is an equal opportunity employer.

Rent-A-Whore fills the void produced by the closing of the Promised Land and of the Honey Pot. An irate customer caused the furor. He rejected an 80 year old offering because she had only one upper and one lower tooth. The Speech Pathology Chairman said in rebuttal "Thank God they meet" and is acting as her counsel. The firm of Sturm and Drang has been appointed as mediator. The last we heard, everyone lost.

The Student Council is listing hot tips on the campus vending machines. The popcorn machines are currently paying the highest dividends, since it has been statistically determined that six times out of ten, money will be awarded, although no popcorn. The popcorn machine outside the President's office can be trusted to yield the greatest odds, although an arrangement must be made with the janitor. The candy machines are quite risky and should be reserved only for those richer students who are known to be philanthropically inclined.

Students with heart conditions or high blood pressure are advised not to patronize the hot coffee machines. It can be quite a shock to insert a coin, get the paper cup shot out in your face, and helplessly watch the coffee go down the drain.

Academic bum, Malvolio, who flunked out of 7 other colleges, pleaded tearfully and in genuflection to the Crumble Admissions Committee to give him one last chance to prove his worth. He quoted such things as "the quality of mercy falleth as the gentle rain from heaven." Ten minutes after matriculating, Malvolio changed into his serrated knee pants and fecal-smeared shirt, got out his placard reading "DOWN WITH THE PRESIDENT," hurled a few boulders through Timkens' picture window, and via bullhorn challenged all administrators into debate as to why they shouldn't be discharged following their hearing.

During Malvolio's retreat, with the campus cops closing in fast with a battering ram, he said to his admiring audience that he was accepting an offer to manage a nudist camp where democratic concepts were much better tolerated.

BACK TO THE FACULTY

Jonathon Lackluster , Instructor in Healthful Longevity, died during a faculty meeting, but nobody paid any attention. Most of the faculty were sleeping. Some awoke and left that evening. Others got up at various times the next day. The janitor who was chasing a squirrel out of the building discovered the body.

The Dean noted that he is now 87 years old and the question of his retirement would come up in 10 years. When asked if anyone had been approached as a replacement, the Dean said that he was recommending his old friend, Elmer Luminescence, but a small problem of several incompetent sphincters delayed his visits.

It was reported that a search committee is being formed to find a new janitor for President Timkens' office. Due to the extreme sensitivity of the position, the search may have to be extraterrestrial.

The resignation of McRooster, Professor of Dead Birds, was refused by the Dean's Council. They want McRooster to recover from a depression that he suffered after being drummed out of the Ornithological Society on the charge that he ate a turkey.

The Dean said that he is looking for a statute that will prevent the Campus Prostitutes Association from having their end of the year sale. Worse, there is a rumor of a senior citizen discount.

Engineering Professor Da Vinci, who made his own alpine tramway from erector set parts, is missing. The faculty is asked to join the search. (Note: If these guys would only look, they would find him trying to get down.)

A member of the Dean's Council said that Ms. Alabaster White, Lecturer in Truth and Purity in the School of Theology, had just given him a copy of the 119th revision of her book, *I was a Captive Whore, What is Your Story?* The Dean added that Ms. White had been given a lie detector test which was inconclusive.

Ms. Horrendous Ovary, Lecturer in Endocrinology, is described as resembling a punctured football kicked into a strong wind.

The Dean stated his pleasure in announcing that Furyissimus Mountainthunder, a dinosauroid of note, will deliver the annual Philosophy Award lecture. His subject will be, "I'd Rather be Dead than Right."

The Council listened to the grievance of Rudolf Hagfish, Assistant to the Assistant Instructor, Hagfish says that nobody in the Zoology Department can appreciate his sound claim for promotion. His specialty is the sounds of Triassic brachiopods. He decries the fact that his road downhill in the last 35 years has included feeding the laboratory frogs, then keeper of the crickets, and now inspector of bulbs in the steam tunnel.

From the Animal House: If you think you have influence, try ordering someone else's dog around.

Professor Veal Cutlet
Department of Romance Languages
Dear Professor Cutlet:

Each year our rule of retirement forces us to uproot rare and ageless men such as you. As an emeritus you will be numbered among the few irreplaceable giants that we ever had in this institution. We shall all miss your warm, human touch. You should know that the students claim you as a professor who really professed.

Tomorrow promptly at 10 a.m. a blockbuster and bulldozer will tear down your office. If you do not have your books and other possessions on the sidewalk before that time, you may as well give them up for lost.

At this time I may note that your house is also on campus property. Obviously, don't bring your books home. We can arrange with the Red Cross to take care of you during the emergency.

Your friend and admirer,
Smiley Timkens

Director, Campus Radio

Your goddam weather announcer better stop predicting showers or I'll tear the friggin' station down. Every time he says rain I have to slap a steaming hydrocollator pad on another joint. The next ten days better be good.

Chief Arsonist,
Malevolent Society

Assistant Professor Scumbucket

Dear Mr. Scumbucket:

Your service to the College has been truly magnificent. You have labored diligently to build molehills into mountains for the last 30 years, and you deserve a final reward.

Our secretarial staff has been inundated by correspondence, and I am now creating a Department of Envelope Stuffing to ensure orderly communication. I want you to be the first chairman of this unit, and your name will be suitably inscribed in our perpetual scrolls. Please report to your new post at 5:30 a.m., Thursday. Bulbs will be installed to enable you to find your way into the catacombs.

With grace,
Smiley Timkens

Psychiatrist Grindle, Health Service

You have been under surveillance for some months, especially since it was discovered that you receive patients only when there is a full moon. Furthermore, your tie is always sprayed with urine.

Since you have tenure, we do not wish to stir up a can of worms with the AAUP by terminating you. We are therefore "disestablishing" you as of this letter. This category is not in the book of rules so you have no recourse.

As you know, we hired you with about the same care that we buy bananas for the faculty club. The point is that you need to disappear with equal speed, but without giving us indigestion.

In dulce domino,
Smiley Timkens

Research Associate Short Zombie
Zoopaleography
Dear Mr. Zombie:

You were given time off for research two years ago, but it is reported that you spend your time fixing go-carts and painting wastebaskets for the neighbors.

According to your Chairman, you state that the fault lies in the fact that your research animal, the ant-eating Brazilian bear, is not available and is too costly.

We have solved your dilemma. You may pick up your severance pay and a complimentary one-way ticket to Brazil at the Bursar's office the end of the week.

Please send a reprint of your first published article to our proposed science library. This should arrive, hopefully, in time for its opening in the year 2000.

For Research First and Your Job Last,
Smiley Timkens

Dean of Men:

Will the student who beat the hell out of me in the Senior Frolic last night agree to buy me an oxygen tank if I give him back his two front teeth? Please arrange the swap.

Horizontal Upperclassman

Dear Horizontal:

As amicus curiae, I have mediated an acceptable solution. Your adversary states with logic that it is only fair that he punch your nose in so that a perfect balance is attained. With your permission I will set up the meeting in the hospital.

FROM THE DESK OF THE PRESIDENT

To: The Faculty
From: Vera Scrum, Trusted Administrative Assistant

It is time to clean the President's desk, so the following gems are being distributed:

The Faculty Committee on Salaries and Promotions has been discharged. The Committee worked 4-1/2 years and submitted a 587 page document indicating a serious need for salary raises exceeding starvation level and for promoting half the staff above the rank of instructor. President Timkens has turned back the report with the statement that it needs a new committee and perhaps 4-5 years of work. Timkens charges that the document is "semantically inadequate." He also notes that a comma was used in place of a semicolon on p. 416.

President Timkens has announced that the faculty is now too large to meet at one time. He will divide them to groups, and the meeting with each group will be unstructured. He defines this term as meaning that the faculty will have great latitude in raising questions concerning its welfare and interests. The Department of English has independently defined the term "unstructured." Its interpretation is that Timkens can with maximum evasiveness answer all questions from a few intrepid extroverts, demolishing them with masterful skill and at one stroke. (Ed. note: Since the general faculty dislikes the extroverts perhaps more than they do our beloved president, a large attendance is expected for the verbal execution.)

The railroad is considering closing the Crumble station. If this occurs, all passengers will have to get on or off at South Cornfield. The College Trustees are working on a compromise plan with the railroad whereby the trains will slow down at Crumble and passengers can jump off into a large pen filled with sawdust. The conductor will throw their baggage after them. This arrangement may be a little hard on the older faculty, but special isometric landing exercises will be given by the Physical Education staff.

The Trustees have instructed their downtown firm of attorneys, Voodoo and Perfidy, to obtain an injunction against Honest Henry, the largest auto dealer in Crumble. He has erected an unauthorized sign at the bottom of Quadriplegic Hill near the campus. The sign reads "We give the best trade-in on acutely outmoded cars." The sign is obscuring the ambulance which is permanently stationed there to crowbar out wrecked students.

The President's Office is investigating the activities of Airwick Prenzer, Assistant Instructor in Finance. There are some peculiar goings on in Airwick's office. In recent weeks the only way to get to see him has been to ring three times, turn into full left lateral view for photography, and in sotto voce say "Have to see Big Louie."

The Legal Division of the Mathematics Department has scored another success. This week, Hermes, our new Greek instructor, who says that he is a messenger of Zeus, was arrested on a charge of presumptive inebriation. He fell out of a saloon and then headed for home, deviating between right and left.

The Department retraced his footprints, finding that he wobbled just as much one way as the other. They triumphantly presented their evidence to the court, emphasizing that on the average the defendant walked a straight line. The judge was forced to admit that the average determines normal behavior.

The State Approving Authority consultants who came here two weeks ago to inspect the program in Agriculture has issued a statement that the buildings were locked. It is their belief that there probably is no curriculum in Agriculture and somebody made a mistake asking them to come. We hasten to correct this impression. These people unfortunately arrived during the annual grundoon hunt. As we all know, no red-blooded student or faculty member could possibly miss this event.

Dean Dingleberry has sharply admonished Instructor Low Clearance of the Department of Chemistry for referring to his class as a group of aberrantly evolving worms. The Dean has also addressed the class with the plea that they cease stating that Instructor Clearance was educated beyond his intelligence.

The Crumble Appellate Court has awarded damages to Nutrition Instructor Hot Coldslaw. The staff member was diagnosed as having a rare syndrome called "Forward Lean." The court took the enlightened view that this was an occupational disease caused by Coldslaw having to lecture over a low orange crate for the previous 17 years pending repairs to his former desk. Powerful support was given to the opinion of the judge by an 1837 state supreme court decision which ruled that an appellant with a pronounced case of "barrel ass" had contracted the condition in the due pursuit of his academic duties while sitting on a wide concave stool. Action was brought to compel the Trustees to change the physical condition of employment.

The Trustees have voted that all dormitories will be named with proper consideration of the financial status of the students. Two dormitories now under construction will be named the Presidential Manor and Abraham's Cave, respectively.

Following President Timkens' order that offices having similar functions and status be placed near one another, the office of the

Dean of the School of Education has been moved next to the Janitorial Service. The permanence of this move is dependent upon the receipt of protests from the Janitorial Service.

President Timkens discussed with the Trustees the functions of a dean. The President noted that a dean must frequently act the part of an idiot and that all his deans have risen admirably to the role.

It was also agreed that the prime function of a dean is between that of a dog and a fire hydrant.

The Trustees discussed the speech in the state legislature of Crumble's implacable enemy, Senator Abysmal Blooper. Abysmal has repeatedly stated that he would like to bury our beloved College, but he hasn't yet found a hole big enough to bury it in. He wants to set up a committee to explore possible sites.

S. Brindle Brown (ask not what S. stands for), inventive genius in Engineering, is proud of his laser cane which has fine optical triangular systems. The laser emits pulses and reflections which are focused on photodiodes. We can hardly stop here. Brindle set out with his laser and his sonic glasses and knapsack to find the Holy Grail, but before opening the front door he tripped over a black shag rug which didn't emit light signals. The hospital monitored his head injury in two minutes with a 30 year old, 10 watt bulb, although twisting his skull around so that it faced front took a bit longer.

The College experimented with the method of sending up white smoke through the chimney of the central heating plant to signal to the town that important elections of administrators had been completed. But immediately following the elections something went amiss. The janitor came up through the chimney, followed by the Dean of Women. The accompanying smoke was green. The procedure has been temporarily abandoned.

The announcement of the State Anthropological Society to lead a safari into Crumble City to study modern ruins has created controversy. The Society President states that no digging will have to be done.

Special Security Agent Hallelujah, who reached 100 years of age this week, was advised by Personnel to crawl over to the Bursar after blowing out his birthday candles and turn in his resignation. One set of recommendations stated that he no longer had both oars in the water. His supervisor described him as undead.

President Timkens issued a statement today as to why he fired his first floor butler, Burton, who has faithfully served our former college presidents for 45 years. Timkens noted that at breakfast the butler was becoming careless. In the past few weeks he had cracked Timkens' pheasant eggs off-center.

The Board of Trustees have expressed their deep regret to Burton that he was no longer eligible for a pension because he still had six weeks to go before he reached the minimum pension age. When questioned by the local paper about his future plans, Burton replied with meticulous logic that the alternatives were well defined in the statutes, namely starvation, a job in the salt mines, or suicide. Burton said he was taking a week or two in order to consider the appropriate decision.

When the Music Department's piano tuner, Opporknockety, broke up a client's piano and asked for a second chance, the lady client said "Opporknockety tunes but once." The acute logic noted herein deserves the printed space that it has so far lacked.

President Timkens' second floor butler has been discharged. Some weeks ago he was found watering the President's beer. His next offense was to send an egg, sunny side up, every morning down the privileged mail chute leading to the President's Bank of England desk.

It was later discovered that he was piping messages every morning at 3 a.m. to Timkens' bed and was organizing his nightmares. Timkens' most recent dream was that he was in a flying saucer dive-bombing the faculty club. The handwriting of the Malevolent Society is discerned clearly in these actions.

Equitus Derriere, who manages the horse barn, just published his tome *There Just Isn't Enough Manure to Go Around.* A good story, but the theme is directed just a bit to the administrators. The writer failed to read the statutes dealing with directions for survival. Insiders have let it be known that Equitus is about to receive his "C'est La Fin" letter along with a tin mackerel to commend him for 40 years of service.

Vice President Rudyard Watercloset, who firmly insists that any faculty action should show the nature of the vote, received a telegram while in the hospital last week. It read "The eligible voting faculty wishes you a speedy recovery by a vote of 343 to 342."

It has been discovered that a former member of the Malevolent Society somehow became the Secretary of the Secret and Sacred Council of Deans. He wrote up the minutes as he pleased before any meeting was held, but he distributed them to the entire faculty only at an appropriate interval of time following each meeting, on the proven assumption that the deans would not be caught dead reading anything they said. The phony documents determined policy for the entire College for two years before a freshman waiter at the meeting who could just make out some basic English decided that something was wrong.

The monthly prize given by the English Department for a model of succinct and logical conversation went to the following student, responding to his instructor:

Instructor to student: You don't know anything.
Succinct and logical student: Of course not. You're the bastard who taught me everything and you don't know a Goddamn thing.

For three days only, Crumble will have an admissions day special. The College will accept any applicant if he doesn't have more than eleven toes. A terrifying barnburner will be the opportunity to watch the Registrar carry Lesser Dean Fuggem Twice on his back while his horse dives into a two by five pool below a flaming heating plant smokestack.

Get your tickets early for the monumental wrestling match between Crumble and the contestants from the state prison. Our tag team, Milkshake and The Coward, will fearlessly face insurmountable odds, The Horned Toad and The Tarantula. The latter two are being temporarily sprung from solitary confinement and will have to keep their chains on. This is the event of the season.

President Timkens will no longer hire student drivers. One of them drove a top down auto in a funeral procession for the President's dog through a car wash.

Psychiatrist Grindle's latest book is on *Circadian Rhythms in Lovers and the Music Faculty*.

In their courtship, lovers, at 10 p.m., can only be separated with a hacksaw. After two years of marriage, at 10 p.m., she says "If you touch me I'll scream rape." The interval time between the phases of the cycle may be variable.

The members of the Music faculty, at 10 p.m., when the symphony concert is about to end with a crashing crescendo, are all in a state of total euphoria. They are higher than a satellite, and love and beauty rule the world. In the faculty meeting, at 10 a.m. the next day, any available musical instrument turns into a potential lethal weapon. Each person would brain his colleague with a Stradivarius if he only had the nerve.

To: Occupants, Crumble Faculty Club
From: Cerebral H. Atrophy

Since receiving my Ph.D. in Paleoembryology, I find that there are only two jobs in the world. At age 26 I am in early retirement.

Because of my need to remain in academia, I am available, wages open, to mow lawns if they are close to the campus, fix baby carriages, or attend bedpans for retired faculty. I have references to attest that I am an expert in telling the age of Caesarian-delivered mummies.

Because of a shortage of electricians, nobody with metal pants will be admitted to the Administration Building until the trouble has been located. The College is enticing Unringable Doorbell, Manager of the Crumble Small Electric and Fertilizer Company, to quickly join the staff.

Dear Dean Dingleberry

We commend you for bringing a branch of the "Dirty Dugs of Duessa" to the Student Union. This charming restaurant indicates that you are attuned to the times, despite evidence that you are a male chauvinist sexist pig.

We deplore the fact that no space provisions have been made for a quiet period of postprandial fornication. Please correct this as soon as possible.

Hazardous Harriet,
President, Society for Augmentation Mammoplasty

Spoiled Pirogi
Lecturer in Phonology
Dear Spoiled:

As you know, our faculty must be faultless and provide model conduct to our students.

It has come to my attention that you have so much to say in

your lectures that you tend to continue your recitation while breathing in for the next statement.

Phonation during inspiration is a faulty vocal habit that is unpleasant to the students. I have consulted our Health Service physicians who state that you obviously have *inspiratio ad nauseum.*

I am therefore remanding you for three months to the Music Department for corrective therapy—without pay, of course. A bill for therapy will be submitted to you at the conclusion of the treatments, the fee to be set in accordance with the success of the results.

No charge for this advice,
Freewhistle Pisspot, The Third
Faculty Guidance Councilor

McRooster, Professor of Dead Birds, was jailed for shooting pigeons that were flying over the Rio grande from Mexico to the United States. He said that he hated illegal aliens. The Society for Dead Birds stated that it never heard of McRooster and he was most likely an illegal alien from another planet. McRooster cleverly countered that he once owned a duck that came from a slaughterhouse in Boston.

Dean Angelina Christmascake is in the pokey for beating her husband. He stirred her cup of coffee counterclockwise. We are awaiting the decision of the court with baited breath. It could change the science of nutrition and possibly even geophysics.

ADMINISTRATIVE OFFICE TIDBITS

In accordance with President Timkens policy of meeting all boats, his household staff has been expanded by an upstairs butler (the nawb of Dir), a janitor (the wali of Swat), and a pastry cook (the mir of Nagar). It appears that in their own countries there were one nawb, one wali and one mir too many.

All is not serene, however. During a furious altercation about who would be scrime boy for the day in the kitchen, barrel tender Barf Doohickey asked the mir if he had ever been sent home for bugs. Barf is awaiting his expulsion order to sweeping the steam tunnels.

Wu Flung Dung, internationally famous detective, is joining the Campus Police. His assistant, Ms. Blue Plate Special, will enroll in the freshman class so that she can be close to the scene of the expected crime.

Curator of the Art Museum
Dear Curator-Type Person

Because of our deep gratitude for your long years of service in the Museum which is noted for its wide regional appeal, an explanation is necessary to explain why it has been relocated.

The Museum was pre-empting valuable space on which we can put a rollercoaster that was bought at a bargain when the traveling circus was repossessed and sold at auction. You can now find the Museum in the rear section of the automotive shop if you look carefully here and there.

College Efficiency Expert

The Trustees have reviewed the purpose of the Crumble faculty and they agreed with the well-known conclusion that it is to cast false pearls before real swine. Both victims need to look for a maxim about Trustees.

Rodney Swillbucket, a pharmacist in the Health Service, is about to be censured by his chief. He has been seen reading the Dreckapotheca surreptitiously. As all medical historians can tell you, this tome lists the useless drugs used by the ordinary idiot throughout the world.

The testimonial dinner to retiring Lower Dean Fetid Canker was a sparkling success. President Timkens toasted him "as a person of invaluable hindsight."

Other remarks of note were:

"He has an innate capacity to add a new dimension to whatever confusion prevails at the moment"—Vice President.

"He could cause consternation in a primate refuge area"—Chairman of Zoology.

"He is very distinguished, probably upper Paleolithic"—Chairman of Anthropology.

"He is a serious opponent to be reckoned with, if you are downwind"—Chairman of Meteorology.

"His vocal folds are in high gear while his brain is in reverse"—Chairman of Speech Pathology.

"He is a master of constructive non-accomplishment"—Pipefitter's Union.

"He ranks with Custer, Watergate and the San Andreas Fault."—Anonymous.

Bounty hunter Schmuppsi brought in less than his quota of students last month and he may be dismissed from the Admissions staff. Temporarily, he has been ordered to attend faculty meetings each week just to make him aware of how tough it can get for substandard producers at Crumble.

Psychology Chairman to his secretary: I have an extremely large number of appointments this week. Check my calendar and find a convenient time when I can commit suicide.

The Trustees have decided on a course of action to keep Education Dean Ollie Underbright in the National Dean's Council. Very simple. The Dean will go to the annual meeting with his mouth taped.

Administrator Twilby is losing caste. For the past few weeks he has not been seen at the meetings of the Committee to Plant Petunias around the Steam Tunnels. According to Zoology Teaching Assistant Humblebee, this is an unfailing sign of loss of status. Humblebee's statements must be taken seriously. He was right when he predicted impending disaster for Biochemist Orcus. Humblebee noted that Orcus had turned in his refrigerated centrifuge for a motorcycle. The chain of events was predicted with awesome accuracy.

President Timkens appears to be getting a bit concerned about the Chancellor's ambitions. But Timkens is up to every challenge. He is sending the Chancellor to represent Crumble at the funeral of every vice-president and dean in the country. A morgue researcher is being sought for the inner presidential staff.

The Publicity Director has been discharged for failure to convince the State Legislature about the College's urgent need for a gold bathtub for President Timkens' wife. Timkens released his own bulletin to the effect that he has appointed Rumble Turnover of the Government Department to the new essential post of Chief College Mythmaker. Turnover's unrefutable view of the worthlessness of saving State funds since they depreciate or are stolen makes him especially fitted for this assignment. His past and shining achievement was to picture the financial picture of the College as so gloomy that the Legislature found it in the obituary column of the Crumble Sentinel.

A letter from Vera Scrum states that upon receipt all faculty members are advised that directives from the President via her desk are to be considered as Holy Writ. This is not to be taken lightly.

President Timkens will depart immediately for an urgent mission to West Africa where he will participate in a special program involving the painting of a ferryboat. While he is cementing our international relationships with a bucket of paint. Vera Scrum will be Acting President.

From the Instructor in Brevity in the Speech Department who was just divorced from one of the Cobra sisters "The screwing you get just ain't worth the screwing you get."

Crumble just lost 85 students and the Administration is in acute mourning. The New York Stock Exchange held up well despite this news.

Faculty salary increases and annual contracts will not be negotiated for another month at least. The Board of Trustees used up all the available time in an exhaustive all-night debate on whether to put mustard dispensers on each table or on each alternate table in the College cafeteria. No decision could be reached and the Board will have to be called in special session.

The National Approving Authority has stated that Crumble lacks the characteristics which identify a college and is therefore outside of its jurisdiction. Professor Sockeye Salmon of Fisheries disputes this nonsense. His rebuttal is that the Approving Authority appears to be composed of intelligent beings and is thus incapable of the necessary illogical judgment.

The National Approving Authority has responded. It has awarded the College another one of its numerous "firsts." The plaque, now hanging in the Great Hall, reads "Leader in Mediocrity."

The announcement by Stradivario Banjoli, the conductor of the Horseshit Ridge Philharmonic Symphony Orchestra, that he is giving a concert in the prestigious South Cornfield convention center, has enraged his arch-enemy, Picololi Frenzo, who was not even invited.

There are rumors that Picololi has conspired to do Banjoli in. When the orchestra reaches the crescendo of an opus, the landlord of the convention center is going to rush up to the stage and demand his rent or out you bums go. One has to applaud Picololi for his diabolic creativity.

Memo to: Students in Psychopathology 576
From: Dean of Students Office

Although I am in sympathy with your complaint that Professor Schlumping beats students on the head when they give disoriented answers, there is little we can do. Professor Schlumping's nephew is head of the Board of Trustees. Schlumping, too, will be beaten on the head if he makes the wrong decisions.

I recommend that all students come to class with helmets.

The Department of Anthropology advertised for a staff member, stating that its need was so great that it would gladly take one with two heads. A man with two heads showed up and has demanded the job.

Nutrition Instructor Short Ration has just completed a three year study supported by a $150,000 grant. Ration's conclusions are that if there is a nuclear attack, the amount of radioactivity an individual will receive through the food he eats will increase if he eats more. We congratulate Instructor Ration and deplore the lack of such insight in our general staff. Ration is confident that his next set of conclusions will have the stature of a divine revelation.

The Music Department announces a change in one member of its symphony orchestra. For the past three concerts the third woodwind has fallen off the stage into the pit every time an aria reached its crescendo. It was his backflip during the presto agito of the third movement of Beethoven's Moonlight Sonata that settled his hash. The forklift and the ambulance motor could not be kept in consonance with the music.

The Great Crumble Tremor last month which followed by two days the discharge of Winter Misery, super-researcher in earthquake control, has been taken by the Crumble Astrology Society to be nature's catastrophic response to Winter's leaving. It is an awesome salute to his universal pre-eminence. The only comparable devastating disturbance known in this region was the terrifying collapse of empty space in Professor McRooster's head some years ago. If the latter event was an implosion or an explosion was never settled because nobody could get out of the way fast enough.

Dr. Strained Stool, Proctologist at the Health Service, has been vindicated by his Department Chairman following a logical explanation of his absence for six months. Stool stated "A great scientist can never be found in his own lab, and a truly great scientist cannot even be found in a lab that he is visiting."

The president of the College parachute luncheon club has just confirmed a universal law of physics: people and salami fall at the same rate.

Scientist Ephraim Shnook has just come back in pretty bad physical condition from a one-month experiment where he lived alone, without the comforts of civilization, on a deserted island. Shnook knew such important facts as air in a balloon shrinks when the balloon is placed in an electric refrigerator, or a black rhinoceros does not get infectious arthritis, and other things that important people must know.

Shnook took along his dog that didn't know any of these facts. However, the dog is the picture of perfect health and tranquillity. Shnook will summarize his findings if and when he leaves the hospital.

Loose Gravel, Instructor in Mental Health, requires that his students know such things as:

Never talk back to an administrator when he is hallucinating.

Never shave while your wife is punching you.

Nobody ever left Bulgaria at a leisurely pace.

When in trouble come to Loose. The consequences are not guaranteed.

Umberto is coming to Crumble. The School of Agriculture is most fortunate in getting the limited services of this expert for the winter session. Umberto's speed record as a chili picker has never been equaled.

Each Department Chairperson will get an assistant whose title will be "Authoritative Source." This will allow the Chairperson to lie like all hell and deny that he said it. It will also cover up his expected stupidity. The idea follows the practice in Timkens' staff; they advise him what to do whereupon he does as he pleases, laying the blame on them mercilessly. For everyone colluding, this goes under the code name "Plausible Deniability."

Wrong Turn while driving President Timkens in the capacity of Timkens' personal and trustworthy auto chauffeur, tailgated a policeman and ran the cop and his auto straight up a tree. A sample of the "conversation" follows.

Cop to chauffeur: You unlawfully followed too close and you wrecked a police car.

Chauffeur (pointing to Timkens): He told me to do it.

Timkens (livid with rage): I'll choke the lying bastard (which he proceeded to accomplish).

Cop (to the rescue and warning Timkens): You look like an assassin. I'm booking you for attempted murder plus the minor charges of wrecking a police car and tailgating.

Editor's Note: The Administration has put a gag order on further discussion. Sorry.

And while we're at it, President Timkens' equal opportunity employee is no longer with us. We heard that he was by time-honored custom thrown out of the window. He served hog maws at the President's dinner for the Trustees.

The janitor who cleans the inner sanctum of the Board of Trustees went looking for paper to wrap the usual banquet garbage in before he threw it all in the dumpster which was hauled away. It was discovered too late that six months' worth of secret documents were gone forever including briefs to fire all dissident deans. Attorneys Voodoo and Perfidy who are on retainer for the College are searching for a charge just short of murder 1 to pin on the criminal.

Pro Bono Publico, the College staff writer, has been censured by the Italian-American students for his recent poem "Ode to a Herring." Pro Bono has promised not to cross ethnic lines and he says that he will try to find something good to say about Christopher Columbus.

Rolf Tomatosmash, a not too well-loved bacteriologist, has been asked to cancel his classes. Every time he lectures, everyone in the room comes down with a bacterial disease. There is no provision in the statutes to deal with such cases, but President Timkens can be depended upon to settle his hash.

From Dean Dingleberry: "Due to the excessive false-alarm ringing of sirens, I have arranged for the College Fire Department to have an unlisted phone number."

The jury members who came to investigate the elevator in the Biology building because of a lawsuit filed by a person who was stuck in it for ten hours were themselves stuck for eight hours. The mechanic could not be found because he had been attending a class on how to fix a stuck elevator, after which he went to his usual happy hour that lasted all night in the local saloon. When the jury first arrived, they had to pass through a classroom in which Ms. Droney Pustule was giving her expected soporific lecture and she didn't know when to shut up because she couldn't find where her notes ended.

At the trial the judge uttered the apothegm "Res ipso loquitor," meaning that the whole damn College is guilty and he allowed personal damages, even to the jurors.

Septic McNasty, brave new Campus Police Chief, came home after a hard day chasing student criminals. All his clothes had labels sewn in them which read "Keep out of the reach of children." Septic swears that the misdeed is the work of the Malevolent Society, whose capture he now considers to be his life's ambition. Following capture, McNasty promises dismemberment of selected portions of their derrieres, the trophies to be displayed in the hallway cases of the Art Gallery.

Murky Cliché, who has an endowed chair as Janitor-in-Residence, in the Psychology Department, says that it is difficult to make prophecies, especially for the future. You may recall that Murky was once diagnosed by Intern Gleep as having terminal diaper rash but somehow overcame the fatal event.

Crumble women are boycotting "Beauty and the Beast," a clothing store owned by an alumnus of the Malevolent Society. The Beauty section is only for the men.

Key to administrative Crumblese:
Strong leader: a term for any administrator who is not unconscious.
Not a bad fellow: he has only one fault, he's paranoid.
He is growing old nicely: transfer his office to the broom closet and see if you can shoehorn him in there. Let him keep his prayer rug.

The Board of Trustees will have to spend an extra session in its biennial evaluation of the performance of the deans. The case of Dean Ollie Underbright is especially difficult. His status will depend upon which of the following categories he fits: half-time idiot, full-time half-wit, or the other obvious combinations.

Infinite Grace, Timkens' consultant in flower arrangement, has a six-year old son, Whitney, who might just become a bad seed. The following is a censored transcript of a meeting between Whitney and a trainee counselor in the Child Guidance Clinic.
Trainee: Good morning Whitney, it's a nice day.
Whitney: Who the hell asked for your opinion?
Trainee: You should be pleasant, respectful and listen to your elders.
Whitney: You just laid three eggs, all at the same time.
Trainee: Let's start by getting better acquainted.
Whitney: Are you some kind of a homo?
Trainee: Why did you throw your seatmate's books out of the sec-

ond story window?
Whitney: Had to. Our home room is not on the first floor.
Trainee: Don't you feel that the teacher is your friend?
Whitney: Shit, no.
Trainee: Why do you swear like that?
Whitney: Poor education in English. I've already been expelled from school.
Trainee: What happened to your upper front tooth?
Whitney: I kicked the dentist and the son-of-a-bitch knocked out my tooth.

(Editor's note: We cannot continue. It's just too painful.)

Kermit Slob, a local veterinarian, lovingly known by his colleagues as the "Old Philosopher," has accepted an appointment as Very Temporary Visiting Soothsayer, without stipend of course. He is starting in the Droll Saying Section of the Department of English. Slob has assiduously collected such universal truths as:

A coed's greatest asset is her boy friend's imagination.

A boil on the stove is worth two on your behind.

The lower you fall in a barrel of alcohol, the higher you get.

Don't praise the day unless you get to bed without being clubbed or fired.

It isn't always certain that the future is ahead of us.

Or from his collections that give evidence of his subtle humor:
Question: Why should you never pass an elephant?
Answer: Because it may clog up the toilet.
Kermit also offers as an additional incentive to prove his worth:
Question: What do you do for an elephant with diarrhea?
Answer: Give it plenty of room.

To: Ms. Scorched Dumpling, Home Economics
From: Vera Scrum, Trusted Administrative Assistant

Your students claim that you cannot boil water. As you know, this is a requirement for their diploma. Appear at my office tomorrow. You will return to me by next week a 10,000 word treatise by Chiron The Centaur who could even teach Aesculapius. This information has to be available somewhere.

Instructor Sigma X^3 of the Department of Mathematics has given experimental verification to the universal attempts to square a circle. He rammed a sidewalk brick up a bull's behind.

Teaching at Crumble has become so bad that corrective measures will be instituted at once. Applause meters are being installed in each room The decibels reached will determine salaries and promotions.

The Malevolent Society, uncontested watchdog of student rights, will institute its own corrective measures. These could be cliffhangers. Hypoinstructors should be prepared to sweep glass out of their rooms and also teeth and hair if their performance doesn't elicit an occasional bravissimo especially from students speaking Italian.

Wet Soap, Instructor in Health Education, has been considered to be the champion of basic rights by faculty consensus. But the Administration would have had to invent him. He objects, but never too loudly, to administrative decisions. The administrators immediately print his quasi-diatribes to show that they listen carefully to the thinking of the faculty.

Wet will most certainly be appointed to the Board of Trustees when he retires. At their meetings he will be given warm milk and body language admonition if he starts to say something other than his name and social security number.

There is controversy in the English Department as to how to name the men's toilet in the developing east wing of the annex.

Chairman Language Mangler, always a strict grammarian, insists on Pee-éria, citing precedent for emphasizing the antepenult. Overdue Scroll, also a Latin scholar, states that one must strive for euphony and he adamantly urges Pee-er-ía. The Chancellor is considering a task force to resolve the question.

REPORT FROM THE HEALTH SERVICE

The Health Service cannot seem to finalize its earth-shaking study on the effects of lollipops versus morphine in the management of wayward children by equally wayward practitioners. Two groups of children were studied. P values at the 1% level of confidence indicated (a) absolutely nothing, and (b) that the crucial experiments will have to be done on Swiss mice.

The Service is cooperating with the Board of Health and the Whorehouse Association of Crumble to deport Tessie the tow-haired teamster, an independent entrepreneur. In the tugboat captains' conference at the College this week, she disabled so many of the conferees that the vessels cannot be moved out of port. Terminal river cities depending on barges could suffer food shortages.

Cranberry Snooker, food taster for President Timkens, was brought into the Health Service for observation. He was evaluating the Royal Chinook salmon and he washed it down with silver polish.

Rudolph Darfschnitten, the new surgeon at the Health Service, has led a checkered career. At one time he was an actor in Hamburg. His greatest role was a troublemaker in "Ruhrig fliesst der Rhein."

The Health Service warns students not to order the Sunrise Special at the Red Stool. The Special is sprinkled liberally with sawdust. The restaurant manager contends that this slows down the diarrhea which occurs after listening to some lecturers too early in the morning.

The Health Service announces that Dr. Andros del Loco has been appointed College Witchdoctor. He was found near a digging site by the Anthropology staff. Loco could be an improvement over Intern Gleep.

Associate Instructor Happy Plague was AWOL for three months. He told the authorities that he forgot what college he had a job in. Intern Gleep has diagnosed this as the Crumble Syndrome and he is collecting statistics on this for his bachelor's degree.

Dr. East Saturday, the College Meteorologist, is resting at the local hospital for observation. He has taken to wearing a weather vane in his hat.

The Health Service has obtained temporary custody of Instructor Grutty's dog, Haggard. Grutty, who is Teaching Assistant in Nutrition in Home Economics, says that he couldn't afford the dog food. Haggard is now walking on three legs and is expected to use all four by next week. Intern Gleep, who once owned a three-legged cow, is in charge of the case and he has been given a badge saying Veterinary Consultant.

Seen in the window of the College bookstore: Our prices are so low that we are ashamed to quote them. So there is no point coming in until we raise them this afternoon.

Crumble will offer a degree leading to proficiency as a "Battleship Repair Estimator." Finding a battleship will be the first duty of the students.

The Philosophy Department insists that both horns of a dilemma are usually attached to the same bull.

Ill-health just dogs the administrative staff. Dean Catcabbage has been diagnosed as having schluckathembewegung (SAB). He gulps too much air when he swallows. According to a consultant from the Department of Zoology, this condition occurs in decerebrate rabbits. The Dean is to minimize elevation of his Adam's apple. Catcabbage is to be looked at by another consultant who is doing research on whether "squirt-signal" consistently accompanies SAB.

The Chairman of the Department of Health Education has gone through a long and mysterious illness in which his head was seriously weighted to one side. The cause was undiagnosed despite exhaustive medical examination. We have good medicine in Crumble, however. Dentist Spitsink discovered that the Chairman had accumulated 5 pounds of tartar in only three left molars and premolars. The Chairman is attending compulsory night classes in oral hygiene.

Dean Frond Graynose of Mortuary Science visited the Health Service to borrow a bandage for his hangnail. Promising young intern Fishmeal felt it his duty to give him a thorough examination. Fishmeal reported that he could elicit a cracked note upon percussing the Dean's head. He believes that the prognosis is ominous. Graynose, however, counters that his parents observed a liberty bell-type ding dong 69 years previously and he would be abnormal without the ding dong. A panel of experts, that the Health Service is never without, will decide the issue.

Note carefully: It isn't the cough that carries you off, it's the coffin they carry you off in.

Psychiatrist Upside Downcake is the new Director of the Great Crumble Madhouse. He says that he will turn everything around. He has his directions mixed.

The Dirty Dugs of Duessa, like the Red Stool, has joined the list of suspect restaurants in Crumble. Take the case of the Senior Citizens Supper. Everyone eating it has assumed a characteristic posture, his knees doubled up to his stomach and a look of writhing torture on his face. A more recent special, called the Sweet Teethlings of Fled, is being analyzed at arms length at the toxicology laboratory. One toxicologist bravely tasted it and started barking like a dog. One patron said that he drank the soup of the day, called Cholesterol Conserve, and he is still thrombosing slowly.

In all fairness it is admitted that the CFO soup is both delicious and non-toxic. The term CFO derives from the fact that these three letters once fell off the shelf and dissolved in the soup below. The flavor was so enhanced that this soup is a favorite. No other letters can reproduce the flavor.

The cook is presently concocting a volcano sauce that is his answer to British Anti-Lewisite. He is also developing a Tunnel Opener. This is a 20-alarm chili with a dash of trinitroglycerin.

Food reports keep coming in. A vice-president is being treated for palate-schmerz. He ate so many exotic foods on his last fully paid trip around the world that the food in Crumble has put him into a stupor. Our staff alchemist is working feverishly with the chief nutritionist to whomp up a heavenly dish that will normalize the vice-president. He is being currently sustained with intermittent blasts of compressed air.

Dr. Tummyrumble, Crumble's famous malnutritionist, has been admitted to the Health Service with acute hoarseness, produced by hollering at himself for 16 hours. He had worked for five years on an exhaustive study of the digestive habits of cannibals and he had completed 3,000 cases. Crumble's last practicing cannibal ate up all the data when Tummyrumble's back was turned.

Kurfurwinkle, certified as fraud-free in his last trial, is back at the Health Service as Visiting Gastroenterologist. You will remember him as the author of "Kurfurwinkle's Diagram." This forecasts quantitatively the different bizarre attitudes that Crumble students will take immediately following every Wednesday night's meal at Freshmen Commons. Age and sex differences have been factored into the graph.

The Health Service is pleased to announce that the man pinned under the machine in the Safety Director's shop will be pulled out shortly. He has been identified as the Safety Director. Everything will be all right as soon as they extract his incisor teeth from the malfunctioning potato peeler.

Dr. Gloomy Swinger of the Health Service has been transferred to the Department of Physics. His aptitude for basic research is being tested by keeping him for two weeks in a constant temperature water bath. He will the following week stand as fulcrum on an analytical balance to check his ability to weigh objects to three decimal points.

We have just found a letter to Myron and duty compels us to print it.

Dear Myron:

Intern Gleep has complained to me that he has to work seven days a week at the Health Service. His spiritual life is suffering.

Suppressed Carnality-Theologian

Dear Suppressed: I have a compromise. On Sundays, Gleep's soul belongs to you. On weekdays his ass belongs to us and we intend to get the lazy bastard off it.

Clinical researchers at Crumble have refuted the theory of focal infection. Their data show that tonsillectomy is not a cure for nymphomania .

The researchers are also following up a report that there is a relative absence of arthritis in persons known to be insane. So far, three of our deans have been found to be free of arthritis. An in-depth study will be made with cockroaches.

Intern Gleep almost had it this time. While smoking a cigarette, he inserted a colonoscope into the anus of a student who promptly passed wind. The methane gas in the wind exploded and the student's entire behind caught fire. Gleep, rising appropriately to the task, sounded the fire alarm to which the entire Great Crumble Fire Department responded. Gleep will be allowed on the service only after an attendant ties his two hands together behind his back.

The Health Service offers instructors a sample letter of recommendation to turn off students who are applying to about 100 medical schools.

"Luckless Fester has begged me on hands and knees for a letter of recommendation to medical school. I can say with all confidence that he does not know the meaning of failure. He persists in it. His record looks like it has been forged so I will not need to embellish it. Worthy of note is that the applicant excels in Elementary Bodily Functions including Romance, both in theory and practice. Somehow he was never suspended."

"It is our sacred duty to evaluate a student with all fairness to him, the profession and the customer, and this letter fills all the desiderata. We would admit him to our Medical School but a seat was removed from the amphitheater by request from the burgeoning program for Elevator Operators."

The Health Service agrees in principle with the view of the Malevolent Society that Crumble is a toilet bowl in search of a clean behind. One of our staff is researching the problem in depth. He is currently submerged.

A new syndrome has surfaced. The malaise begins about six months after suffering starvation on the faculty. Upon seeing anyone on the campus with a three-piece suit, supposedly an administrator, the susceptible faculty member develops tics, spasms and grimacing of the facial muscles. A diagnostic sign is coprolalia, the compulsive shouting of obscene words. Exhaustion follows, remissions being proportional to the square of the distance from the antigenic perpetrator. The victim can be desensitized by injections of pooled blood from retired administrators.

SOME RECENT UNPRINTABLES

We include the account from our intrepid roving reporter about events of interest occurring in the jungle. The commotion to be described involves a missionary from Crumble who was caught.

Tribal cook (in his native tongue, of course): I have the victim in the pot. Shall we light the fire?

Tribal chief: Large crowd tonight. Have you done your homework on the proposed dissection?

Cook: We can get ten good chunks.

Chief: Some unexpected relatives are showing up for the banquet. We will need more pieces.

Cook: Hold everything. I need to consult our tribal mathematician.

Chief: Is he good at chunking?

Cook: Excellent. He's a Yale graduate.

Do you recognize the guy who, at the close of an invited seminar speaker's talk, asks the speaker a question, then proceeds for the next 15 to 20 minutes answering it himself, before turning the floor back to the hapless speaker? This guy turns the entire 360 degree arc before sitting down so that everyone can remember him as a person of quality and light. The seminar speaker has no recourse but only to say "That's a good question" while holding on to the podium to keep from collapsing. The moderator has to quickly declare the meeting closed before the local bullshit artist dreams up another question.

The Dean of Men reminds all students contemplating suicide about Borgia's law that two poisons are better than one.

Ms. Rusty Bedpan, gynecologic nurse, is regretting her cause, "Take a Friend's Husband to Bed Week." She says that she was snookered into sponsoring it in Crumble. The people at the Bible and Catfish store won't speak to her. Last week she fell out of the Worm store and she believes that someone removed the steps just before she came out. She has been excommunicated from the Great Crumble Tabernacle and being a religious woman she has appealed to the Holy Rollers to take her in.

Dr. Marvin Earwax, a Crumble otologist until his license was revoked because he couldn't blow air in a straight line through two ears of a vice president, has joined the Health Service. Earwax is practicing as a nutritionist and he has attained national prominence by inventing the maneuver of putting lemon juice into tomato juice to make it taste like orange juice.

When Dean Dingleberry recovers from his most recent auto accident, he will be questioned by the District Attorney. A sample of his breath taken at the scene of the disaster was found to disorganize the ciliary activity of oyster gills.

He who laughs last had better not bet on it—Smiley Timkens

Policeman to Crumble student just stopped for speeding: "I've been waiting all day for someone like you to come charging down the highway."

Polite Crumble student: "I came as fast as I could."

MYRON'S CORNER

We have come upon the following series of letters from Myron, the sage of the Health Service, in the course of pruning our rubbish.

Dear Myron:

Since you are the closest approach to the Oracle of Delphi, I submit this question. I am a slob who is permanently red-tagged by the Board of Health. If I attend your seminars, can I become an expert in Clean Room Technology? I have heard that it is a lucrative field.

Dear Slob: You appear to be several light-years away from eligibility. The course you need is for incorrigibles. One is given at the city dump, mudslide entrance. You will be quarantined so as not to contaminate the rats.

Dear Myron:

Every time I have to go to the Health Service, I get sicker. When I get too sick, they throw me out. Please comment. Disease Pot—Sophomore Coed

Dear Disease Pot: The frequency of visits to our Health Service is directly correlated with the subsequent severity of student disease. It doesn't matter how trivial the disorder, just expect the worst to happen. My advice is that you have your room-mate knock you out, using a rubber frying pan or any other sublethal device at hand. Your primary symptoms will disappear and be replaced when you regain consciousness by a condition that can be treated with aspirin and wet towels.

Dear Myron:

My husband keeps insisting that Crumble can escape annihilation only if President Timkens is executed. How shall I proceed to avoid the grand tragedy? Wife of Paranoiac Psychology Major

Dear Wife: The strategy is simple. Persuade your husband that Timkens is harmless and that he should start his execution with the vice-presidents. When this is agreed upon, then persuade him to execute all the deans. Having switched his interests, you may if you like persuade him to do in the department chairmen. In this way you can ultimately cure him. At the very least, you will have saved the life of President Timkens. As for the deans, they have now become disposable since we have joined the Rent-A-Dean Service.

TO: Public Domain from Myron

Anyone interested in buying a pair of new skis should come to the intensive care unit of The Great Crumble Hospital. Ask a nurse if George is conscious.

Dear Myron:

I am an A+ student in Business and Economics. Recently, I invested my next two years tuition in a sure-fire Hot Dog and Waxed Shoelace store downtown. I have lost 40% of my entire fortune and am having nightmares. Please advise. Bewildered Sophomore

Dear Bewildered: Declare bankruptcy at once. Pay off 40 percent of your assets and you will feel 60 percent better. Following this action write me again.

Dear Myron:

My roommate says I should see a groinecologist. What is that? Dripping Coed

Dear Coed: He is a person who works where other people play. Keep your feet together and your head down.

College Dentist Obscene Marshmallow was given stern advice from Myron, who can really dish it out, following the complaint of a coed that Obscene tried to fill the wrong cavity. It may be said that the coed is not taking it lying down.

Dear Myron:

My horse started to lean critically to the southeast yesterday and there was no wind. Today I started to lean to the northeast. Intern Gleep thinks we have kuru. Urgent confirmation needed. Princeton Scraggs

Dear Professor Scraggs: Bring your horse to the Health Service tomorrow. Push him through the front door. You come in through the back to avoid spreading disease. We will first try calcium supplements which you and your horse can share on alternate days, If your horse doesn't respond, we will make arrangements for it at the glue factory. As for you, if you should backflip suddenly, crawl to the infirmary. I questioned Gleep about kuru. He said that he asked a professor of Higher Education about it, but the professor didn't seem to know about kuru or, for that matter, about anything else.

Dear Myron:

In response to your theory that right-handed men who sleep in double beds tend to sleep on their wive's left, I have negative evidence. It depends upon whether they are facing the pillows or the bed.

What is your response? Anonymous

Dear Anonymous: I suspect that you are a troublemaker.

Dear Myron:

Everything my six month old baby eats turns to shit. Is this unusual? Unwed Freshman Coed

Dear Unwed: Our Research Staff states that this also happens to adults. Do not panic. When your baby reaches age 21, you will no longer be legally responsible for what happens.

Dear Myron:

I am the outstanding financial forecaster, not to mention whoremaster, of the Economics Department. I am recently out of mistresses and my business is not in the hole. Is that good or bad? Superfluous Hamhock

Dear Superfluous: This is either good or bad, depending on the translation. I would not tell it to anyone else if I were you.

Dear Myron:

My supposed friend who is a judge and whose home I visit often ruled against my claim for personal injury in a brick-throwing bash which I lost. He said it wasn't a direct hit. Please advise how to get even with him. Henry

Dear Henry: The next time you are at his house, pee at him and if you miss, tell him the same thing.

Dear Myron:

Although I am now an expert at cleaning barns, I need genetic counseling to develop my genius potentialities in science. My father is a brilliant phenomenologist, one brother is a niche-lover, and a second is a dilettante. My four-year grade point average is D minus. Scientist with Overwhelming Possibilities

Dear Overwhelming: I ran your imposing credentials through our computer. You will be a quick and dirty cream skimmer. Change your major at once-to hotel management.

Dear Myron:

What do you think of my marrying a mermaid? My friends tell me it won't last. Fisheries Major

Dear Fisheries Major: Statistics are on your side. There is no authenticated record of a man divorcing a fish.

Dear Myron:

My roommate claims that electric shock is a hazard to health. I disagree. Can you suggest a crucial experiment? Doubtful

Dear Doubtful: Try a current of no less than 20 amperes. The threshold value is very important. At the point where you find yourself "frozen" to the conductor, please don't beg your room-mate to do anything until spasm of your respiratory muscles produces impending asphyxia. If at that time you feel that the point is proved, I suggest that artificial respiration be started. Write me about the outcome if you are able.

Dear Myron:

I now realize that I was snookered into coming to Crumble. I signed the contract before the chloral hydrate wore off. Now I am hesitant to leave because of the jeers of my peers. Please advise. First Term Freshman

Dear First Term: Crumble is purely an act of faith. After you are here awhile, this gives you an excuse for all your later failures in life. You never have to explain further. Very comforting thought. I suggest that you remove the ants in your pants, fill your shoes with booze, and settle down to a long two years of atrophy.

Dear Myron:

In my family are four people: my mother; my father; my brother, Freddie; and of course, me. My mother is absolutely gorgeous. At least that's what her boy friend says. My father is confused about the issue. My brother, Freddie, says she is a good cook. What do you think? Mixed-up Sociology Major

Dear Mixed Up: I agree with your brother Freddie. Your mother is a good kook.

Dear Myron:

While admitted to the Health Service yesterday, someone knocked on my door and then came in. She said, "I'm your doctor. Take off your clothes." I asked her if I had to take off my pants and she told me that was included too. Then she examined me from head to toe and told me to go back to bed. "Now I ask, what is your reaction." Puzzled Freshman

Dear Puzzled: "Why did she knock?"

Dear Myron:

Should you talk to your wife while you are making love? Unsophisticated married sophomore

Dear Unsophisticated: You should occasionally if there's a telephone handy.

Dear Myron:

We want to know who in the hell appointed you Sage of the Health Service. Please answer promptly. Greasespot.

Dear Greasespot: I wanted to become a sex maniac but I couldn't pass the physical.

Dear Myron:

My husband says I am going up to see a certain fellow in my class too often, and he will bust up this fellow and anyone else who I will go up to see. Can I come up to see you and talk this over. Misunderstood Sophomore

Dear Misunderstood: Do not come up to see me until I have completed my course in karate and machinegunnery. I would encourage you to go up and see my old-time enemy, Dr. Camoogy Eclair, the belligerent psychiatrist at the Great Crumble Madhouse. He has it coming to him.

Dear Myron:

I am only 17 years old and getting bald. What is your advice? Henry

Dear Henry: Come to the clinic very early next Tuesday and we will castrate you. Baldness rarely occurs in eunuchs.

Dear Myron:

I just fell down an elevator shaft. What shall I do? Worried Professor

Dear Worried: Send a message to your wife that you'll be home late for dinner.

Dear Myron:

My seven year old adopted son has acted in the most bizarre manner from the time we got him. Details are submitted. Please advise. Frantic Sophomore Mother

Dear Frantic Sophomore Mother: I analyzed the case history in great detail. The answer is simple. His real mother threw away the embryo and brought up the placenta.

Dear Myron:

I am prematurely losing my pubic hair. This could detract from my hard earned reputation with my public. What do you suggest? Popular Sophomore

Dear Popular Sophomore: There are two solutions. First, you could keep your fly closed. If this retards your relationship with your more intimate public, we can schedule you for a transplant. Your photograph shows that you still have enough hair around your ears to fill in the empty spaces. Our plastic surgeon, who is an expert in calligraphy, will even insert a nice monogram at no extra cost.

Dear Myron:

You work with a wild man named Fendrick Poltroon. He hates nearly everyone and everything. Is my assessment correct? I need to know because I am getting a job taking care of maniacs. Very perceptive coed.

Dear Very: Your assessment would have been perfect if you had deleted "nearly' in the above sentence.

Dear Myron:

I trust your judgment so that I eagerly await your advise. My clinical thermometer keeps telling me that I have a fever but there are no other sign or symptoms. Please advise. Octopussy

Dear Octopussy: Break your thermometer in half. Your temperature will come down precipitously. Don't let anyone know that I advised you.

Dear Myron:

I don't like your advice and I hereby challenge you to a fist fight. I obviously can lick you since I keep in shape by restricting my food intake to one pound of steak daily. My elimination is two pounds. Barch Frusioni, Weight Lifter

Dear Barch: I can only think of one answer. It is impossible to eat one pound of steak and put out two pounds of shit.

Myron's instructive lecture to the Baby Carriage and Salami Crowd that husbands should be periodically deprived both sexually and at table was received with wild applause. There is no telling to what heights Myron will rise. According to his enemies, he could soar right out of the Health Service.

From now on there will be a roving campus attendant to take care of the increasing aberrant behavior. You will recognize the attendant by his white coat and net. Walk carefully and discreetly as you go by him. Your entire future may be at stake.
Health Service officials can report only superficially on what happened there yesterday. A hospitalized coed was seen jumping out of a second story window followed by a long-haired medical technologist wearing sandals, urine-stained dungarees and a sweatshirt with his arm and hypodermic syringe and needle extended for intravenous sampling. Since the Director of the Health Service was in a hurry for breakfast, he did not stop to ask if he could help.

ABSOLUTELY ESSENTIAL UPDATE FOR THE STAFF

Editor's Note: We are not sure how the above differs from "essential."

From the Unwealthy Graduate Assistants: Don't buy anything that eats.

McRooster, Professor of Dead Birds, has asked for professional advice as to how best decline the job as Academic Vice-President which has not been offered to him. McRooster feels that if he does this often enough, his political future within the College will be assured.

The new buzz word is "overachiever." Since this comes from the School of Education, the word carries the force of authority. It means that the overachiever knows twice as much as his instructors and thus four times as much as the dean.

In the Crumble public schools, overachievers are claimed to have less intelligence than the losers since they create three times as much trouble for the principal. Instead of mainstreaming the losers, the question will be whether to mainstream the overachievers. We have great faith that the School Board will solve this question with infinite wisdom.

Word has reached us from Bongoland that our Foreign Resident Center is having trouble putting up billboards advertising Crumble City Junior College. The angry natives are complaining that the signs further spoil their currently uncivilized scenery. President Timkens says that he intends to bring the matter to the attention of the United Nations. The Registrar, who is putting up the billboards personally, has been told to resist all efforts to prevent his work. The situation is fluid.

From the ante-bellum Chairman of the Political Science Department when Crumble was in its glory:

Democracy is still the best show in town. It permits the exercise of so-called rights that have a universal touch of humor. The actual story of a two-month pregnant prisoner is a good illustration. The mother saw no reason to keep her developing fetus (now assumed to be a living person with legal rights) in prison for seven months more of the pregnancy when it had committed no crime. Jurists, who couldn't even dream up this situation, are asked to demonstrate their capacity for Solomon-type wisdom to render a decision. They could sit in the box forever.

Shindo Singsweet, pigtailed and unshaven psychiatrist at the Health Service, has proposed an effective mechanical treatment for schizophrenia. He repetitively wallops the head of the patient with a rubber mallet. Singsweet theorizes that a profound molecular reorientation occurs which just balances the existing disorientation. Singsweet first demonstrated his treatment before the "Crumble Downtown Seminar Group." The Group contains several naturopaths, one metaphysician, three accountants, two butchers, and a clergyman. Approval of any scientific theory by this Group is highly sought after and is immediately recognized by the Board of Trustees. The Group has unanimously endorsed the technic.

Duoquinto Septimus, College garbage collector, was named by his father who once knew a high school instructor in algebra. The father says that the world is not ready for Duo. However,

Duo's mother is more realistic. She says that triangulation has not been able to locate Duo's brain.

Dr. Alpha Coenzyme of the Department of Chemistry, recently retired, seems to grow smarter by the week. When questioned about his increasing smarts, he attributed it to complete isolation from the plethora of misinformation freely dispensed in his former Department.

The Archaeology Museum, built in Alligator Swamp, has posed a problem for our undaunted Architectural Service. All personnel have been issued knee-length irrigation waders and off-shoulder ditch spades. Timid students are advised to lease amphibious tanks until a helicopter service is established.

The biochemists are pleased with the appointment of Assistant Professor Apple Pan-Dowdy. He has had considerable chemical experience, the last ten years being spent in stuffing contraceptive jelly in tubes.

The austerity program initiated by an efficiency expert in the Department of Buildings and Grounds is satisfactory, according to President Timkens. Timkens was especially impressed with the efficiency demonstrated by a painter who was painting two walls with both hands, mixing two buckets of paint with one foot in and out of each bucket, and simultaneously painting wheelbarrows traveling by behind him on an assembly line, with the use of a brush held in his external anal sphincter. (Editor's note: Very busy person.)

Inger Binger, Instructor in Hurdy Gurdy in the Department of Physical Education, received his warm letter of recommendation entitled "To Whom It May Concern" from Timkens yesterday. Binger got the point and is spending the weekend applying to Horseshit Ridge High School.

Pascal Celery
Ex-Salad Chef
Dear Pascal:

You are threatening to file suit on the grounds that the secretarial job in the Physical Education Department was given to a female, basing your protest upon reverse discrimination.

A review of your eligibility test shows that you did not know that 12 leptons and 36 different forms of quarks have now been isolated. Obviously, you are ignorant of the fundamental picture of matter. In regard to the broad spectrum of knowledge essential to a typist, you had no idea of when Lao-Tzu founded Taoism in China. Surprisingly, you did not know how to predict an earthquake. And even on the local scene, you knew nothing about toothpaste analysis.

If you wish to apply as a student in our Sociology Department, you will gradually develop powerful problem solving capability. In four years you can reapply for the position as typist.

Cautiously,
Smiley Timkens

The Geographic Society by extrapolation says that Crumble City is at the end of the world and people should avoid stepping off at the city limits. Fences are being erected until the matter is settled.

Language Mangler, Chairman of the English Department, was called to the Dean's office to explain why his students failed to receive their course grade despite their continued requests. The Chairman explained that his dog ate up the grade book.

The Malevolent Society practically destroyed the attendance at the last football game. Their pilots came over the stadium in a helicopter and with pinpoint accuracy dumped a half-ton of shit on spectator Dean Ollie Underbright. The Dean managed to crawl out of the sludge whereupon he was quickly run out of the stadium by the police for contributing to a nuisance. A little old lady nearby said that the Dean must have done something awful to deserve such a fate. A CIA agent in the crowd noted that he would like to recruit the pilots for service in Nicaragua. The Dean in a post-cleanup interview lamented that nobody is safe anymore.

L'Enfant Terrible, our perpetual sadsack and Lecturer in French, is now complaining about his treatment in America. The Corps of Engineers arrived one morning with full equipment and poured tons of sand over his house. Something about reinforcing a levee. Crumbleites have turned this into a recreation area termed the sand dunes.

Although his house is underground, the city has sued L'Enfant for delinquency in paying his taxes and the local bank is threatening to jail him for failure to amortize his mortgage. L'Enfant counters with a useless statement that nobody asked his permission to bury his house. He has petitioned the State to bore a hole so that he can retrieve his overcoat.

A window cleaner working in the Philosophy building threw the Chairman out of an uncleaned window. The window cleaner said that this was an economy measure. Also, he said that he had a discussion with the Chairman about Aristotle and that the Chairman demonstrated such poor logic that there was no way he could continue a dialogue with him.

The mayors of Crumble and Horseshit Ridge have been engaged in a ceaseless controversy that we almost didn't want to publicize. We cite only the briefest current exchange:

The Honorable Mayor of H. R.: The Government says that we

have to reduce our pollution. Please close Crumble at once and especially when the winds become unfavorable.

His Accidency, The Honorable Mayor of C: Just like not carrying coal to Newcastle, it isn't necessary to heap up more shit in Horseshit Ridge.

Rebuttal from H. R.: Your remark suggests one way out. Emigration from Crumble is stopped as of this statement. Detour all your traffic through Bad Eggsville.

Logical retort from the Mayor Of C.: Please forward your remarks in writing on tablets. Our City Archaeologist will translate them. Meanwhile I will request the Governor for a neutral border patrol.

Crumble's gangland leader was turned away from FLOG A DEAD HORSE, the town's most fashionable evening restaurant, because he wasn't wearing a tie. The shooting that took place later inside had to go on without him. The Civil Liberties Association is about to protest the restriction of individual freedom of movement for Crumble citizens.

Engineering Diener Higgledy Piggledy, who invented the unmatchable robot eraser, would gladly send his robot to the scrap heap if he could approach it with an axe, and even better, a high intensity bomb. The robot erased his four-year, 1800 page thesis on "Writing My Way to Promotion." This had just been accepted and was returned for corrections on pages 2 and 7. Higgldy had not made a duplicate copy.

The robot is carefully totaling Higgldy's lecture notes and it hisses menacingly when Higgldy approaches. Higgldy would like to drown it but he would settle for its irrecoverable castration.

The manuscript by the staff of the Department of Philosophy entitled "The Accumulated Wisdom of 300 Crumble Faculty

Members" has been rejected everywhere. One editor said that the wisdom might be applied by rectal absorption if the manuscript were printed on lighter paper. Another said that his cat refused to urinate on the document and that was his customary test.

To: Director, Home for the Aged
From: Smiley Timkens

We are auctioning off two staff members who taught taxonomy here. They could fit better in your institution than they have the past 45 years in ours. No need to come early since there will not be a rush.

The staff of Anthropology, whose grants for research total 2 million dollars this year, has voted that Dean Dingleberry will henceforth take orders from them since the Department obviously pays his salary.

Crumble has been officially designated as Brand-X college. It will be used to illustrate that any other college can do better.

If students want to learn only how to add and subtract, they may register for Math 101. If they need to know how to multiply and divide, they will have to wait for Math 102. If our brilliant students want to multiply and divide in Roman numerals, arrangements can be made to transfer them to Shebanse Polytech.

Erratum Feedbag, Tutor in Remedial English, who lectures in the closed-circuit television course "How To Look Like A Nordic," has been asked to take a vacation. Erratum gets 5 o'clock shadow at 9:30 A.M. To keep Erratum in character, it has been decided to cast him as an Eskimo dog in "Nanook of the North."

Dean Ollie Underbright to an instructor (while the Dean was

walking down the aisle in the last faculty meeting), "Good morning, it is indeed a pleasure to see you again."

Instructor (under his breath), "The hell with you, too."

The Geology Department is conducting an experiment on the effect of changes of climate on man. To obtain homogeneous control, members of the staff will live in a barrel for 12 months. We commend the Department for evolving such delightful simplicity of experimental design. The Department of Zoology is watching the experiment with interest, since animals are costing them too much.

Baggy Elbows, Gerontologist
Department of Rehabilitation
Dear Baggy:

You have performed with predictable disgrace on the semicentennial test for retention on our distinguished faculty. You did not know the method to characterize silicon-doped, gallium arsenide insulator/semiconductor surfaces. Also, you had no idea what a backwash turbidimeter is used for. On the other hand, you were astonishingly bright on how to maximize fraud and to expeditiously disappear through a campus steam tunnel.

The Bursar and the Physics Chairman, in that order of importance, ask that you retake the entire exam. Our staff must display knowledge in modern fundamental concepts, or they will not be able to hold an intelligent conversation with our teaching assistants.

Splat
Faculty Counselor

Professor McRooster has become agitated greatly about the decrease of his fiefdom in dead birds. Another assistant has been taken away. McRooster has announced in trumpet style that the extraction of additional bodies from his staff will be tougher than pulling a kangaroo's tooth. In pursuing his get-tough policy, McRooster said that his next meeting with the Chancellor will be an eyeball to eyeball encounter in which he has no equal.

The Crumble kindergarten class voted to have as its theme song, "Bounce a ball off baby, tra la la la la."

Philosopher Discontinuity concludes from serious observation that when two seemingly harmless administrators get together during school hours, they become a lethal anti-faculty weapon. The trouble worsens if there is an idle secretary with a typewriter nearby.

In accordance with Crumble's custom of offering specialized services to fill everyone's needs, all coeds who have declared themselves to be nymphomaniacs on their registration forms will be housed in the just completed dormitory, The Bear Trap.

Assistant Instructor Emeritus Wet Cornfritter manages to retain his dignity. Despite bankruptcy in his bistro, The Lonesome Star, which was almost as inactive as a Maytag repairman, he bounded back and is now whisk-brooming affluent customers in the men's room of the Great Crumble Hotel. The retiree says that this job is less demanding in the post-intelligent years of his life.

President Timkens, always demonstrating his innovative genius, proclaims that all administrators must have a dog. If the dog gets more publicity per semester than its master does, even if it is only per bite, then it is shape up or ship out for the master. Still another first for Crumble.

Two faculty members who attempted to form a "Get Timkens Society" were apprehended by the Campus Police in a conspiratorial meeting behind the steam plant. One was tape-recorded as saying "Let's blow the whistle on the skunk." Dean Dingleberry has expressed amazement that his faculty would use that kind of language.

The Department of Philosophy announces that its course in Intermediate Truth will be canceled because it doesn't appear that the instructor will be available. Something about shoplifting. We hear that the slammer is a good place to be if one has to revise his lecture notes.

Rectangular Hyperbola, prize logician in Mathematics, will not be charged for his compulsive habit of tearing pages from back to front out of library books. He explained, as expected from a logician, that you can rip out the last page because the preceding page will then become the last. The Department agrees that his reasoning is flawless.

Report of the Educational Policy Committee to President Timkens:

Disciples of internationally famed Professor Feebish Thronk have asked that a building be erected on the campus to honor Feebish forever, perhaps even longer. The Committee responds as follows:

If the College wishes to institutionalize Thronk it may feel free to do so, but without the complicity of our Committee.

To: Chairman of the Committee
From: Timkens

Vox Populi Vox Dei. (The voice of the people is the voice of God.) I always obey the call of the democratic consensus. The building is caput.

There is one question. Does the verb "institutionalize" have a double entendre?

In Glorification Day at the College, 96 per cent of the teachers who were rated worst by 100 per cent of the students rated themselves among the top 25 per cent of all the teachers at Crumble. The Mathematics Department will put these figures into an equation whereby the worst teachers and the student ratings must match inversely, thereby serving as a non-refutable instrument of accountability in determining promotion and salary increases. The deans will simply press a button and pull the data for each staff member out of a buzzing slot machine like bottles of soda pop.

The Accounting Office, whose staff is totally uncreative, has been told to keep the hell out of it. Also, no more pictures will be allowed in the daily College paper showing a research professor teaching a class of four smiling students who are eating watermelons while busily taking notes under a verdant peach tree.

Famous last words: "Trust me." We quote this verbatim from long-gone Scrambled Eggs who once confided in her chairman.

Miss Pipsi Terrific, Assistant Professor of English, has been asked by Dean Dingleberry to attend a remedial English class until she shows evidence that her defects in comprehension are neither incurably genetic nor the result of sensory aphasia. She reported to the Dean that she received a letter from President Timkens that was vague and enigmatic and she could make no sense of it. Timkens seemed to be trying to voice a most touching farewell to her with a poignant note of regret and sadness, together with gratitude for her unmatchable 37 years of devotion to Crumble. He had cried all night. Ms. Terrific, during her visit to the venerable Dean with the letter, said to him "I must go to President Timkens at once. It sounds like a convulsion. I think he's dying." The Dean advised Miss Terrific against flying at once to Timkens, noting that it is good rule never to take an administrator by surprise.

The Rusty-Trusty hot plate, purchased for $3.25 in 1917 by the Department of Chemistry has broken down, affecting six sections in General Chemistry. In view of the acute emergency, the

Dean has granted permission to the Department Chairman to wear dark glasses and a sign reading "blind" and to sit for the weekend with a tin cup in front of the local 5 and dime store.

Things went badly at the last symphony concert. The leading lady started to sing soprano but instead sang lenissi monagatto. This upset the rafters cat and it fell on the conductor's head, who fled abruptly. The singer then fielded a tomato thrown by a music-loving freshman and she descended to profundo basso. The audience left, some chomping peanuts.

Assistant Bursar Endicott Virtuoso is in deep trouble. A fire broke out in his wastebasket the morning of payday. He poured gasoline on it. The loss includes a wing of the building and S10,000 in bills.

Visiting Lecturer Schrenzel Floo, who also owns the local Furnace Blowing and Chimney Cleaning Company, was called out in the middle of his public lecture on "The Abstract World of Symbols," due to a sudden freeze in Crumble City. The last half of the lecture will be rescheduled in the summer.

Lecturer Green Bottom, expert in archaeology, has been called before the local tax collector. He paid his city dog collar tax in 1 obolus, 10 denarii and 3 logs.

The Physics Department is contributing increasingly to our local news. Assistant Instructor Mickel Mickel (nickname: Mickel) has developed a physical theory of how administrative personnel are selected. He states that it is a matter purely of specific gravity. Scum rises to the top. The theory is attracting national attention.

Filgie Toodle, Group Leader in Astrophysics, had a difficult time of it last night. Despite his superb help in correcting the course of a missile headed for the moon and guiding it into the sea of. lunar tranquillity, he was unable to fix the plunger on his toilet hopper at home. Directly following the flooding of his downstairs living room, he nearly suffered violent death at the hands of his wife.

The weather predictions of the College Climatology Station are becoming suspect. The President's Office had to listen for one hour yesterday to a little old lady who said she had to shovel two feet of partly cloudy off her sidewalk.

The one-legged janitor at the Cafeteria caught Fleetwing, the All-American track star, escaping with a hot apple pie. The track coach is negotiating an athletic scholarship for the janitor.

The new Vice President for Instruction says that he would never have taken the job if he knew there were faculty and students on the campus.

Secretaries are needed in the Philosophy office. Because of the low priority of the Department, the roof leaks badly and will continue to do so until there is some evidence of students in the building. The Department therefore requires that all applicants possess a good backstroke in addition to proficiency in shorthand.

Phonetician Raspy Chirp has fallen into hard times. On the basis of his theory that everyone hears a sentence the way he wants to, he said to every person coming through a receiving line at a friend's wedding "I just killed my grandmother." Unfortunately, his grandmother committed suicide while baby-sitting at Raspy's house during the wedding. Raspy is currently in the Bastille with a murder charge hung on him.

The regional evaluation committee, after visiting lecturer Freebisher's class, has decided to withdraw accreditation from the

Department of Mathematics. One of Freebisher's hour exams contained such questions as:
What substance divides into two unequal halves?
Draw a square twice as long as it is wide.

Students will pair up in threes before doing the following problem.

E. Dundee Pinball, the official traveling missionary for the School of Theology is in serious trouble. He contracted to save two souls to the gallon of gas and of late he has failed to meet his quota. His case is under advisement.

A jurisdictional dispute in the Applied Plumbing section of the Department of Physics has been settled. Foutch Silcock will henceforth become Professor of Plumbing Up To The Trap and Arley Turnbuckle will be Professor of Plumbing Above The Trap.

All staff members are encouraged to read the Timkens Treatise on Universal Apothegms. Can you believe that he said "The faculty is the faculty's worst enemy?"

Mandarin Duck
Diving Instructor Physical Education
Dear Mandarin:

Your manuscript "South of the South" has been aseptically disposed of. It was incinerated along with a dead pigeon.

Do not feel bad if you didn't keep a copy. Think of it this way: (1) the manuscript wasn't worth the powder to blow it to hell with and (2) your wife can use the vacated desk to store sardines in.

We simply cannot wait to read and destroy your next opus.

Servant to the Faculty,
Forby Doo Doo, Editor, The Great Crumble Press

The Campus Police are seeking a dangerous gang of grass snatchers. Last night this outfit stole three acres of grass surrounding the library and two other buildings. They left a note warning that President Timken's lawn would be next. The State Police may be asked to enter the case and find out who has been buying spades lately. Notices have been posted asking anyone who has seen the missing lawn to bring it back. The Sheriff has offered a reward for capturing the grass grabbers, dead or alive.

Hookbeak Goosefeathers, who is McRooster's arch rival in the field of dead birds, has been invited by the local Birdwatcher's Society to speak in the Great Crumble Tabernacle (Hallelujah). Hookbeak says that when he is in a sacred place, he reverts to telling the truth and consequently he will have to state that McRooster is a high degree idiot; this will occur whenever his talk requires touching on the subject, which could be frequent.

McRooster counters that he will throw a dead bird, or three rotten eggs (which he considers to be the equivalent) at Hookbeak if the bastard adheres too conscientiously to his script. An enthusiastic crowd of ruffians is expected.

An Art instructor is in a squabble with a student who claims that he unfairly received a grade of D in Ceramics on the basis of an exam in which he made a pot. The student demands an A because his pot does not leak. He says that the purpose of the pot was unspecified and he knows that it would make an excellent urinal. His mentor is confusing good looks and usefulness. The instructor, now the defendant, is awaiting a committee's decision with apprehension.

The recent colloquium in the Mathematics Department was adjourned with no definitive conclusions reached. The discussion centered about how much trouble quantitatively four psychopaths (now sociopaths) could stir up in a faculty meeting as compared to two psychos (a tolerable number). It was argued that when two new parameters are introduced, their effects have to be multiplied rather than added. The faculty meetings would be unsafe unless rubber bullets and pressure hoses were available when the sane ones became insane and embarked enthusiastically on an all-out homicidal attack.

From the English Department: The difference between "good" and "well." There was the traveling missionary. He came to do good and he did well.

The Health Service advises caution in ordering the recommended "spectacular" fish of the day when having dinner at the Red Stool restaurant. The last time anyone even read about a fish in Crumble was their appearance in the last Ice Age. Prospective customers should read in detail reputable textbooks of Geology and Evolution. Also, look carefully to see if there are icepicks and shovels around the premises. Do not take this caveat lightly.

The International Council of Electricians has awarded its annual prize to physics diener Fenwick Tossiewasher, for his invention of the Handy-Dandy Fuse Blower. Fenwick was cited as doing more to increase the average annual income of electricians than all other advances put together in the past century.

Igneous Rock, Geology Chairman, has been temporarily put out of commission by an unexpectedly righteous Assistant Dean. The A-D received continual complaints from all the Geology staff that Igneous talked with them only as the mood struck. He would summon each one into his chambers if he had his own complaint, e.g., his wife chasing him out of the house with a hatchet. He always took out his watch and dismissed the staff member exactly three sentences after the latter started to air his own gripes.

Igneous tried this on the A-D, with the fatal mistake of not remembering that the sacrosanct and inviolate rights of even a lesser dean take precedence over those of a chairman. The exasperated A-D swung a "Good-Night Irene" punch at Igneous which floored him, after which the janitor was instructed to throw Igneous into the dumpster for a quiet convalescence.

The staff hopes that this might catalyze an attitude adjustment for Igneous, at least until his contusions and abrasions heal adequately.

The Crumble city auditor has found a deficiency of $1.85 in Mayor Slusher Weakling's accounts. He demands that District Judge Muchmore Wrongo convene a grand jury. Slusher has learned to think fast and he has driven the city hall, which is a trailer, to Bad Eggsville; this is out of the county and Slusher is in a safe jurisdiction. He says that when things die down, he will return and fire the auditor for expenses involved in making an unauthorized telephone call to the judge.

A psychopathologist says that he now believes the maxim "Never sleep with a woman whose troubles are worse than yours."

Archie Cornmuffin, an authority on nutrition in Paleolithic animals, was called out of a conference where a 1/4 million dollar grant was being considered, which he lost because of his absence. He was asked by a freshman who called him out how to spell neoechinorhynchus.

Iambic Pentameter, Poet-in-Residence, has been receiving frequent notices from the President's office about how to apply for civil service vacancies for janitors. Iambic is consulting local oracles for an interpretation. An oracle is to employed by the Psychology Department to fill a growing need of this nature.

The official College explorer, who lives on North South Pole Street in Crumble, is under investigation. For the past month he hasn't been able to find his way home.

We sadly submit the following memo, a copy of which was pinned above the hopper in the men's toilet.

To: New Chairman of Government Department
From: A Committee of Aggrieved Instructors

You are a world-class son-of-a-bitch. Which one of our superadministrators cloned you? This is probably the wrong question since at Crumble the fact that one mother can produce five normal children has been corrupted to five administrators copulating verbally and producing one bastard.

At the next Department meeting please come naked so that we can more readily determine which prehistoric monster you evolved from.

This memo complements the communal catharsis that we all just had in the toilet bowl. We may have to deck you at a later time since reinforcement works best with a diverse therapeutic regimen.

Wrong Substation, Crumble's leading economist, says that Paleontologist Eohippus who is working on dinosaurs is 100 million years behind the times and should be given another shovel to repeat his work. Eohippus counters that Substation's last epochal statement was predicting success for the Edsel. And this is as nothing compared with his apocalyptic pronunciamento that no President would ever think of tampering with Social Security.

Rusted Terrarium of the Museum is having a funeral service for his pet snake. Sheds of its last molt will be passed out to each mourner as a permanent remembrance.

The Malevolent Society's Disloyalty Song "Don't stay with the champ when he's down" won honorable mention by the Board of Trustees. The song got less than enthusiastic reviews at the recent meeting of the Ex-Vice Presidents Club in Grogan's Grog Shop.

Distorted /r/, of the Public Speaking staff, who teaches One-upsmanship 101, will lecture on how to maximize one's possibilities. /r/ describes himself as being the only person on the faculty who would have been able to sustain a conversation with Aristotle.

The eulogy was delivered yesterday in the chapel for Napoleon Speedworthy, Instructor in Driver Education. The chaplain bemoaned the fact that Napoleon was driving 90 miles per hour with a 15 mile per hour brain. He stressed Nap's bravery in the face of such odds.

Distorted Mean, noted statistician, claims to refute the notion that Crumble City is a menace because it has the highest death rate in rural America. Mean says that this illusion must be corrected since Crumble's death rate according to him is 100% like any other nice place.

The Statistics faculty has found that residence in Crumble can reduce a child's IQ up to 25% of its former value, depending upon the duration of exposure. All faculty families are urged to emigrate quickly.

It was also determined that professors should never marry professors. This only begets idiots and in turn more professors.

Assistant Dean Unhappy Apple of the School of Agriculture believes that he has fallen from grace. A letter from Timkens directed him to vacate his office and relocate in the Rabbit Warren on the College Farms. Because of antivivisectionist pressure, the rabbits will be given first choice as to where they will locate in the room.

The Mayor of Crumble has notified President Timkens that Procrastination Week has been postponed until next month.

Flemm Pretzeltwister, Cook Trainee at the Cafeteria, didn't obey the advice of the sages "fish or cut bait." He was dragged under water by an unidentified monster and has never been heard of since. Ecologist Twinkie Scudgebucket says "We must look at this in a global sense; Flemm has contributed to the food chain in nature." Flemm's wife threatens to cleave Twinkie with a meat cleaver and turn him to manure if he happens to pass by. She notes that she is not sure whether this will be good or bad for growing vegetables.

Angelina Christmascake has been reappointed as Dean of the School of Theology. The Trustees believe her to be eminently qualified since she always looks like she just fell out of a church organ.

We will have to report that Ms. Christmascake's behavior is not always exemplary. Last month she karate-chopped her boyfriend through a plate glass window because he bought her a car without a light in the glove compartment. Only last week she broke his arm because he installed a plunger on the left side of her toilet bowl.

Red Clamchowder, culinary consultant in the cafeteria, reports that he doesn't like Amish cooking. After salivating copiously over a stolen shoo-fly pie, he went back to the scene of the crime and complained that the pie was good but not great. The essential kicker seemed to be missing. Reports have it that Clamchowder was chased full speed with the Fooderclangers in hot pursuit right up to the state line.

Crumble's mayor, Slusher Weakling, has been accused by the City Council of rushing the city precipitously into the 12th century. The introduction of a sewer was just too much for one alderman and he suffered a heart attack during an uncontrolled blubbering fit over wasting public funds.

Eldridge Pigeonshit, Curator of the Bird Sanctuary, is accused of malfeasance to high authority. During a meeting in which Dean Dingleberry was busily gumming his munchies, Eldridge went from his depressive to a manic state watching the driblets fall from the Dean's ears. Since he needed his salary which required precautionary sanity, he only picked up the container with the munchies and pulled it over the Dean's head. The case is being heard by the College attorneys with Eldridge under temporary suspension from the recess table.

Og, Instructor in Primeval Medicine at Lollipop Lane, is joining the Crumble faculty. He was the one who asked the fox to guard the chicken coop. He was the one who asked the elephant to pass the peanuts. He was the one who in 1960 sent a friend with emphysema to Gary, Indiana.

During the recent grundoon hunt, in which every red-blooded student in the School of Agriculture participated and the building was locked, a wrecking crew appeared there by mistake and completely demolished the structure. The wreckers left a nice sign, informing the grass cutters to water the lawn frequently.

Dean Catcabbage has his desk on the sidewalk with an umbrella over it, pending his hearing before the legislature. Upper Dean Dingleberry swears that the whole caper was the work of zombies from the Malevolent Society. The Women's Christian Temperance group says it is the work of drunken students and it is putting a drinking fountain on the site.

The campus is aghast at last night's events. Dean Dingleberry was kidnaped, gift-wrapped and sent C.O.D. to President Timkens' house. This is clearly the work of the Malevolent Society. Timkens admitted having thoughts of rejecting the package, but he finally unpacked Dingleberry after grumbling about the express charge.

Primal Soup
Observer in Astronomy
Dear Primal:

Since our telescope rusted, you have been mostly in coma status in the observatory, except when you feed the cat. You will soon have trouble moving your red blood cells through your sluggish capillaries. We are therefore reassigning you as Faculty Building Representative. This work is curative and should restore you to full health.

Your day tomorrow will begin by formulating recommendations concerning the following important problems:

1. Reducing the office space of each faculty member to 4 x 4 feet. Although this may reduce the available oxygen, every chemist knows that a gas under pressure does more work.

2. Reducing the abrasiveness of the toilet paper, but only for the higher administrators.

3. The urgency of moving the faculty club to the boiler room.

As quickly as you show promise by appropriate answers to these very complex problems, we will clinically review your capability for gradual return to academic work. As a start, I will need an assistant, not too smart, in my research on the fate of the third molar in griffins.

Take it from your best friend,
Canned Beans
Zoology Graduate Student;
Fourth Assistant from the Bottom to the Director of Buildings and Grounds

It is now essential to know the meaning of an epigram: "To tell you the truth, I've always lied."

The March meeting of the Great Crumble Historical Society was just not a success. The topic was the selection of a theme for the monthly festival. The senescent members asked for recognition of the first patent granted for false teeth. The political science group insisted on recognition for the Carthaginian fleet defeated by the Romans in the first Punic war. The self-righteous contingent wanted to celebrate the date of the return of the turkey buzzards to Hinkley, Ohio. The paranoid-schiz group, proportionate in number to that of mental defectives expected at any meeting, demanded celebration of the first massacre of English settlers in America by the Indians.

The chairman broke his gavel after striking head blows to the first several members he could reach in the first row. One member was still in the room three days later, claiming that there was no parliamentary vote for adjournment. (Editor's note: The above is not unusual. The Sociology Department does this all the time.)

Visiting Exchange Professor Umberto Diaperpin, authority in delayed adolescence, may have to be returned. Today he insisted in his class that the D in schmo is silent like the X in herring.

Although it is July, Umberto comes to class with his overcoat and explorer's bonnet on because they will not fit in the bus station lockers. His chairman worries that this is a prelude to his becoming like the rest of the faculty.

Midweek at the Health Service

Starring Intern Gleep who asks a student: Is your complaint indigestion?

Unfortunate student: Yes, sir.

Gleep: Urinate on your hands and rub it over your face.

Student: Of course.

Gleep: Now defecate on your hands and rub the crap on your face.

Student: Your wish is my command.

Gleep: Just as I thought—sour stomach.

The Crumble Players are staging a new extravaganza designed to humiliate by comparison all former writers. Just to titillate the reader concerning the great fortune in store for him, the hero, Malocclusion, is thwarted at every turn by the arch-villain, Deaf. Both have the same girl-friend, Babushka. Just as Malocclusion is letting his audience know who really runs history, Deaf writes on the wall "Mene, Mene, Tekel and Parsin," the curse of Nebuchadnezzar. Malocclusion is thrown against the ropes.

Now Babushka knows that the only antidote for the curse is to shout back "Abercrombie and Fitch." Does she do it? No! But wait. Her grandmother swings a mighty haymaker from the floor up and fells Deaf, thus coming in line for the highest accolade of the evening. This turns out to be a full bottle of well fermented wine thrown from the third row by a satiated bum who prefers isopropyl alcohol. But enough. See for yourself. We won't spoil the story.

Never lend money to friends. It spoils their memory.

EXCERPTS FROM THE LAST MEETING OF THE DEANS

The deans began by singing in croaking chorus "Don't think of your dean as a boss. Think of him as a friend who is never wrong."

The Chair stated that all new staff must undergo an extended quarantine period such as they give dogs prior to their being released on the campus. The novitiates will be examined for ectoparasites, adaptive staying power for the cafeteria food, and whether the incumbent is allergic to deans. A pilot study placing the novice and a lesser dean together in a cage without food and water has been found to be prognostic.

The Chair reluctantly recognized Lesser Dean Fartsey who then explained the cause of the crackling sounds that emanate from his behind when he moves in his chair. Even though nobody believed him, the Health Service proctologist has diagnosed the condition as "defectus lubricatitus," a syndrome known to exist in Triassic mastodons. Engineers ordinarily soundproof Fartsey in the dean's conferences, but today they were called to soundproof a vice-president.

Incidentally, the "Green Apple Quickstep," written by the proctologist, who is also a composer, should attract attention in the musical world of folk medicine.

Adolfo Monomaniac has been stopped from selling tickets for the brouhaha this weekend in Psychology Hall. The event of the evening was to be a fight between a deaf albino cat and a waltzing guinea pig. Adolfo has been placed on high probationary discipline. This means that he cannot speak to his wife, even to say "Pass the potatoes."

Dean Dingleberry has been given new powers appropriate to his exalted office. He now has the authority to solve any problem by declaring it to be non-existent. The following account of yesterday's meeting demonstrates the wisdom of this new policy.
Zoology Chairman: We cannot get any more dogs for experimentation because of the opposition of the local Antivivisection Society.
Dingleberry: Do you have any dogs now?
Chairman: No, Your Lordship.
Dingleberry: Then there isn't any problem.

We have just been informed that Dean Catcabbage has requested an Assistant Dean who will have the function of clouding all issues prior to their consideration by the Dean. This is consistent with the responses given by the Dean to his faculty.

The Engineering Dean stepped into a hole while unloading a piano. A bulletin from a chiropractor states that the Dean's two sides just don't match. Mathematicians have been brought in to apply vectorial analysis to the problem.

Dean Ollie Underbright is recovering nicely in the Great Crumble Hospital. In keeping with his expected dignity, he had a well organized convulsion. It had something to do with an unfirable professor who came to the annual School of Education prom attired in a bright yellow jockstrap.

Bizarre Central has just announced its approval of a new and exciting course, Construction 101. Prerequisites for students are a wheelbarrow and a hose. Crumble needs to upthink its course offerings.

From the Fisheries Unit: It is well know that caviar comes from a virgin sturgeon. The Unit thinks that this observation needs updating.

Being appointed to the Deanship at Crumble is at first considered by the appointee as the equivalent of being sprinkled with holy water. After the first year, the exalted one my be given a sweatshirt painted with the Scarlet Letter. He has patently become a ding-dong to the general staff and not much of a prize to the higher administration who dwell in the campus Taj Mahal. The faculty, who usually possess less than divine wisdom, tend to be the Dean's worst problem.

STUDENT REPORTS

Half Nelson, who according to his pediatrician was named for the condition of his brain, has announced his engagement to Wanda, presumably a female. Half is the fellow who while running at top speed on a trestle to get away from a train stopped to pick up his hat.

The College has admitted its first student of royal blood, Bluntwitted the Stupid. He traces his ancestry to Boneless the Viking, a person who just loved to fight but who had to be carried into battle in a basket. It is rumored that Bluntwitted has a penchant for beating up unrecalcitrant professors.

Bufo the Bloated, second team wrestler, has been advised to get a quick divorce. He has developed "bruit de clapotement" which is a splashing sound every time his wife punches him in the stomach.

Freshman Emerging Chestnut, a major in Botany, claims that the Registrar is interfering with his right to fail courses. The case has been adjudicated. He will be put into the Zero Possibility Disadvantaged Program.

Thieves Hideout and Preretirement Home, situated peacefully in the Great Crumble Forest, may reject student Vile Hooch. He was caught too many times, thus demonstrating a stupidity that could bring shame on the Hideout. They do not wish to sully their impeccable record of not getting caught, by admitting a moron.

Four recent graduates, all loyal alumni of the Malevolent Society, have stoutly maintained their sacred vows. One just opened a women's store called "Britches for Bitches." A second specializes in stolen wheelchairs, but only from administrators. The third retains his deep sense of humor. Yesterday, he spent a day prior to his arrest mixing up the groceries in the carts of 100 customers in the Great Crumble Supermarket. The fourth is opening a bomb store downtown; the City Council says that this could catalyze a much needed urban renewal.

Graduates Growlybear and Sweetpea have marital problems. Sweetpea had a plumber install a toilet for her own use in their one room house. It will be difficult for Growlybear to top this.

The History Department finally got even with superstudent McClangabang. He did not know what Empedocles' first name was.

An Eskimo from the North Pole, who had just matriculated, was asked how he found out about Crumble. He said that he saw a poster nailed to an iceberg. We compliment our Director of Admissions.

Collectively Bananas, a professional 10-hanky weeper, will represent flunking students at the Deans Judgment Table. Bananas' assistant, Alma Sackcloth, will add to the confusion if asked. In the last unhappiness session she was rated 0.5 on a scale of 1 to 10.

President Timkens is having no end of trouble with his basement cooks. Last night the latest one assassinated a New York strip steak. Until the cook's deportation papers are signed, everyone will eat raw tomatoes.

Mayor Slusher Weakling proposes to unslum the neighborhood around the college by deporting the students there to South Cornfield. Garbage trucks will accompany the exodus. An emergency meeting of the exurbanites in South Cornfield is being held on how to repel the invasion.

Banality and Jargon, student tutors in remedial English, are being sued by a elementary school pupil because not one of the three of them knew the difference between a subjunctive and a pluperfect. Neither did the principal. The pupil flunked his entrance exam to the Great Crumble School for Barbers and may have to go to Fawchee Subnormal.

One of the local high school pupils has decided not to come to CCJC. He could have been tried for high treason by the City Council except that his attorney proved conclusively that there was no opportunity for the pupil to fulfill his life's ambition, clam digging.

The police at The Great Crumble Bastille have had enough of Fernando Blowtorch, an emeritus Crumble freshman. The chief slipped him a hacksaw and told him not to leave any forwarding address.

Tattered Tom, contender for the most impoverished freshman, was driving a stolen car to the courthouse where he was to appear because of stealing a bushel of potatoes when he was hailed at a stoplight by a chauffeur in a Rolls-Royce who asked Tom if he had any Poupon mustard. Tom said that he was fresh out of Poupon because a bag lady had outraced him to a trash barrel and she would castrate him if he persisted in invading what by neighborhood agreement was her private landfill. The chauffeur elected not to pursue the matter further.

Student Peachblossom was dragged off to the slammer and booked for "Over-Enthusiasm" at the weekend Drunkathon in the

Great Crumble Saloon. She was throwing the cops into the municipal fountain next to the peace statue.

When her protective boyfriend protested to the cop at the desk that Peachblossom was a sweet southern belle, he said "She claims that she was bred in old Virginia, but right now she's only crumbs out here."

The Political Science staff reminds us that mercy whirred up with justice does not always make a palatable drink. In war, drugs may at first be excluded from the blockade of an enemy country because their troops have to be kept in good health, otherwise they may not shoot accurately at our soldiers who are playing the role of the bullseye. Also, their supporting population has to be kept strong enough to shovel ammunition onto the trucks headed for the front.

Advice from a senior administrator:

Never let the truth get in the way of your popularity. It could destroy your chances for promotion.

Ichabod Dumpster, Sophomore Class

Dear Icky:

We congratulate you for being elected College Malingerer by your class. Your dedication to this cause is unsurpassed. Yesterday, one hour before your exam in basket weaving, you turned up at the Health Service with 8 major symptoms and 5 minor ones. Two weeks ago, just before an exam, the subject matter admittedly difficult, on how to pack an orange crate, you came here complaining of 3 major symptoms and 15 minor ones.

Your complaints are dramatic and our consulting surgeons wish to notify you that upon your next visit they will admit you to the Great Crumble Hospital for an exploratory operation. This entails a novel approach. You will be slit down the front from throat to penis. If necessary, a circular incision will also be made, from bellybutton full circle clockwise back to bellybutton.

Make an appointment at once. You will be paid on an hourly basis for enhancing our surgical research.

Cordially,
The entire staff

Dr. Pillnik, latest refugee plucked from a life raft by the College Recruiting Service, is asked to take a course in introductory biology. While lancing a student's eardrum, he went right through to the opposite ear. If this were a department chairman, we could understand. Pillnik claims poor team support. He says that in Europe his surgical team included proficient nurse Cold Borscht, Merlinovich the Magician and, necessarily, an astrologist who could accurately predict the free-for-all punching match that usually followed.

To: Raggsy Diddle
From: The Bursar

Your bill for mowing the lawn sent by you and your friend Dog-Ears is outrageous. What is your explanation?

To: Bursar
From: Lawnmowing Incorporated

My colleague and I have bought a new lawnmower for $85 and as you can see we have incorporated. Prices must now reflect our prestigious position in the field.

Ragsworth Diddle, Esquire
Chairman of the Board

NEWS FROM THE HEALTH SERVICE—MOSTLY BAD

The Health Service reports the following admission. Stockroom Assistant Cerebrus Minimus had a bad day. He tried to visualize five dimensional space with his one dimensional brain. This badly discombobulated the straight line arrangement of molecules in his brain and he decided to hang himself. He wrote a letter to his dog describing how he would do himself in. However, he didn't know whether the word he wanted was hanged or hung. He thereupon repaired to the Crumble library, but the Bowowski dictionary there had all the words out of order. He decided to reconsider his demise, but on the way out of the library a chandelier fell on his head. This effectively postponed any additional career planning for the day. We haven't the remotest reason for continuing this report and we abandon it abruptly.

We report important news today about Intern Gleep. First the good news: Gleep was awarded a bronze plaque for his adroitness in managing dying patients. For example, he reassured Instructor Total Relapse a terminal cancer victim, that he was more normal than most people his age; he had 20/20 vision. Next week Gleep will give Total the watch-tick test.

There is some bad news. Gleep's physician wife has been censured. In examining a student who complained of groin pain, she grabbed his testes without introducing herself.

The Health Service may lose a pulmonologist, Dr. Blue Bloater. At President Timkens' annual Denouement Dinner, Bloater was seated downstream from the saltshaker. We cannot explain his fall from grace but the situation does not bode well for him.

Lukewarm Rompers, once a pediatrician at the Health Service but now a Lecturer in Speech, can phonate in two languages by delicately manipulating his external anal sphincter. Needless to say, he lectures facing the blackboard. There is always the danger that a student from the Malevolent Society may give him a barbed wire enema and produce an anal dysarthria, thus ending his teaching career.

Whitemop Cloverleaf, secretary of the Junior Class, has just been released from the infirmary. While driving back to CCJC from the Thanksgiving holiday in his open roadster, he unwisely failed to heed a road sign that said "Watch out for falling rocks."

We sadly report the following. Intern Gleep has been banished for two weeks from the Health Service. He must keep at least two blocks away from the building. His examination of student Subminiature Brain for nosebleed cost the College about $1,000. Gleep had tests run for high density lipids, polycythemia, typhoid fever, tumors, syphilis, ulcers and all the other things he heard about in medical school. The patient's mother called and said that after beating the hell out of Subminiature for picking his nose, he was immediately cured.

Now to Myron, the sage of the Health Service. He has found that students with two or more mat burns on their behind will have gonorrhea with three times the frequency of non-mat burn students. The work is epic.

Myron also has the following letter.

Dear Myron:

I have not heard from my diabetic son whom you kept in the Health Service for two weeks. Please discontinue for a moment your only physical activity which consists of retching and send me information about his condition. Determined Mother

Dear Determined Mother: We discharged your son, who came to us too late for diabetic treatment. He turned into a Hershey bar and we sent him to the chocolate factory for further processing.

Advice to People Who Coule Get Shot:

A student majoring in Logic was having an affair with his married seatmate. One afternoon, at her home, the husband came in early. The student, being alert, hid under her bed. After some suspicious conversation between the spouses, the husband searched the premises and discovered the student under the bed.

Husband: "What the hell are you doing here?"

Bright Student: "Well, everyone has to be somewhere."

(Editor's Note: We leave this narrative hastily.)

THE FACULTY AGAIN

The Psychology Department's alcohol-fed baboon went on one of his increasingly frequent rampages yesterday. Before deciding to quit, the baboon twisted the chairman into a pretzel and had him sign a paper that he is resigning The faculty is divided on whether to kill the monkey or reward him with extra strawberry jam.

No Eggs, expert in dairy husbandry, will serve as a consultant to the Agriculture Department as soon as he can be cured of a boll weevil infection. After leaving a third world country whose agricultural ills he worsened, he left by night and was rescued from a boat wearing only a T-shirt with the insignia "I love ducks."

President Timkens thinks that the deans in the lesser administration building are seeing things in reverse. He will first approach the problem in the vertical dimension by turning the building upside down.

Tallyho Sheepdip has been appointed Faculty Meeting Raconteur. This is to keep everyone smiling when they have just been told that there will be no pay increases for the next three years.

Two things might just destroy Tallyho's unbounded sense of humor. One is that he found out that he is included in all no-pay announcements. The second is that every time Tallyho delivers his intended bellybuster story, he explodes with his own laughter during the punchline and sometimes before, while the grim silence of the expectant audience deepens the disaster.

"Even a fish is safe if it keeps its mouth shut." This is from an instructor who objected to everything, but who seems to have matured ever since he started to pack bananas for a living.

The feasibility of stocking the River Crumble with dinosaurs was discussed at length at a recent meeting of the Anthropology Department. Highly unpopular Curator Milchcow of the Museum was assigned the task of collecting dinosaurs or else admitting his lack of ability which could be followed by his resignation.

The Geology Department announces the appointment of Galileo Hogwash. Gal did his graduate thesis on "Avalanches in Kansas City." It wasn't his fault that they kicked him out. His major professor was never allowed out of the asylum for long enough periods to direct the problem.

A Primer in Clinical English:
Intern Gleep to constipated freshman: Take this castor oil freely. It will make you move. Come back tomorrow.
Victim (second visit): Didn't move.
Gleep: Take bigger doses. See me tomorrow.
Victim (third visit): Didn't move.
Gleep: More castor oil. Come tomorrow.
Gleep (fourth visit): Did you move?
Victim: Moved today. Whole dormitory full of shit.

Zoologist Elmer Clucker has gone out of the frog rearing business. He stocked his backyard pond with tadpoles and then put in two ducks. The catastrophe defies description. (Editor's note: In the words of Leon Harris, Clucker appears to have "a remarkable capacity to snatch failure from the jaws of success.")

The Philosophy Department has finally agreed to the demotion of behavioral deviate Cedric Breakwind from Associate Professor to Assistant Instructor. According to a witness, Cedric once started a fight in an empty auditorium. The Dean agreed that the incident wasn't a good career move. There is also controversy about Cedric's lecture on "Happiness Can Be Cured."

An 11-year-old, Snotnose Harry, has written to the Political Science Department, asking when his faculty appointment begins. Snotnose has produced a tablet from his infamous ancestor, Pseudo-Smerdid the Usurper, carved in Persia in 315 B.C. The tablet states that by divine decree an unfortunate descendant to be named Snotnose must be given the Polisci chair in a so-called college by the name of Crumble. The writing has been authenticated by Staff Cryptographer Rumpled Carrot. The opinion of Carrot carries great weight following his convincing demonstration that he could fix a Timex watch.

Toujours L'Amour will chair the new program in Cosmetology (which for the very backward reader means cutting hair). But we will all have to wait until someone fixes his undescended testis.
A cleaned-up excerpt from Mayor Weakling's commencement address:

The general stupidity of the College along with its exalted faculty mirrors that of the surrounding community. Despite the belief that the local scholars have the cure, the apple doesn't fall far from the tree.

Syllabic Babble, Reader in Speech Pathology, whose class has not been attended by any students for 15 successive periods, is being considered for discharge. With logic, Babble demands emeritus status. He claims that he appeared, thus fulfilling the terms of his contract. This could be a benchmark case and it will be watched keenly by unnecessary staff all over the country.

A Teaching Assistant, name withheld to protect the innocent, is suing the College. He claims harassment by a janitor. After he and his girl friend were chased out of a Zoology closet, his sperm count dropped by 40 million per ejaculate. The College attorney is willing to settle, quickly.

The College Treasurer has explained with logic the disappearance of $35,000 from the Bursar's office. He explained that the money had simply become commingled with his own $25 on the way to the bank. He has not yet found the time to uncommingle the funds. Not to worry.

Fearless Alfie, Consultant in Tactics and Strategy, and also the bravest member of the Crumble faculty, went for a Sunday drive. He asked over his CB system if any smokies were in the vicinity because he wanted to speed like any true-blooded American. Unfortunately, Superbastard, Crumble's most feared cop, heard the conversation and told Alfie that all was clear and to open the throttle and enjoy the breeze. Alfie came roaring down the pike and was cut off by Superbastard who proceeded to lecture Alfie on the stupidity of criminals. Alfie then informed Superbastard that he was bringing him in on a citizen's arrest for dirty tricks. He instructed Superbastard to remain calm while he was going to handcuff him and bring him in to the police station.

The rest is unclear since Alfie is not too coherent through the openings in his skull bandages. He vaguely remembers being powed in several directions, apparently simultaneously. Superbastard brought Alfie home and when Alfie's wife did not answer, Superbastard threw him through the window after informing him that he would book him after sufficient wound healing. Alfie says he will meet his classes in the hospital. He thinks he will not press charges.

A special administrators' meeting was held on how to keep in check potential faculty pretenders to the throne. The special object of attention was Allsworth Kingly Tartrate, an archetype of the professor most desirable at Crumble. His height, weight and three-piece suit fitted the picture. He walked erect, not like his colleagues who resembled Pithecanthropus, and he always looked as though everyone else smelled badly. When he got on his mythical podium, which he did upon meeting any presumed serf-type instructor, his speech was accepted as "It has been said." Allsworth, as expected, was The Great Teacher, Great Research Scientist, Great Advisor to the Governor, plus a few other titles dug up when he met with his worshipers.

President Timkens offered the logical solution. Every three days a convocation would be called and another honor would be conferred upon Allsworth. This would put him in the category of Pooh-Bah, the comic Lord-High Executioner. It might be just barely possible that Allsworth would see himself as a buffoon and begin his retreat into anonymity.

Nightletter, To: President Timkens
From: Satan, Superintendent of Hades, Hot Springs Section

We have one of your deans down here, an unloved inmate known to our more rational inhabitants as El Stupido Grande. This guy has incorrigible bad manners at table. We voted to get him the hell out of here.

If you agree to take him back, I will use our hotline to St. Peter and get permission to have him reconstituted and then kicked out. I appreciate the fact that it will be hard on the Earthlings, but space is getting very tight here.

Please carve your reply on a flaming tablet and we will pick it up before it cools. Don't use the U.S. mail.

Fractured History: As Madame LaFarge said to her husband when he told her that his girl friend had hyperglycemia, "Let her eat cake."

Campus crews are working overtime to solve a strange problem. Every time that Logic Chopper lectures to his class, the automatic distortion of facts analyzers in the Physics building three blocks away go haywire. Lights flash, bells ring, and all classes on campus have to be canceled. President Timkens suggests that Chopper be given an indefinite leave, preferably between two mountain ranges. This supersedes the orders of Myron at the Health Service who recommended a laryngectomy.

Superbly Oblivious
Department of Physics
Dear Mr. Oblivious:

Please resign. To begin with, your colleagues swear that you do not know how to liberate a quark from a hadron. You are also deficient socially. At the President's box lunch, you distributed the three piece order of fried chicken unequally over your three piece administrative training suit. When the butler served you the Robert Mondavi Cabernet Sauvignon wine, you dipped the bread in it. The last straw was when you asked everyone to be quiet and then gave a talk on how to pluck a pigeon. And we can hardly forgive your remark when Dean Dingleberry passed you that "Big winds come from empty caves."

Turn in your keys to the gatekeeper as you leave the campus.

In the President's absence,
Vera Scrum
Trusted Administrative Assistant

We include here Myron's suggestion of an inexpensive and non-invasive test of personal importance: You are sinking into oblivion when you can no longer insult everybody and get away with it.

Lady Swampbottom, Professor of Speech Aptitude, who gave more than 100 talks this year on Color Blindness in Postpuberal Turtles, has filed a grievance because she was not promoted to something like Exalted Professor. She walked into the chairman's office one week before the semester ended and asked where her classroom was. It is rumored that in the last pay period the Bursar sent her a phony check.

Daisy Hoot Toot insists that there are not enough women on the Crumble faculty. She asks that appointments should be an equal opportunity tragedy. Dean Dingleberry, always rising to the occasion, has established a fact finding committee, headed by Assistant Instructor McDoodle. He says that he will have his report ready for typing first draft in about two years, barring unfortunate incidents such as failure to find his shoelaces. McDoodle is a good choice for heading this activity. He once taught an entire semester without having his fly open. This is a quality person.

Roughdry Clothesbasket has been designated as best dressed member of the faculty. His chairman, however, says that no matter how many shirts Roughdry wears, you can always see his bellybutton.

All-purpose Instructor Luke Trashworth is being reviewed for possible demotion following his inept management of the homecoming parade. He disobeyed the universal law that you never put horses at the head of the parade. Dean Catcabbage, the Marshall, was unable to find a pair of rubber boots.

We have no urgent reports at this time so we'll leave a blank space for you, the reader, to fill in on the margin. Nothing dirty please with our book.

The new History instructor can really research the literature. Example: Quintus Fabius Maximus, Roman Generalissimus, outfoxed his enemies by having them agree to postpone the crucial battle until he completed his feast period, April to September. He also got the battlefields changed because some of them aggravated his asthma.

Dean Dingleberry, in an attack of goodness, recommended the faculty for a 0.05% raise. In the emergency meeting that followed, one administrator theorized that Dingleberry is becoming addled and he explained the Dean's absence from the current meeting on the view that he was at home hallucinating. He also heard that Dingleberry may have the mange. Worst of all, the administrator showed a picture of the Dean's most recent weekly auto accident in which he crashed into the adobe hut of Princeton and Wellesley Scraggs who are being cared for by the Red Cross.

The Second Vice President for Trash Removal is in serious trouble. He has been asked to turn in his key to the executive washroom. The VP was seen urinating in the same gribble with a faculty member, which is a demeaning experience.

An Emeritus Professor of Astronomy has been sitting in the bus station for three weeks with a hydrogen rocket up his behind. He says that he is waiting for favorable weather when he will take off for *Tau Ceti*, about 12 light years away. He thinks he may have to change his straw hat when he gets 2 million miles up.

Gumbo Soup, retriever of the scraps in the cafeteria, was ejected from the Preceptorial, the most sacred discussion group in the Theology building. Gumbo had insisted that Aristotle and Aristophanes were pro-abortionists. He was immediately remanded to the Defectory for purification. Gumbo is appealing to the Dean of Theology and he also wants to stand penance in the Refugium because it has a window. We can only hope that his book, "A Profane History About Everyone" is never discovered.

The worst teacher of the month is Wimble Diddy, elected by unanimous acclaim. The students' citation reads "It isn't worth the powder to blow up his lecture notes." He has been ordered to meditate about his sins in a can for two weeks, surrounded by sardines.

Roadway Turd received the most distinguished award, a push-pull broom, at the plenary session of the Great Crumble Janitorial Assembly. It was a glorious affair. When the coon pie was eaten, all level 3 personnel were given their choice of finger bowls with lemon juice or hot shibori towels.

Flash from Downtown: The president of the Great Crumble Bank was talked to sternly today by the three visiting holdup men who came in and could not find their usual reserved seats in the lobby. They prefer shooting from a sitting position. Their leader stated that it was a depressing afternoon. The president of the South Cornfield Bank and Worm Store had told the leader to take his life because he was saving his money for his old age.

Biochemist Hocus Pocus, world class publisher of 800 articles and 40 books, just died at age 32. A Hocus Pocus Center will be established to re-publish completely what all the authorities thought he said. This should give 10 otherwise starving, would-be authors a living for the next 15 years.

The Math Department will also hire two researchers to figure out how Hocus Pocus carried this off since he was traveling around the world 300 days per year to lecture on his discoveries which he said occurred in his work at the bench. His death occurred when he fell off a yacht in what he claimed to be his vacation time.

The following could be thought of as a tragic report, but this depends upon which side you're on. The Director of the Institute for Inland Waterways at the College invited his friend, the Safety Director, for a trip down the Great Crumble River in the 60-foot yacht just purchased by the College.

All went well until they radioed Felix Cudowiecz, the drawbridge tender at the just completed bascule bridge, to raise the bridge so they could pass through. As usual, Felix was asleep in full hyperextension.

The Director couldn't find the manual on how to pull the control to stop whereupon he went to Plan B. This involved climbing to the top of the boat's flagpole where he could observe the impending crash without drowning as the boat disintegrated.

The Safety Director was compelled to opt for Plan C. He jumped overboard and swam for the pilings, keeping speed admirably with a school of mackerels that just happened to be in the neighborhood.

The yacht and the bridge are now history. Felix threatens to firebomb the College. The Mayor of South Cornfield is exuberant. He says that Crumble is hopefully separated forever from his idyllic village across the river.

Delirio Inkfog, who has never been given a dinner to celebrate the clarity of his lectures, has been elevated to College Speechwriter. As soon as funds become available, a cryptographer will be added to his staff.

President Timkens' personal wine steward has been demoted to Civil Service Class Zero. We can only find out that he served improperly beheaded shrimp with the vintage Comtes de Champagne Blanc de Blancs. The sommelier blames it on a crooked fishmonger.

Language Mangler, our English Department Chairman, says that the next time someone says to him "Long time no see," he will anesthetize him and package him off to an Indian reservation for remedial treatment.

A member of the Music Department is being watched. It seems that he is writing chamber music for Whorehouse Row. The complaint is that the music is of second quality.

The symphony concert was a disaster last night. While Picololi Frenzo was conducting the orchestra to the crescendo of an opus, an usher climbed to the stage and told him that his two-day-old Mercedes was just totaled in the parking lot. The subsequent sons-of-bitches uttered by Picololi could not be fitted into the music.

"Someone is always spitting in the soup," Kaiser Wilhelm.

The conference of administrators on faculty rights ended with the expected conclusion and with the weight of history on its side. To wit: As Bismarck said "When the eagles agree, the sparrows have to be silent."

Heard at the College chapel (author unfindable):

Usher to outsider: You can't come in here. You have no I. D. card to show that you are a student.

Outsider: I need to give a message to a friend.

Usher: O.K., but don't let me catch you praying.

Tranquility Smoothbottom, an undaunted secretary in the Theology building, went to complain to a subdean about her boss. By mistake she got into the office of a vice-president. Infuriated by being mistaken for an underling, he ran her out with a broomhandle inserted accurately into a nonskid region of her behind. Tranquility did not take this lightly. She returned immediately, to look for a book to hit him over the head with. This was a major mistake. There are no books in a vice president's office. In fact, the number of books expected varies inversely with the promotional distance from an assistant instructor. Rising to the occasion, Tranquility took the vice-president's diploma off the wall and almost debrained him.

In the ensuing court action, the judge declared that the attack on the vice-president was a necessary hazard of his job. The question was one of property damage, i.e., diploma destruction. Tranquility stated that the diploma came from the School of Education and even the paper wasn't worth recycling. She also had proof that he bought the diploma in a flea market. The case was dismissed. The claimant said that if he had hung up his original podiatrist's license, he might have had more credibility.

Scrimpton Screw, Comptroller of Petty Cash in the Bursar's office, is suing his wife for divorce. His records show that she cost him an average of 87¢ per day over 17 years. Some surreptitious ice cream cones have recently jumped this to 89¢. Scrimpton claims that this upsets his entire balance sheet and his yearly forecasts, causing him insomnia and infinite anguish. The judge agrees with attorneys on both sides that incompatibility with the human race supports Scrimpton's case.

The Chief Accountant in the Business Office says that he has a foolproof system to distinguish the debit from the credit side of the ledger. He keeps the debit side in his desk drawer nearest the spittoon.

Foaming Butt
Hot Tub Circle
Crumble
Dear Foaming:

I am returning your manuscript "Don't Screw Around With Gypsies Or Hopalong Cassidy." You will need it to be admitted quickly to the Great Crumble Madhouse.

We need your further cooperation. Please submit a manuscript at once for my secretary. She is in a profound depression and you might just counteract it by provoking an attack of uncontrollable rage.

Our secretary is so excited about receiving your therapeutic manuscript that she is presently hyperventilating.

Possibly grateful,
Forby Doo Doo
Editor, The Great Crumble Press

The College has been placed on an emergency state of total lockdown, even stricter than that seen in the South Cornfield maximum security prison after a riot. An unknown villain(s?) has been getting into all campus buildings and writing on every blackboard "Timkens is a son-of-a-bitch."

All classes are restricted to the central frog pond and students must keep their hands raised in an "I surrender" posture while on campus.

Dean Dingleberry, in a terse press release, states that the situation is under control. However, anyone caught with chalk could be shot on sight.

Memo: From the Bursar

Due to financial exigency, we will have to nickel and dime it for an indefinite period. All faculty members who need to see a dean will have to go through turnstiles now being transferred from obsolete subways to the deans' offices. The toll will vary according to the prestige level of the dean visited.

From the College Research Service

Pound for pound, Crumble is the outstanding school in the world. Our faculty weighs more in total than that reported anywhere else. We will all weigh in once a month to ensure keeping our prestigious position.

Princeton Scraggs has informed Dean Dingleberry that his situation is critical. The month always runs out after the end of his money. Our Home Economics research team is working in 24 hour shifts to formulate a survival kit. This should satisfactorily keep Scraggs and them with something positive in mind.

Feckless Bushwacked
Visiting Sage in Political Science
Feckless (and you deserve the name):

Our reviewer in Agrisex, Felix Chamberpot, took with him on his vacation your manuscript "Grits and Tits, The Threat to the South." Felix writes that in a one-boat accident which occurred while he fell asleep but the boat didn't, the manuscript accompanied the boat to the bottom of Foggy Dew Creek. Contrary to a Newtonian law of gravitation, he noted that the manuscript disappeared before the boat did.

We will never know the full details of the threat to the South. Felix won't tell us because we fired him for his third unrecoverable manuscript. As for you, take a couple of years off and write another tome, this time preferably about the North. By that time I may have been chased out.

Unlimited sympathy for your future,
Forby Doo Doo

Turbid Backwash
Plumbers Conspiracy in Crumble
Dear Turbid:

Thank you for your lucid manuscript "Bathtub Refurbisher's Lung." We were especially impressed with your account of how you accomplished the spot to spot excision of turkey feathers from the windpipe of the thoracic surgeon Unfiltered Puree who failed to call you for a consultation about the hazards lurking in his bathtub.

With admiration,
Forby Doo Doo

On Crumble's annual Disappointment Day, Professor Trashworthy was named the College Contrarian. He had just got even with his enemy, the whole city of Crumble. On National Philanthropy Week, he had all his money plus the vault moved out of the Great Crumble Bank. He then evicted the Boy Scouts from their headquarters and put in a tank of crocodiles. He took back a grizzly bear that he had donated to the zoo and let it loose on Main Street. He sued the Police Chief for letting it be known that he bayonneted a guy who retrieved a lost quarter on the sidewalk just before he, himself, dived for it. (Editor's note: This fellow was clear winner in his special talent and we should be proud that we have another Crumble First.)

MEETING OF THE COMMITTEE THAT CONSIDERS POTPOURRIS

Hang Only Five, Great Crumble Judge and part-time College Historian, opened the meeting by reporting some disturbing facts. He just discovered that the commencement orator at Yale told the class of 1912 that he had two messages for them. The first was that half of what they were taught wasn't true. The second was that they probably didn't know which half it was.

Hang continued on a pessimistic note by reporting that Pediculosis Pubis, Preceptor in Lower Anatomy and Greek, and also self-acclaimed player of cosmic music, is being sued. A neighbor claims that Pubis' music of the spheres has given her son intractable diarrhea. Fortunately, divine intervention has terminated the dispute. Pubis, while riding his tricycle and humming cosmic music, disappeared down an open manhole. There is reason to believe that the neighbor left the cover open to accommodate all her son's shit.

According to Hang, the bust of the present Economics Chairman will be placed alongside other suspects in the newly donated Hall of Infamy. The Hall is another Crumble first and has already received national awards. This is not altogether a pleasant report. Hang presented the case of Crumble's most brilliant graduate, up to last week a candidate for a Ph.D. in Sociology. She appeared before her Committee to defend her thesis, but she couldn't remember what the topic was.

Hang also noted that Dean Dingleberry may have lost several million dollars for the College. While the Governor was addressing the Crumble staff, Dingleberry was in his characteristic coma gumming his cookies. Worse still, he came to the meeting wearing his scruffies. Hang said that if President Timkens had noticed this, he would have wiped out Dingleberry with the customary lime Bavarian.

The report continued all downhill. It was just discovered that the Brotherly Love Elementary School run by the Department of Education was torn down seven years ago, but the principal and 17 teachers have made out payroll forms continuously. Presently, all staff claim that they are being treated at the Health Service for loss of long-term memory.

Still more. Dean Ollie Underbright has been said by committee to be a pathogenic virus that was miscloned. This fact would be of interest to nobody except that Ollie planned the new Education building to be upside down. And this may only be the tip of the iceberg. President Timkens advises cautious optimism.

A committee member noted that President Timkens has been named in a lawsuit claiming that he breached his fiduciary duties to the class of minority people called the faculty. The defendant allegedly diverted one-half million dollars in the budget to pay for walking his dog.

Hang noted that the student cafeteria director may be placed on disciplinary warning for following too closely Pawkey Panfry's famous law that "Soup tends to be watered in direct proportion to an increasing number of customers." Hang consulted the Mathematics Department which recommended that exponential factors be added to Panfry's equation to take care of the responses of angry students, and possibly the police following the fracas.

Hang deplored the fact that Lesser Dean Fartsey had stated publicly that the faculty had more bullshit artists than he knew when he was working with patent medicine salesmen. Fartsey is slowly catching up with Fendrick Poltroon in the rate of accretion of enemies. Hang wondered whether an international agreement might be reached to exchange Fartsey and Poltroon for some prisoners of war.

Another never to be resolved case is that of Ex Cathedra, College truant officer. Ex is truly conservative. He wears both suspenders and a belt, but this has no relation to the fact that his fly is open frequently. Dean Dingleberry is calling Ex in to give him a choice of additional remediation or out he goes. The meeting should be interesting.

An administrator asked Hang how to handle faculty discontent. Hang told him to do anything he wanted to. The faculty bitching would stop because there would always be the inevitable next disaster to divert their attention. If the disaster were delayed, one could be created by the faculty mythmaker.

Hang said that the weekly freshman prize to find errors in English sentences hasn't been won in 32 weeks. A student may yet win the cumulative pot and have all expenses paid for the year with money left over to buy waxed shoelaces. The sentence this week is: "The villian unloosened his tie irregardless of the cold, but this is his perrogative."

Hang adjourned the meeting on what appeared to be a discouraging note. The College will be given funds for an additional storage library, but it will be located in Horseshit Ridge where nobody ever goes near an unfamiliar building. The only ones in the present library are people who own eyeglasses. The others are coaxed to go in so that they can see what can be done with the alphabet.

FROM THE PRESIDENT'S WASTEBASKET

Dear President Timkens:

We invite you to represent Crumble at the inauguration of our new President, Quinton Queazy. It is a cause for public rejoicing to have our Trustees select such a knowledgeable and radiant superperson. We just know that our beloved college will be a first because of his remarkable imagination and proven leadership. Again, our Trustees are to be commended for their almost supernaturally inspired wisdom.

You may pick up your regal purple gown and peaked miter at the auditorium preceding the convocation.

Cordially,
Coconut Macaroon, Vice President
Shebanse Polytech

(Editor's note: Six months have elapsed since the receipt of the above.)

Dear President Timkens:

We urge you to join our Judicial Review Committee at once for the impartial trial of the worst leader in our history, Quinton Queazy. The son-of-a-bitch has alienated the faculty, depleted our treasury, caused our students to transfer to Lollypop Lane, and we think that he set fire to our coed dormitory.

Severely distressed,
Coconut Macaroon

Dear Coconut:

I accept your invitation to the execution. But stay calm. The entire scenario is normal.

—Timkens

Halacious Mudfence, a psychiatric consultant for the faculty, has set down rules of action for a staff member bringing his particular problem to a dean:

I. The Encounter. Walk in boldly. Try not to trip over the barbed wire as you approach the dean's desk. Be mentally set to have the dean reduce you from a lion to a lambchop. The dean is prepared to preserve all institutional rules that will wall him off from your problem, whatever it is. He will sternly cite the rules in alphabetical or numerical order, whatever the way he memorized them.

II. Your Turn. You have to shrink the dean to pygmy size. You obviously tried to make your point, but in vain. So say nothing thereafter. Firmly look the dean in the eye, never wavering, and maintain a grin using both corners of your mouth. Make no other moves until following a noticeable unnerving of the dean, he kicks you out.

III. Completing the Shrinking. The following day send the dean an anonymous letter, purportedly from President Timkens, on presidential paper stolen by your girlfriend, a secretary once dismissed from Timkens' office. Your letter should start on page 2, confusing the molecular arrangement of molecules in the dean's brain. The letter might read as follows:

Page 2

and because of your unseemingly behavior to several members of our proud faculty, I refer you to the first paragraph of this letter which states specifically the consequences of your actions.

You will institute at once the corrective measures stated on page 1.

Sadly,
Smiley Timkens

The following was overheard at a meeting of repentant dropouts with the Registrar to evaluate their ability to return to Crumble:

Registrar (to an exceedingly disheveled bum): Are you a dropout?

Bum: Not to worry, Doc. Its raining outside and I only came in to steal an umbrella.

Nobody has been able to get to the Physics building all summer. The structure is now completely covered by vegetation and can be located only by a team of explorers.

A conservationist found a flower at the front door of the building with nine hitherto undiscovered petals and the rare flower has been declared an endangered species. An injunction granted by the court to spare the plant may hold up entrance for at least two years.

The Physics instructors say that since most of them are leaving for other jobs, the few remaining are also an endangered species and they have so petitioned the court. The judge has hastily taken a vacation for parts unknown.

Instructor Live Steam's chairman hasn't yet figured out how to get rid of him. Steam has been stamped and notarized by the administration as a chronic troublemaker. He stated in a lecture that a chairman is the last person you go to if you need factual information about subject matter in the chairman's field. The chairman is always very busy diligently seeking travel information about international meetings, not to mention warding off hostile takeovers when and if he is back.

The best route is to cozy up to a student teaching assistant. This utilizes statistics which involve the chance that the assistant may be right half the time.

The Malevolent Society did it again. The College administrators are in hot pursuit. On the morning of the semiannual Demolition Derby, the Society members stole all the administrators' cars and entered them in the contest. The carnage is just too awful to describe. It even includes President Timkens' Rolls Royce.

The National Wolfsnake Association is holding its convention in Crumble. Although its members serve as admirable models for the lowest common denominator in intelligence studies, they must invent some other group as being even crummier. Failure to do this throws them back into apehood and this reversion could endanger their residual mental status. They will spend the week trying to pinpoint an imaginary group victim so that they can go home uplifted in spirit.

From: The Registrar
To: The Admission Committee

A boatload of refugees is coming up the Great Crumble River tomorrow. Grab everyone you can as potential matriculants. We'll assort them later. The worst ones will do as Teaching Assistants in Chemistry.

The administrators complain that no other college has ever heard of Crumble. Advisors at the Bacchigallupo School of Riveting say that Crumble's plight is explainable by cladistic theory. This means that other colleges cannot identify Crumble because they operate by a logical scheme in which Crumble does not exist as a category. The mess is semantic and the answer awaits more powerful tools in the field of illogics.

Joco Sodbuster, Instructor in English for Agriculture Students
Dear Mr. Sodbuster:

Our Committee To Find Hopeless Teachers has completed its search. You are the nominee. Your lectures are so bad that we are initiating a bed check to see how many students stay awake. You may have to give away a set of dishes to maintain your enrollment and at your own expense. Also, such statements as "I live on the floor above the floor below" or "It's going to be winter next summer" confuse your more stupid students.

Start looking elsewhere,
Vera Scrum, Trusted Presidential Asst.

Chicken Little,
Instructor in Husbandry of Stolen Pigeons
Dear Mr. Little:

It is no accident that you are the recipient of our annual "Most Horrible Animal Industry Award, The Mixed Bag of Tar and Feathers."

Once you were an eagle but you have turned into a turkey. We are painting out your name on your once coveted parking space. Everyone will know that you have screwed up.

A word of caution. It will be dangerous for you to appear at this year's Presidential Turkey Shoot.

Not too tearfully,
Vera Scrum

Special Announcement:

Guiseppi Thawed-Pizza, whose hyphenated name obviously marks him as being of nobility, has joined the Psychology staff.

The Great Crumble Travel Agency must be congratulated for its bold and visionary approach. In Crumble, it emphasizes the glorious vistas and boundless wildlife of Bongoland, not to mention the naked women walking upside down in front of their matchless thatch huts. Sumptuous food is provided during the watch.

Upon arrival in the promised land, one encounters flashing red warning lights put up by the same Travel Agency. The signs urge the natives to leave both pre- and posthaste, either scenario being only one-half hour before the first typhoon strikes. The sign on the following block tells the victims-to-be to get out and enjoy the verdant unspoiled hills and valleys, the never-to-be-forgotten caves, and the posh hostelries in Crumble.

Instructor Flipside has been getting up late for his 8 a.m. class and has had to use his racing car to make up time. He comes roaring onto the campus, with everyone diving into the nearest bushes. His weekly casualties average two pedestrians and three vehicles. He says that he can do better than that. All early risers are asked to send him alarm clocks.

Nux Vomica, a student member of the City Council, told the truth about why trash removal is never on time in Crumble, but he is paying heavily for his transgression. Even his best friends declare that nobody ever heard of an elected official telling the truth and they want him considered insane. The mayor says that Nux needs to learn how to perpetuate confusion through ambiguity. This will mask his stupidity and give him charisma.

Degassed Tapwater
Campus Reservoir Maintenance
Dear Mr. Tapwater:.

We have had enough of your telling visitors, every time you drive them by the office of our President and his staff, "This is where Ali Baba and his 40 thieves work."

We have evidence that you are not exactly a pillar of truth and piety. Our janitorial staff complains that the lawns cannot be watered because you took all the silcocks home, but not obviously to unclog them in your spare. time. You should take a week off to dream up how they found their way into the Great Crumble Pawnshop. Because we have to equalize the crookedness on all sides, thus preserving democracy, we must all preserve calm and dead silence.

Broiled Meatball.
Ombudsman

Temperance Lecturer Oligo Quibble has just been released from the slammer. He was physically attacking everyone, friend or enemy. The judge in bountiful mercy remanded the defendant to his wife with the provision that she keeps him on a short leash when they are outdoors. According to the city leash law, he will be no worse off than his dog.

Mayor Slusher Weakling is now displaying enough creativity to warrant supporting him for any position in the next election, starting with dogcatcher. Slusher wants the whole College to be emptied out and start all over again. The proposal has merit. Slusher wants to ascertain how much grief he would be in for if he runs for the position as the next College President.

To: Dean Dingleberry
From: Dean Corkscrew, Fawchee Subnormal

Our Cultural Exchange Program is progressing well. We now need professors since the ones we have left here cannot be differentiated from our students (and we use the terms professor and student in their broadest connotations).

To start the second phase of our profitable relationship, we are currently willing to exchange three of our students for one Crumble professor. Neither side will have anything to lose or to win either.

If I do not hear from you by Tuesday, I will submit the same offer to another member of our consortium, Shebanse Polytech.

The Board of Trustees has still failed to confirm Mrs. Boilercrud's application to work at Crumble, on the grounds of nepotism. There is a question as to whether a plumber and a janitress, who are husband and wife, can be employed.

The problem is just too overwhelming for the Board and it may have to be directed to the State Supreme Court.

President Timkens is getting excited about the Animal Rights movement and alternatives to animals being used in experimentation. He has instructed the Physiology Department to set up a project on the effects of diet on blood cholesterol. For six months, the dogs will eat Porterhouse steak and the staff will eat dogfood.

The acknowledged smiling sex queen of the faculty didn't get her tenure. The members of the Promotion Committee were being watched by their wives.

We have an Assistant Dean who is a self-proclaimed stand-up comic. He has two sets of stolen jokes which he delivers alternately at 50 mile distances from the campus. He figures that nobody will be present at any two of these sessions. Since we hate the bastard, we are squealing on him. We realize that this could set off a firestorm with faculty members who use the same jokes in their lecture notes for 30 to 50 years.

Geographer Fishbone's vacation to a glorious Caribbean island didn't wind up in accordance with the advertisements. Two blocks back of the beach he was beaten up by natives who then proceeded to advise him never to go two blocks away from the beach.

The talk by 200% Confused on "Freedom at Crumble" was

greeted with less than enthusiasm by the Administration. Confused said that freedom at Crumble is like working for the post office in Bongoland. Confused's next lecture has been edited. The title will be "Whistles and Bells."

SOME REMARKS FROM PRESIDENT TIMKENS TO HIS STAFF

Never share bad news with the faculty. They will find it out soon enough from the students, who nobody pays attention to.

Always ascertain which policies of the state government are traditional and maximize the crooked ones faithfully. Keep in mind that the race belongs to those with all-purpose creativity.

Always hire a department chairman who is more stupid than his dean. Firing the former will then present no problems.

Never fault a colleague if the fellow owes you money.

Pay no attention to our retirees. They had it coming to them.

To: Luckless Beerfoam
Third Zoology Diener from the Bottom
From: Dean of Men

We are told by the Health Service that you have a venereal disease. We don't really care whether you have gonorrhea or a toothache, but we are God-fearing people at Crumble and we must know how you got into such trouble.

Submit a detailed report of your whereabouts for the past three months. Block each day out hour by hour and leave no spaces. Even a 20-minute deletion could raise our suspicions.

Submit the report to my secretary. But first run it through the autoclave in the microbiology laboratory. Both of you will be supplied with disposable masks, gloves and boots.

President Timkens says that it is presumptuous to have "Hail to the Chief" played by the College band when he comes in to visit its rehearsals. When he visits the College symphony orchestra, he is silent about "Venite Adoremus."

To: All Crumble employees
From: The Bursar

We are enclosing raffle tickets for the most exciting chance of your life. We have decided to give our Art Museum to the lucky winner. Nobody has been seen in it for the past two years.

Brick for brick you couldn't get a better buy. Please send in your money before the cold weather sets in and destroys the statue of Hermes.

POTPOURRI

Our commentary today is on the problem confronting Veritas Kinky, Instructor in Truth and Purity, due to the misbehavior of his four-year-son. The son was discharged from the Cub Scouts for wetting his pants during a paramilitary exercise on how to aim a water pistol on overly sweet adults who pat children on the head.

The son formed a competing Teepee and Tomahawk Club, which now includes three members, all of whom were kicked out of the Cubs for wetting their pants or some similar serious deviation from the mores of those with better bladder control. The motives of the members are uncertain but suspicious.

Veritas has taken the side of his son. This is a bad mistake since the use of the ethnic title for the club is demeaning to a proud and noble race. The Great Crumble City Council has been unable to find a statute that deals with the situation. The problem has been referred to the State Supreme Court; these people have always settled disputes with infinite wisdom, especially when they are on television.

Excerpt from Mayor Weakling's address during the annual Crumble Cemetery Week: "Everyone who has been anyone is buried here in the Great Crumble Cemetery. None of us can wait."

Anyone telling the truth on President Timkens' staff is bathed in a gravy concocted by Vera Scrum until he or she is cured of this bad habit. All persons so treated are tested periodically with a battery of machine-gun rapid questions and graded in direct proportion to the deviousness of their answers. A poker face accompanied by weeping and handwringing adds to their likelihood of being restored to grace. Do not apply for a staff job; Timkens will call you.

Harry X. Schlemm
Instructor in English Literature for Coal Miners
Dear Harry:

I reviewed the essay that you submitted in competition for the faculty annual literary prize and I find it common. Being of noble descent, I use the word common in its most charitable sense.

My secretary flushed your MS down the hopper with great care and skill. Don't send us any more.

Cést finis,
Wimbleton Tout Répare
College Literary Critic

Dear Tout Répare or whatever the hell your real name is

Of all the horse's asses I have known, you compare very favorably, in fact in the first ten. This is obviously a compliment, but I also feel quite charitable today. If you need a reference when you are booted out of here, please feel free to use this enthusiastic letter.

How do you feel now?
Harry

National Brotherhood Week was a dismal failure at Crumble. Sophomore Honker in a fit of connubial love blew his nose on the sleeve of his overdressed girl friend. A fight spread through the entire hall. The campus police tear-gassed everybody including two vice-presidents who were too fat to escape through the windows.

Little Miss Muffet, Instructor in Home Economics, brings her

Little Red Riding Hood basket filled with little red cookies to school every day and passes them out to the staff with the hope that some day she will be promoted for services rendered. In the past few weeks she has omitted Lecturer Chippychaser from her itinerary, This has seemed strange since Chippychaser comes from a long line of Chippychasers who have served Crumble faithfully, even if not with distinction, or for that matter, honor.

Our eagle-eyed reporter has discovered that the current Chippychaser has fallen out of favor with Dean Catcabbage. According to the law of the jungle, this means that anyone seen closer than three feet from Chippychaser will be automatically linked with whatever crime Chippychaser allegedly perpetrated and will be treated accordingly. The faculty alienation is practically total.

We commend Little Miss Muffet and we urge that she be promoted at once to the post of "Early Warning Detector Officer."

Chicken Tender, Manager of the Poultry Research Center, has successfully fended off all attempts to fire him. One would not classify Chicken as a nice guy. His dog has made several attempts to kill him and the reverse is also true. He once got a letter from Attila The Hun that stated "You are not on my good list." His dean once tried to banish him by way of a 20-year exchange fellowship in Ouadougou, but that didn't work. There was also a plot to send all his mail to a hypothetical address, el barrio North Pole, but the chief conspirator has been put in jail for shoplifting paper clips. There is rumor that Chicken's endurance is related to the unfortunate fact that Quick Fix, the District Attorney for Crumble County, is his uncle.

The Speech Department presents herein the full text of the talk at its weekly convocation. The visiting lecturer signed himself in as "Anonymous Invitee." He wouldn't give his right name. We caught up with; him as he was running out from under a sheet. He yelled that brevity is the soul of wit. His talk follows.

Dear Audience (which followed a three-quarter hour introduction by the Speech Chairman):Since you all seem to have head colds which I might catch, my advice is that you go home. There is no charge for this prescription which is worth more than an hour's lecture.

Something is cockeyed with the goings-on in the Dead Eye Dick Institute at Crumble. Eight people have been working there for the past seven years purportedly collecting and publishing all the goodies about Dead Eye's shenanigans. They estimate that another 12 years will be necessary to collect, collate and publish all the data about this very important person who has contributed so much to Americana.

There is a glitch. One of the staff members of the Institute has been found to be a ghost writer. At the weekly bash at the Institute, he admitted that he dreamed up most of the supposed facts that were published. He supports his position, however, on the view that it is extremely difficult to be creative for at least 12 years more. Also, because of the artistry of his bullshit, he is well worth his pay. The Administration holds that his logic is irrefutable and that Crumble is delivering a first in its contribution to the scholarly world.

There is the story of our Admissions Officer who was told to get around the State and rip out advertisements about other colleges listed in telephone directories. He was apprehended in a library while at the same activity.

(Editor's note: There is a positive side to this: necessity is the mother of invention.)

The proposal to hire an inter-campus chancellor is not having smooth sailing. The Marco Polo branch says that its troubles decrease inversely with the square of the distance from anyone on the main campus at Crumble. The branch staff obtained this equation from a resident physicist who has very little else to do. In fact, he agrees to make up equations if the price is right. We hear that the tar and feathers are being made ready should the unfortunate proposal materialize.

Disconnected Chickenbones is coming up for tenure. It is up or out for him. The review committee says that he is a lucid maniac, which makes him no different from the rest of the faculty and they tend to favor his continuance.

The State engineers are meeting in secret conclave on the question of how to exterminate Emeritus Stockroom Assistant Banjoface. He is only 65 years old but his brain is 95. The engineers cannot proceed with planning a bridge over a campus ditch because Banjoface has discovered an ant with whiskers under the ditch and he has had it declared an endangered species. Although faculty members slide head first into the ditch on their way to class and have to explain that they did not pee in their pants, the work has been halted. Banjoface says that he intends to live forever to halt the desecration.

The Safety Engineer had a hard day at the power plant. He was told that he was first in the country to test the newest, most powerful, self-propelled vacuum cleaner yet to be introduced on the market. The mayor and other dignitaries were on hand. He proudly started the engine which at once went up a tree with him on it, then relentlessly sailed to the top of the smokestack, whereupon he let it go, watching the monster smash to pieces several hundred feet below, while he waited for a rescue helicopter or a parachute, whichever came first.

Attack Dog
Consultant in Sex Education
Dear Attack:

We selected you as our honored guest at our annual coed awards banquet, but this is our third letter to you without your reply. Could you let us know at once whether you can accept our invitation.

Holding our breath,
Jumping Tealeaves
Coach, Women's Pole Vault Team

Dear Ms. Tealeaves:

I accept the invitation. Start the festivities without me, but rest assured that when the screwing begins I'll be there.

Stay calm,
Attack Dog

Protector of the Public Health
City Hall, Crumble
Dear Protector:

Our house drinking water is from a well and I just found out that chemical wastes have been dumped near my backyard. As you will observe, our water analysis shows VCs, MEKs, EBs, and I guess XYZs all above maximum permissible limits. What are you going to do about it?

Very Irate Taxpayer

Dear Irate:

Not to worry. In accordance with its sovereign power, Crumble has multiplied the permissible limits by two. Your figures show that you are now perfectly safe.

Your Protector

Dear Protector:

I hate to appear to be a troublemaker but now I find that Crumble butchers are selling dog meat and labeling it choice steaks. What is your next step?

Very Irate Taxpayer

Dear Irate:

Our Better Business Bureau believes that all Crumble citizens must make a living and this includes butchers. Also, the Bureau logically wants to match the people and the products sold. Our formulas are obviously successful. You could shop in Horseshit Ridge where you will get what's coming to you.

To: Smiley Timkens
From: Henry Gehenna, President
Bacchigallupo School of Riveting

Dear old friend and counselor. We have a serious problem here and I am seeking your unerring advice which I always follow. We recently hired a number of extremely smart faculty members, but our students are as stupid as usual; in consequence, they are leaving in droves to matriculate at our competitor, the Lollipop Lane School for the Feeble Minded. How can we stop the exodus?

To: Henry
From: Smiley Timkens

You came to the right man. Our situation is well in hand because our faculty and students are equally stupid. No trouble has ever come from a perfect match.

My advice is, burn the place down. It is too late for any other solution. And, of course, run for your life before your superiors discover what happened.

RECENT VERY NOTEWORTHY EVENTS

Dean Ollie Underbright,

I sense a lack of confidence of your faculty in your ability to inspire them to the international achievements that we expect of our Crumble staff.

Being of fair mind, I have devised an "Early Morning Survival Test" to evaluate how well you relate to your faculty. Beginning tomorrow, I am assigning you an extra office hour, from 2 to 3 a.m., Sunday off. You will be rated on a scale of 1 to 10, depending upon how many faculty members come to visit with you at that time. Six is passing.

In about two weeks I will review first your intra-departmental social popularity and come to a preliminary conclusion as to whether we should put you to work in the steam tunnels.

Dean-type courage, my good friend,
Smiley Timkens

Chipped Beef
Consultant in Cosmopolitan Cooking
Crumble Cafeteria
Dear Chipped:

This is your fourth trip to mainland China, all at our expense. At your next visit to the Great Wall, bring your own sleeping bag, which you can use in the grass below the Wall, since you will be on your own.

Also, why China, Siberia and Nicaragua? In your impending explanatory visit to my office, you will wrap yourself in American,

State and Crumble flags, in that order from top down. Your hat is exempted.

Stay home and reduce the national debt,
Smiley Timkens

Dear Myron:

I just joined the faculty and I have been directed to you for advice on how to determine who the bastards are among my colleagues. They got me on my last job which explains how I had to degenerate to Crumble.

Naive Roland, Assistant Professor

Dear Roland: You bring up an important point since the bastards are usually the ones who are assessing you early on to see whether you will fit their life style.

There are some indices. First, find out if the suspect's spouse has had enough and is concocting a poison. This index does not apply if wives who are questioned are masochists. Second, ascertain whether the suspect even says hello to anyone except those who can promote his/her one upmanship. Third, beware of staff who have too many flags on their premises or who won't let the Corps of Engineers build a recreational toilet because there is a six-notched toadstool near it that might be trampled on. Fourth, find out whether the suspect has a junkyard dog. Fifth, check whether he/she is always super-jolly in a carefully selected group of quasi-friends, while in the early A.M. he/she is coughing, spitting, and generally disgusting.

Overall, the diagnosis is skewed if you are also a bastard or trying too hard to appease one. The latter option is not usually successful. Finally, don't search too hard; the bastards are never too shy to hide their one talent.

Instructor Cedric Throwaway proudly announces that he is the only person in his department who has been legally declared to be a certified moron. His colleagues accuse him of boasting.

Cedric says that when he becomes chairman, it will be up or out for any uncertified staff.

The Dietetic staff solves nutritional problems logically and expeditiously. By a vote of 6 to 5, they affirmed the tenet "Don't put bananas in the refrigerator."

Nimble Bimble, in an attack of fearlessness, publicly disagreed with President Timkens. The following is what happened subsequently.

Timkens to Nimble:

I summoned you here to let you know that you are an ungrateful bastard, not just to waste my time emphasizing your built-in stupidity. When we hired you there was a question whether to appoint you as head janitor of the steam tunnels or as a vice-president. Our phrenologist, after examining your skull, thought that you would do the least damage in the latter capacity.

I am granting you 30 minutes to get the jar of cookies out of your desk and make your escape from the campus. Our security officer here at the door will kick you in the rump to expedite your departure.

Timkens to the Press:

Bimble has been a most valued administrator for 20 years and only an acutely sore external anal sphincter has led to his decision to leave us. We hope he can walk. He will be eternally irreplaceable.

Nimble to the Press:

I regret leaving this dear College and especially my best friend, President Timkens. Only a sore sphincter, which might become chronic, has led me to this decision. Do not ask me to stay since another climate will be definitely more favorable for my convalescence.

Arboreal Dogbane, an expert in preventing anyone from cleaning out tin cans from the College forest, was hired by the city to chase the rats out of the municipal dump He succeeded admirably, except that the rats are now hiding in everyone's house. Let us all be thankful that squirrels don't become a problem.

In an incredibly brave decision, the faculty has submitted a resolution that Crumble administrators stop using bilingual English, one recognizable in grammar texts and the other uninterpretable in the quasi-democratic messages distributed to the faculty.

Dr. Aloysius Bedpan, Proctologist
Great Crumble Hospital
Dear Bedpan:

We are cautiously sanitizing your fecal-smeared manuscript entitled "Horror At The Colo-Rectal Sphincter." It is being returned to you by our carrier pigeon and it will be dropped off on your roof.

When accepting this editorship, I took the sacred Crumble oath to prevent nondegradable garbage from entering the public domain. Members of our affiliate, the Board of Health, were present at the ceremony and they support me fully. Our recommendation is that you request the federal government to bury the manuscript in a safe waste dump not too close to anyone's house.

Vox Populi Vox Dei,
Forby Doo Doo

Boiled Grass, Veterinary Nutritionist, in a superb lecture to the Agriculture faculty, said that to control a cockroach, one has to think like a cockroach. He noted that this shouldn't be too difficult for the faculty at the animal farms.

To: Genghis Khan, Official Crumble Explorer
From: Deputy Chairman, Department of Physics

Your letter to President Timkens in which you demand full compensation for your trips to several cities in the Far East has been referred to this Department for judicial review.

You submitted no paid bills to substantiate your claims, so we are forced to use the immutable laws of physics to mediate the dispute.

The great Einthoven stated that for electric currents, when potentials are measured consecutively along a set of points and they come back to the starting point, the vector addition of the sum of the potentials is zero. We can logically extrapolate to your case and state that when you purportedly traveled to a series of places and eventually returned to the place you started from, the sum of the forces describing your journey equals zero. Since you are here and therefore your resultant displacement is zero, we can only conclude that you never left Crumble. Sorry about that and quod erat demonstrandum.

Ms. Hubba Hubba Hubba (nickname: Hubba), washroom attendant in the Economics building, has written a probable story as to why the Geology Department's glowing annual report of obtaining funding for petroleum research is a bit puzzling. The Department Chairman says that Hubba's survival in the institution is, at best, dubious.

According to Hubba, you must always analyze the Department's statement of success just the opposite of the way that the Department does. First, examine the federal government's contribution. This keeps increasing in direct proportion to its lack of knowledge about what's going on. Next, see if the State has, in a subtle manner, very slightly decreased its funding each year, while publicly praising the value of the research to the people of the State. Finally, note very carefully whether the petroleum companies involved have sharply decreased their funding each year; these are the ones who manage to awake early from their stupor and abruptly figure out the idiocy of remaining with the losers.

Observe that the federal money overshadows for a time everything else and allows the Department Chairman to keep eating Chateaubriand as he travels around the country, although making discreet inquiries here and there about another job.

To: Muck Slopbucket, Head of Janitorial Service
From: Smiley Timkens

We need your enthusiastic support to spearhead our drive to reduce salaries so as to keep our budget in balance. In keeping with universal policy, we are starting with the janitors. Because of your key position, it is essential that you let the workers know of the importance of their small sacrifice for Crumble.

To: Smiley Timkens

I will like hell get involved in this new monkey business.

To: Muck:

We obtained your records from the Health Service and Myron has confessed in our torture room that you are a delayed ejaculator. If this became known, you would only be able to consort with nymphomaniacs. We are both reasonable people and I am sure that you will do your best for God, country and Crumble.

To: Smiley Timkens

Your logic is clear and unassailable. As the Kaiser once said, "Deutschland Uber Alles." I am calling a meeting this week to urge that we must all tighten our belts for the good of Crumble.

Magnum Opus

Ex-Literary Consultant
Dear Magnum:

As everyone knows, our experimental laboratory of cardiology in the basement of the feed and grain barn is internationally famous. The delivery boy at the Great Crumble Drugstore repeatedly tells us this.

We are currently injecting a new heart drug into pigeons, but the local hunt club has acutely reduced the supply of the birds. We hear that you are now starving and we will pay you at non-controversial rates to substitute for the pigeons. The only side effect of the drug is cardiac arrest.

An offer you can't refuse,
Hi Treason, Chief Researcher

Dear Hi:

I am collecting diseased skulls. I will cooperate with you on an even swap.

Magnum Opus

Hodge Podge
Instructor in Remedial English
Dear Hodge or Podge:

Your manuscript entitled "Wet Banana, A Poignant Love Story," is off the wall, all 600 pages of it.

You will now need to come here "quam celerissime" and separate your pages from the other refuse on the cutting room floor. We clean the place once a month and your unfortunate contribution to the classics could be lost forever.

Inaccessibly yours,
Forby Doo Doo
Editor, Great Crumble Press

The fastest thing in Crumble is a professor fleeing from a building directly after his last semester lecture, outdistancing the students and even the track team.

The hardest task in publishing is to get permission to reproduce a text figure from the book of an author who stole the picture from another author. The silence is deafening.

Horace Microbuck, world authority on the psychology of starvation, has been given the task of administering truth serum to staff members who say "If I got paid more, I would work harder." Horace is eminently qualified since he was fired from nine other positions when he said "Either you raise my pay or I leave."

Overheard on the train to Crumble:
Good neighbor seatmate to an incoming freshman: "When you get to the campus, I want you to introduce yourself to a good friend of mine."
Victim: "How will I recognize him?"
Good neighbor: "He'll be in the library."

The Physics instructor who just gave A's to all his students because of their flawless performance may have to appear before the Board of Inquiry. In line with the Board's new directive to review possible grade elevation, the Board asked all the A students the following question: a thermos bottle keeps hot water hot and cold water cold. Explain how this can possibly happen. Everyone flunked. Some turned in blank papers.

A bluejay has got Visiting Lecturer Boggs into deep trouble. Every time Boggs drove his auto up his driveway, the bluejay would play Russian roulette and dart out of the way a split second before it became a bird statistic.

This week the bird got it, square in the mush. It is convalescing painfully on a very low tree stump, a safe spectator distance from the driveway.

The bluejay has complained to the Great Crumble Ornithological Society and, of course, to the local Antivivisection Society. Boggs has been charged with cruelty to animals, but this does not satisfy the two societies which want him boiled in oil, slowly. The college community expects the punishment to fit the crime.

To: Forby Doo Doo
From: Language Mangler, English Chairman

I keep hearing the expressions "true" and "absolutely true." Which in your expert opinion is correct?

To: Language Mangler

It depends on who is doing the most lying. Incidentally, there is always a small charge for my advice when acting as an expert.

On the annual "Release of Tension Day," a shouting match will take place between the faculty and administrators. No rehearsals are necessary.

The faculty hopes that it can surpass the decibels put out by two administrators in a sealed room, vying for the same promotion.

Dean Catcabbage, in a spirit of camaraderie with the students, entered the bimonthly greased pig contest. After about five minutes, nobody was sure whether the Dean was the pig. The pig roast had to be delayed until positive identification could be made of the Dean.

Dean Dingleberry greeted a foreign minister from the third

world, visiting America for the first time to see how Crumble grows rice for its starving faculty.

Dean: Do you like this country?

Minister: Not what I see here.

Dean: Don't you know that America is the land of the free and the home of the brave?

Minister: We have some of those, too. Not too many, however.

Dean: Why not?

Minister: The rule is that when you attack the leader, you have to be able to cut his head off, and pronto. The free and the brave didn't memorize the rule.

Dean: Have you met President Timkens yet?

Minister: Yes and I like him. He speaks with a forked tongue.

Dean: Is that good or bad?

Minister: Very good. He says that at 50-mile intervals he can shift the articulatory position of his words and different sentences come out that fit the scene. It keeps everybody happy. Not too creative, but it brings in votes.

(Editor's note: Space limits this discussion. We wish the minister well until he gets banished by a new generalissimo.)

Posted over a classroom door:

I am dismissing classes. The Nobel Prize committee is meeting in Stockholm today and I need to be close to the telephone since my guru is confident that I will be chosen as a laureate. One cannot always trust the judgment of the committee, however, so I may be back tomorrow.

Freeze Dried

Visiting Assistant Instructor in Biochemistry

Excerpt of a conversation between Dean Underbright and a hapless instructor who was summoned to receive a prophylactic bawling out:

Dean: We cannot continue to tolerate staff members who refuse to spend some of their salary to travel abroad and thus maintain an expected degree of worldly sophistication. You not only have not been to the great cities of the world, but there isn't any record of your having been to Prairie Dog, Texas.

Hapless victim: If you were a jerk before you went, you're still a jerk when you come back.

Dean: I take this as a personal insult and I will present this evidence to our Review Board for appropriate punishment.

Less Hapless: To be insulted requires a threshold degree of sensitivity and intelligence. You have yet to reach this critical level, so you have already blown your case.

Dean: This meeting is closed until I find another charge.

To: Forby Doo Doo, Editor
From: Eliot Corkscrew, Expert Staff Writer

I am returning my review of Instructor Yucky's book manuscript "How To Avoid Drowning In A Crowded Hottub:"

"This writer has given birth to an overstuffed compendium of more mistakes than even the physicians make at the Great Crumble Hospital. At one point, 53 pages of errors appear without the author ever repeating any one of them. This is a brilliant performance and it warrants stretching the text to 1,000 pages so that it can be published as a "Complete Book of DysEnglish," competing favorably with our national street language and allowing the illiterati their first chance to enjoy reading. I recommend the book enthusiastically."

The Theology staff has succeeded in halting construction of a proposed saloon to be called "The Brick Shithouse" on the technicality that it wasn't even brick. The staff is to be commended by the Philosophy Department.

To: Deans and Vice-Presidents
From: President's Blue Ribbon Task Force

We have evolved the ultimate solution for the unwarranted discontent of those faculty members in rampant starvation. All personnel will now receive a 10 percent raise. This will please all administrators by increasing still more the disproportion between their actual salaries and those of the peasants. It will please the faculty and effectively silence their undesirable bellowing. It will confirm our democratic efforts since the single number 10 does not differentiate among any of the parties.

One of our committee members brought up the question of who will pay for this increase, but he has fortunately resigned. Obviously, janitors, secretaries and all other maintenance personnel will be classified as luxuries in faculty offices and will be terminated.

We applaud President Timkens for selecting us.

Notice of Physical Education instructor vacancy: Applicant must be a superjock. Perrier swishers, male cinderellas and bearded beachcombers need not apply. Also, we do not think that bald is beautiful. Applicant must be kindhearted to subliminal English students who are good swimmers.

If sufficiently sparkling and of sterling quality, send complete vita to the College Cosmic Search Committee. Do not delay since in P.E. the race belongs to the swift.

Ms. Tomato Surprise, Lecturer in Behavior for Genteel Young Ladies and also part-time waitress at The Fin Rot will have her infinitesimal class enrollment reduced to zero because she will be kicked out when she is released from the bastille.

Tomato got roaring drunk at The Hope for the Best saloon in downtown Crumble. When the fearsome bouncer, Shipwreck Jack, attempted to evict her from the premises, she tossed him over the bar, demolishing the huge mirror behind it along with about 100 bottles of liquor. The backup bouncer, Hurricane Harry, was tossed over the bar next, which accelerated remarkably the pileup of broken bottles.

The Crumble coaching staff in a secret meeting has agreed to invite Tomato to disguise herself as a student when she gets out of the bastille and join the weight-lifting and javelin-throwing teams. An attorney says that he can get Tomato freed on the grounds of sex discrimination. An equal number of males, probably five, should have been thrown out with her.

The first scholarly exchange program between Crumble's exemplary professor to a prestigious college and the coming to Crumble of an anthropologist from that college just didn't work. The cultural shock both ways was just too much.

The anthropologist explained that he would first have to visit an intermediate civilization so that he might recognize what he was digging. The Crumble professor fell off a sidewalk because he never saw one and he is temporarily disabled.

We are asked to remind you to buy tickets for the Crumble policemen's ball. You might just find your car shoved over a cliff.
From The Crumble Foundation

1. The Ploy

Dear Emeritus Instructor:

We know that the previous fund raisers for our beloved Crumble have neglected you for too many years. It is because of this that we cannot find your name, although we have retrieved your address from the scratch pads in the Alumni Office. One of the more concerned workers did identify you as "occupant. "

We must never again neglect you. We are certain that you want fervently to support to the fullest the construction of the proposed new house for President Timkens.

Please fill in the enclosed form, stating how much you would like to have withdrawn monthly from your retirement check for the next five years.

Your cordial college brother,
Yorkshire Pudding

2. The Response

Dear Puddinghead:

I am sending you a cup and a pair of dark glasses. I suggest that you stand in front of the Five and Dime store downtown. I am charging you nothing for this advice. Credit the gifts above to my new account at the Foundation.

Nothing but loyalty for my friends,
Innominate Discarded Staff Member

Frank Finagle didn't do too well in his maiden sermon required of all Theology majors. He told the students "May you live all the days of your life."

The Crumble deans and vice-presidents are weeping in their handkerchiefs that their salaries are below those with equivalent rank at General Motors or Exxon. Urgent action is demanded. They will hold a prayer session in front of the Governor's-office at the State House with full confidence that he will at once correct their sad plight.

The faculty is ominously silent, expecting the worst to happen by what is now called "rearrangement" of funds. This costs the State nothing, which silences the Mathematics Department.

Little Miss Muffet has finally expressed her special talent—a mediator of disputes between faculty members. In the last faculty meeting, two fiercely antagonistic instructors were at it as usual. Miss Muffet kept turning from one to the other, offering her solution to the controversy. Both instructors picked her up, threw her out the window, and shook hands.

To: Retiring Faculty
From: The Board of Trustees

We regret that you no longer have pensions. We bet all your contributions on a horse race, but how could we know that our invincible horse would drop dead just before the finish line? This is an act of God and we are confident that you have complete faith in His mysterious ways.

Just to be safe, all of you should look for another job.

Students for Clean Government support the Mayor of Horseshit Ridge who says he likes things the way they were in the 12th century. Certain people have moved into town who are upsetting the idyllic city. Some of them have mowed lawns on the Sabbath.

Farthingale Drone
Poet-in-Residence
Dear Farthingale:

We have rented a paleontologist to dig up past files of borrowers of library books in this State and we find that you borrowed a book, "The Little Engine That Couldn't" in 1913 and never returned it. You now owe $2,000 in accrued fines and interest.

Pay up by next Thursday or your salary will be garnished for the rest of your life, leading to your ultimate starvation. Since my ascension to the position of boss here, criminal laxity is a luxury of the past.

Seriously,
Agatha Prim
Chief Librarian

We pause in our hard day's work of reporting events at the College to repeat a story that pleases our bizarre sense of humor:

A bird came home to his mate looking like a steamroller ran over him.

Mate: What happened? Did you just get released from the emergency hospital for birds?

Husband-type bird: I was flying home from work, very low altitude, and minding my own business when I got caught in a badminton game.

Our reporter was able to ascertain what happened to Vice-President Wet Soup at President Timkens last dinner. All the invitees were given tags to wear. These were numeralized from 1 to 10 in accordance with what Timkens thought about their national esteem. The 10s were carefully screened so as not to be adulterated by the lesser ranks. Soup was separated off with the 2s. After dinner he came home and broke up everything starting with the front door. His dog doesn't dare to come into the house.

The Great Crunble Energy Delivery Company has complained that the winter seasons are becoming increasingly mild. Their profits in supplying gas and electricity have dropped to something less than astronomical. The company hired Professor Flip Flop, self-proclaimed all-around genius, how best to mishandle the situation. Flip has ended his research on zebra muscles in order to develop a refrigerant that lowers house temperatures below freezing. He says that when the toes of the occupants develop gangrene from lack of circulation and turn black, he will be immediately available to adjust their thermostats. He neglected to mention that he won't be around since the company has already figured out when to terminate him.

In downtown news, the Clerk of Crumble County says that

his predecessor didn't leave enough money for him to steal. The job is not sufficiently productive and he is resigning.
Advertisement:

Available to help big family with household chores, babysitting and errands, in exchange for room and board. References unobtainable but don't worry.

An Ex-Assistant Dean

There is evidence that the newer administrators must once have been students. An assistant dean, choking and turning blue, was rushed to the Great Crumble Hospital. When questioned by a physician, he blurted "Got something in my craw, chief."
Advertisement:

The College Forestry Department will now cut down trees on residential streets. There is no charge if your house is hit. We recommend that you leave your auto two blocks away during chopdown week.

Rebuttal from concerned citizens:
Dear Mayor Weakling:

All of us on Hoopla Street have bought baseball bats and are prepared to maim these forestry clowns if they show up in our neighborhood. Send them to Horseshit Ridge which needs to be leveled so that it can start all over again.

Ephraim Applesauce, Lecturer in Big Business, has won acclaim throughout Crumble County for his sage observation that "When you sell something, somebody else buys it." He is sure to be invited to join the permanent faculty.

The debate at the City Council last night ended in a hung vote. Three councilmen voted that it isn't worth flooding the entire College campus to get a new reservoir and three voted that it is. It was discovered that Mayor Weakling had asked the English Department to formulate the question.

At the last general faculty meeting a minute of silence was observed for 16 faculty members deceased in the past year. The faculty secretary reported that he met almost all the deceased in a dream and they said "Thank God that 15 of us are here. An assistant dean didn't make it." Dean Dingleberry quickly went on to the next subject on the agenda.

Deluvial Grayfish
Lecturer in Embalming
Dear Deluvial:

Your obnoxious detective story "Who Put The Smoochy-Boo Paint On Mrs. Beck's Stairs" is the pits even in the realm of the losers. Your main character, Sheriff Vacuum Cleaner, miserably failed to solve anything and the solution remains a mystery. So will your manuscript copy since we intend to do it in as soon as we repair our shredder. Our defense is "pro bono publico." The remains will be returned to you.

You could start from square one and write another story that has a solution commensurate with your brain. We suggest a title such as "Where To Find The Coldest Beer In Crumble." Then submit it to someone at your level of comprehension. We recommend our bitter enemy, Myron, at the Health Service.

Forget quickly that we are here while we are waiting for an unlisted telephone number.

Forby Doo Doo, Editor, Press

The Zoology Faculty invites the faculty to a seminar by Shad Roe. Shad promises exciting revelations in his talk "How to Clean a Fish with your bow tie.

When a high-level administrator tells a characteristically idiotic joke in the auditorium, he is said to "quip," indicating an extraordinary sense of humor. Everyone roars, particularly on body signal from the next highest administrator who orchestrates the cues. Once a lower administrator was flat on his back, in mouth-to-mouth resuscitation position, roaring so vehemently that he had to be decompressed with a bicycle pump on the draw.

If a plebeian from the faculty tells a joke to the same audience, a deafening silence ensues. Then stage whispers follow and one hears such statements as nauseating, embarrassing, obscene, or have the security police get him out through the back door or any convenient window.

Editorial Note: How many articles should one churn out per year?

When a good teacher who has motivated many hundreds of students gets fired because he hasn't published at the pace of a sausage machine, nobody grieves. He deserves his punishment.

When an overpublished researcher is exposed as a fraud, stuffing his manuscripts with contrived data, everyone strangely tries to shut up, with commitments in Europe to fulfill. This is especially true for the coauthors who were never sure what was in the publications.

When a college president, who acted as judge on both cases above, gets fired because he screwed up everything in his line of sight, his incapacity to have ever published anything is inconsequential and is never mentioned.

To: Eric Bulbsnatcher, Electrician
Maintenance Department
From: Forby Doo Doo, Editor Great Crumble Press

We fortunately had nothing to do with your book "Malcolm Blew The Fuse," but your sequel "Malcolm Strained His Pooper," which you had the effrontery to submit to us, borders on a first rate disaster in pornography. We heard that your first book sold seven copies and the publishing house is in receivership.

I am urging President Timkens to quarantine you on some uninhabited Pacific atoll to neutralize your capacity to abruptly worsen the world literature.

To: Forby Doo Doo
From: Eric Bulbsnatcher, Author, Composer and Electrician

I am the only one on campus who knows where the electrical transformers and cables are. If I am exiled, the entire college will be plunged into total darkness, perhaps for years, until archaeologists come up with a successful dig. It will be all your fault. Obviously, my contributions are much better than yours.

Crumble's most popular nightclub, SCREW YOU TOO, is putting on a student bash. Admission is half price for anyone showing a certificate of release from the county jail. Two bands, The Whirling Earthworms and The Discards, will titillate the assembled half-wits.

Dry Martini, consulting wine taster for President Timkens, has been dismissed for recommending inferior olives. This is his second offense. He once failed to detect urine put into the wine served at a Board of Trustees banquet.

Chemistry instructor Doberman Doomsday, who gives apocalyptic opinions to each student about his dismal fate, was found above the Chemistry building tied to the weather vane and rotating smoothly with the changing direction of the breeze. Doomsday says that it is the work of the Malevolent Society. He demands that ex-Chief Ketchum of the Great Crumble Constabulary get the villains or resign his ex-status. The College meteorologist is not complaining since he can tell again which way is north.

Advertisement:

The Sociology office is for sale. The new owner will be responsible for removing the garbage. The red tags can be removed only by permission of the Board of Health.

To: Medical Student Meatball
From: Intern Gleep

As of the receipt of this letter, and even if you don't receive it, you are hereby kicked out of the Health Service.

You told one of our patients that he had a deficiency of 4-methyl-umbelliferyl-beta-D-mannopyranoside. Now how the hell am I supposed to know that? I have been reading the literature furiously and I am only up to 1907.

You are dangerous even as an observer. Go back to the classroom where you will forget progressively what you have learned. This will give you more respect for hard-earned ignorance as you enter the profession.

Assistant Professor Prime Rib, a garden-variety egomaniac, never spoke to Associate Professor Spongebutter in the adjacent office. Prime always slithered by Spongebutter as though he were a vapor, often barely missing him in the narrow corridor.

It's a small world. Spongebutter somehow got appointed to a 10 year irrevocable term as "Plenipotentiary Head of the Salary and Promotion Committee." The next year Prime received no salary increase and he stayed in the same rank. He decided to eat crow and do some cringing before the now omnipotent Spongebutter.

Prime: With my talent and universal reputation, why haven't I been elevated to Full Professor, with top salary in the College?

Spongebutter: I can't remember seeing you before. Are you sure that you work here, perhaps in the kitchen?

Prime: My office was next to yours. You couldn't have forgotten.

Spongebutter: Oh, yes, now I vaguely recall this. I thought that you were being wheeled in and out of our Wax Museum to keep you from crumbling. Then I changed my mind when it became obvious that you were full of shit.

Editor: We are not going to report any more of this except to state that the two are now talking to each other—in the foulest language that they keep looking up in international dictionaries.

To: Dean Dingleberry
From: Euripides, Department of English

You asked me to comment on the students' evaluation of Biology Instructor Fieldmouse. I do not agree with the characterization of Fieldmouse by one student as an "immature skunk." In my best judgment he is a full-grown skunk. I trust that this will be of objective help to you in finalizing the impending tragedy

A collection will be made for Assistant Instructor Heave-Ho Gutbucket who took his 25 years of savings and bought a super-luxury auto. A day later, while it was parked in a shopping area, a fight broke out between two thugs, entrenched on either side of his car. They threw broken bottles at one another through all the closed car windows, chased each other over the hood and top with their spiked boots, and ripped off fenders to throw at each other. The fight ended on top of the dented car roof when they both fell and had to be carried away in an ambulance.

Both combatants sued Heave-Ho for parking his car outside of a white line and thus causing them to be injured in a space ordinarily reserved for such fights and they won the case. Heave-Ho is without car, in debt for the rest of his life, and he received a parking ticket from the police.

To: Idiot (No other name fits so well)
Stockroom Manager, Chemistry
From: Chemistry Staff—Unanimous

Your placing explosive chemicals in the laboratory refrigerator, next to the sparking on-off switch, will cost the College 3 million dollars to replace the roof and the entire top two floors.

We have been scraping students off the walls for the past several hours. A "Premeditated Murder Group Without Profit" is under consideration.

We know of no way to mete out comparable punishment except to feed you to the lions at the downtown zoo. Your alternative is to swim the Rio Grande into Mexico.

Postscript: We just found out that you told your assistant to smell the chemicals in the unmarked bottles so that they could be rearranged alphabetically. Fortunately he had to go to the bathroom and he didn't reach the Cs where the cyanides were shelved.

To: Sublimis and Profundus, Great Crumble Barristers
From: Griselda Fireball, Lecturer in Crime and Justice

A fellow instructor, who just loves to play games with females, always waits for me in the morning to locate the last parking spot just before my class and then pulls into it triumphantly. What is the penalty for putting a bomb under his auto?

To: Griselda
From: The Barristers

Destruction of property is a high crime and is severely punished. Wait for the criminal to leave his car and then aim a small disabling bomb right under his ass. We thought of hiring a flamethrower, but we prefer reducing the punishment to fit the crime.

The Safety Inspector had his usual bad time, yesterday. He went to the Chemistry building to investigate a complaint of faulty ventilation and he got sucked up the fume hood. Upon being retrieved by workers dismantling part of the roof, he is dictating his report of quality control from his hospital bed.

Research workers developing a powerful windmill have petitioned President Timkens to lock the Inspector up during their experiments.

A profiler has been hired to determine the status of the staff, independently of the chairpersons and deans. He won't last long because he has recommended removing the deans from Mahogany Row and putting them in a common bullpen. The deans counterpropose that the profiler be put in the human centrifuge and be whirled around until his brain molecules become rearranged to Crumble normal.

Janitor Fishcake, a firm believer in innovation, saw an advertisement proving that it was far more economical to dispose of things than to provide continual cleaning and maintenance. Every P.M., after a teacher returned to his office from his attempt to dispense the wisdom of the ages, Fishcake appeared for his usual scavenger hunt and threw the teacher instead of the rubbish in the dumpster.

Fishcake convinced his foreman that this alternative saved several hours of useless repetitive equipment cleaning caused by the staff member. Fishcake said that you logically eradicate the weakest link. His foreman was impressed. They are coauthoring a manuscript for the Journal of Expeditious Disposal.

Did you ever have to attend a Best Teacher of the Year Award

Banquet where the worst student in the class was assigned to present the Award? Do not be surprised if the presenter proclaims endlessly the virtues of the worst teacher in the College who is then given the prized diploma.. The awardee is very likely to state "I really don't deserve this honor; there are many teachers here who are just as good as I am." Then the worst Dean in the College, who staged the entire charade, from the winner to the diploma, will say "This is what the College is all about" and he will adjourn the meeting.

Note on faculty toilet door:

Will the person who stole my false teeth, wig, crutch, face mask, and all my clothes while I was showering please return them. I am trapped in here, maybe indefinitely, since nobody using the room will pay any attention to me. There is no longer respect for age.

Emeritus Professor

STUDENT NOTES

Half Mast, fiercest professor in the College, had his last hurrah. At the first meeting of a class, he always informs the students, "By next Tuesday two of every three of you will be flunked, as you richly deserve. My decisions are absolute and irrevocable."

The next Tuesday the current class, by prearrangement, yanked him off the podium where he was just about to pontificate, whisked him away in a horse blanket and deposited him in the city dump.

The deans in full fury demanded an emergency meeting with President Timkens and urged that the entire class be expelled following their being boiled in oil. Timkens noted that he was busy with important matters of state and to come back in six months. At that time he would consider with great care who should be thrown out and that might include Half Mast. If the deans stayed too noisy, they might also be included.

To. Resizzled Porkchop
From: Ex-Agriculture Student, Cracked Wheat

I want to express my appreciation for the exceptional commentaries you gave in your course in Human Relations. Some of my favorites were:

Singing in the rain—which you dedicated to the homeless.

When you are the president, it's never too early to look for a retirement home...which the president never believes.

Where there's a will, there's a relative...which you so eloquently presented in the joint session with the Great Crumble Bar Association.

If I hadn't flunked out this semester, I would have retaken the course.

This is an allegory about Snickerdoodle Hangnail, an instructor who functioned mainly as Professor McRooster's shoeshine boy. Snickerdoodle was appointed Head of the Student Graduation Committee. He immediately asked four other clones to join the Committee. Each of the clones functioned with a few loose neurons and even these were in progressive Wallerian degeneration.

The Committee's first act was to call in a student, Walter Gloomp, who was three days from graduation and to inform him that the former Department Head, two years previously when Gloomp matriculated, had allowed Gloomp to take one year of Hop-Scotch to satisfy his physical education requirement. The Committee was changing this to two years of Hoop-Rolling, to be taken one course each year. Gloomp would have to satisfy the new requirements. Also, the Committee. gleefully informed Gloomp that there was no recourse since Daniel Webster had made sure that the actions of agents of a college are inviolate once the flaming tablet bearing the revised rule cools down.

We have followed this sad tale on occasion and can give you both the good and the bad news. Snickerdoodle has been in and out of straightjackets at the local madhouse on Screwview Avenue, and Gloomp is still a year away from completing Hoop-Rolling.

The students would like to interact with students at other institutions, but the question is what could they win without cheating. The student body president, Howdy Doody, will meet with a clinical psychologist to discuss the problem.

A member of the Malevolent Society snatched an assistant dean, then dumped him out of his car, and was immediately arrested by a civic-minded policeman for littering the highway. Both the victim and the student pleaded nolo contendere.

Overheard in a stroll on the campus:

Dejected student (speaking to his temporary-type girlfriend): My English instructor may not give me the A grade I deserve.

Rootie Tootie (girlfriend from Boilerplate Point, not the best section of Crumble City): What did da turd lay on you?

Student: He thinks he'll flunk me.

Rootie Tootie: Let's go up and destroy the S.O.B.

Student (in elegant English worthy of an A grade English student): When?

Sophomore Miniwit has been put into a Remedial English class. He was misspelling dirty words and these constituted most of his vocabulary.

To: Hwang Ho, Sophomore Class
From: Smiley Timkens

Because of your outstanding academic achievement despite desperate poverty, I am awarding you a special emergency scholarship. Since our funds have all been allotted for the remainder of this year, I am reducing your Dean's salary proportionately which will keep our budget in balance. Rest assured that the Dean on my urging will profess great pleasure in contributing to such a worthy cause.

Promising student Pothole has been forbidden to continue his epic research problem. His delegated executive rat developed an ulcer and the antivivisectionist club in the Zoology Department torched all his equipment. Pothole is requesting permission from the club to work on a problem using Canada thistles. He promises not to tell the conservationists in the Botany club.

To: Bumptious Mudball
Instructor in Bushwacking Technique

From: Oscar Loserville
Class Valedictorian

I was scheduled to graduate from Crumble this weekend, but I have been informed that I received a flunking grade in your course. This is a terrible mistake since I got all A grades in your course and an honors plaque. I need to see you tomorrow at the latest since I have a job in Africa next week and I will lose this if I do not graduate.

To: Oscar Loserville

I am sailing to Europe tomorrow afternoon, but I will pencil you in one month from this date. In my own experience the race never belonged to the swift.

To: Bumptious Mudball

You need to have someone shit in a hat and dump it over your head. I am penciling you in for tomorrow morning and I have appointed myself to bring the hat. Prepare for the fitting.

The Criminal, son of a famous alumnus, The Paranoid, has been admitted to Crumble. The Criminal graduated from a Half-Way House and was almost admitted to a Two-Thirds Way House, but he regressed. Crumble admitted him with the promise that he would commit all his crimes off campus.

Oxslime is about to graduate and he wants to leave town this week, but there is a major problem. His dirty clothes, which now weigh several tons, are under everybody's bed in the entire 18 story dormitory. His girl friend, Dootsie, who is a runner-up in the residual filth department, has the same problem. She is trying to retrieve enough clothes to avoid being arrested for public lewdness.

The Dean of Students is asking all students to donate enough money to hire an 18-wheeler to take away the dirty clothes. Some will be sent to Mexico.

The Board of Health threatens to condemn the dormitory. Also, vision is being obscured and students on the upper floors could get killed.

Lucretia Functionalis, Instructor in Logical Methodology, received some free personal instruction yesterday. The Malevolent Society sawed a circular hole in the floor where she stood for lecturing, then camouflaged it, bringing up to her desk a rope that triggered opening of the trap.

Lucretia, on lecture day, saw the rope and informed the class that one always methodically tests unknown objects, whereupon she pulled the rope, abruptly sailed to the classroom below, and landed on a lecturing instructor's head. Both are hospitalized in a state of euphoria.

The Maintenance Department wants her salary check withheld on the grounds of stupidity and wanton destruction of property.

Chemistry Lecturer Job, in a raging fit resembling status epilepticus, told student Lousewort that he didn't know his ass from first base. Lousewort said that he did and he proceeded to embark upon a detailed description of his ass and then of first base. (Editor's note: What is your verdict?)

Student Assistant Grindle has requested a leave of absence from Wrestling to study Zoology. His interest was aroused by a spate of monumental studies on why a barnyard hen never outruns a rooster. Grindle has read all of Sigmund Freud's works to get the answer, but Siggy appears to have missed that one. If Grindle can find a cooperative hen, he is ready to start his new career at once.

Betty Bountiful, matriculating freshman, has upset the entire orientation week procedures. She arrived at the College with a transcontinental furniture van which included among other items 20 trunks, a king-size bed, and a grand piano. Since the 10 by 10 dormitory room was obviously inadequate, Betty's father, skilled by long practice in space logistics, threw the prospective roommate's bed and bureau out the window, kicked out a drywall which separated an adjoining room, and quickly took off, which was his usual practice. (We don't have the space for further details.)

Sludge Cake, voted Sophomore Class Slob, has capitalized on his prestigious title. He will be an on-line dust collector in a pollution study of the cafeteria. Each evening he will be shaken into a bin by an impartial member of the Board of Health.

Ms. Leaky Keester, Instructor-Designate in Hygiene, is proving to be too much for the janitorial staff. She eats incessantly in every room and throws apple cores, banana skins and also immediate past lecture notes over her shoulder. Even a boy scout could pick up her trail.

Negotiations are under way to get her an exchange fellowship at Horseshit Ridge High School where she would be welcomed enthusiastically.

There are now so many students at Crumble with causes that it is becoming necessary to sell programs so that everyone will be able to find out under whose window a given protest meeting will be held.

There will be a wrestling match in the gym to see who gets a date with Roof Doggybag, voted to be the ugliest tempered coed in the senior class. The loser gets her for the evening or some part thereof.

Knocko Molasses, grocery tycoon, is sending his wayward son, 85% Molasses to Crumble. An accompanying truant officer has orders to see that 85% is bathed at least once per week in Knocko Wonton Soup.

The Dean of Freshmen is a bit concerned about what will happen in the dormitory. An anti-riot squad is polishing its helmets for the ready.

Slum landlord Jeb has been taken off the approved listing for student housing. With the unexpected increase in student enrollment, Jeb became very ingenious. He built additional rooms on his houses with tin cans. He is especially fond of Campbell's soup cans. Jeb says that the new architecture allows instant rearrangement of houses and he asserts that his innovation rivals the invention of the wheel.

The School of Education has grudgingly given permission to allow the following quotations to be printed. They first demanded type readable only with a magnifying lens.

A school teacher is a disillusioned girl who used to think she liked children—Anna Herbert.

In the first place God made idiots; this was for practice; then he made school boards—Mark Twain.

The English Department may have to hire another instructor, 1 on 1, to take care of illiterate freshman Dum Dum. He says such things as:

I unsolved the mystery.

Or when angry: I'll go upside yore head.

When confronted to pay his tuition: I'm fresh out of cash.

In the intelligence test during orientation week, when asked, If a pail lets out water when it leaks, why doesn't a boat do the same thing, he said, That's heavy; I'll ask my mother. She paints docks.

And one of his historic statements: When I become a writer after this English course, I'll buy a pen.

The Crumble football team played a top-notch conference team that needed an interim doormat to wipe their feet on in between the tough teams on their schedule. But they reckoned on normalcy. The conference team couldn't figure out what game Crumble was playing and they became so disoriented that Crumble won. The coach said that this will teach people not to mess around with a team from outer space.

Advertisement in student newspaper: Furnished apartment for rent. In red light district. Former owners have fled. Very good condition except for the mattresses.

A sacrilege has occurred on the campus. A student bumped into President Timkens and said "Who the hell are you?" The area of the incident has been closed until it can be properly sanitized.

A tailgate party will be held before the next football game on Saturday if the committee succeeds in stealing a pig. Our past success has been phenomenal.

Advertisement:

Typewriter for sale. Works normally after 5 p.m. if you keep it in the sun.

Advertisement:

Sleeping single in a double bed. Roommate wanted, either sex.

To: Student Stokehole
From: Jack Ripper, Assistant to Intern Gleep

Please do not tell the physician who heads this Service that I diagnosed your head cold as acute heart failure. I am allowed only one major mistake and 12 minor ones each week. I am sure that you will appreciate my predicament since I understand that you have repeated the freshman year three times.

The theme song of the terrorist section of the Malevolent Society is "He didn't steal that airplane. That airplane just followed him home."

The following note was reported to us by an atheist: Coach Mongoose's basketball team has lost every game to date. But God will take pity on them. Look for the next game to be fixed.

A gifted bioengineering student, trying to advance his status in the Malevolent Society, has developed an ejection seat for the desks of teachers. Woe betide the hapless instructor who is delivering the expected substandard lecture. In rooms without windows and doors at expedient intervals, the projectile velocities need more study to avoid flying instructors from damaging the ceiling.

President Timkens' comment was first a grunt and then "This is an idea whose time has come." He would like the administrators to test the system first.

Student Lecture in the Political Science Department:

In the war on drugs, all the drug warlords should be induced to change to pinstripe suits and have several dark maroon ties. This is the first step in switching from guerrilla-type operators of bandits residing on the wrong side of the jungle to becoming agents managing federal handouts on the right side. History favors this solution. In the present post-Crumble era, one only has to read about HUD, Savings and Loans, and sundry other high-return activities that maintain a basic complement of beautiful people in the peaceful, affluent neighborhoods. The communists don't seem to learn this as well; they just bash each other and learn to live without caviar.

The Comic Editor of the student newspaper was ordered to come up with five pages of funny by the next issue or hand in his keys to the washroom. He says that he can only think dismal since his landlady threw him out and his typewriter after him.

At the varsity basketball dinner, Stubbed Toe, the men's coach, introduced Ms. Fearless, the new women's coach, as incandescent. He also noted that she is a known bitch and this quality produces good team discipline.

Ms. Fearless rose to the occasion. She poured her hot soup over Stubbed's head, observing that he, too, could become incandescent. Also, this substantiated his second point. She was pleased to be in full agreement with him, whereupon she sat down.

Student Groundhog has flunked 9 out of 10 exams in Alleyway Construction and the instructor doesn't want him anywhere near the cement mixer. He is suing the instructor and anyone else who was in the vicinity the day the alleyway caved in. He charges the defendants with career obstruction. His attorney has included damages for his client's pain and suffering, not to mention extra lawyer's fees for the impossible case.

Students are in no rush to sit down and let a lecture begin. The following conversation shows a refreshing exception to honored custom. A freshman at his first class in the College became increasingly annoyed at the instructor who was discussing some kind of nonsense to his secretary after the class bell had rung.
Student: Are you the teacher?

Instructor: Who else?
Student: Then start teaching.

The soup chef at the College cafeteria throws only those bits and pieces into his bouillabaisse which he has researched to be the winners in their natural habitats. The students claim that the soup tastes like it contains only the losers.

An impartial committee is being formed to determine the cook's fate. The cook says that he reserves the right to contest the membership. He is opting for persons with ageusia and anosmia (no taste or smell).

The ombudsman who arbitrates faculty-student complaints cannot come to a conclusion as to whether Instructor Witless is firmer than a custard with his students or an unregenerate killer. The class evaluations are mixed. A committee will be appointed to solve the question.

Dean Catcabbage, whose office is now on the 20th floor of the new tower building, received a parachute with an unsigned note "We suggest that you learn how to use this. Try it out with our compliments."

The Malevolent Society denies any involvement and they can always be believed. However, they state that any student coming up with the best reason for this nice present will receive a diploma that cannot be distinguished from a real one.

The Crumble football coach, a member of the Malevolent Society when he was a student, expressed his dissatisfaction with the decision of the referees in a game by urinating on the 50 yard line in front of 20,000 cheering spectators. According to the referees, they couldn't find a penalty for this in their book of rules. The coach said that he chose mid-field to prove that he wasn't biased.

A sad-sack student, Wee Willie Winky, not to be confused with a nice guy who we all know from Mother Goose, is in a serious dilemma. He had his former girl friend's name, Gwendolyn, tattooed deeply on his behind, in bright orange. But he is no going with a girl named Becky. He welcomes all suggestions except a derriere-ectomy.

This is a very old story but it happens all the time in Crumble. A horse died on Catastrophe Corner and a policeman was dispatched to make out a report. He couldn't spell Catastrophe so he dragged the horse to Hill Street.

Okie Dokie, senior class valedictorian, with all A's in his record, will not graduate this semester. He flunked CPR which he had practiced for one month on his roommate. But Eanie Meanie, a kicked-outee from the Health Service, and now the most vicious examiner in the College, brought in an asphyxiating flounder as the test subject. No makeup exams are allowed.

Male seniors were asked to wear suits at the Commencement exercise. Since a head count showed only two suits in the entire class, the deans recommended that the suits be worn in individual succession, starting the Commencement one month early and running six to eight sessions per day. Tailors will be in attendance.

An Instructor in Nutrition is on board, but probably not for long. In the middle of every lecture he tells the class to talk to each other, whereupon he proceeds to unwrap a ham sandwich and a pickle which he ravenously devours. His physical health is good, but we have yet to hear from Myron and Gleep, respectively, about his mental health.

There is a teacher in the next room who comes to class in overalls and with a pitchfork. He has hay all over him. The diagnosis will be more difficult.

Advertisement:

Pre-owned auto. 50 dollars. A rope is available for you and your friends to drag it out of here. The mileage is unknown but we can rearrange anything you need for later resale. Bring a pen so that you can sign our anti-litigation clause, because it could roll down a hill, with or without you in it.

The Friendliest Folks on Lower Main Street.

TOWN, GOWN AND ALL AROUND

It seems appropriate to start this report with an excerpt from the scriptures—and God addressed his unruly people and spake in thunderous tones ("spoke" was not yet invented in a meeting of high school principals) "The last thing I saith to you is thank God its Friday."

And while we have your attention: A minority person was buried in the Great Crumble Cemetery. All the dead bigots got up and left. The real goners rolled over.

Rip Van Winkle
Department of Physics
Dear Rip:

You are one of our rare Full Professors and we promote only geniuses to this rank. A review of your contributions shows that you have never discovered a universal law. Indeed, you have not yet discovered how to get to your classroom. Our computerized staff rater equates you with our garbage collectors, but they have a better service record than you have.

I am remanding you to our shops to help fix cracked sinks. If you succeed, I will no longer have to apologize to our Board of Trustees for your salary, except to reduce it so that it matches your creativity.

Repair the sinks or down the drain you go,
Smiley Timkens

Calamity Jane took the student anti-rape bus last night and

was raped by the driver. The College disclaims responsibility, saying that he stole the bus and has since departed for the valley of the unknown.

The brighter staff has compiled a list of people who should be isolated in a locked dog cage until they develop the smarts. Some of their offenses are listed below.

1. The dean who calls an obligatory faculty meeting at 5 p.m. Friday, the day before the Spring vacation. The known escapees can be axed at an appropriate time.
2. The chairman who calls department meetings at will, sending out notices the previous afternoons. The agendas, which duplicate exactly the problems that arose when universities first began, and with the same non-solutions, are argued to exhaustion particularly by those faculty members whose intelligence represents the least common denominator. At the seemingly useless closure of each item discussed, when the combatants are recovering their subcerebral energy sources, the chairman asks if there is further discussion of the item. This spurs on the lunatics and the discussion of the single item again goes on to exhaustion. The chairman repeats the call for further discussion. After another interminable period on the unsolvable question, whose answer would be meaningless at best, some unknown benign inertial force, which clearly needs more research, terminates the item.
3. The professor who is compelled always to come through as an intellectual, never changing his act. No matter what and where the discussion, he enters it, citing unknown but proclaimed authoritative texts and great historical persons. He never fails to gravely submit the final word on the question. He does this even if the topic is about tomato soup.
4. The above is the tip of the iceberg. Faculty members seeking revenge can send us more items.

Slum landlord Mildew is being sued by a student for false

advertisement. Mildew wrote that his house came with a pool. It did, but only when it rained, particularly in the living room. Mildew claims innocence since this is a question of semantics and its not his fault that for Crumble students English is a foreign language.

Mayor Slusher Weakling, at the last City Council meeting, delivered a Jeremiah concerning the fate of Crumble. If the trash gets increasingly mountainous in front, back and along the sides of Citizen Misfit's restaurant, the city will fall into a black hole. Slusher was reminded by a spectator, very smart because he was a graduate of Crumble, that black holes are only in outer space in the sky. Slusher replied that we could go both ways since the grease was flammable and was getting explosive. The Council voted to seek advice from an expert, obviously from out of town, and the item was tabled until the next full moon.

This is the big one. The Bursar will undergo the first brain transplant in medical history. He has been giving students their money back. The operation is still experimental in frogs.

Two music instructors, both in line for the single promotion spot in the departmental area of sacred music, just happened to meet in the gun store. Each admired the other's prospective purchase, with mutual compliments on the beauty and effective fire power of the weapons. They both left the store, got on opposite sides of the street, and killed each other.

The program for Catch Basin Cleaners is being abruptly discontinued. Horseshit Ridge High School has complained that it duplicated a course there in Sewer Trap Service. Front sewer hose reels along with the staff will be put on sale at Crumble as soon as markdown sales tags become available.

To: Myron, Sage of the Health Service
From: Despairing Chairman, Department of Philosophy

We need your advice since you are Crumble's greatest problem solver. We hired an instructor for unintelligent but compelling reasons. It is now clear that his neurons are totally short-circuited. How do we unobtrusively get rid of him while I still keep my job?

To: Chairman, with deep sympathy

If this fellow is a nice guy except for insufficient horsepower to connect his neural transmission, simply raise him to a position one level higher than he now has. Use all the right compliments. Admittedly, this will take time before he screws up the works, but his dismissal will be gradually understandable to everyone.

If the intended victim is both stupid and vicious, the formula changes. He should be elevated by the administration three levels above his intelligence. The faculty will scream since they should not be made privy to the plot, but the disaster will be quick and certain and the man's resignation "for health reasons" irrefutable.

I will keep in touch should the battle plan need revision.

To: Myron
From: Chairman, Department of Psychology

We have a member of our faculty who is a good teacher and scholar, but his behavior would be bizarre even in an insane asylum. Please advise us how to handle this problem short of vaporizing the character.

To: Chairman

Your problem is universal and its solution requires skill and dexterity.

The usual method is to palm off this type to an unsuspecting chairman elsewhere. You praise the lecher everywhere you go, especially to your best friends. Emphasize that he is an unusual team player and that you desperately want to keep him, but funds are being withdrawn from your budget.

When he is hired by another victim, absent yourself from all outside meetings until you hear that the next chairman has gotten rid of him by the same technique

Our roving reporter went to the staff dining hall and he eavesdropped the following conversations:

At President Timkens' table, his sycophants were cautioning him not to tear down the old tarpaper barracks. They were worth millions in sympathy. The horrible scene caused state legislators to cry and then vote for funds. When the Governor came to town, faculty were selected to stand outside the barracks, hopefully in the rain, decrying the conditions inside which they said included eruptions of poisonous vapors and plenty of rats (borrowed for the occasion from the animal quarters).

At the next table, the usual professors were engaged in Nobel Prize talk, at decibels calculated to catch the attention of Timkens. All kinds of discoveries were evaluated with authority and many were verbally trashed because they didn't quite come up to the present professorial standards.

At the far end of the room, next to the steam pipes, the unproved faculty peons were in animated discussion. They knew the batting average to three decimals of every baseball player in the big leagues, from 1935 on. They knew who had a sore shoulder after each game and how this changed the odds of the bookies for runs in the eighth inning.

At a table where all women were seated because they were not yet in the race for promotion, the discussion centered on complaints about their maids. At home, the maids were complaining similarly about their employers. Some of the women worried about the antics of their husbands who had to take jobs 500 miles away.

Mayor Weakling has called a meeting of the Council to see if its members would consider selling the city. The 1910 fire truck needs replacement and this would produce bankruptcy. Weakling says that he has an alternate possibility. He contacted the Mayor of Horseshit Ridge who might buy the fire truck since his village is just coming into the twentieth century and the match would be perfect.

English is a complex language. Today's lesson is the "double entendre." Assistant Professor Hagfish, who hates grammarians, answered a sign posted on the bulletin board, reading "We will take care of your plants while you enjoy your vacation. Our guard dog will let nobody else in." Signed, Honest John.

Honest John and the dog did a remarkably efficient job. When Hagfish returned, the plants and everything else were taken care of, one might say completely. Where John and they disappeared to has not been ascertained.

Our reporters get the news just when it happens and sometimes before. This morning, a crook sold President Timkens' house to Dean Ollie Underbright. We will report more on the action when the President comes home this evening.

The Athletic Director has the foolproof system to protect himself when he gets fired—which is an eventual certainty. Every week he invites an outside seminar speaker, ostensibly for the enrichment of his staff and there is no question that they need it. The key to his industry and planned success lies in the Director's careful selection of those visitors who could facilitate his quick getaway to another haven when the jig is up at Crumble.

The Great Crumble Press has published an important book called "Strategies for Promotion." This informative tome tells how many Brownie points a nauseatingly ambitious faculty member can expect by various bootlicking maneuvers and at what level each tactic should be employed. This taradiddle is a must for any staff member who could easily be unemployed.

Students Ooey and Gooey, who were acclaimed to be the most blissful married couple in the College, had jobs as Teaching Assistants in the Chemistry Department. One day they had a furious argument in the laboratory, hurling beakers and sundry equipment at each other and even at a stray dog. The students proceeded, in accordance with time-honored Crumble custom, to throw them out of the window. The students later explained to the Chairman that this accelerated peacefully the completion of their assigned laboratory exercises. The Chairman agreed that the students acted with logic and precision. Ooey and Gooey have been reassigned to pasting pages in torn books in the basement archives of the library, Ooey in the cold-storage area and Gooey behind a furnace.

Ancient Proverb: Don't praise the day in the morning.

The nation's leading anthropologists convened at Crumble to consider Professor Knockwurst's finding that his 12 years of local digging in the city dump gave 90% proof that man evolved from a rat. The convention ended with the conclusion that the only 90% proof was the alcohol that Knockwurst consumed, shrinking his brain.

Nobody knows what to do about the fellow who keeps roaming around the campus with a powerful, battery-operated searchlight. He says that he is a descendant of Diogenes and is looking for an honest man.

Mr. McRooster, Professor of Dead Birds

Dear McRooster:.

Your published birdshit has piled so high that it has created a severe shortage of paper on the campus. Since paper is currently worth much more than birdshit, I am ending this letter abruptly. You can fill in the expletives that I had to omit, on your living room wall.

Not your admirer,
Anonymous starving English instructor
(This paper was stolen from the supply room.)

To: Clogged Gravy, Instructor in Food Destruction, Home Economics
From: Dean Dingleberry

I am pleased to appoint you officially as a role model for our subthreshold "you're probably finished" students.

We selected you because you were such a perfect match. Depending on your results, application forms to rejoin the faculty are available in this office.

To: Wooden Nickel, Consultant in Global Finance
From: The Editor, Student Newspaper

I will publicly apologize in our editorial column for referring to you as an imbecile. You are a terminal idiot.

To sell ice cream, it is de rigeur to put an entirely unintelligible name on the container. This obviously improves the taste. No Splinters Chopstick, creative Assistant Instructor in Economics, has joined the game. His ice cream has the name "Yoogna Schlimaerna." The nationality is never-never land and totally untraceable, even by the CIA.

The women with little children are complaining to the City Council that there is no place for them to sit down at the park. The benches are occupied by unemployed, sleeping Ph.Ds. The women want the bums removed.

Dense Cloudbank, known as the most sullen and disagreeable

member of the faculty, smiled yesterday. He was rushed to the hospital by his colleagues. A neurosurgeon will open his skull at once to determine the cause of his new strange behavior. We hope that a brain tumor is not producing this mental confusion.

A blue-ribbon panel of investigators from the State legislature questioned the College Bursar about continual disappearance of funds. One panel member asked the Bursar if he was personally involved. The member was summarily dismissed, with the words "Social Disgrace" stamped on his wrist. The other members expressed their deep apologies to the likely suspect for such unseeming conduct of their panel colleague. The meeting was adjourned with the official conclusion that the missing money undoubtedly vaporized in the hot temperature of the storage vault. The Bursar was thanked for his loyalty and cooperation.

Dean Dingleberry may have to evaluate seriously an incipient insurrection at home. When he finished a 15-minute invocation at dinner last night, his five-year old great granddaughter was heard to say "Mother, let's fry the old bastard."

Priscilla Prig, most upright faculty member in the College, has a sign on her door:
No Eating
No Drinking
No Smoking
No Sex.

Underneath the sign is an anonymous student's rebuttal: But not necessarily in that order of importance.

Child Psychologist Suboptimal leaves his sandbox at 3 p.m. sharp every day, goes to his cubbyhole to play with his treasured bear, then proceeds to his long nap. Equally predictable is the custodian who awakens him with an unmistakable clarion call and evicts him from the building.

Last weekend, a night not to be remembered occurred at President Timkens' home. The wine steward's assistant forgot to hose down the cellar and the dry corks allowed the wine to evaporate from three bottles of $5,000 Chateau Rouget 1962 (Pomeral) vintages. The international banquet for visiting highest level dignitaries had to be topped off with cocoa, and the welcome sign "Enjoy—Buon Appetito" had to be removed. Timkens would like the culprit to be indicted on a charge of Murder 1, but the District Attorney has been unable to find a precedent.

We hasten to report a trivial event that occurred directly following last night's Zoology seminar on "Reciprocal Altruism," which is an extension of evolutionary theory. The term implies an exchange between partners that benefits both of them. It was best exemplified in front of Zoology Hall when two of the professorial speakers shot each other dead.

Updating Mythological Creatures of the World:
Egypt: The creature Ammit was a composite of crocodile, lion, and hippopotamus.
Greece: The Centaur was part man, part horse.
Crumble: Dean Catcabbage—Pick your own mixture, but be merciful. Start with the knowledge that his cow had a nervous breakdown.

Agriculture Consultant Quackgrass was arrested on Christmas day following the complaint of his wife that he threw the refrigerator at her. He was just about to follow this up with the chandelier. Quackgrass is suing the Crumble police on the grounds that they severely restricted his ability to practice his religion on a holy day.

We like the story of the man who fell through a roof of a bank that he was trying to enter and rob and then sued the bank for failing to maintain its property or to post signs indicating unsafe avenues of entry, especially after dark. The story arouses local sympathy since it is consistent with the thinking of any fair-minded Crumbletonian. Our College attorneys hold that negligence on the part of the bank is obvious and that the safety of our criminal citizens is no less important than that of any honest man. Our Political Science staff say that it is guaranteed by the Constitution.

Tired Bullshit, which is the only pseudonym that his outnumbered enemies will use for him, is considered by administrative and faculty consensus to be the great communicator of the College. A true Daniel Webster. He always speaks (while wrapped in Crumble flags) of the outstanding accomplishments, most of which could not have happened without his unfortunate absence from his own work in order to give his sagacious advice to the Administration.

Tired's most noteworthy current contribution is to the Crumble public schools. The term "first grade" will be eliminated and all pupils will henceforth start with the second grade. This academic advancement should act as a catalyst for the rest of the country.

A new faculty member in the School of Education wanted to know what the difference is between the Departments of Higher and Lower Education. He asked the right man and was informed that Higher Education is on the top floor.

English As A Foreign Language

Administrative-ese: The Vice-Presidents hosted a banquet in Hawaii to interest manufacturers of inflatable chairs to locate a branch in the Physics Department at Crumble.

Translation: The dinner was superb and a good time was had by all.

Everything in Crumble is tilted downhill. Even the Great

Crumble Whorehouse is up for sale and its occupants need to be relocated. Buy one and get one free.

To: The Ombudsman (who rights all wrongs)
From: The Misunderstood Minority

My fellow students in the Theater Department have taken a solemn oath to castrate the Director, and to ovariectomize the next leading lady who resorts to whispering when the scene gets emotional. The Director explains that this relieves him from all responsibility to set up a positive situation that we can all empathize with. This usually consists of the actress hollering. The reliance on a reduced air pressure from the larynx of a supposedly overstressed heroine is unnatural and certainly a bit much for the sensitivity of the auditory apparatus of those listeners whose hearing is in early senescence. To worsen their problem, the interference of accompanying music isolates them completely from the production. This is of course merciful if the fiasco is put on air and a commercial follows.

Additional Floss While We're At It:

An issue somehow arises each week which stirs up students into two major camps plus sundry subdivisions. A quiescent period for too long is ominous and occasionally lethal. Windows start getting broken downtown, potential rapists surface, and the spell ends in who can break the most noses, students or police.

The student newspaper is the most effective instrument to create a controversy of most probable current interest and to catalyze inane letters to the editor until some force in physics called inertia is balanced by a force in biology called fatigue and this results in a short period of silence and convalescence.

A controlled cycle will now be a function of the College

Mythmaker. He or she will stir up a whole mess of imaginary troubles at appropriate intervals corresponding to natural biologic rhythms. The mythmaker's permanence will depend upon whether a high administrator escapes from being an unfortunate centerpiece as a result of the mythmaker's concoctions.

The Mythmaker has also been selected to create at least one new buzzword per week. He could foul up the universal language of administrators except for the fact that buzzwords fall into obsolescence when the authorities at national meetings act as erasers by creating a new set.

The Seminar

An invited seminar lecturer from out of town spends 55 of his allotted 60 minutes defending the validity of his methods that brought him to his dubious conclusions. This gives the audience 5 minutes to attempt to discover what the hell he was talking about. Some months later, another researcher of great fame arrives and annihilates the methods of the first lecturer, then proceeds to his own grand fallacies.

Apparently, the truth is frequently as evanescent as the fellow departing on the next plane. But all is not lost. The seminar affords a great opportunity to fall asleep, if you don't snore. You also gain brownie points since your attendance reflects a burning desire to be right there in the forefront of the newest knowledge.

The premedical students, who enjoy crybabying their way through any course not requiring a stethoscope, kidnaped Tutor Chickenscratch, Coordinator of Remedial Writing in Chemistry. This is a required course in the Department. Chickenscratch told the Dean that in accordance with the normal curve in his course, he flunks everybody but two students. He explained that he is performing a public service. One is that there are too many premedical students. Their elimination will supply manpower to fill the urgent need for pants pressers, fence viewers, and people still called janitors.

The Dean observed that student numbers are equated with power and therefore the student repeaters will greatly improve Chickenscratcher's chances for promotion. He also noted metaphorically that love is better the second time around.

Our observant reporters have intercepted this intercontinental message:

Deans of the world unite! Fendrick Poltroon has overdone his denigration of our genetically determined positions in the cosmic scheme. Add the proposed teachers unions to this and we could be equated with faculty.

Rush your donations to Crumble. With this fund we can hire a hit man to castrate Poltroon. His Robin Hood attitude could become cataclysmic. We have established a Super Cerebration Committee to conjure up eloquent platitudes against the unions.

Councilman Pandemonium of Horseshit Ridge came up with a barnburner to rescue the village from its impending disasters of every description. The solution is so simple that it borders on greatness or insanity, depending on which side you're on. All the towns within a 500 mile radius are to get together and form one megalopolis. This will be the largest territorial city in the world. There is only one difficulty. Nobody is paying the slightest attention. Pandemonium has been advised locally to enter a stage career and play the role of a confused herring.

Defective Gene
Tutor in Genetics
Dear Defective:

Your complaint that you were not listed as one of the 37 multi-authors of the book "Chromosome 21," brings tears to our eyes. However, if you read with a magnifying glass the fine print on page 2, you will see "et al.," and you can bet your boots that you are in there someplace. We might retrieve this with computer assistance.

Any author of our books must be held in esteem by people other than pygmies in at least two other colleges. We found one professor at Crumble who fit this category and we listed him as an author even though he had nothing to do with the book. You obviously understand this logical explanation.

We regret that your "blood, sweat and tears" will produce only a greater loss of these vital fluids and you could wind up in the Great Crumble Hospital, tied to a gravity bottle for indefinite transfusions.

If you could discover something, let's say like the Superconducting Super Collider, we might in a flight of fancy consider putting your whole name among the first 20 in a manuscript.

Happiness is anonymity,
Forby Doo Doo
The Great Crumble Press

Councilman Elfish Deliverable agreed to sell the Crumble city hall to an out-of-town farmer who wanted to use the building for cold storage of apples. Elfish told him that the structure was an abandoned barn. The farmer is suing Elfish for failing to close the deal on the date stated in their contract. Elfish counters by noting that the Mayor has taken to sleeping in his office and it would be difficult to awaken him and explain what was happening.

The manager of The Red Stool, where you play Russian roulette when you eat, is seeking legal advice as to whether he can refuse admission to customer Hogwash. Every evening, Hogwash orders the red plate special, then goes to the potted plant and buries it there, chants a short prayer from the bible, returns to his seat, and empties an entire new bottle of catsup into his plate, which he slurps up and then exits.

Hogwash insists that everyone is entitled to life, liberty and the pursuit of happiness, especially life. He intends to stand between the food and the poison center at the hospital, for the benefit of all. The Board of Health will present him with a bottle of pasteurized milk on Good Citizens Day.

There is nothing to match a cause for murder in the mind of a wife of an assistant instructor with a 30-year service record who has to sit at an obligatory banquet honoring his chairman who has just returned from a paid trip around the world. All this while she is watching the Dean's wife, who is seated at the elevated head table, gnawing triumphantly on a turkey leg and occasionally beaming laser-type glances at the peons below.

At the customary brouhaha last night, in Psychology Hall, when the hootenanny was at its height, Diomedes Cornfritter, Instructor in Rehabilitation, rearranged one eye and two teeth of Hobbit Herman, Instructor in Optokinetics. Hobbit says that he sees north and west simultaneously. It has some advantage in visualizing what his teeth are doing. He is seriously considering dismemberment insurance prior to the next meeting.

To: Reticent Rolf, Assistant Instructor
From: Dean Catcabbage, Agriculture

All faculty in our College except you have contributed to the fund to plant scallions in front of President Timkens' waterfall. The faculty challenges you to match their donations. In this College we meet all challenges fearlessly.

To: Dean Catcabbage
From: Rolf

I just adore the buzzword "challenge." All patriots thus addressed should meet the common enemy with swords, pistols or, in this case, with cash.

This is the seventh in the series of different challenges that I have received from your office this month. Being a peaceful man, I would prefer to let the warriors rise to the challenge. However, I will compromise. I challenge you to increase my salary which hasn't changed in three years. When I receive the increment, which should be later this week, I will personally plant a scallion anywhere around the waterfall.

The "Committee for Pure Rainwater in Crumble" has just discharged its advocate, Foot Dragger. Foot claims that his battery acid is more fit to drink so he is setting up his own business and selling his water to the Great Crumble Grocery. He says that the Committee is angry because it didn't think of it first. An arbitrator is being selected from the Chemistry Department.

The quotation used to characterize recommendees "I recommend the applicant with no qualification" has divided the interpreters in the English Department. Since English is a foreign language in the Mathematics Department, its faculty have remained aloof from the controversy until the sentence can be converted to an equation.

Ms. Muffin Marshgas, Tutor in Chemistry, had an argument with Dean Underbright and bit his ear off. At the court hearing, the judge reminded Muffin of the city leash law. Muffin will be restrained indefinitely with a dog trainer holding a rope around her neck when she comes to work.

To: Dean Dingleberry
From: Professor McRooster, Department of Zoology

Your letter, which lacks endearment, informs me that I cannot hire a biologist to teach the course in Evolution in our Department. Evolution appears to be a non-four letter, dirty word, at Crumble. I see, however, that there is an ample supply of recently hired career bananas hanging from trees, waiting for a so-called course to be created which they will profess to teach. I will restrict all further remarks to dead birds for which there is no controversy.

The following is a conversation between two instructors in Victorian English who were summoned to the office of the College ombudsman to adjudicate their differences.

Alleged victim: I was quietly having lunch in the cafeteria when that guy came along and shit in my breakfast cereal.

Obvious criminal type who would do it: You will observe that the defendant has no grasp of Victorian English. I will couch my statements in elegant language. For no reason he came after me with a low-slung hatchet and attempted to cut my water off.

Ombudsman (showing the wisdom of King Solomon): Here are two loaded guns. Go down to the town dump and see if you can kill each other simultaneously.

WISDOM OF THE AGES FROM THE POLITICAL SCIENCE DEPARTMENT

When you are elevated beyond the number of your neurons to a high political post and you proceed to screw up everything, buy a clean shirt and necktie, comb your hair so it doesn't face downward, practice looking very honest, and make a television appearance. Immediately following some introductory inane statements in which you wish the entire world good health, say "I'll take responsibility for the whole mess." BUT ... never utter the second half of this statement, which is "Let the punishment fit the crime." You could land in jail. Also, consult lawyers to make sure that there is no punishment, particularly if your buddies have not shredded the evidence. In that event, owning up to your bungling will have everyone crying in resonance—unless you have snitched a loaf of bread for your seven children.

Alumnus Cracked Dome once wanted to be a neurosurgeon, but he changed his career to a commercial airline pilot. Somehow he can no longer find a copilot brave enough to fly with him. He has already bankrupted several airlines. He says that he may change his specialty to rehabilitation, with special reference to suicide prevention for the destitute. His current diet of slow-speed squirrels has kept him in caloric equilibrium for the present.

Eric Bulbsnatcher is giving a seminar to the maintenance personnel on "How to keep the electrical equipment from short-circuiting your career." Although Eric stole the title from sources that are reputable, the uncontrollable display of aurora borealis-type sparks should be awesome. Please bring helmets, visors and fire axes. Also, prepare to run for your life.

The Crumble Administration has made a momentous decision to patent Dean Underbright. His super capacity for bumbling has made him a unique vehicle among the primates for the study of the mechanism and unexpected effects of stupidity. Our beloved College always has another first.

In spite of Underbright's incapacity to join the human race, President Timkens refuses to drop him in the nearest dumpster. Timkens reminds one of Lyndon Johnson's refusal to fire J. Edgar Hoover on the grounds that he would rather have him inside pissing out than outside pissing in. (Editor's Note: Somebody told us that this statement should be credited to Abrahma Lincoln.)

Dean Catcabbage does not want Dean Underbright, who is his worst enemy, to survive at Crumble. Catcabbage has dreams in which he wrestles Underbright. Just as Catcabbage pins Underbright to the mat and asks him to say "Uncle," Catcabbage wakes up. Catcabbage says that this is very unsatisfactory and he is looking for a dream doctor to solve his problem.

Vice President Shadrach, one of whose biblical ancestors was reported to have come out of a fiery furnace, has disgraced his proud genetic line. He fired Wildwater Rapids, the most gentle staff member in the College, simply because Wildwater used the electric pencil sharpener without signing in.

Wildwater, in his first known fit of rage, says that he has irrefutable proof that Shadrach came from a surrogate mother that was a rat. When Timkens heard of the dispute, he said "So what's new?"

A cardiologist at the Great Crumble Hospital has added to

Crumble's never ending advances. He is the first anywhere to have a disorder that he calls "negative three-pillow orthopnea." He places his head three pillows below his feet which permits blood to flow from his ankles to his brain as the need arises, which is every half-hour. This allows him to keep working and to make decisions in line with what is expected of any cardiologist in this gravitational position.

Visiting Assistant Instructor Cloudburst is very proud of his best student, Purple Fish. Cloudburst has advised Purple to go to a graduate school and for his thesis develop an ultrasensitive balance that will weigh pros and cons. Cloudburst says that this will be a benchmark in the promotion of multidiscipline research.

Oat Fungus, Assistant Diener in Curricular Development, is always in the forefront of scientific advance. He bought a home computer and in accordance with accepted practice he uses it as a doorstop.

Wahoo, an electronic genius, invented a remote control device that cuts into the lectures of people he detests and it says "Don't believe the son of a bitch."

Letter to the Editor:

I am an efficiency expert on the State Board of Education and in this diatribe I propose that the teacher is an unnecessary obstacle in the college curriculum. His role as a crutch to the students diminishes their responsibility to learn anything by themselves. He gives administrators a headache. He comes home unfit to live with his spouse, usually peaceful if she has been de-clawed. Take away his textbooks that someone else wrote and throw his notes out of an auto while on the crowded expressway and he is reduced to basic idiocy.

Upon reflection, I suggest that you forget the whole matter since nobody agrees with me.

Permanently banished professor

To: Permanently Banished
From: The Editor
I agree with your last paragraph.

Research Student Muckworm has been asked politely to evacuate or get off the pot. His thesis has been to quantitate how long "Two shakes of a lamb's tail" are. Muckworm has been deliberating for two years about what kind of an instrument he should use to attack this elusive problem. Muckworm's major professor claims that he never heard of him.

The new psychiatrist, who claims to be the real Numero Uno, and can trace his lineage as the 195th descendant of the Sabbatei Zevi of Izmir, will assume the Distinguished Lectureship Chair in the-Defectology Section of the Psychology Department as soon as he passes the insanity test.

Instructor-Designate Fulvous Overdose, who was just hired at Crumble, delivered his pre-arrival seminar in which he decimated all critics in the audience by such rebuttals as "The research by internationally famous Professor Wellsaid has exploded any vestige of the truth, if there ever was any, in what you said," or "Your theory was last heard of by a proponent banished on a raft in 1614."

Stockroom Assistant Felix Failure was fully up to Overdose. Felix stated "If the speaker had read this week's article on prehistoric poisons in the Journal of Folk Medicine, he would have found his same talk, but with the prescription "What to do when the charlatan arrives." Felix asked to be excused so that he could go outside and vomit. He believed that the absorption of all the bullshit into his digestive tract might just lead to some incurable disorder.

The Trustees have approved the construction of a bombshelter that is for the exclusive use of the deans. They are the most likely targets at Crumble when the eventual riot occurs. Assistant deans are on their own. Vice Presidents, being more remote from the scene of the crimes, although comparably culpable, will have more time to plot their escape route. The shelter will be stocked with dean-type food and toilets.

The Zoology Chairman had a rough time yesterday at the educational television station. He began his talk with brilliance by observing that the most characteristic property of bone is the fact that it is hard. The more brilliant station manager broke in to announce that due to an unforeseen but now obvious problem the remainder of the half hour would be filled in with chamber music.

There is some disturbance among the administrative personnel. This is due to Daphne, the wife of the newly appointed Sociology chairman. Daphne is the daughter of the 18th Duchess of Diddlydump and she is used to serving hot scones and tea to about 50 acquaintances every afternoon. She sends the bill to the College Treasurer whereupon he goes into a quasi epileptic attack and has to be restrained by being placed in a harness that has been set up in his office. The Malevolent Society has advised the Treasurer to have cockroaches planted in her pantry and await the outcome serenely.

Dr. Thirstbuster, Desert Physiologist, has sued the Crazy Crumble Chronicle for stating that he is a graduate of CCJC. He has since been a victim of taunts and titters at national meetings. The College has sued Thirstbuster for his involvement in worsening its ignominy. The Chronicle editor, Derailed, retorts that the

College and Thirstbuster are matched perfectly, like ham and eggs, and the Chronicle could come to no conclusion other than it did.

The judge was last seen in the worm store, buying bait for a long fishing trip which he expects will last until his boss changes the venue in which he should have presided. The local anticipation is greater than that which occurred when the fellow who was peddling recycled gargle from the back of a truck was found to have AIDS.

A frog fell off a beam in the animal quarters and bounced off the head of a five-term freshman. The frog was badly injured. A resuscitation team from the local anti-vivisection society must be applauded for reaching the scene within minutes.

The City Council has sealed off the "Evacuation Route," the fastest way for people to get out of town when the buffaloes come rampaging through in the breeding season. The street is now being cleansed with compressed oxygen.

The students freely translated the street sign to mean a free public toilet. The English Department refuses to accept the blame, but its chairman, Language Mangler, is in deep trouble.

Transparent Noodle
Maintenance Department
Dear Transparent:

Your book manuscript, "Boom Boom, Bang Bang," has an appropriate title and I like that. It sounded exactly the same when I threw it out the window and it landed on a passerby's head.

If you should decide to take a stroll on the campus, you may, with misfortune, re-collect the pages if you determine the wind direction by holding up a wet finger.

Kiss-off,
Forby Doo Doo
Editor, The Great Crumble Press

We submit the following just to prove that we have done our homework today:

One sheds real tears when one loses one's own money—from Decimus Iunius Iuvenalis, 60 to 117 A.D.

We keep finding letters to Myron since our trash collectors have gone on strike. Here is another tidbit:

Dear Myron:

I have been advised to have a brain transplant to correct my inborn stupidity. Should the surgeons use tissue from other donors or from what might be non-stupid sections of my own brain?
Flooded Dory

Dear Flooded: The disadvantage of your own brain as donor is that you would most likely reinfuse stupid cells and worsen the problem. This is a good possibility judging by your letter. Stay as you are and become a high governmental official.

President Timkens is facing a serious challenge from the new Chancellor Greedy Gumbo. Greedy knows how to spend money, if it isn't his. In his last position, he had a $150,000 salary plus a paid mansion, an auto and a maid. He made a fatal mistake. He paid 25 cents one day driving the auto through a toll booth and he submitted a bill for this to be paid by the college. When he found out that he might be shot one dark night if his paid assassins could figure out how to get away with it, he disappeared with good logic and surfaced, you guessed it, at Crumble.

The marriage counselor has his own problem with the syndrome, "ménage a trois." He has a male lover with whom his wife is also in love. (We choose not to pursue this in a book as nice as ours.)

Crumble was hit by a tsunami (catastrophic water waves generated by a volcanic explosion). The disaster occurred when the Chairman of the Geology Department dropped bombs into the Great Crumble River to vent his rage because he wasn't allowed to fire his superdumb secretary. The Dean will somehow try to solve the problem so that Crumble will no longer be in danger of gravitational collapse.

Academic Rules for Beginners:

Be careful not to break the immutable law of academia that one must never raise his voice above a universally acceptable level in any formal faculty meeting, even if you are being crucified. The transgression upsets sorely the administrator conducting the meeting and it could precipitate a neurologic disorder.

The penalty is that the criminal's name is held in the shit-list file of all administrative offices until the criminal dies. In fact, clearance can be granted only when the undertaker informs the appropriate dean that the body has been pumped full of embalming fluid.

At that point, a eulogy is composed, extolling the untimely death and extraordinary accomplishments of the dearly departed; this is easy to write since standard forms are available.

Disease Pot, a Crumbletaurian who is always in the forefront of every local epidemic, now has to sit in a specially designed portable second balcony chair which she steers along a mountain-type cable in all assemblies at the College. Additionally, her "Disease of the Month" is posted prominently on campus bulletin boards.

Endless Dishbuster
Pantry Butler, President's House
Dear Endless:

We are impressed with your credit record so that we are extending an invitation to you to come to France before the crowd does and purchase at an unbelievable price the most promising property and landscape in the entire country.

This prize is the Palace of Versailles. You are among the upper six finalists to receive this offer. There is no need to bring your wife. She will be surprised at your good luck.

Rest assured that your presence in person to claim the Palace will be greeted with intensity. Indeed, even shots may be fired.

Your best friend,
Sawtooth Filch, President
Gangho Realty Corporation, Worldwide

Dear Myron:

My boyfriend is ordinarily very lovable, but on occasion he beats on his chest shouting "I am Tarzan" and he then proceeds to change the area that he thwacks mightily and he beats me up. What is my next step? Unresolved Coed

Dear Unresolved: I have to consider seriously what a wag once said. "God created your friend on an off-day." He has acutely fulminating attacks of megalomania. Find a coy female who is also a prizefighter and match them up. Tell her to carry brass knuckles just in case the situation deteriorates unexpectedly.

To: President Timkens
From: Lustrous Lunchmeat, Horse Farm

It's about time that you packed your toothbrush and headed for Mexico—permanently. We need a new leader and I fit the job admirably.

To: Lustrous
From: President Timkens by way of his downstairs janitor

I was asked to reply to you. We are referring you to the sad story of Icarus who soared too close to the sun and damn near lost his wings.

Next week, which gives our Business Office time to process your departure papers, we are soaring you to our Marco Polo branch. Bring your long underwear.

Our roving reporter has submitted the results of his sidewalk interviews with random passersby. He asked them what a noun and an adjective are. One person asked if he was talking about a sick horse. An English teacher from Horseshit Ridge High School said "Whaddya, some kind of a nut?" Our interviewer left abruptly because the police were closing in on him for insane public behavior. He says that he now knows why the name "Grammar School" was changed to "Elementary School" or other lowly titles.

And while we're at it, the Principal of the Great Crumble Elementary School was the speaker at the cap and gown Commencement exercises for those who completed the first grade. He deplored the early dropout rate, especially the fact that he could be unemployed if some of the pupils didn't someday get as far as the sixth grade.

Nothing compares with Crumble's emotionally charged and highly spirited student torchlight parade the night before the football game of the year against Fawchee Subnormal.

All alumni, students and guests were invited this year to breakfast with Dean Dingleberry on the morning of the game. Only three persons showed up. Fortunately, the Dean didn't have the slightest notion as to what year it was and he was in a semi-coma until late afternoon.

Michelangelo Brushswiper, who was appointed Artist-in-Residence on the faculty because his first name proved that he was great, is now suing the College for threatening to throw him out, mercifully feet first, when they find out where he disappeared to. His attorney says that his greatest achievement was painting LADIES AND GENTS, THIS WAY on toilet doors. The defendant agrees fully, stating that he painted these signs with the flourish of a great master, baroque style, and this puts him in the category of a timeless genius. Prior to his vanishing he had painted on his office door KEEP THE HELL OUT in boldface characters, no flourish. He is without doubt a versatile painter.

Aesop Bugzapper, Researcher in Entomology, has received several major grants for research since he demonstrated how to reduce the number of shoo-shoo flies in his kitchen. He eats steaks only at the major hotels with his endless travel funds (public money). This week his wife summoned the police who threw him into the slammer, effectively preventing him from catching the next plane outward bound for a convention in China. His wife's complaint was that she paid 30 cents a pound more for steak than he allotted in her budget (his money, of course). She had to spend that night in the home for battered women.

Surplus Stool, Expert in Diseases of the Anus, may never be able to publish anything again outside of Crumble. He wrote that book reviewers are pygmies who never completed fully what they should have done in the bathroom. The residue has to come out in their critiques even without the benefit of prunes.

Unopenable Fly, Consultant in Health Education, is an easy person to locate. He is in line for some sort of a medal. Unopenable is a toilet dweller and he had a private telephone installed in the privy since he uses it as an extension office. All personnel, which includes administrators, staff, students, and even attendants with whiskbrooms, must converse with him in the men's room, between locked doors and only between Valsalva maneuvers (look it up).

Dr. Flubbedydub, a spare-tire type cardiologist at the Great Crumble Hospital, examined a 96-year old woman and gave her an appointment for her next visit two years later. We admire his bold approach and we intend to use him as our physician.

The Marriage Counselor claims to have an infallible, 10 second, noninvasive test to check whether two prospective marriage partners should go through with their marriage plans.

The Counselor presents the following so-called joke to each of the two individuals: "If two are company, three get egg rolls." If both laugh at this, they are perfectly matched, most likely at a high-grade moron level. If only one laughs, the other should leave at top speed. There is also a false positive where neither laughs.

The debate between Professor Righteous Flagwrapper, by consensus the "Great Communicator (GC)," and Assistant Instructor Dilly Dally, the "Great Procrastinator (GP), " was declared a draw. The subject was "Who would you prefer to be with on a desert island?"

The conclusion was that GC was all bullshit and a yard wide. Anyone with him would freeze or starve, worsened by the mental torture endured just by listening to his all-smiles drivel, delivered non-stop during the death throes.

The GP would emit a different type of bullshit. Freezing and starving would occur, but amidst solemn promises of "Leave it to me," after which both parties would quietly expire.

The talk by the Psychology janitor, entitled "Is There A Difference Between A Troublemaker And A Pain-In-The Ass" will be the central theme of the departmental colloquium this week. An in-depth presentation is expected since the janitor has had long experience with the staff and miraculously has never had a fist fight.

The FBI may have to be called in to investigate the Photography Department whose Chairman advertised "Let Us Blow Up Your Mother."

The staff members of the English Department haven't yet translated the statement of the court defendant "To the best of my recollection, I cannot remember anything." The Mathematics Department still cannot reduce the remark to maxima and minima simultaneously so they are staying off the battlefield.

Crumble's new roving sports announcer is sensational, He gets to the scene of the action while it is in progress and tells the roaring crowd how he sees it. The following will exemplify how good he is:

The rodeo (The Crumble senior has just been thrown violently off horse):

The announcer on his foghorn; "Did you observe the skill and the grace of the rider, especially during his triple somersault? He deserves your kudos. Clap, clap, clap, everyone."

The victim (twisted like a pretzel from a bakery going out of business): "You sonuvabitch, call an ambulance."

Or, at the regatta (The captain of the Crumble Sailboat Club has just been hit by a loose boom and is using the breast stroke with his good hand to keep from drowning):

The announcer (right there in a powerboat and directing his foghorn to spectators on the pier): "What a captain! Did you observe his remarkable parabolic trajectory as he went flying toward the water? Let's all give him one or more rousing cheers."

The victim (to the announcer): "I'm drowning. Get a rope. And when I recover, I'm going to kick the shit out of you."

Hematologist Leucopenia, who comes to the Health Service when it is too wet on the golf course, was nominated unanimously by the Deans for the "Great Teacher Award of the Year. " The students, prior to their weekly riot, said that they had no recollection of ever seeing him in a classroom or even when they were ill. Leucopenia retorted that since he was a person of considerable humility, he was refusing the nomination, but he recommended that it be given to his best friend, Dean Catcabbage. President Timkens announced from on high that the award will be postponed to the next century.

We want to update our readers about Whitney, the unregenerate son of Infinite Grace, Consultant in Flower Arrangement. Whitney has been expelled from several reform schools and he has been locked out at gunpoint by several others. Infinite's friends are using their influence to get Whitney back in. They are dressing him in rompers, a bow tie and a Tyrolean hat with a feather to outmaneuver the admission officers. We are all hoping for the best, for the community at large.

Alpha Hydroxy, Diener in Chemistry, appeared before the City Council to explain how to deal with pollution in the Great Crumble River. His masterful presentation started as follows:

The River Crumble is again emitting its noisome vapors. The effluence of 100 years of overflowing sewers deposited in the slimy sludge bubbling with its gaseous emanations in the river bed gives off its stewy effluvium from the shallow, drought-sluggish waters; boaters abandon their boats and the citizens give voice to their angry lamentations.

At that point the presiding officer informed Alpha that all members of the Council had forgotten that they had other appointments. He, himself, had to go to the bathroom.

A graduate of the Forestry Department at Crumble who was hired to cut out tree stumps is being sued for leaving holes in the ground. The defendant claims that he is following accepted practices of the Tree-Stump-Cutters Union. If he touched the hole, he could be shot by the Hole-In-The-Ground-Fillers Union. The judgment is going to be a close call.

Student Flinchless argued that of two conflicting answers he gave for a quiz question, one turned out to be correct and he should have received full credit. The English staff said that this is not the way to write a book. The Philosophy staff disagreed and said that all sides of a question should be considered until exhaustion causes all the participants to go home. The College attorneys said that weasel wording protects the client from self -admission of guilt and they referred the beleaguered instructor to the Constitution. The Physical Education staff said that the instructor's decision should be based upon the size and physical potential of the student for bashing in the instructor. The Mathematics staff, always reliant, said that if the student ran a business, the profit he gained by being right half the time would be offset by the losses suffered in being wrong the other half. The net gain would be zero and that's what the ignorant bastard deserves. Q.E.D.

Our own beloved Myron, always cerebrating at high gear, has updated his method of evaluating whether a staff member has a proper sense of personal importance. If he is present too often to teach his class instead of being in London or Tokyo, one has to suspect a flaw in his character, not to mention a misplaced sense of duty. It is always necessary to obtain a grant, with 90% travel funds. If something should happen to this system, such as some obnoxious outsider trying to shift the available funds to unwed mothers or similar situations, the pandemonium among professors could be earth-shaking.

Dean Dingleberry is in a quandary. Someone is sending him very absorbent underpants and he doesn't know whom to thank. We suggest that he observe very carefully who is now sitting closer to him at his bridge club.

To:All Staff
From:The Janitors Union

From now on, all elevators will have padded walls in the Psychology Building. The instructors have been beating the shit out of each other during the ascent particularly. The residual debris is just too much.

Intern Gleep's new research patient, Stockroom Assistant Savage, may make Gleep famous. Savage's ferocity, especially to full professors who he chases down the hallway, has been unexplainable. However, Gleep imaged Savage's brain and found that several tomatoes were growing there and were much larger than what was conceivably a brain. The discovery could supplant hydroponics. It may never be duplicated except that Gleep is prescribing tomato seeds to an experimental group of freshmen. In a former experiment, Gleep prescribed apple seeds, but his subjects got cyanide poisoning and are all dead.

Wife of a member of the Board of Trustees: All my husband's friends are crooks.

Wife of a Crumble vice-president: My husband is one of his friends.

Advertisement from a Writer's School:

New authors wishing to upgrade their skill, i.e., their capacity to contribute to a black hole, are upscalable by us. Our graduates are authorities on the antics of dorks who have even become television stars. Such success permits our writers to fall into the delusion that they are employed.

To: Professor McRooster
From: Smiley Timkens

Don't get power-mad. At the present height of your power, the only way to go is down. Even presidents learn that their secretaries have a much longer survival time.

Further, don't protect your staff too vigorously. Your certain demise almost always comes from within. Your supporters will sympathize with you for a period of time predetermined by local custom.

To: Lefty Louis
From: President Timkens

We regret that we cannot hire you for our legal staff. You should not have brought your sawed-off shotgun to the interview.

To: President Timkens
From: Modred, Provable Descendant of King Arthur

In response to your flip remark that I shut up since I don't own the Department of Psychology, I will continue to let you know that my side of the case is right. I have no interest in the other side.

To: Modred
From: Timkens

Since you appear to know only one side of your peers' opinions, I hereby with responsive logic demote you to one-half of your current rank and salary. I have consulted the Mathematics Department and I have been advised that when ratios are equalized, as above, all balances are preserved. As always, you will observe that I try to treat both sides with quantitative fairness.

Harvey Crocked, Manager
The Chateau Crumble

When I checked in last night, your bellhop lost my baggage, apparently forever, just from the front desk to the second floor. I have to give a lecture this afternoon to the Ladies Association for the Purity of American Speech and all I have on is a pair of dungarees with several holes in each knee. I am also unshaved. As soon as this message is delivered, I shall rush like a fullback into your office to get paid. I promise to kick the shit out of you if payment is not forthcoming in full and ass on the table. Have an ambulance standing by just in case you're thinking about getting argumentative.

Justice will surely prevail,
Smedley Bonkers

The College cafeteria is becoming a mecca for sightseers. If you can get under a table and stay quiet, you can dependably catch an unrehearsed performance of the campus cops chasing the poorer students who have just stolen the shoo-fly pies or, if you can tiptoe unseen into the International Room, you can see a Central American commie chasing a former general's son while threatening the latter with an open bottle of Tabasco sauce.

The Economics Department is not too popular at present. It recommended to President Timkens that to firm up Crumble's financial picture the College should follow sound business practices and sell off the dogs, particularly the Psychology Department. These services could be provided better by the Bacchigallupo School of Riveting. This might allow the cash cows, i.e., the Economics Department, to provide more milk. Timkens is busy trying to prove that there are any cash cows at Crumble.

Ms. Silly Putty, Crumble's fairy tale analyst, has irrefutable evidence that the frog claimed to be kissed by a fair maiden upon which it changed to Prince Charming was actually a tadpole at the time and only attained froghood when the fair maiden had already been cremated. There is also the version in which Prince Charming kissed the fair maiden and turned into a frog.

Edgar Glut, Crumble's leading inventor, in fact a genius, is going broke and is joining the Crumble faculty which will allow him to keep his family in wheaties. His last invention didn't excite global recognition among the jet set. It consisted of gold-plated toilets surmounted by digital read-outs which warned the occupant how close the spray was rising to his keister. A previous invention, fireproof egg cartons, also failed to live up to expectations.

Advice from the old pro:

Never make your office too comfortable or inviting. It is a sure-fire prologue for seizure by a crony of your boss. According to current statistics, you will be moved nine times in four years following your first fall from grace. Your office will be downscaled each time until you get unceremoniously fired. The higher you are as an administrator, the more important it is to keep the expected schedule in mind. Close to your seventh move prepare to advertise the sale of your twin-engine Cessna and your 48-foot sailboat.

College professors generally are downscaled to 10 x 10 foot rooms, no window, where they remain if they are tenured until their cerebral degeneration just equals that of the dean.

Psychiatrist Madwort at the Health Service has adopted a dog, but the dog refuses to acknowledge it. It is urinating messages on the window, hoping to catch the attention of the police.

From the Great Crumble Hospital:

Mangled Glob, Instructor in Health Education, is totally immobilized by both Parkinson's and Alzheimer's diseases, but he is otherwise in good health. (Our comment is "Mirabile dictu" and it doesn't matter if you can't translate it.)

At its sixtieth reunion, Chuck Glockenspiel was elected Class President. He wasn't seen or heard of in the entire 60 years so he is the only one who hasn't developed any enemies.

And while we are at it, the class members will have their meeting in bed, feet slightly elevated to bring blood back to the brain. The tea dance has been canceled. Even the tea may be a bit too stressful.

An entry, whose authorship we have been unable to find, is interpolated at this point because it can titillate those with a perverted sense of humor. The substance is that a cockroach in the Animal Quarters asked to see the Director.
Director: "What is your complaint?"
Cockroach: "We've got ants."

> *(NOTE: We have great sympathy for the Director. Recall the great Animal Quarters famine of '59. It was he who asked the rabbits to distribute the lettuce.)*

The Crumble Faculty is now forbidden from joining the City Fitness Walk. The faculty members fall into holes or, somehow, trees fall down on them at least once during the Walk. The more legitimate ambulance customers, especially the repeats, are complaining that they can only get busy signals on the telephone.

Caveat emptor: Inept Sheatfish, the Economic Department's consultant in pitfalls to avoid when purchasing a house, paid $50,000 to repair his own home. The 93-year-old vendor guaranteed the repairs for life. Unfortunately, Inept failed to read the fine print on the contract that it was the vendor's life, which Inept discovered when the vendor died three months later.

Instructor Meatball and his wife are not going to take the twins, Yummy and Yucky, to eat out any more. While dining at a restaurant on the pier at the Great Crumble River, Yucky fell out of the window and was luckily fished out of the river by a fellow who was on hand because he hadn't yet caught his quota of catfish. During the confusion, Yummy thought it was great funsies and he jumped into the river. Police sirens were screaming and people were running with nets all over the place. When tranquillity was eventually restored, Meatball was kicked out of the place and warned never to return.

The choral group in the Music Department has been banned from further appearance on the campus. Their singers, who have taken the classical Athenaeum name "The Bullfrogs of Aristophanes," sound too much like their name. Their collective croaking is discouraging students from majoring in the Department.

From: Chairman, Department of Log Rolling

In order to take the course called Log Rolling, it is mandatory to take six prerequisite courses in this Department. This explains why the final course number is Log Rolling 701. We submit this explanation here so that students will not be confused.

Assistant Instructor Hypnopompic
Department of Astronomy
Dear Fellow Scientist:

We are pleased to invite you to join the Cosmic Society of Famous Astronomers. This invitation has been limited to 50 astronomers in the world.

Our journal "The Sky Is Falling" will keep you current with all the happenings in the solar System. You will receive the first three issues at 10 cents per copy, after which the price will rise imperceptibly until it reaches 25 dollars per copy, this could take another six months but it is necessary to maintain our prestigious headquarters. Your initial savings are incredible.

Superb Snook
Chief Executive Officer

Dear Superb Snook:

I have now been a member for three months but I won't be for the rest of forever, As far as I am concerned, you can relabel your journal "The Sky Has Fallen." I can't even find Mars in any of the pictures.

Don't send any more of this crap because you will pay the return postage. If more of us great scientists do this, you may even have to give back to the repossessing Sheriff the red carpet leading to your desk.

Officially a non-participant,
Hypnopompic

Our archaeologists just uncovered tablets from Mesopotamia written by King Teetertotter. Message reads "Harem sweating. More ice blocks needed in fornication suite. No taxes involved; read my lips."

To: Quarterback Nawrocki
From: Your Coach

I cannot honor your request to keep you in bread for being on our team. As you are aware, our college does not pay athletes. I do vaguely remember seeing something that looked like a bundle of hundred dollar bills buried under the north edge of the 12 yard line. Feel free to look into the situation. Please do not make little hillocks since our playing fields must stay flat.

Ms. Fatling, who prefers that nobody translate her name too literally, has just won the Happy Slurper Award in the cafeteria. The cook is trying to prevent her from entering the Bean Soup Contest.

The Chancellor had a reverse self-fulfilling prophecy. He

dreamed that a stockroom assistant beat the hell out of him. The next morning he found himself on the bedroom floor and he heard his wife tell the maid "Let's get the bum out of here. He's late for signing another rule against the faculty."

To: Dr. Mottled Enamel, Dental Division, Health Service
From: Smiley Timkens

This is another incident at Crumble involving your attempt to fill the wrong cavity of a coed. You are banished to a vacant tent near the steam tunnels until Intern Gleep tells us that you have been castrated. The medical punishment is light and also curative. In regard to your new living quarters, remember that Pythagoras, the light of Magna Graecia, lived for a time in a cave.

Fantoe Fleabane, who for 20 years stacked packing crates at the Maintenance Department, got bored and went up to the roof to commit suicide. He fell off just as he was about to change his mind, but a stiff breeze came up and he soared as nice as you please to earth, to the cheers of the plumbers and electricians. Fleabane's credentials are now impeccable and he will soon become an associate dean.

Crumble is always looking for a first and is very successful in obtaining its unsuccessful choice. This time the Wicked Witch of the North was hired. She will be the new Weather Woman. Clucks and cacophonic screams will be heard on the hour in accordance with Crumble's democratic principle to keep everyone on campus fully informed. The Witch should be a howling alternative to the humdrum chimes of the chapel.

The Chairman of Philosophy has been asked to write a historical account of the accomplishments of his Department in the last 25 years. He has been leaning over his desk for two days without food or water and he is still on the upper part of page 1. Everyone else on the staff has mysteriously disappeared and there are no volunteers. The offer to rent the Philosophy building to make jig saw bushings still holds and it may have to be accepted.

The Malevolent Society sent a surreptitious note to Dean Catcabbage that one of his faculty members was lucubrating continuously. The Dean called the culprit in and fired him. At the subsequent meeting of the grievance Committee, the Dean was told that lucubration means to undertake scholarly study until late in the night. Catcabbage has been sent to Horseshit Ridge High School to take freshman English until a sophomore tutor signs a release for him.

A student president of the senior class in the School of Education was assigned to formulate a class motto, using Latin to prove that the students were educated. The president, who was secretly a member of the Malevolent Society, chose the imperative "Arbellite" which the Romans translated to "Let's all masturbate." Dean Underbright wrote that he completely embraced this motto because it could be trumpeted at high decibels and with a sense of macho. The class could open all its meetings by bellowing this masterpiece of creativity.

Following the expected leakage to the press, Underbright had to do penance, first by sending three months of his salary to a starving group of nomads at the north pole. Secondly, he had to put an advertisement in the local newspaper stating that he was applying for certification as a full fledged idiot and he might not even be qualified. Underbright said that he didn't know any Latin; the class president added that Underbright didn't even know shit from shoe polish.

Farthington Bullrush, State senator, demolished even his most vociferous critics at the College political forum this week.

Farthington glibly quoted his initiation of public projects that he never heard of himself, but these were in the woods where the audience never went. He would even cite the most detailed costs of the mythical projects, for example, 12 million dollars and 36 cents. He hadn't the foggiest notion that he could be 6 million dollars away from anything that might possibly have happened, but neither did anyone else. The audience agreed that he was superman and worthy of reelection forever, maybe even longer. The Chairman of Political Science, a self-proclaimed expert on politics, says that Bullrush is so good that he would have to be invented.
This Week's Lesson on Strategy and Tactics from the War Department:

If you are coming to Crumble as a high administrator, there are alternative paths to follow in your relation to the faculty. The first is to do anything you please, pretending that the faculty doesn't exist. In this route, roughly estimate when you will be kicked out. However, you may be able to take only a few years at Crumble. Also, very few other institutions that you may want to escape to will ever ask the reasons for your demise and your best friends, if you have any left, will resemble you so closely that they will lie appropriately.

The other route is to regard everyone in sight as a happy family. To encourage this, tell them that you prefer to be addressed as Chuck, Bud or Buzz—although never with anything beginning with a Z—even if your first name is Igor. You will also be kicked out and statistically this will take about the same time as though you followed alternate path 1.

We may have referred previously to the professor who had two speeches and he gave them all over the United States. If two colleges on his route were less than 50 miles apart, he alternated the speeches. Since there are well over 3,000 colleges in the country, the professor has been extremely busy and we can update our report that he hasn't been seen in Crumble, even by his wife, for more than three years.

Lame Duck, Instructor in Economics, may have to change his department to English. His students complain that he is teaching mythology. Lame retorts that he studied with the best geniuses known, the economists in the White House.

A great ship is steaming up the river to the Port of Crumble. It is carrying relief cheese from Africa.
(Editor's note: It's Friday afternoon and we had to clean the room, which explains all the trash above.)

Travel agencies are about to advertise trips that include London, Paris, Rome, Amsterdam and Crumble. Rave notices extol Crumble as being a newly-discovered part of the prehistoric past that no sophisticated traveler can afford to miss. Special rates are offered to anthropologists, archaeologists and clam diggers. There is a word of caution; serious bible students should stay away. Unlike Sodom and Gomorrah, Crumble has not yet been destroyed by fire.

Our creative career counselor has devised a simple one-minute test to direct a student toward an occupation that should be most fitting for him or her. The test consists of the following question: What words in your judgment describe what trait is most essential in your proposed choice of occupation? Do you possess the appropriate traits? A few samples of this innovative test are listed below.

Physician: Some empathy; good golfer
Judge: Lofty; likes children
Teacher: Good vocal folds; hates children
Store clerk: Undiscoverable; mean when caught
Automobile dealer: Poor mathematician, initially superfriendly
College dean: Keeps wrong company. Redemption possible

High school principal: Likes secretary to run school
Marine captain: Usually charges up wrong hill

A janitor crossing the campus and carrying a crate of bananas to an administrators' meeting bumped into Dean Dingleberry who asked the janitor how his wife and family were. The janitor was so overwhelmed by this conversation with a super-being that he fainted on the spot. Dingleberry beckoned to two passing students to drag the janitor over to the water fountain and dunk him which he read was appropriate therapy and he continued his walk, hardly missing a stride.

The campus trash collectors have discovered that Downstate University has been depositing its wastes nightly on The Crumble campus. Nobody ever noticed the difference.

President Timkens, in his usual superior capacity as an arbitrator, has recommended a compromise. Either blow up any Downstate garbage vehicle approaching the campus or charge hopelessly inflated prices per ton, cash on the barrelhead. The Trustees will finalize the choice. There is talk of Downstate using laser weapons to penetrate the barrier.

Mismatchum Malarchy, who is heavy into research, says that he is the undisputed authority in Crumble on kavakava. Malarchy is a firm believer in being undisputed and if another authority shows up, Malarchy will change his specialty to smallpox in Triassic apes. There is a problem. In the light of Malarchy's unique capacity to continue the discontinued, he might start an epidemic that never existed.

Malarchy has a friend, Emeritus Instructor Peanutbrittle. He does what you expect a friend of Malarchy to do. He buys hopelessly unpublishable manuscripts and processes them into packing for bird nests.

From the Department of Economics:

We emphasize this month's dismal prediction by falling back on two well known jeremiahs:

(1) We agree with anonymous graffiti that the future is not what it used to be. And

(2) As the butcher said, the wurst is yet to come.

Forby Doo Doo, Editor
The Great Crumble Press
Dear Mr. Doo Doo:

Because I always take painful deliberation in assessing a book manuscript as a reviewer, I needed two years to return this evaluation. I hope that you remember my name.

The title of the book, "Mack the Rat," is a bit provocative and I recommend the more youthful title, "Mickie Mouse." Since the prospective readers are not biologists, nor much of anything else, they won't know the difference. Also, because the entire book is an indecipherable smorgasbord of trivia, the title could just as well have been "The Psychopathology of the Earthworm. "

I recommend that the book be published in loose-leaf format so that the reader can easily shred for cat litter any section that unduly enrages him. This will all the more quickly minimize our increasingly useless trash problem.

I abhor swearing unless I do it myself and the book abounds in this substitute for paucity of language. To clean it up, I have deputized my 7- and 9-year-old children as associate editors to locate obnoxious passages. Even though their mother is worse at swearing, this book has variations that they need to verify in dictionaries for literary accuracy. Having now cleaned this up, the book is presently 99.8% pure, like Ivory soap.

I considered making paper airplanes out of the manuscript pages and throwing them at our occasional house guests, but some of them carry sidearms and could retaliate.

I suggest that we have an editorial party, all dance around the mulberry tree, throw the manuscript pages up in the air, then collect the pages in whatever disorder we find them and send them as is to the printer. Ample nude pictures thrown in here and there would divert the usual reader from the text and the book could become a best seller.

A review well done, wouldn't you agree,
Ferdinand Lower-Bound
Adjunct janitor

To: Students who talk back
From: The Health Service

If hit in the mouth by an angry dean, carry all your knocked-out teeth in a wet handkerchief or placed under your tongue to our dental service. We are usually very busy, so we suggest turning your face and presenting your skull to the killer dean. A concussion is more amenable to treatment. Moreover, being dinged may not interfere with your customary performance. There is an additional advantage: dementia pugilistica is better than shock treatment or lobotomy in improving your behavior when confronting a dean bigger than you.

There are rumors that a vice-president has defected to the Malevolent Society. We can only wait and see. The fate of the whole College hangs in the balance.

The Board of Trustees has designated Prime Mildew, who has been at Crumble 18 years, to be the first tenured student. You can be sure that he will serve to the best of his inability.

According to the laws of thermodynamics, if you attempt to spray carbolic acid on a marauding cat at your garbage can, it will run at high speed away from you while members of the local antivivisection society will run at high speed toward you. The effects of a collision among all three participants has not yet been worked out. It would make the usual master's thesis.

Keeping your cool while under severe stress (from the Home Economics staff):

Did you ever try pouring ketchup liberally on your expensive steak while a waiter royally garbed in a tuxedo is staring at you?

There is violent controversy about appointing Wonky Flushbox, currently Director of Latrine Safety, to the position of Vice-Chairman of Philosophy. The Administration declares that the faculty who oppose Wonky's appointment are a cult, bigoted, self -serving, plus an additional laundry list proving without a shadow of doubt that they are incapable of comprehending the ideals of entrenched interests.

The faculty who are supporting Wonky are said to be brave, intelligent, far-sighted, and possessed of all the known virtues. The students couldn't care less since they never heard of Philosophy.

Since Wonky's rise in the hierarchy represents an administrative appointment, the neutral faculty know who is going to win and they expend no calories by getting involved in the great debate.

Physiologist Fogged Diaper says that orange juice is of no known value and should be discarded as a food. He bases this startling conclusion on the fact that orange juice failed to inhibit the stretch reflex in a crayfish claw.

Decision making (from the Labor Relations section of the Economics Department): You are a student in an instructor's class and he employs you by the hour, for the first time in his home. You agree to be extremely careful about his treasures. In your high level job at mopping the floors you move his antique roll-top desk which has been inherited through seven generations of his famous ancestors. The King of England has personally autographed it. The legs of the desk fall off and the entire desk becomes unglued. All you can see is lumber everywhere. What is your next move? Do you ask your employer to pay you for that hour?

A more complicated case: This is about the student worker who was hired to mow the lawn of an instructor who lived on a hill overlooking the Great Crumble River. The student was riding a just purchased, very expensive tractor. He was piggy-backing his girlfriend, lost control and he, his girlfriend and the tractor went at high speed downhill into 80 feet of water.

The girlfriend is suing the instructor for destruction of her jumpsuit, loss of her contact lenses, and she wasn't sure where her bra went and at what time. The student "worker" who has several bumps on his skull has a separate suit claiming that there were no written instructions about what to do in the event of a disaster. The instructor is in a dilemma about the cost of retrieving his tractor. A diver and a rescue ship may be necessary.

The saddest case yet: This is about the premedical student, a waiter at the College cafeteria. He was fingered to serve breakfast at 6 a.m. to a visiting delegation of medical school deans of admissions.

The student, who was a sad sack that it had to happen to, tipped over the table, liberally spraying all the guests with an assortment of goodies including egg yolks, jelly, sausages in grease, all topped off with nice hot coffee and cream. The student gave CPR to one dean with heart trouble and the fellow died.

The Economics staff say that the student's chances of getting into a medical school are worse than a snowball in hell. The odds are somewhat better in the Caribbean.

State Veterinarian Braunschweiger in a seminar to the premedical students explained that the size of a textbook is often inversely proportional to what is actually known about anything in it. If a disease has been thoroughly investigated, a couple of lengthy paragraphs characterize it fairly well. If a disease is not well known in cause or treatment, a 1,000 page book is devoted to lying about its contents.

A citizen living a block away from the Crumble city hall refused to stop insisting that the building depreciated his property and particularly when the City Council was meeting in it. Mayor Slusher Weakling obtained a subpoena to haul the citizen into court for municipal defamation of character. Other charges are obviously in the making. The citizen didn't gamble on "good-old-boy" justice at the courthouse and conveniently disappeared. The mayor is considering hiring a bounty hunter to fetch him back.

The Mayor enjoys round-table discussions of worldly importance. He speculated whether it would make any difference if the world population of college presidents decreased by one. The city attorneys, Muck and Mire, at the round-table were fully up to this. They advised the Mayor that it would be like a spit in the Great Crumble River.

From the Physics Department: If you are up in a satellite and think you are catching a cold, call NASA. They will come right up and take you home.

The Great Crumble Insurance Agency is one of the city's proudest assets. When your auto has just been in a collision, you will find the insurance agent under your car just as you crawl out (if the car isn't wrapped around you). As soon as he brushes off his new Brooks Brothers suit, he will have you sign a release form while he gives you a check to cover all the damages including your statement that you have suffered a bad back.

Psychology Lecturer Obtuse is quantitating the sensitivity or grossness of people by their behavioral responses to what he has set up as 10 levels of humor. His base level is as follows: In a family outing a man watched his mother-in-law fall off a cliff, swearing every inch of the way to the bottom. The man nearly died laughing. If you respond similarly, you are a low, crawly rat, probably genetically unredeemable. The other nine levels are under research.

According to Mudslinger, a member of the Malevolent Society, Dean Quackgrass would be of much greater value to the College if he were transferred as chicken flicker in the henhouse at the Agriculture farms. The Dean responded by firing a warning shot across Mudslinger's ears. This is a time-honored custom that the Dean once learned when he was cleaning cannons in the navy. We doubt that the chickens or he will be derailed from their usual pursuits.

The Political Science Department has scheduled a debate on the topic "Which group is the greater threat in Crumble, the illiterate slobs or the literate crooks?" The representation in town is about equal and a noisy crowd is expected.

The educators have done it again. Following a national meeting in which intense cerebration occurred to find a reason for the meeting, it was agreed by acclaim that all teachers should be monitored for the number of gesticulations they perform in any one hour lecture. These include body-swaying, arm-flinging (the excess of which, if you use one hand, is called hemiballismus), and also oblique and other rotational movements of the head beyond a critical value called sine theta. An excess number, agreed upon by the national experts, could be cause for dismissal from the faculty. The entire staff is now practicing restraint, although the penalty for absurd movements by the students, e.g., throwing spitballs, sending up flares, sleeping over desks with their heads inclined more than 45 degrees to the horizontal, and other usual student maneuvers, has not yet been addressed.

Did you ever notice that when the crazies initiate their new pronunciamentos, they sign their names with large bold-type flourishes, fully expecting the names to appear in a hall of fame along with the signers of the Declaration of Independence.

Somehow their names never get under a glass case in a museum. As the stupidity of their actions gets increasingly obvious, the whole venture very quietly dies. Somebody spirits away the documents with the names on it and nobody can ever remember that any such actions existed. If a troublemaker keeps bringing up the subject, the disclaimer is that they were historically displaying the proclamations of King Louis the XVIth.

There is an 80 year old Assistant Instructor in Physical Education who has an infallible test to determine if he has Alzheimer's disease. Once a year his wife asks him the same question that she asked the year before. If can answer it, he's home safe.

Botany Instructor Water Hemlock has aroused the ire of the Malevolent Society by giving one of its members an F (failure) when he deserved an F+ (high failure).

Every morning when Hemlock bicycles to his class and is riding at full speed toward the large fountain in front of the Biology building, an inclined ramp is thrown in his way. Hemlock and his bicycle travel predictably in a parabolic trajectory which ends in the center of the pool around the statue of the fellows who invented the pill. Hemlock always emerges soaking wet and two minutes before his class meeting. It is useless to pick up his water-soluble notes.

The Society in its usual spirit of merciful forgiveness believes in a limited period of punishment, but incrementally. This logically explains why the members sent Hemlock a rubber suit and diving helmet, prior to total cessation of therapeutic behavioral management. He will be watched to see if his facial muscles suggest repentance for his crime.

President Timkens has declared Ephraim Null, Instructor in Symbolic Logic, to be surplus property. This makes Ephraim available to anyone crazy enough to bid for him in the annual auction of disposable State property. Since Ephraim points his legs in one direction and his brain in another but refuses to retire, Timkens' action should solve the problem. Timkens charges that Ephraim's wife has to leave him in the Kiddie Corral when she brings him shopping with her in the Great Crumble Supermarket.

Language Mangler, Chairman of the English Department, is in danger of being mortally attacked by his listeners if he continues in his evil ways. When a staff member comes to him with a problem, Mangler proceeds into a profound discussion in which he never finishes any single sentence, but upon approaching the ending which might just conceivably make sense, he switches to another thought. This continues interminably until the exhausted faculty member escapes from the room.

Mangler is not without creativity. His second ploy is to plunge with unceasing vigor into a sentence which, if it were in writing would fill two typewritten pages. During this unbroken monologue Mangler puts the verb(s) somewhere in the sentence where the deciphering could occur only by sophisticated computer analysis.

Acrimonious Sadie, who for years cleaned the President's office, lived up to her name, particularly since she was granted special immunity and executive privilege. Many a vice-president precipitously fled the office when she assumed battle-ready position with two mops, not one. The only person she didn't outrank was Vera Scrum, Trusted Administrative Assistant.

President Timkens' advisory staff, ordinarily your typical goon squad, did not escape Sadie's wrath and in an uncharacteristic fit of realism they searched for a solution to the first part of the problem which was to shut her up.

McRooster, Professor of Dead Birds, was put on the case. McRooster was once an authority on evolutionary theory but he was excommunicated when he became a creationist. However, remembering his high school biology, he concluded that Sadie may have descended from plethodontids with freely projectile tongues. On this remarkably observant deduction, he exercised option 1. This was to surgically mobilize her tongue indefinitely by slamming the door on it while it was in full protrusion. Sadie's subsequent silence has been gratifying. Since McRooster's had to be silenced also, he was granted an eternal leave with full pay.

New magazine from the Journalism Staff: This staff is enthused with their new creation "Non-Sparkling News." The first issue will carry choice items that every knowledge-hungry (or is it knowledge-thirsty?) professional person needs to know to maintain a meaningful conversation at dinner parties. A few samples of the best wit of the writers will whet your reading desire:
The dull life of a college professor
The duller life of his once exciting wife
The even duller than that life of a professor's student
How to avoid the first 55 minutes of a one-hour seminar, any subject you name

How to match gloves in the chemistry laboratory with the horrible effects of given percentages of sulfuric acid. This alone is worth the price of the magazine since there are nine glove models with choices of six different materials to protect your skin for 20 seconds against enough of the fuming acid to knock your respiratory system out of commission before you can glove up. Some people lose interest in continuing the search. The next issue of the magazine will come out if the Department has not been disbanded for losing money.

The "Best Teacher of the Year," selected by consensus of a faculty committee whose members were carefully selected by the dean, has disappeared. His students said that he was so bad that they would vaporize him if he showed up just once more. At his last meeting with them, several of the students came in with blowtorches.

Crumble administrators are in confusion in hiring a fellow who says that he is a Nobel prize contender. He is real big at meetings, but his wife, who is about to kick him out, is flunking him.

If we get too many more letters to Myron, we are going to start charging him for the space:

Dear Myron:

I have not seen any of your smart-aleck remarks for some time and I wonder if you are now dead. If unfortunately otherwise, I have decided to put the finishing touches on your superego. My silencer is, "How high is up?" Disloyal

Dear Disloyal (and who the hell cares?): The answer to your hackneyed question is just too simple, "You will know when you start to come down."

Special meeting of the Aristotelian Society:

The Head Honcho started the meeting by stating sternly that time is precious and all the participants stated that they needed to get back to their lectures on time. He repeated this interspersed with other nonsense for about one-half hour, ending up hoarse. This forced him clinically to introduce the first speaker. Nonsense #2 followed in which the speaker repeated the need for brevity, taking about 10 minutes in this venture.

There is always the summary of the Head Honcho in which it is the custom to repeat just about everything said previously. Then in the interest of the preservation of democracy every person therein is polled to see if he has some of his own infinite wisdom to add. Usually, the members present have to send messengers to their class to cancel them due to the unforeseen gravity of the meeting. The students and janitors mark this as a positive contribution and go downtown to see the pornographic movies.

Horseshit Ridge High School is hiring five principals. This policy is now in fashion, however, and Horseshit Ridge will not be last if the benefit is sufficiently dubious.

Our research economists say that there are two ways to look at this. One is that the teachers have no way to win, one against the magnificent five. They are busy concocting impossible scenarios during their executive breakfasts while the teachers are busy ducking erasers or other flying objects in their classrooms. The positive aspect is that the expected disaster that any single principal could dream up alone requires four other principals to prevent or quietly bury.

To: Stuck Hingescrew, Master Carpenter, Maintenance Department
From: Smiley Timkens

Although you know more about building a dormitory than our architects do, your fist fight should have been restricted to the meeting in the Administration Building. Your subsequent extracurricular battle on the sidewalk in which you threw two of our architects into the frog pond has earned you no kudos with my advisory committee whose members respect rank faithfully and always vote for slowing efficiency but equalize this with logic by promoting catastrophic disasters.

Your statement to the architects that you know five times what they do is nonsense since five times zero is zero. If you had somehow figured out how to divide zero by five, you would have come out infinitely better than them. You are obviously deficient in mathematics which necessitates recommending a tutor, to start immediately and as you would expect at your own expense. I am also recommending a professional pugilist to upgrade the viability of the architectural staff. Striving for such evenhandedness is the hallmark of a superb president.

The Safety Inspector has had too many accidents and is taking no more chances. He now takes his psychiatric afternoon nap in a horizontal desiccator cabinet on the eighth shelf, covers himself with a Class A fire blanket, and puts on his bright orange, biohazard gloves.

To: Cinnamon Monomaniac, Executive Secretary, Brakes and Shock Absorber Laboratory
From: Tiger Pelopidas, Titular Monarch of Civil Service Personnel

The secretaries in your office complained to me that you are treating them as if they were a subhuman species. Let me remind you that by protocol I am the only one empowered to do this.

We are making a sign for you to be posted prominently on your desk. One side will face your staff and the duplicate message on the opposite side will greet incoming visitors. A preview of this message will give you time to calm down and assume your new role:

Cinnamon Monomaniac, of recent unsound mind, due most likely to a misbehaving gene, locus on chromosome unknown, do renounce my errant ways, especially to the lovelies in my office and they may feel free to walk up and over me to reach their typewriter tables. They may leave any unfinished work on three days of their choice and particularly on Friday afternoon to visit their hair dressers. I will finish the overload, all smiles and to their critical satisfaction. Following a six-month probation period, I agree to genuflect before each one of them and request a position commensurate with my new talents.

The dilemma: Who do you quickly consult when you hear that somebody in talking about you said, "I've got him between the cross-hairs."

Loopy Pointless, Visiting Assistant Instructor in Chemistry, is trying his best to attain a place in the Crumble Hall of Infamy, another one of Crumble's firsts. He has this semester flunked 98% of the class, all premeds, who will now have to apply to medical schools in the Caribbean.

Dean Dingleberry's advisory group, a veritable think tank, is certain that Loopy has a killer gene and that he have it out or leave. Loopy has acquiesced to the group's demands and he will enter the Great Crumble Hospital where a molecular biologist who thinks he's a doctor will undertake the sequencing of Loopy's genes. Prior to this, the Nobel-type biologist will spend the entire next year on a shake-out period to see if anything works on his analytic instrument. There is no telling what he may ultimately churn out of Loopy's chromosomes.

Advertisement: Candidate is being sought for a tenure-track position in Computational Non-Cognitive Aptitudinal Pseudoscience. Applicants with experience in Applied Vacuumology will be given preference.

(Editor's note: Our experts have tried to decode the above but sanity prevents any conclusion other than that the advertiser already has his candidate selected and no other need apply. It is clear that no terrestrial interloper can supply the non-credentials demanded in the job statement. This advertisement has a cat box odor.)

Personnel Officer to applicant: What one word best describes your innermost character?
Hapless applicant: Honesty
Personnel Officer (jotting down his evaluation): This applicant is nonpromotable. He has no idea of "collegiality" at Crumble.

The Health Service physicians report that Ms. Public Latrine, a freshman, has repetitive attacks of virginity. This is the only such case in their current files and is worthy of an article in the Student Journal of International Misbehavior.

No Return, once a conductor on the trolley line between Crumble and Bad Eggsville, has been hired as a pilot for the newly formed Great Crumble Airline. He owes his success to his experience in never failing to collect a ticket and also to the fact that only three people fell off his trolley in 20 years. Airline workers are removing trees and relocating houses within three miles of the airport, any direction.

Troubled Dogmeat, a five-fanged witch, has been hired to restore discipline at the Maintenance Department. Her first act was to immobilize the head painter and cut his water off. (Editor's note: She's never been near a water meter.) Morale must have improved since the whole area is extraordinarily quiet.

Notice posted on the door of a foreign student: Don't shut this door when it's not open. The student's tutor, offering a correction: Don't use a double negative in English. Your notice should have read, Shut this door when it's not open.

> *(Editor's note: This tutor teaches a course called English in the Fifth Century B.C. He is highly paid since this is a Crumble first.)*

The sommelier who guards President Timkens' wine cellar swears that he saw a woman with a hatchet in levitation above the best vintage barrels in the sacred underground vaults. The steward says that it looked like Timkens' seventh wife who Timkens banished because she asked him for a quarter while he was flogging a butler. Timkens is ordering that bear traps be placed all over the cellar.

The students pitched a dean out of the window during the Love Fest last night. The dean is still unidentified because in his disheveled state he looks like your typical student except for his statement that he is a dean.

The College is taking severely restrictive, punitive measures. The condom machines in the coed dormitories have all been padlocked. The local movie is cooperating by hiding its popcorn machines. Recreational sin will be very hard to come by until the criminals come forward and confess their part in the crime. The Malevolent Society denies any involvement, but its members wish that they had thought of it first.

Instructor Upchuck, who says that he is the world's authority in medieval history, has taken to strolling around the campus wearing a king's crown and a bejeweled royal robe. The cops haven't definitively figured out how to dismantle or invisibilize him. Their latest plan is to kidnap him and drop him 90 miles away in the Impenetrable Forest, with a six-month supply of nuts.

The Women's Temperance Committee is protesting slot machines and a condom dispenser in the foyer of Crumble's recently opened luxury apartment house. The Committee has filed a class-action suit in the Great Crumble Court. The owners retort that the Temperance Committee is limited by charter only to smash up bars and it is exceeding its designated mission. The students say that watching this will be more fun than trashing Main Street the next few weekends.

Mayor Weakling states that he and the City Council will have to be on an extended trip visiting nursery schools around the country and regret that they cannot help arbitrate the dispute.

Digression (and badly needed too): Untacked Fumblefinger, precision toolmaker at the Maintenance Department, is destroying all his screwdrivers in the electric buzzsaw. Please send him your old ones.

Home Economics has hired a "Restaurateur in Residence" for the fall semester. His first lecture will be on his revision of the Tyrolean Sub. This will consider in detail the pathophysiology of a mixture of creamed ham, pepperoni, provolone and hot chilies, garnished with strawberry ice cream. He says that he isn't to blame for what happens, but survivors of free samples will be granted free tuition if they can make it for the rest of the semester.

A fugitive race car driver easily eluded the Crumble constabulary, but he had no idea that he was going to land on his head on entering the normal mudslides in Horseshit Ridge. The natives say that his mistake was not stopping at the local tourist bureau to get avoidance data eliminating the village. Most strangers get an entrance permit which states explicitly that the village cannot be sued for what is going to happen to them.

Dean Dingleberry is sending a team of agricultural experts

headed by Consultant Billingsgate, once Misdirector of Public Affairs, to Rome. The experts will try to get an international agreement stabilizing the price of Italian tomatoes. The effect of this on world fertility will be the theme of a subsequent tidal wave of university administrators.

Illwind Boarfish, certified by the Political Science Department to be a competent anarchist, is being sent to find the reasons for disorder in Bongoland. This was once a tranquil region except for the mid-morning lions looking for a few people to eat. This mysteriously changed abruptly following Illwind's earlier visit there. Now, everyone ducks fast and shoots when entering a bar or restaurant. Illwind, the only experienced expert, will guide the impartial fact-finding team from Crumble.

A simple test of your capacity for logic:

It is scientifically possible to prove that an event can occur but not that an event cannot occur.

Would the less sophisticated reader and any logician who likes to fight skip the above and await more acrimonious statements that follow:

The foreign student who waded into shore from a raft and was assigned to be Teaching Assistant in Chemistry has been in trouble that has defied clarification until today. He placed his daily student grades in a container that was marked "Direct Deposit." The janitor (now promotable to Special Detective Status) found that this was a trash can for partially digested meatballs, left over coffee that suspiciously was not mountain-grown, and toothbreakers advertised as hard candy for the sophisticated palate. The course will start all over again on Monday, this time in English.

Flotsam and Jetsam, a pair of derelicts, presumably human (although this is debatable), have been hired by paleontologists in the Geology Department to serve as base controls, like Brand X, against which all other known vertebrates (species with backbones) can be compared. The major problem that may blur the data is that they refuse to get washed. The scientists are trying to coax then into an auto, top down, which they can run at low speed through a car wash equipped with a highly directive steam outlet.

Random thoughts while in a coma: Your reputation as a genius rises with your promotions to positions of increasing importance until your actions eventually prove that this should be in reverse. At this point you will settle back in tune with your appropriate wavelength in the societal spectrum.

Our most recently crowned Betty Coed won the first prize hands down in innovative costumes at the annual Halloween ball. She came dressed as herself in her usual classroom clothes. Representatives of the leading women's designers in the world are coming to see her. This is another Crumble first.

The secret has been discovered as to why the police at midnight had to fish Dean Underbright out of the bottom of a huge dumpster behind a downtown restaurant. The dean on his ascent was liberally covered with assorted garbage. Underbright had been summoned alone to a top secret dinner by President Timkens where he was ordered to torch the office of an unnamed professor in the Physics building. Timkens scribbled the professor's name on a paper napkin. Underbright, as usual activating the small number of neurons present in his brain, wiped his face with the napkin and the waiter removed it along with the dirty dishes. This ended the proposed covert action, although Underbright's fate hangs in the balance. Timkens has announced that he is ashamed of such actions by a subordinate and he promises tighter control.

Rodney Doubletrouble has returned to his ancestral home in Crumble and he has been appointed to the faculty as Lecturer in

Upright City Government. Rodney traces his family lineage all the way back to Seth Tripletrouble who wore three guns to save time reloading. The family name was downscaled when Seth hanged the sheriff of Crumble in the village square for disturbing Seth's poker game when he was winning. Tripletrouble was chased by the cavalry and it is only recently that his descendants under cover of darkness and a thunderstorm returned to Crumble. The present sheriff says that if they get fresh, there will be no Trouble at all.

We are not enthralled with the coin-fed soda pop machines for apes at the Great Crumble Zoo. The animals are robbing anyone who is stupid enough to enter the zoo.

To get rid of a filthy roommate requires more innovative thinking than our editor can conjure up. Probability values show no sex difference among the incidence of slobs, making your chance of meeting up with a slob greater than that of contracting a venereal disease. If you marry a slob, at least one of your offspring will carry the disease as a dominant trait. Then you will have two or more slobs who are beyond any known cure.

Bringing in rats will do you no good. The slob has already brought them in. The attempt to get rid of both species will have to be a five-star performance. A dubious ploy is to throw all the food out of the window along with half the clothes on the floor. Remain totally silent during the ensuing scene, but be prepared to run. Keep a hot poker on the stove if your life is at stake. Complaining to the house master in a dormitory is useless because he may be dirtier than the roommate. Our advice in extremis is to contract a disease where you vomit perniciously over everything in the pigpen.

Henry Whistleblower, a Health Service psychiatrist, scrupulously followed the advice of his personal witch doctor and never did any of his colleagues in on Friday the 13th. (This superstitious fear is known as triskaidekophobia; everyone knows this term and the ultimate consequences of disregarding it, even deans who call p.m. meetings on normal Fridays.) We recommend that all whistleblowers read the above with due seriousness to avoid being categorized as bad apples and damnation from earthly misconduct.

The Horticulture Department is having a pansy hunt this weekend. Since this is February, all participants should bring enough food until June.

Tellum Truth, famed author and adversary of everything in Crumble, came to a forum to explain why he is the writer of reports that degrade nice folks like deans, although he includes everyone else at Crumble. Tellum is accused of lacking the college spirit expected by others, for example, the wholesome freshman madly exhorting the football team that is winning 83 to 0 to kill their opponents even if poison gas is necessary.

A single excerpt of the brouhaha follows:

Tellum: A university is a microcosm of the universe despite its self-proclaimed trappings of beauty and truth. Its most benign aspect is the well-mowed grass around its buildings if you can outline them at a distance from all the parking lots. All the optical illusions make anything negative that may happen within it so unexpectedly aberrant in the minds of unsophisticated beholders that the disbelief produces the same basis for humor that derives from all human frail ties. Crumble is simply a special invention designed to reveal the worst, but it may catalyze our imaginations a bit much.

Dean Underbright: Your analysis and explanation are a lot of crap. I seem to be a favorite object of your obscene remarks which now exceed 90 degrees from my true worth. That gets my higher up. (An observer was heard to whisper, 90 degrees off zero.)

Donald Quackgrass (a janitor in the Agriculture building, sitting in for Dean Catcabbage who selects his substitute to attend meetings according to Catcabbage's assessment of the importance of the attendees) What the hell are you talking about?

Chairman of Meeting: The conversation has reached its expected low point. I regret, Dean Underbright, that you are being kicked out.

Editor's Note: It was decided that it wasn't worth the time to continue disemboweling Dean Underbright and everyone pitched in to get the cots ready for the participants' communal nap.

The end of the semester teacher evaluation decisively put the damper on the promotion of Chemistry teacher Ms. Fireball Bitchfield. She was characterized as "She's as jolly as your mother-in-law stuffed in a trunk."

To: Owner
License Plate Number Awash 216-840
From: Friendly Fred, Manager
The Royal Treatment Towing Company

We flattened your auto both sides to the middle. The job was extremely effective in widening for traffic the alley in which you parked the auto two hours overtime. Our rites are moderate when we identify you. Rest assured that you can use the remains as a fireproof cover for a bomb shelter.

Combined research from the Physical Education and Nursery Staff:

If you are prescribed walking exercise for a specific distance per day, let's say 1-1/2 miles, walk one statute mile with your dog.

You could do the same 1-1/2 miles by walking 1/2 statute mile with your three-year-old son.

Muggsie Knotgrass, Instructor in Textiles, has been given an extended leave of absence. Her clothes give her the appearance of a mini-warehouse close to a coal mine. She will spend the leave with a wardrobe consultant who will try desperately to recoordinate her in time for the next semester. Her coed students are fearful of what this might do to them.

To: Ilsa Puny
From: Intern Gleep

Your application to join the staff of the Health Service as a medical technologist has been rejected.

You did not know that the liver weighs three pounds. Also, you localized love and bravery in the liver when everyone knows that they are functions of the cardiac muscle.

We are returning the results of your hearing test since you may need them for positions in welding or where you may have to use a jackhammer.

To: Elvira Sheepdip, Lecturer in Mammalogy
From: Howdy Doody, Class President and Monitor of Faculty Behavior.

Your evaluation of a student reads "He is on the lower end of an exponential decay curve." We object to this. Our Shakespearean contingent, who prefer the advice that the quality of mercy falleth as the gentle rain from heaven, has softened your last hurrah to "He is on the bottom rung of a broken ladder." Please accept our much better evaluation or we will spray your lecture desk with molasses.

The exciting Home Economics recipe called "The Tie Spoiler"

is a weapon guaranteed to heat up the connubial conversation where it has dulled at the dinner table. This culinary delight which has an unexpected high-speed spray of tomato sauce and indelible ink is an invention that any swiftly retreating wife can employ if she can subsequently get back into the house while her husband is occupied in trying to treat his now non-functional vocal folds with hot steam.

It is increasingly difficult to keep a job at Crumble since one's entire past history is now being investigated. We submit only two unhappy examples. The first, Aphrodite Kallipygos, who traces her unsurpassed family tree through 20 unsullied centuries, was once crowned "The Goddess With The Perfect Behind," and she has now been dismissed as "0fficial Coathanger" from the women's gym.

The second case should serve as a stern warning to all. Visiting Assistant Instructor Lupine Leafmold, a successful practicing sadist in the Chemistry Department, was found after exhaustive conversations by Crumble agents with his relatives to have stolen a jar of senf-gerkins when he was 9 years old. At age 10 he was a hardened criminal. He was kicked out of the public library and he wasn't even whispering.

Author unknown but it could happen anywhere in Crumble:
Farmer: If you cross that pasture you better be able to do it in 9.8 seconds.
Brash trespasser: How come?
Farmer: The bull can do it in 9.9.

Advice from the old pro:
If the Crumble Audiovisual Service does not have the latest state of the art equipment and you have tomatoes thrown at you in the middle of your fouled up presentation which you are using to get a better job, there isn't a goddamn thing you can do about it.

Honeycuddle, lovable secretary during daylight, and even more lovable orgiast at night, was declared missing by the campus police after several torchlight searches in the Crumble River. She surfaced today and declared that the three-day blowout at the fraternity house was a howling success.

Most dastardly deed of the week: The Malevolent Society stole Maestro Avocado's violin, sawed it in half, and returned it with a bottle of Elmer's glue.

Advertisement: The College Automotive Service is selling its surplus vehicles. There is one that will be given away to anyone coming early. It is a liftback, originally 5 speed, driven only by the Safety Director. Currently, it has one speed. The roof is not badly bashed in. We don't know what happened.

Advertisement: Home for sale. Great location, only 5 minutes from the campus. Drawn pistol will get you readily through the combat zone. Helmet thrown in if requested. See Slum Landlord number 120, College approved.

Advertisement: Bake sale by sorority, Sigma Beta Dish. Contributions invited from sympathetic sisters. Anything submitted by the faculty must be brought first to the Board of Health. Male students are to keep the hell away until we sound a trumpet. They can then come in like the Oklahoma Sooners, claiming food and a coed.

Intestinal Fortitude, Nutritionist, is among the bravest men on the Crumble faculty. He has agreed to taste everything served at the cafeteria prior to its being served to the specially designated "Honor Students" who sit in a group and sneer at the common horde. All other students have sworn to do them in since the invidious grade comparison jeopardizes the comfortable survival of the unfit.

There is a high technology crook in the Psychology student body. Every time that the students assemble for departmental exams, all lights go out, pens and pencils float to the ceiling and instructors wearing wigs find themselves bald or whatever. The Chairman says that if the crook identifies himself, he will be made a full professor. The Department needs to be brought into the 20th century by a creative crook.

The debate between the incumbent mayor and his political opponent in the Crumble elections proved that His Honor is up against a forthright and powerful foe. We cite only one of the exchanges to illustrate our conclusions:

Moderator: Both candidates will give concise answers to questions posed by me so that their clarity of responses will reveal even to our illiterate citizens what their position is on public issues.

Moderator to Mayor Weakling: What will you do about new taxes?

Mayor: No problem. We do not believe in new taxes. We simply raise gas and electric rates, let the bricks fall off the school house, and collect garbage semi-annually. Time prevents me from giving an additional and exhaustive laundry list since I was elected on a no-riot platform.

Moderator to fierce opponent: What is wrong with our beautiful city and how the hell can you begin to fix it?

Fierce opponent: I have a sewer in front of my house and when it rains the sewer turns into a spillway. I have a power launch, rev up the motors and leave the neighborhood. All of us must display such creativity and meet the changes resolutely and with great courage. Remember that the future always gets behind us.

Moderator to an impartial citizen who is emerging from a saloon toward the gutter: Which candidate do you think won the debate?

Impartial citizen: Fierce opponent did, hands down. He answers questions with no hesitation. Also, I believe in kicking out everyone after one term, even though the Mayor is my brother-in-law. Inability to steal the whole city is good for democracy which is still the best show in town.

Interlude for an axiom: If anything works, prepare for its demise.

The College is pleased with its Hall of Infamy in the non-penetrable Physics building. The Physics Chairman did not get his picture hung as the founder of the Hall, in the foyer. This was in spite of the fact that he had flunked all his students in three consecutive years and he was hanged in effigy in the stadium at half-time in the last football game. The whole thing may blow over since President Timkens is removing funds to heat the building. Most students don't know where it is and some said that Physics was a purgative.

We advocate visiting the Hall. We were impressed with the list of salaries posted for basketball players and their cost of living increases which were necessary to match the inflated needs of their girlfriends. We make haste to add that teachers will be spray-gunned if they approach the. Hall. They have a known propensity for making trouble.

The Scum-Run, an annual sub-poverty fund raiser in Economy Dorm, has been postponed. Monsoons have raised the water level in Alligator Swamp and only students who can swim are allowed to leave for classes. Arrangements are still inconclusive for water taxi service by the Coast Guard.

Not yet rehired Assistant Dean Outward Bound sent Dean Catcabbage a complimentary copy of his article, "How To Defend Oneself Against Crocodiles Dressed Like Administrators." The

Dean said that he liked the article and could he get a reprint to send to President Timkens. Outward isn't sure how he can erase the title by some remote control instrument.

An award for compassion has been presented to sophomore Cornball Stud. He said that he was for sexual harassment but he was iffy about provable assault.

To: City Clerk
From: "Slum Landlord," born "Snatch Anything"

I have had enough of your notices to me addressed to "Slum Landlord 120." I might just go to your office, turn you upside down 'and bump your head on your desk, say 3 or 4 times. This should silence whatever molecules have been disarranged in your brain for a reasonably indefinite period of time. Prepare for the worst.

To: Slum Landlord 120
From: City Clerk

All your relatives, and they all have the same surname, now collectively own 50 percent of the city. Addition eventually of legitimate and illegitimate children could overwhelm our files. Logic demands that we specify you by the three terms above since this will allow early retrieval from our computer.

Due to cautious experience, we employ two large and hungry bums who will intercept you at a 30 foot mark from my office. They will drop you in the stairwell and you will have time to recover, although two floors below, in a reasonable period of time. The bums are fed on a basis of their caseload per diem. Ambulance service is available, but we advise bringing a slum relative who can assist with the stretcher and the oxygen.

We have researched the advantage of being a Nobel laureate.

He or she can obtain a fee for a one-hour lecture, most of which is unintelligible to the audience, that equals the salary for a whole semester of a Crumble Teaching Assistant who has to instruct semi-comatose students in English As A Foreign Language every day for 17 weeks. This is also unintelligible to the audience.

Broccoli, cauliflower, cabbage and mustard contain allyl isothiocyanate which is carcinogenic particularly in male rats. If our male deans are willing, we suggest that they now devote their life to a worthy endeavor and volunteer for confirmatory experiments. These are underway by a zoology major in his second year who says that he is on the brink of a major discovery.

As the hen said to the egg, "I've had enough of you. From now on you're on your own." This is from a Resident Counselor of Student Custodial Care who was just lightly dipped in tar and feathers by the dormitory pranksters.

Assistant Instructor Slowball, who is fixing to stay at Crumble for life, writes that administrators never suffer from poor logic or irrationality; these are afflictions of the faculty, A poll of the students indicates that in all fairness they are neutral on this subject. One of them said that his answer might determine his course grade.

The Psychology faculty is impressed with the new revelation that when simple statements are presented to students in light sleep, their ability to learn is increased if and when they wake up. In point of fact, all Crumble instructors have known this from the day they started to teach. The psychologists, who refuse to stop, are searching for the causative excitotoxin.

A Health Service research team, which gathered data to find what the most common disease is on the campus concluded that it is the staff. The students were a close second although most of their complaints could be classified as constipation or the high price of condoms.

Intern Gleep, who says that he follows all his patients until their expected demise occurs, is up for an award by the International Population Control Society, The Crumble Medical Society is a little less enthusiastic.

Advertisement: Cheap crook wanted to help steal automobiles. Experience not necessary. Equal Opportunity Employer.

> *(Note: There is reason to believe that this want ad was put in by a former head of the Malevolent Society.)*

Three newspaper accounts were sent to us by the Social Justice Department since their substance is timeless.

A twice stolen parrot turned stool pigeon and told the police the names of both crooks.

A boy murdered his parents and begged for clemency because he was an orphan.

The safest way to rob a bank is to become its President.

Remarks from a Sociologist who spent his travel money for the year:

Everybody talks about "literacy." This is one of the great boons to those professors who need to replenish their stock of new titles so that they can maintain their traveling and continue to be recognized as a "Mr. Big" in the overcrowded lecture circuits. But who is lecturing to the increasing hordes of illiterates, who are filling the bars and poolrooms and who are not always thought to be one's most desirable seatmate in Mr. Big's audiences?

Student Free Verse will have to consider his future as a trombonist. He was playing the trombone while blissfully chomping on linguini in clam sauce and his irritated dorm mates tried to ram the instrument up his behind. Although their attempt was a failure, they have warned him that they are perfecting their technic. It remains to be seen whether Free is a careful listener.

Orientation Day for new staff is a must. Obtaining a list which faculty members to avoid is de rigueur and it can be received surreptitiously from the usher wearing the bright orange and green blazer. Spurn everyone on the list, particularly if an administrator is passing by. Physiologists know that an administrator can even smell around corners. Their vision is poor, however, although they have not been known to bump into the main library. There is a case on record where one of them did this, but he was skiing downhill and went out of control.

Forby Doo Doo, Editor
The Great Crumble Press

I am submitting a book manuscript to you which I am certain that you will classify at once as an opus superbis.

How soon may I expect publication? I need the royalties.

Resident Counselor Sleaze

Economy Dormitory

Dear Sleaze:

Our classification started with opus magnum but our staff had hit the bottle too hard. When the party stopped, the staff reclassified your untidy mess of papers as "disposable." The only questions were where and how soon.

The only strong point that we find in your so-called manuscript is that it is or was only 78 pages long. Three of us were able to read it and direct it through our sink disposal before we left for dinner. It can never be said that the material wasn't kept clean to the bitter end or that it could reach the hands of the great unwashed out there.

For the remainder of your life, think even smaller so that your works can be packaged vacuum-sized. This mechanism on a large scale could reduce the paper trail which is overwhelming the entire country.

In the meantime you could go into wastebasket sales, an occupation that is flourishing. We should have saved your *opus* to stuff your first wastebasket.

Sic transit gloria mundi, especially your crap,

Forby Doo Doo

Adjunct Lecturer $C_6H_{12}O_6$, who comes from a long line of chemists, is contemplating suicide. The clerks at the Business Office cannot get his name straight and all of his salary checks have been lost or cashed by other chemists. He is in a state of severe malnutrition and his lectures are even worse than those of his department chairman.

Tidbit From The Physics Department:

Torricelli said that nature abhors a vacuum. If it occurs, an ubiquitous character named Murphy rushes in at top speed and proceeds to make it worse. Speaking of vacuums, another fellow that you should pay attention to is Bernoulli. He says that if you chance to be walking in a narrow alley and a high wind abruptly arises, the near vacuum between beginning and end of the alley greatly increases the velocity and you will find yourself in helpless flight until you are deposited unceremoniously at the expanded far end. It is just possible that we may issue another scientific bulletin tomorrow if only someone will print it.

Irate parent to teacher: Why did you give my son Mudbum a zero in your course?

Teacher: I consulted with the Math staff and we couldn't find a mathematical way to give him less.

Vice-President Coldtoast is demanding salary and a yearly contract for his cat. He claims that it keeps mice out of the offices of the high brass and that this has done more to improve the image of the occupants than anything else he can think of.

Serious advice to colleagues who wish to become comics: Don't sit in your office thinking up funny situations. The vacuum in such a sterile environment may cause an implosion, making the funny section of your cerebrum even smaller. Go into the hallways and listen to what the personnel say in all seriousness to each other. Listen especially to those who are telling their colleagues that they are going to massacre someone. If the proposed victim seems to be a dean, follow them down the hall. Your routine will be greatly enriched. Some of the best material has come from teachers who have been thrown out of windows, first by students and then by a vice-president to whom they came for sympathy.

Remark from one of the certified paranoiacs on the faculty who is about to be discharged, "The paranoiacs are after me."
From the Political Science staff on how to do in a candidate with the assistance of the most respected and impartial reporter on national television: Thus, a question from invited interviewee, who knows what the answer will be:
"What are Schnookerhooker's chances of becoming the nominee of his party for the President of the United States? Do you think that he will lose?" (Note that this is English for destroying the candidate.)

Impartial Reporter: The polls from Upside Down Falls in Idaho didn't give him much chance. In all fairness, however, let us not be definitely pessimistic until we receive more unfortunate information."

Selected tidbits from the course in Remedial Writing:

Manuscripts submitted for publication are ordinarily first evaluated by reviewers with extraordinary wisdom. Any reviewer preserving this myth has to find fault with several items per page. An author who wants to be smarter than the average bear has to outwit his opponent, the reviewer. The easiest recipe is to select words such as "the" or "and" and spell them backwards, liberally sprinkling such errors throughout the manuscript. In correcting these, the reviewer will be highly pleased with himself. Indeed, correcting anything on a more complex plane will not only give the reviewer a sore brain, but will lead to his producing a diatribe of horseshit that can be countered only by a dialogue from the prospective author involving equal anti-horseshit (or is the more proper word "bullshit?"). This wastage of superior talent can only be deplored.

Editorial note: Our next column was intended to be on "Advice to the Lovelorn," submitted by the Reproductive Physiology staff. Their advice was unintelligible, even to us. We are sending the material in the next rocket to Mars, with the notation, "Reply immediately."

Dear Myron:

Your letters, although directed nicely toward third-graders, are becoming unequaled in ferocity. Explain your unmannerly behavior. Howdy Doody, Class President

Dear Howdy: My mother had sex with a junkyard dog. Don't come anywhere near here unless you are completely enclosed by barbed wire.

Nurse Cratchett at the College Health Service. who despite being without top title, is more feared than Abdul-el-Bul-Bul Amir. She even outranks in authority the current Mother Superior who is close to the Pope. She may have run Intern Gleep out of his job despite his contacts with the Governor.

Gleep has been chasing with a bat the Research Executive Rat, and he has put a dozen ferocious cats on the night shift to do in the Rat even if it tries to sneak in through a secret tunnel on the roof.

Gleep complained to Nurse Cratchett that the Rat has been fighting with an even more popular, although still somewhat untested, upstart rat. But Gleep failed to know that Nurse Cratchett had appointed the first Rat to Executive status. Now, however, post-battle, it was missing several toenails and half an ear. The Executive Rat told Nurse Cratchett that Gleep had diminished its quality of life. The Rat demanded the death penalty for Gleep. The Rat had heard that Gleep wanted to do a liver transplant on him. Nurse Cratchett is considering the whole affair very seriously while Gleep has been placed on half rations.

And while we're at it, our favorite nurse actually answered a call bell from a patient who complained that her back was giving her excruciating pain. Nurse Cratchett said, "Why don't you do something about it?" and left the room.

The members of our unbeloved Malevolent Society need instruction on how to terminate the bloopers they generate. Whimsy Blimp, one of their mutants, was invited to a party, but nobody had prior knowledge of his misadventures. He slithered over to a group that he had never met before and he said to one of the girls, "Did your grandmother get paroled?" He then disappeared promptly without waiting for the ensuing confusion.

The lecture on Developmental Stages of Poverty by the unsinkable Princeton Scraggs was well received. He described how delighted his parents were when they could afford a second set of loin cloths. Their upward mobility was even more obvious when they bought a tent. Scraggs explained that his recent reversion to a diet of fish heads was caused by the repossession of his raft and pole.

The Malevolent Society has temporarily gone underground and we doubt whether its members will surface for some time. The last straw was in the Men's Executive Washroom, always a sanctum sanctorum. A new sign over the urinals read "Stand close and face forward." The stalls then proceeded to spray India ink over two deans who were obeying the messages, but who were unfortunately about to go out following the delivery and co-host an oral delivery on "Cleanliness is next to Godliness."

The expectant audience in the adjacent auditorium was told to leave by a janitor who was also totally covered by the ink when he logically tried to test the stalls to find out what was wrong. It can be said that democracy prevailed since nobody could distinguish the deans from the janitor.

The Safety Director at Crumble drove to his attorney's office to discuss an auto accident in which his car somehow got into the river and demolished a motorboat. To get there he was caught traveling backward down a one-way street.

While parking his car at the barrister' office, the Director knocked two fenders off the car of the man he was about to see. When the Director was unceremoniously ushered out of the attorney's office after confessing to the latest accident, he knocked both fenders off the front of the attorney's partner's car. There was a fight, during which everyone involved landed in jail. The Safety Director was put in solitary confinement for his own safety.

Intern Gleep is banned from talking with disturbed students who come in for psychiatric counseling. Gleep asks such questions as "Did you ever kick your twin brother out of the uterus?" Or,

"Did you have the need to slosh around freely when you were a fetus?"

Social Worker Peeaway is obtaining irrefutable evidence for his thesis to confirm Lombrosio's view that most people are born criminals. He stands on a busy corner and asks every third person, "Why the hell did you do it?" No other questions. Some confess. Others disappear into the crowd with unbelievable speed. Peeaway's methodology is unimpeachable and he has a brilliant research future but we don't know where.

Miraculous Goldplate reserves a central seat in the faculty dining room. The seat is raised on blocks to enable him to preserve a commanding view and hold court with his revering sycophants. When asked about his health because he keeps hocking lungers into the adjacent spittoon, he inevitably answers "super."

Today is the celebration of God, Country and Crumble Day. We pause in our unpleasant historical story to join in this sacred event. Please pray silently for a moment, enough to fill the space below. Wait for the Amen sign to appear. This service is non-sectarian.

AMEN

(Approved by the Council of Deans)

And while you are still reeling from patriotism and theology, the Health Service advises caution. You could suffocate.

Fractured History of Medicine:

It was Plato who wrote that you can always blame your ill-omened character on the poor quality of the water. Now you have it from good authority.

The recently appointed Whistleblower, whose duty was to identify fraudulent researchers, died, presumptively from a heart attack caused by overwork. The coroner stated that the bullet found in his brain was probably an accident, done harmlessly by an unattended child playing in the next yard. Or perhaps from an unidentified flying object from Jupiter. Nobody has applied to refill the position. The administration is resigned to the fact that a certain amount of fraud is a reasonable expectation and that Crumble researchers make only honest errors.

Assistant Instructor Trailblazer, without question in the forefront of the discipline of Logic, his professional area, asserts that his field is now obsolete since he has solved all the problems. The departmental promotions committee has not yet reached a decision to upgrade him to Associate Instructor or to hand deliver his letter whose envelope reads "Out You Go."

The English staff has held three meetings to clarify the difference between "typically" and "very typically." The fourth meeting is canceled because the Chairman, Language Mangler, was rushed to intensive care at the Great Crumble Hospital. The diagnosis is stress endured in failing to obtain endorsement from the faculty for the superlative form of the expression. He had trouble in the past when the difference between "the sun shone" and "the sun shined" was unresolved.

For the attention of the English or Mathematics Department:

Laboratory Instructor Hold The Line will not be able to hold class today. He was maimed by a student who insisted that 2 x 2 = 6. The student has a hand calculator powered by solar radiation, but it has been cloudy for several weeks.

Toute de Suite is being worn down by interlopers who keep changing the department of the only subject he knows. He no sooner graduated as a nuclear physicist than the clearly unethical chemists seized the field and called it nuclear chemistry. Then the engineers, who had plenty of time to go out stealing fields, took over what was left. Toute is back in graduate school where he expects to spend the next eight years in two different colleges so that he can get a job somehow before the field grabbers can make him a permanent academic bum.

Hilarious Meconium was voted as the most hard-hearted fellow in the sophomore class. He left his fiancée as collateral in a pawnshop.

Will the secretary who threw a typewriter at the Instructor in Logic please come to Surplus Property and pick up some more of the machines. Nobody knows what a typewriter is any more and this is the most practical way to reduce our inventory.

The Safety Director can be counted on to provide entertainment to any gathering. At the weekly outdoor pigout his 18-wheel truck ran wild, pursuing the fleeing guests relentlessly, but all of them managed to reach the other side of the river, even those who never could swim before. No date can be set to reconvene the event since every invitee says that his schedule is filled for the next several years.

Sign up for the Deluxe Private Suite at the Great Crumble Hospital. Your friends will marvel at your comfort before you died.
An excerpt from the minutes of a meeting of the psychiatrists at the Health Service:

Psychiatrist Grindle (moderator): The topic today is "Depression, How Can We Quantitate It?"

A physician (i.e., name for a person at a medical meeting who has no standing whatsoever): The answer is simple; the victim has to be at the level of whale dung.

In-House Resident to Physician: Who the hell let you in?

Grindle to Physician: Interesting dialogue. Why is whale dung a threshold value?
Physician: Because it's at the bottom of the ocean.
Uncompromising Resident: So's a lot of fish.
Grindle: We better all get out of here. I left an undiagnosed patient who started choking to death two hours ago.

We like Groucho Marx's reply when he was told that there was a question about where students will sleep in a college with unfinished dormitories. He replied, "Where they always sleep, in the classroom." He added a side remark that there was a question of what to do with professors who make it up as they go along.

Instructor Hiram Pillbox
Department of Philosophy
Dear Crotchety (I mean Pillbox).

I am taking time out from an impossibly busy schedule to let you know my deep feelings for you. Your inestimable service to the College cannot be put into words so I won't try. We'll leave it by saying that your acclaim is national.

Please sign the enclosed unemployment compensation forms.

With obviously great sadness,
Smiley Timkens

To: Instructor Cheesecake, Cement Construction
From: Ex-Student Fogarty

I am inviting you to spend part of an evening with me, say ten minutes. Your grade knocked out my chances for retention in the cement mixers program and I would like to return the favor by knocking the hell out of you. I am a fair man and you should be able to return to work no later than one weekend in bed. Stay healthy until we meet.

A law of Physics states that nature abhors a vacuum. Thus the vacuum tends to shrink. But our beloved Myron has his own opinion. After observing Intern Gleep's behavior, Myron is convinced that Gleep has a hole in his head and that it is non-fillable unless with sawdust. Myron would like to chair a national meeting on the subject between physicists and biologists.

From the Zoology Department:

Do you know that kangaroo milk has a low content of lactose? It is very safe for kangaroos. We had to say something since the Pschology Chairman is smugly pleased with his own pronunciamentos.

Instructor Klutz is donating the wrong items to the persons holding the periodic community Selldown. This is the fourth time that he has entered his wife. There have never been any takers and she is returned by eviction at closing time. Klutz complains that she is displayed in the worst geographic position, next to homeless cats which quickly attract takers.

To: Head Janitor Brillo
From: Smiley Timkens

Our internationally famous faculty members, and they also say this themselves, meet for lunch daily at table 000 in the Student Union and their discussions are only at Nobel-type level. They have urged that I direct you to the peons table adjacent to the boiler room.

When the group considered Clausewitz, you said that his uncle lived in your neighborhood. The group members dread to think how you will demean them when they get to talk about Herodotus, Machiavelli and Thucydides. Using the imperative case, regard this memo as a cease and desist enjoinder. Also, quam celerissime (which you are to look up and answer as directed).

Yesterday the annual selection by students of the dullest teacher on the campus was held. The winner (loser?) was Horace Pitviper, lecturer on good teaching. There were several runner-ups, but following their identification they were totally ignored, which was in keeping with their performance.

When a reporter asked one of Crumble's brightest students to characterize Horace, the student answered, "He's Dead Sea, man."

The Great Levelers:

1. When your doctoral dissertation, filed "permanently" in the library for serious researchers to read, is returned to you three months later, with the notation on the back of scrap paper "We need space for a statue of the Dean."

2. When your book, which took you three years to write, is selling for ten cents three years later, on a discarded book rack in the Student Union.

To: Head of the Maintenance Department
From: Precious Moron, Currently Free-lance (Editor: Euphemism for unemployed)

I am applying for the position advertised as foreman of the construction crew for the new "Intelligent Student Depository." My credentials are historically impeccable. My ancestors built ziggurats in Mesopotamia. My skill in measuring in cubits has never been matched. Who now among us knows that there are 28 finger widths to the cubit? Please answer by next Tuesday or my asking wages will increase incrementally each hour.

To: Language Mangler
Chairman, Department of English
From: Anonymous Troublemaker (true name; born with it)

What's the difference between "essential" and "absolutely essential?" Can a person be "dead" or "very dead?" No hurry please with your answer. You could in haste be "wrong," or "absolutely wrong," or most probably "all wrong." We do not want to upset your departmental lexicographers who are still wrestling with prepositions. We hear that they never practice circumlocution or anything else either. Please address your answer to me at the College Cafeteria. My title is Can Opener, Mainly Sardines.

At our age, which is better suited for bears in hibernation, we could not find the author of the following entry, but his/her logic cannot be faulted. To wit, according to the unstoppable calorie guzzler who just reached 400 pounds of body weight "If I am a prominent citizen of Fat City, I might as well be Mayor."

To: Athletic Director Knucklebender
From: Executive Secretary, Society for the Preservation of Athletes Salaries

We were told by our Downtown Seminar Group that you did not know there were fighting kangaroos before Adam and Eve were invented. This ignorance is hardly bearable from one with your expected encyclopedic knowledge. Now we learn that you do not subscribe to the Journal of Educology. There is not even evidence that you ever took a course in Dragline Technology.

To: Knucklebender again
From: Discipline Committee, Above Society

We request that you shut down your useless research. You are to cease your attempt to find why tomato ketchup is impossible to pour when it leaves the refrigerator, but pours all over you when it is shaken. Your assistant confessed to swigging from the bottle, which skews your data. Further, you are ignorant of the advances in physics on this other wise important subject.

A student called the Immigration Service. He said that he couldn't understand the foreign Teaching Assistant in English and he wanted him deported, the sooner the better. The Assistant claims that he cannot understand the Crumble natives. The standoff is approaching the national norm.

Following the directive of President Timkens, Psychologist Tunemeout is visiting classes at random to test the intelligence of Crumble students. The report below from a class in Logic is a representative sample of Tunemeout's data.

Tunemeout: "A man swam two-thirds of the distance across a lake, but he knew that he couldn't make it so he swam back. Are there any comments about this statement?"

Answer from both instructor and students: "The sentence appears to be correct."

Second question, directed to a student who didn't seem to have trisomy 2l: "How old are you?"

Student without prior clinical signs: "I am two and one-half years older than my brother."

Tunemeout: Mr. Instructor Failproof, there is no need to waste your valuable class time administering the written section of the intelligence test.

The Humane Association of Crumble has summoned a notoriously filthy student, Crinkum Crankum, for a hearing. Crinkum lives on the 18th floor of Economy Dorm. A hungry rat died of exhaustion climbing up there. It knew that it wasn't allowed on the elevator. Crinkum will be accompanied by his attorney to the meeting.

The Secretary of the College Honor Society has researched the most effective way to get responses from posters announcing future meetings. He hangs them in toilet stalls. These prove to be the places where faculty and students do their serious reading.

Anthropologist Cockatoo, who likes to visit any jungle he can find, so long as his Department will pay for the trip, recounted to his class a harrowing experience he had in his early days at jungle hopping. He was captured by cannibals and was about to be cooked for the usual tribal midday snack. The casual conversation at the cook-out went like this:

Gourmet cook: The pot is ready, chief. Would you like this unsavory looking character lightly steamed or well done?

Tribal Chief: Let's try twice baked.

Cook: Where the hell did you get that recipe?

Chiefy: A friend sent me a Mafia cookbook from Chicago.

Three years later: Cockatoo told his admiring class that while the tribal members appointed a committee to solve the dilemma, he was able to escape. He wrote to the chief, apologizing for not saying good-bye.

From the Business Program: Today's subject is two more ways to get rich.

Develop a product, particularly a totally harmless pill. A total of 100 to the container will simplify computations for the office staff. State prominently on the label that 20 are free. Then jump the price 20% more than that of your nearest equally thriving competitor.

Develop a product that you can hype enough to sell. As your vat dries out so you can make some more, subtly reduce the number of ounces in the container, best by blowing air into it to make it look larger. Never neglect to raise the price since nobody can relate ounces and money.

The Poet Laureate of the College was booted out of a Chinese restaurant where he had been moonlighting. His job was to compose sentences of great wisdom, put them on paper and insert them into fortune cookies.

We submit just a couple of his cluckers: "Faint heart produces no mashed potatoes". Or "He who has last laugh obviously will have no other one."

The restaurant owner has countered with a more powerful ancient proverb, "Man with hatchet not necessarily your friend."

The Zoology staff members are observing the antics of a vice-president who, when sounding off at meetings, raises his hands to his temples, thumbs pressing at right angle to each temporal bone, while wiggling his up-raised fingers in and out like an inside antenna. The technic is supposed to reinforce the vacuous statements which the administrator cannot verbalize using only the English language. This simulation of a rabbit on the defense is under research by our evolutionists.

Angelina Christmascake, Head of Theology, has had to straighten out the thinking of Brother Ingrate and she is fully capable of this task. Ingrate said that God is disorderly. Every time a person puts his life into nice, even pigeon holes, some great disaster breaks up his well-planned system. If he is enjoying tranquillity in his old age, he is croaked. Ingrate said that it is high time to invent a new plan. Obviously, he won't be able to do this while he is in the service of God, Christmascake and Crumble. He has thought about becoming an unemployed atheist.
From the Most Respected Logician in the College:

When the official historian tries a put-down and asks you what a specific famous person did, and of course you don't know, answer with supreme bravado, "He was a world-class villain despite his known contributions. You will be right 99 percent of the time. The biological startle reaction displayed by the historian can be depended on to stifle any further probing.

Heard on the Matriculation Line for Entering Freshmen:
Foreign student, just arrived for the first time in America, speak-

ing in very broken English to the next student in the line: "What do we do now?"

Next student, born in Crumble City: "Hell man, I don't know nothin."

Foreign student: "You have an accent."

From the Small Business Bureau:

The fastest way to get your chairman back on track after he returns from a convention in the South Seas is to tell everyone that he screwed up the works before he went and got paid for it.

The Logician again:

The safest way to hedge your bet, especially when asked if you are sure, is to answer, "Just as sure as there's a heaven." This will endear you to everyone in earshot while scaring the pants off your opponent.

Washee and Smashee are Crumble's most recent commercial cleaners. We welcome them but suggest extreme caution and a rider on your household insurance.

A little knowledge is a dangerous thing, especially if your companion has none. The Architecture lecturer told his girlfriend that she was as graceful as the caryatids of the Erechtheum and she punched him in the nose.

Fiesta is the noisiest coed on the campus. She is a veritable cacophony of shrieks and shrills. Her boyfriend, Fidolio, has evolved a cease and desist system, admittedly a temporary holding action. He starts 20 yards back, works up a full head of steam and tackles her from behind. In the clawing and punching that follow, she develops an oxygen debt and can't talk for the next 30 minutes. The scene is predictive even to the point when they politely bid each other good night. Fidolio is working on field tests with innovative therapeutic methods. His more impatient friends advise desensitization, preferably with a club.

From Smiley Timkens
To: Whoever On the Faculty Knows Its His Turn

Since the Governor mysteriously became more powerful than me and is now "feeling his oats, we are in danger of having our budget sharply reduced. In anticipation of this, I am developing several scenarios. One of them is to fire every one of you, which is quite logical according to my advisors in the State Legislature. More expediently, I am instituting "Occam's Razor." This maxim points out that we can do without the more worthless bums on our faculty. Why have more when we can accomplish as little as presently with less. We might start with the deans. I will initiate meetings, convening in buzz sessions with a ratio in each of two deans to three faculty members. This should ensure full democratic treatment.

The Great Crumble Funeral Parlor, which has just relocated next to the Surgical Center of the Great Crumble Hospital, has been cited by Mayor Weakling as being the most enterprising establishment of the month. The Parlor has erected a sign that reads SAME DAY SERVICE.

The ferry has been enjoined from crossing the River Crumble ever since the boat started to list 45 degrees to the starboard. All passengers have had to sit with weights around their necks, and only on the port side. The only way to reach the opposite shore is to drive the Unhappy Hollow Road for 97 miles and play Russian roulette attempting to cross Humpback Bridge at that point. The Great Crumble Post Office advises everyone to stay calm. The mail will get through. The Post Office has a carrier who swims with one hand and keeps the mail sac above the waves with his free hand outstretched. The postmaster assures the natives that the mail will be dry when it reaches their relatives, unless the mailman sneezes. The postmaster hastens to say that the problem of settling debts among the now trans-Crumble relatives is not in the purview of his Department. It is feasible to yell at one another across the river with megaphones.

Dear Director of Admissions:

Melted Clinker is the best student I ever had. Admit him unconditionally. These are my last words.

Corrigible Pismire
Emeritus Professor of Paleopsychology

Dear Director of Admissions:

Pay no attention whatsoever to the note above from just defunct Professor Pismire. He died in the Emergency Room of the Great Crumble Hospital while Clinker was nipping him with forceps to keep him conscious long enough to write the letter during the Code Blue.

Imploringly,
Everybody in the College

The astronomers are becoming the worst troublemakers in the institution. Just when everyone agreed that he could get a good night's sleep, Instructors Fluky and Clodpate started throwing mini-asteroids and meteorites at each other in the departmental faculty meetings. All other faculty members have had to crawl down the aisles to their seats, motorcycle helmets being de rigueur.

The new Chairman, Chiron, is mediating the dispute that asteroids are asteroids and comets are comets by declaring that asteroids can turn into comets, and besides, who the hell cares. As a convincing measure, Chiron is having two barbed wire compartments built to separate the combatants while still permitting free speech; he has a cousin who is a lawyer and who told him that this would avoid constitutional problems. The wire would also be useful in case an occasional maniac from another department slipped in and joined the fracas.

The geologists in the basement can now relax. They complained that the fights were setting off their seismograph. Indeed, their most prolific researcher was about to submit a manuscript indicating renewed volcanic activity in Mt. Vesuvius. He has been temporarily restrained, however, by banishment to the steam tunnel.

An excrement-load of students from Horseshit Ridge High School is coming down the river and over the rapids to see if they want to matriculate at Crumble. The boat is being piloted by ex-Midshipman Fimbry Noggin, their English teacher. Little do they know that he has never been in a boat before and that when he sees the rapids, he will be the first to jump overboard. Despite his good vision, there is a problem with his brain. We may continue this story when the kangaroo court convenes to hang him.

The Trustees, in a fit of democracy, have also decided to let the students submit their ideas about a new logo for the College stationery. The logo should clearly identify the character and mission of the College. Two choices have emerged. One shows students being sucked into a black hole, most of them upside down. The second shows a blank, dirty dishrag which its proponents claim will cost the least money and tell the whole story. There is a third entry, currently only a runner-up, showing trucks from various other colleges unceremoniously dumping their students here and there on the Crumble campus and quickly turning to fetch more emigres. Undefined people shown on the sidewalks, presumably taxpayers, are shaking their fists at the developing waste heaps.

You decide who is the more effective English teacher:
New teacher, still very respectful: "In speaking or writing, remem-

ber the adage that brevity is the soul of wit."

Old crotchety teacher, all punched out: "In speaking or writing, shit or get off the pot."

The English Department is offering a prize for more than two translations of the following: "I don't know nothin from nothin."

Tidbit from a conversation overheard between two freshmen:

Number 1: What's your name?

Number 2: Rocket Bullchip.

1. Well frost my pumpkin, I have a live-in boyfriend with the same last name.

2. What's his entire name, from left to right?

1: Warmspit Bullchip.

2: What's his ambition?

1: He would like to play tackle for Oklahoma

2: What does he do while he's waiting?

1: He stands around most of the day adjusting his jockstrap

2: Doesn't sound like he's too career oriented

1: Well, ta ta for now. As the poet said, "Boots, saddle, to horse and away." My bald hairdresser is awaiting me and he can't wait to spill the spicy lore of the day.

Read carefully today's wisdom from the Speech Department:

No kudos for the famed lecturer from elsewhere who is a frustrated would-be comic and who enunciates his words clearly until he reaches the punch line of one of his tales. At this point he screws up. His voice drops to an unintelligible guttural level, or he cackles, or the microphone has screaming feedback, or he milks the audience to a premature roar of laughter where they' re all slapping their pants immediately prior to his climactic statement. The developing deaf senescent people in the audience sit in grim silence or force a sick smile. They suffer almost as much as when they are at a Shakespearean play with the dialogue in Beowulfian

English and a freight train is passing by. They never find out why Beowulf stabbed Grendel.

The Board of Trustees has not yet finalized its decision to change the College logo on the official stationery to "Light, Money and Truth." Its the priority arrangement of the words that bothers them most. Also, the one Latin scholar among them proposes "Lux, Lucre et Veritas."

Visiting Dean Curmudgeon from Fawchee Subnormal had the afternoon off and he came to have tea and crumpets with his old friend, Dean Dingleberry. He had to climb seven stories in the Tower Building since the elevator wasn't operating and the repairman was stuck in his own elevator waiting for his assistant to jack him out. The assistant is illiterate, however, and is reading the repair manual upside down.

Back to Curmudgeon before another diversion occurs and this account begins to resemble a faculty meeting. Upon reaching the top step, his tongue hanging out longer than that of a Great Dane after a dog track race, he slipped on a banana peel put there by Assistant Dean Merryperson who is a very low order type jokester. Curmudgeon hurtled down considerably faster than he climbed up, gyrating circularly such that his red and white blazer resembled a confused peacock trying to emulate a bluejay that had just been shot. Two observant student spectators were laying bets on what floor Curmudgeon would land.

Miraculously, the Dean survived not much the worse for wear, except for lots of huffing and puffing. He proceeded to scream to Dean Dingleberry's secretary every swear word he could remember and he ordered her to transmit them accurately to Dingleberry. The quick-witted secretary responded that Dingleberry was out of town for the month. He would be too busy to talk if and when he returned. There is little point dwelling on this episode further since the rest of the day was without hooha in the building.

Student comedian Stovepipe has found that being funny takes guts since the victim of his story is always lurking behind a bush. Stovepipe's satire on "Long Life to Nanky Poo" was attacked by an otherwise sane cardiologist who complained that Stovepipe was recommending the wrong prescription. Stovepipe could be indicted for malpractice and without a license.

Crumble's Office of Irreducible Nonsense Strikes Back:

The colleges that call Crumble students illiterates have students who become professors who write unintelligible books and treatises that disappear as soon as the desperate publishers can partly recover their costs or fade into bankruptcy.

The Crumble students write graffiti in readable scrawl which everyone pauses to read. This is because the verbless sentences send pointed messages about sociopolitical issues which strike the core of the universal problems that professors argue about, depending upon who pays them.

Student Wretched says that he resents being called Wretch for short. He was christened Wretched and he wants proper respect. He is much less concerned about his surname, Slotear.

Emeritus Assistant Instructor Dingaling says that he is hearing things upside down. The otologists at the Great Crumble Hospital have scheduled him for an operation, as usual the first of its kind. A surgeon will turn him upside down while others with the help of anyone nearby will hold his ear in the same place. This is truly negative creativity of the first order of magnitude. It ranks with the concept of negative entropy in physics.

Crumble's enterprising eatery, The Red Stool, is full of surprises. It is instituting a nightly special called the "Unnamed Horror, designed to titillate the most creative imagination. We will not reveal its nature since your stomach with holes in it may be the only thing you have left.

Open Letter: To The Head Scrawler Of The Malevolent Society
From: Harriett Entrails, Secretary for Vera Scrum, our Trusted Administrative Assistant

We are locking our wastebaskets so that your spies can no longer suction our daily reports up the presidential chimney. Also, our janitors must now burn the hanging flypaper since we have found sensors encoded in the glue. Vera cerebrates at genius level and she is determined to do you in or kick you out, whichever comes first. I am nailing this communique to the campus telephone poles until we find where to dig you up. We will nail you when you surface probably with a family of raccoons.

If you don't know what DNA is, don't bother to ask. Chances are great that it won't make a damn bit of difference in your family conversation.

Parboiled Cliffhanger, recently elevated to tenth in line for the position as Assistant Instructor of Neuroanatomy, has sharply increased his eligibility for the position. In spite of existing opposition from the right, Cliffhanger insists that intractable pain in the toes can be permanently alleviated by surgical removal of the brain. His fierce opponent, Herman Vermin, says that high energy researchers such as Cliffhanger are appreciated only when they are dead. Herman suggests that Parboiled should consider early suicide. All of us are breathlessly awaiting Parboiled's reply.

The History of Art teacher says that graffiti did not originate with the dispossessed persons besmirching subway trains and brick walls in the cities where our true culture is said to reside, everywhere else being stunted corn and horse manure. Cicero, circa 50 B.C., being teed off with Julius and his pals running Rome, scrawled in elegant fashion on the walls of the forum "Throw the bastards out, velocitas maximus." This translated to the faster the better, but it also advised Cicero to start running at marathon speed (no torch, please) toward the Alps.

Isn't it sad that whatever college you flee from or escape to, the worst villain you encounter is the head of your new department.

When you have exhausted your research on the trivia and minutiae concerning the three-eared bear and all the journal editors throw your unopened manuscripts over their shoulders into the wastebasket at the far end of the room, exulting in their accuracy, turn your attention to another field. We suggest that you rush out of an observatory shouting that you just discovered a wobbling planet that is hotter than a mashed potato. You are prepared to plot the cooling rate for the next ten years and its effect on rodent populations in city dumps. You could become the director of a new public agency dealing with this exciting problem.

Do not minimize the shit storm that will be stirred up because of your sage advice. You can expect a flood of insulting correspondence that you can practice throwing over your shoulder to a target until you attain a satisfactory degree of accuracy.

To: Halacious Thwakaway, Roofer, The Taj-Mahal
From: The Great Crumble Press

Your "Handbook for Poisoning Pigeons" can be found in the Great Crumble River where we threw it, although it seems to be clogging up the spillway. The proofreaders thought it would be readily degradable in running water. The beavers were expected to help in the destruction, but they wouldn't touch it.

There is a favorable aspect to your now outmoded manuscript.

It never got any worse from start to finish. It couldn't. Visiting hours at the River for mourners end sharply at sunset. Since the Coast Guard can get nasty about pollution, don't confess that you wrote the book. Also, don't look for trouble by attempting to write anything else.

No charge for the advice,
Forby Doo Doo

From: Intern Gleep, In the absence of the Dermatologist, Health Service

"Your hair is the first to get the shaft. You're next."

Exhaustive research of the staff of the Economics Department has led them to state unequivocally that unemployment exists when people are out of work. The Department Chair is now certain that this confirms the opinion of the world's greatest economist, Calvin Coolidge. The Chair states that it is too bad that the results are not yet in the public domain.

Student Felix Dirtpan was lucky. He tripped over a book mainly because he didn't know what it was, thereby missing an exam which he would have flunked. This allowed him to take a makeup on Moron's Day when the mentally defunct are given 75 out of 100 points free on any exam of their choice. Any fair-minded clone would have to admit that Crumble has another first.

Logic and Economy in English:

Coed 1: I'm hating you.
Coed 2: I'm hating you right back.

Protocol for Teachers of Mathematics:

A self-respecting math teacher refuses to lecture in any room that does not have chalkboards completely around the room. He starts at one end, writes formulas approaching the speed of light, usually in a clockwise direction unless he is left-handed, with the students circling in their seats like vultures, in the appropriate lines of sight. When the teacher reaches the last available space in the 360 degree arc, the lecture is over. Nobody dares erase anything until the teacher is out of the building and hasn't left his hat.

Oedipus Rex, fearless Chairperson, frequently telephones his faculty at about 4 a.m. to come immediately to a meeting which if not held would result in serious jeopardy to the survival of the Philosophy Department. Since nobody answers the telephone, Oedipus calls the Dean to tell him that his staff must be carousing all night in various subterranean grottoes and they should be discharged for moral turpitude. The cautious Dean usually counters with some suggestion such as that a more logical move might be mass castration. Oedipus does not call the Dean until after 10 a.m. since that is not a wise move unless the Dean is to be informed that his house is burning down.

Red-hot tablet found at the site of a recent volcanic eruption in Crumble:

To: Occupants, Administration Building at Crumble
From: Mephistopheles, Hades

We are having a serious problem in regard to increasing overpopulation here. Regard this preliminary notice as a plea to change your evil ways and we promise to do our best to get you into a half-way house.

The fracas about a tuition increase for students has been settled and to the satisfaction of all. A blue-ribbon study panel found that a 2 percent increase was needed. Based on this, plus the usual fudge factor, the Crumble Vice-Presidents in plenary session asked for a 28 percent increase. The Chancellor, acting as defender of the students, on white horse and flaming sword, swore that he would, under no circumstances, permit more than a 14 percent increase. Historically, as seen from success stories with gas and electric companies, this proclamation from a fair-minded referee settled the issue. The students gained the 14 percent, the Chancellor came out as a heroic figure, a good candidate for Congress, public confidence in the democratic system was warranted, and no College buildings were burned.

The X-Ray Technology Program got off to a bad start and was terminated this week when the County Sheriff presented an order from the Governor to padlock the door to the Dean's office.

The first student graduated x-rayed a patient for a sore toe. He told the victim to inhale and hold his breath. The only glitch was that the technologist went home but forgot to tell the patient to resume breathing. The compliant patient died, very blue all over.

The stamp-licker in the Zoology office has developed xerostomia (no saliva). Since the telephone with the wheel is also caput, all external communication has come to an abrupt halt. The Department has hung out "Closed for the month" signs and it is giving away its armadillos free, with first preference to the President's staff where they will have compatible company.

Missing Link
Anthropology
Dear Missing:

When you finished discombobulating a skeleton and we reassigned you to clear the algae out of the former glorious pond surrounding my office, the worst again happened. It is now an impenetrable rain forest and we have had to hire an experienced safari guide to help visitors hack their way through the underbrush and try to locate the door to the building. You could become the greatest expert on eutrophication in the western hemisphere.

It is timely to congratulate you on this still unsung honor. Your seemingly endless succession of honors resulting from your unsurpassed oneupsmanship makes you a serious contender even for the college presidency. Your honors are now thick enough to cut down to pie-piece size. It will require a large knife which I am enclosing. After you resize your diplomas, you can use the knife to help cut yourself down to an appropriate size, let's say a pygmy. To diversify your rehabilitation, you are hereby appointed Campus Fence Viewer. We can then think about your early retirement.

Problem resolver, Smiley Timkens

Instructor Lout Meatball, a truly creative person, invented a powerful aggregometer which pulls everything together. Although married, he got stuck naked with his clandestine girlfriend, in his creative laboratory. The usual glitch occurred. He left the directions to turn off the machine at home on his wife's dresser and he doesn't want to call in his secretary to summon the fire department to ax the machine. Things are about to get more sticky especially since he invited Dean Dingleberry in to see his new creation.

The Safety Director was invited to make the keynote speech at the world introduction of the super-powerful popcorn machine now being unveiled in the huge display window of the Great Crumble Department Store The Director started by singing "The world is so full of such wonderful things, I think we should all be as happy as kings" when he fell into the roaring machine. The enthusiastic crowd applauded the Director as he went popping in every direction, occasionally waving for someone to save him.

From the English Department:

If a President officially calls a bear a cow, it is a cow until whatever it takes to reverse the nomenclature occurs. Dictionaries, unlike bibles, do not have God to protect them from administrators.

There is a rapist running amok on campus. Detective Wildly Implausible of the Great Crumble Constabulary insists that the rapist must be a Crumble faculty member because he is so smart. Wildly says that the suspect must have a wet processing tool that leaves no footprints. Good idea to leave this report.

Instructor Forgivemenot has solved the problem of staff members strolling into his office without RSVP invitations and disappearing into the night with his pencils, cocaine, diplomas on the wall, and whatever else that acquaintances believe to be communal property. Forgivemenot bought a junkyard dog, pure Doberman, and always foraging for a tasty meal, humans not excepted. Nobody goes back especially at night.

TELEGRAM. To: Vera Scrum
From: All the faculty except three

Convened in special meeting, we have voted to designate you officially as "The Wicked Witch of the Southeast." All other compass points seem to be filled. You will receive shortly an appropriately designed sweatshirt.

We requested that this telegram reach you at 5 A.M. so that the birds can chirp along with our glad tidings. Enjoy. All of us have escaped for the weekend, leaving your adrenalin surge enough time to recede by Monday morning.

Our Flight Instructor at the control tower of the airport reports a conversation with a co-pilot of a plane apparently trying to approach the airport. We have to use non-aviational English herein:
Tower: We need to speak to the pilot.
Co-pilot: He's outside.
Tower: What the hell are you talking about?

Co-pilot: He fell out of the window. I'm holding on to him, trying to pull him in.

Tower: Par for the course. Who's flying the plane?

Co-pilot: Damned if I know. If I turn around my pal is history.

Tower: We can't follow the directions you're flying.

Co-pilot: Right now, everywhere. But not to worry, we're not upside down.

Tower: We'll expect you soon. Right now we're finishing our ham sandwiches.

From the Theatre Department:

When you go to a play and the couple in the seats just in front of you are talking about the price of fry pans and the players on the stage are no longer audible, lean over and say, "Nice dialogue but we don't see your names on the program." Be cautious as you complete the message. Hopefully, you are seated next to a very big guy who looks like he's your bodyguard.

Caveats in seeking a new apartment (From the Behavioral Sciences):

If you are out searching for an apartment to rent, back off if the sidewalk abruptly narrows to allow barely one person to walk. The landlord may have the same behavior.

Another element in behavioral diagnosis is when you tell the landlady your name and she asks, "In what country do people have that name?" You could answer, "Only royalty in Tasmania. Are you royalty or a commoner?"

You could encounter a third type, a landlady who greets you with a bittersweet smile. Her zygomaticus major muscle, which in nice people draws the corners of the mouth upward, has been frozen solid by long practice in mid-excursion. Tell her that you forgot to bring along your paramour and then leave while her depressor anguli oris muscle takes over to uglify her back to normal expression.

0385-KAPL

To: Faculty of English Department
From: Language Mangler, Chairman

All our staff members will henceforth be required to read the commercial circulars that tell the recipients that they have already won a million dollars. The only requirement is to buy at least 200 tubes of shaving cream. Some of the circulars allow a grace period of 24 hours to claim the Rolls-Royce thrown in or it will be given to the next victim.

Despite the fact that only one in 10 million may win a prize, the language in the messages is clear, stupidly simple, repeated with increasing sympathy for those who don't reply, and extraordinarily motivating. This is in direct contrast with the moaning messages of despair from our faculty who deplore student apathy, increasing illiteracy, and an uncontrolled capacity to become insulted when asked to state the difference between a noun and a pronoun.

We would do well to discharge our faculty who are known nonsense spewers and substitute the people with savvy in commercial writing who are successful predators because they understand the appeal of appropriately written English. Since as Chairman, I am presently occupying the head tent, I will recommend that all students and faculty here read Mother Goose. Its appealing rhymes waste no time or space in the delivery and directness of its messages.

Crumble is suffering a recision. For those among you who never consult a dictionary, this is a term which politely informs an institution that some of its funds are being taken back. The State, in the present case, failed to say that the entire mess was caused by the blundering Governor and his accomplices.

The Crumble Board of Trustees has risen to the occasion and

in full accordance with faculty expectations. The Department of Sociology was dissolved but the staff members were given a week to recover from spinal or other neurological shock. The Trustees showed that they were not displaying favoritism since they voted to have the Department Chair remain and teach the 14 courses listed in the catalog. A portable potty will be installed since there could be very little time between classes for excremental trivia.

To: John People-Eater, M. D.
Health Service, Surgical Service
From: Smiley Timkens

Your throwing an amputated liver from a student over your head is despicable. What's more, you missed the trashcan. You are clearly on the downalator. Hold on tightly as you sink into oblivion.

President Timkens:

I am a man of few words and I can only note that I have a legitimate claim to fame. I once cured a disease that never happened.

On the way down,
John People-Eater

Ms. Quirkus Maximus, Tutor in Latin, won the "Sad Sack of the Year Award," with acclaim. She traveled from Crumble to a meeting in Mexico and subsequently went to another meeting in Alaska. Then she took a plane home. Back in Crumble she remembered that she had left her auto at one of the two meetings.

There was a close runner-up for the above title. This was Tinkle Bell, Emeritus Teaching Assistant in Logic and Profound Theology. Her sub-award was entitled "The Final Desecration." She was a tourist in Jerusalem and a street vendor got her into a well known scam prior to his disappearance. He sold her God's telephone number.

Senior Chairman Language Mangler proposes usage of the word "Polychotomizer" for staff in faculty meetings who answer a question by dividing it into at least a dozen diverging questions. This ploy spreads a 12 minute meeting to about four hours, with a half dozen more meetings scheduled to address the original pointless question.

To: Penurious Paul, Mayor of Horseshit Ridge
From: Frond Graynose, Dean, Mortuary Science

Our students, who need more practice than you can imagine, buried your mother-in-law. We sent you a bill for six dollars. So far, we have not received payment. If we don't hear from you by next week, up she comes.

Did you ever wake up from your sleep in a faculty meeting and notice that a dozen new rules were established? Read the annals of the Department of Mathematics in which you will find that the number of existing rules is directly proportional to the number that have to be broken. Fortunately, for those who cannot read graphs which depict the same thing pictorially, the equation descriptive of the situation is linear. The more sophisticated among you will demand an exponential treatment to satisfy the foolishness seen on the y-axis of the graph.

Rules obviate the need of faculty members with small cerebral hemispheres to do any thinking; they can hide behind any rule needed to subdue an angry student. It is possible that an overzealous faculty perpetrator could be hit over the head with some nearby primitive weapon by a student who is espousing his own causes. A state of unconsciousness that could result from the attack might be more effective than a cease and desist order for the rule, put out by an administrator who has just awakened from a Rip van Winkle sleep. Cease orders issued from above only bring about more faculty meetings and another dozen rules.

Biology Instructor Eohippus described "parthenogenesis" to his awe-struck class. This is a process in which body cell fragments lacking nuclear control of development, e.g., those of sea urchin eggs, are treated with chemicals, a known example being highly mineralized sea water, after which the body fragments undergo cell division and do so up to a point like a primitive dividing embryo. Great Grandmother Nitwit, who was auditing the class, asked Eohippus if she should stop going swimming. Her great grandson, El Stupido, who was class delegate, pleaded with Eohippus, "Tell us more about the body."

To: Compilers of this entire rubbish about Crumble
From: Multidirectional Belch

You are sickees. I cannot burn your book since the fumes may corrode my tin trash barrel. Burial is an adequate solution. To improve your world-class lack of perspective, read my book, "Administrators are Nice People." Contrary to Populist propaganda, they are not fat and they do not burn easily.

President Timkens says that it is getting a bit tiresome to attend the daily nonsense power lunches of his staff as well as to stay cordial at the black tie dinners for the moochers coming to his evening feasts. Timkens is also concerned with the outcry for Crumble's elevation of status to a university, since at that point he and the whole faculty might be carted off in the nearest wheelbarrows.

Timkens sagely observed that if a university was not established about the time that the Pilgrims bounced off a rock at Plymouth or when whoever claimed to have grounded a ship earlier in Virginia, its administrators and staff could never land on level ground with the beautiful people who are dispensing the true educational experiences.

The local Crumble gentry in hot pursuit of status argue whether to establish a medical school before a law school. Since the Crumble physicians deprecate the local attorneys as a necessary band of predators, Timkens in his high priestly role thought it essential to emphasize a moral story from fractured history that while physicians were uselessly lancing boils on George Washington's derriere, lawyers were framing the Declaration of Independence. We pause in this sordid tale to return immediately to the main jungle where reality is rearing its ugly head.

AND AS THE SUN SETS IN THE GOLDEN WEST

To: Forby Doo Doo, Editor, The Great Crumble Press
From: The Great Crumble Writers of this book

We are submitting all these reports about our beloved College as a permanent testimonial to its unique infamy. The collation is clearly of genius quality.

To: The Great Crumble Writers and their truthless collaborators
From: Forby Doo Doo, Editor

I sent your magnum opus to our three most distinguished reviewers instead of dropping it into a manhole. The following are their obviously impartial evaluations:

Reviewer 1 (Ms. Purity Prude): I only hope that God is too busy to read this material. He might submerge the whole place in the Great Crumble River.

Reviewer 2 (Professor Birdhouse): I am returning my review and this consists of five blank pages. Being a friend of all parties, this will emphasize my neutrality. I stand ready to submit additional blank pages if you need more confirmation.

Reviewer 3 (Ex-President Cloud Nine): The opus is benign. The real story of Crumble is far worse. I would put The Great Crumble Writers on salary plus more to keep two investigators busy. Also, put aside funds for a bomb shelter for all of them.

From: Forby Doo Doo

As usual, the last word is mine. Since democracy must prevail,

I turned the manuscript over to my cleaning lady. Her broad spectrum of interest in the world's greatest literature, e. g., Nick Carter, The Dreckapotheca, The National Enquirer, and others give her an international authority. You should hear within two years but don't hold your breath.

ANTICLIMAX: THE SHIP IS DESERTING THE SINKING RATS

The year 1969 was not a good one for the College. President Timkens has disappeared and rumor has it that he is abroad consolidating some Swiss bank accounts.

Mayor Weakling is trying to sell the city. Horseshit Ridge may buy it if it secedes from the College and the latter is blown up on July 4th. An alternative is to convert the College to a chemical waste dump; this could satisfy the students since the patriots among them could remain and wave flags protesting the presence of a dump until the cops start turning them into hamburger.

Myron was unsaged at the Health Service. He now wants to be a stand up comic at the White House. The ones there are not getting rave reviews. One of the Political Science staff wants to join a revolution. He claims that the work is steady, history being on his side.

The Psychology Chairman said, "I wanted to retire since I was 30 years old but my wife threatened to exchange me for a dog. Now I have an excuse."

Scraggs said, "My colleagues gave me a tin cup. If they give one of the vice-presidents a bell, we can be partners in a new business."

Fendrick Poltroon is collecting material, probably from outer space, for another script, scenario to fit the purchaser. To keep himself in Cheerios, Fendrick is temporarily vending patent medicine off the back of a horse-drawn wagon.

Every evening in the monastery on the hill, Brother John looks down on the vanishing campus and chants the well-known verse, "God's in his heaven, all's well with the world."

THE LAST RITES. END OF THE GOLDEN ERA AND IN LOCO PARENTIS. CIRCA 1970

Our prime misinformer, Fendrick Poltroon, in a final statement, regrets his inability to add details about the fall of Crumble from glory. He was advised by the College constabulary, "We are asking you politely, leave town." In ancient Rome the directive was "Frater ave atque vale." In lower Rome, particularly, it was "Verbum sat sapiente." No need for the translation since it all means "Leave town." In a last poetic statement which Fendrick pulled out of his stockpile, "We are as a wind that blows through Crumble, a current that moves from the future into the past." Poltroon's pilfering has style.

An observer from Horseshit Ridge said metaphorically, "Crumble was a humpty-dumpty complex. It fell off the wall and couldn't be put together again."

President Timkens did not heroically say, "I shall return." In his latest disguise, a supreme creation of his former couturier, he is about to enjoy anonymity on a sun-swept beach in the South Pacific. Vera Scrum, his trusted administrative assistant, cannot be recognized in her Fu Manchu hairdo.

Dean Dingleberry retired to the baronial estate of his cloned nephew, Rotten-To-The Core Dingleberry.

Ollie Underbright is a migrant worker in a peach orchard. His arch-rival Dean Catcabbage is collecting welfare.

0385-KAPL

Other administrators have drifted Off to Never-Never Land and have eluded trace.

Santayana observed that the more things seem to change, the more they remain the same. The ghosts of Crumble are likely to surface in some form or other, essentially the same wine in new bottles.